Babes in the Darkling Wood

BY THE SAME AUTHOR
ALL PUBLISHED BY HOUSE OF STRATUS

FICTION

ANN VERONICA
APROPOS OF DOLORES
THE AUTOCRACY OF MR PARHAM
BEALBY
THE BROTHERS *AND*
   THE CROQUET PLAYER
BRYNHILD
THE BULPINGTON OF BLUP
THE DREAM
THE FIRST MEN IN THE MOON
THE FOOD OF THE GODS
THE HISTORY OF MR POLLY
THE HOLY TERROR
IN THE DAYS OF THE COMET
THE INVISIBLE MAN
THE ISLAND OF DR MOREAU
KIPPS: THE STORY OF A SIMPLE
   SOUL
LOVE AND MR LEWISHAM
MARRIAGE
MEANWHILE
MEN LIKE GODS
A MODERN UTOPIA
MR BRITLING SEES IT THROUGH
THE NEW MACHIAVELLI
THE PASSIONATE FRIENDS
THE SEA LADY
THE SHAPE OF THINGS TO COME
THE TIME MACHINE
TONO-BUNGAY

THE UNDYING FIRE
THE WAR IN THE AIR
THE WAR OF THE WORLDS
THE WHEELS OF CHANCE
WHEN THE SLEEPER WAKES
THE WIFE OF SIR ISAAC HARMAN
THE WONDERFUL VISIT
THE WORLD OF WILLIAM CLISSOLD
   VOLUMES 1,2,3

NON-FICTION

THE CONQUEST OF TIME *AND*
   THE HAPPY TURNING
EXPERIMENT IN AUTOBIOGRAPHY
   VOLUMES 1,2
H G WELLS IN LOVE
THE OPEN CONSPIRACY AND OTHER
   WRITINGS

Babes in the Darkling Wood

H G WELLS

First Published 1940
Copyright by The Executors of the Estate of H G Wells

All rights reserved. No part of this publication may be reproduced, stored in a retrieval system, or transmitted, in any form, or by any means (electronic, mechanical, photocopying, recording, or otherwise), without the prior permission of the publisher. Any person who does any unauthorised act in relation to this publication may be liable to criminal prosecution and civil claims for damages.

The right of H G Wells to be identified as the author of this work has been asserted.

This edition published in 2002 by House of Stratus, an imprint of House of Stratus Ltd, Thirsk Industrial Park, York Road, Thirsk, North Yorkshire, YO7 3BX, UK.
Also at: House of Stratus Inc., 2 Neptune Road, Poughkeepsie, NY 12601, USA.

www.houseofstratus.com

Typeset, printed and bound by House of Stratus.

A catalogue record for this book is available from the British Library and The Library of Congress.

ISBN 0-7551-0392-0

This book is sold subject to the condition that it shall not be lent, resold, hired out, or otherwise circulated without the publisher's express prior consent in any form of binding, or cover, other than the original as herein published and without a similar condition being imposed on any subsequent purchaser, or bona fide possessor.

This is a fictional work and all characters are drawn from the author's imagination. Any resemblances or similarities to people either living or dead are entirely coincidental.

Contents

Introduction – *The Novel of Ideas*   i

Book One – The Easy-going Cottage

1	Unrevealed World	3
2	Church Militant?	31
3	The World's Harsh Voice, is Heard Off	55
4	Conference of the Powers	83

Book Two – Stella has Time to Think Things Over

1	Experimentalist in Moeurs	125
2	Stella has Time to Think Things Over	157
3	Search for Reality	205

Book Three – Nightmare of Reality

1	The Guide and Friend in the Deep of the Forest	255
2	Gemini in Poland	277
3	Gemini in the Shadows	301

BOOK FOUR – TRUMPET BEFORE THE DAWN

1	Psychosynthesis of Gemini	333
2	The Killing of Uncle Robert	375
3	Reveille	383
	Tail-piece	453

Introduction

The Novel of Ideas

It is characteristic of most literary criticism to be carelessly uncritical of the terms it uses and violently partisan and dogmatic in its statements about them. No competent Linnaeus has ever sat down to sort out the orders and classes, genera and varieties, of fiction, and no really sane man ever will. They have no fixed boundaries; all sorts interbreed as shamelessly as dogs, and they pass at last by indefinite gradations into more or less honest fact telling, into "historical reconstruction", the *roman à clef*, biography, history and autobiography. So the literary critic, confronted with a miscellany of bookish expression far more various than life itself, has an excellent excuse for the looseness of his vocabulary, if not for his exaltations and condemnations. Unhappily he insists on adopting types for his preference and he follows fashions. My early life as a naïve, spontaneous writer was much afflicted by the vehement advocacy by Henry James II, Joseph Conrad, Edward Garnett and Ford Madox Hueffer, of something called *The* Novel, and by George Moore of something called *The* Short Story. There were all sorts of things forbidden for *The* Novel; there must be no explanation of the ideas animating the characters, and the author himself had to be as

INTRODUCTION

invisible and unheard-of as God; for no conceivable reason. So far as *The* Short Story went, it gave George Moore the consolation of calling Kipling's stories, and in fact any short stories that provoked his ready jealousy, "anecdotes". Novelists were arranged in order of merit that made the intelligent reader doubt his own intelligence, and the idea of "Progress" was urged upon the imaginative writer. Conrad was understood to be in the van of progress; Robert Louis Stevenson had "put the clock back", and so on. Quite inconspicuous young writers were able to believe that in some mysterious technical way they were leaving Defoe and Sterne far away behind them.

There has been no such "progress" in human brains. Against this sort of thing, which for many reasons I found tiresome and unpalatable, I rebelled. I declared that a novel, as distinguished from the irresponsible plausibilities of romance or the invention in imaginative stories of hitherto unthought-of human circumstances, could be any sort of honest treatment of the realities of human behaviour in narrative form. Conduct was the novel's distinctive theme. Was and is and must be, if we are to have any definition of a novel. All writing should be done as well as it can be done, wit and vigour are as God wills, but pretentious artistry is a minor amateurism on the flank of literature.

This present story belongs to a school to which I have always been attracted, and in which I have already written several books. The merit of my particular contributions may be infinitesimal, but that does not alter the fact that they follow in a great tradition, the tradition of discussing fundamental human problems in dialogue form.

The dialogue, written or staged, is one of the oldest forms of literary expression. Very early, men realised the impossibility

INTRODUCTION

of abstracting any philosophy of human behaviour from actual observable flesh and blood. As soon can you tear a brain away from its blood and membranes: it dies. Abstract philosophy is the deadest of stuff; one disintegrating *hortus siccus* follows another; I am astounded at the implacable scholarly industry of those who still write Textbooks of Philosophy. And your psychological handbook is only kept alive by a stream of anecdote. The Socratic Dialogue on the other hand produces character after character to state living views, to have them ransacked by an interlocutor who is also a character, subject to all the infirmities of the flesh. Plato's dramas of the mind *live* to this day. They may have inspired – it is a fancy of mine for which there is only very slight justification – that kindred Socratic novel, the book of Job. For that magnificent creation my admiration is unstinted. I have made a close study of it; I have in fact not only studied it but modernised it, traced it over, character by character and speech, in *The Undying Fire*. The Book of Job has been compared to a Greek tragedy, to the *Prometheus Bound* of Aeschylus, for example, but I see it myself, naturally enough, from the angle of the writer. It was written to be read.

Manifestly the novel of ideas and the play of ideas converge. My friend George Bernard Shaw has lived a long, vivid life, putting the discussion of ideas on to the English stage, to the infinite exasperation of generation after generation of dramatic critics, who insist upon puppets with heads of solid wood. Then they can get the drama of pure situation within the compass of overnight judgments. From opposite directions Shaw and I approach what is to us and, I submit, firmly and immodestly, to all really intelligent people, the most interesting thing in the world, the problems of human life and behaviour as we find them

Introduction

incarnate in persons. We have no claim to be pioneers, but by an inner necessity we were revivalists. *Hamlet* is evidently a dramatic dialogue about suicide in face of intolerable conditions, and *Julius Caesar* a treatment of political assassination. But by the time Shaw began dramatic criticism, ideas had vanished from the English theatre for generations. Mallock and Peacock, however, had kept the dialogue alive through the darkest period of the three volume novel.

I found myself, and I got to the dialogue novel, through a process of trial and error. The critical atmosphere was all against me. As I felt about rebelliously among the possibilities of fiction, I found certain of my characters were displaying an irresistible tendency to break out into dissertation. Many critical readers, trained to insist on a straight story, objected to these talkers; they said they were my self-projections, author's exponents. But in many cases these obtrusive individuals were not saying things I thought, but, what is a very different thing, things I wanted to put into shape by having them said. An early type of this sort of book was *Ann Veronica*. She is a young woman who soliloquises and rhapsodises incessantly, revealing the ideas of the younger intelligentsia round about 1910, ideas I had found very interesting indeed. Before then no one had realised there was an English intelligentsia. The book is not a dialogue, simply because no one answers Ann Veronica. It interested a number of people who did not realise fully what bad taste they showed in being interested.

I made a much nearer approach to the fully developed novel of ideas in *Mr Britling sees it Through*. I was getting more cunning about the business. I made him a writer and I used the letters home of his son to say a number of things that could be said in

INTRODUCTION

no other way. In *Joan and Peter*, I did what I think was a better book than *Mr Britling;* it is a dialogue about education, and I centred the discussion on the perplexities of the guardian who had to find a school for these young people. All my most recent books, *Brynhild, Dolores* (apart from the scandalous misbehaviour of her dog and a few such uncontrollable incidents), *The Holy Terror*, are primarily discussions carried on through living characters; it is for the discussion of behaviour they were written, and to cut out the talk would be like cutting a picture out of its frame.

And now I will come to the plan and purpose of this present book, which is the most comprehensive and ambitious dialogue novel I have ever attempted. I will try to explain certain devices I have had to adopt, and certain unavoidable necessities of the treatment. At the present time a profounder change in human thought and human outlook is going on than has ever occurred before. The great literary tradition I follow demands that this be rendered in terms of living human beings. It must be shown in both word and act. This I attempt here. So far as my observation and artistry as a novelist has enabled me to achieve it, there is not a single individual in this book that you might not meet and recognise in the street. If you have had any experience in writing fiction, I think you will find that you can take any of my characters out of this book and invent a meeting between them and the real people you know. But because of the very great burthen of fresh philosophical matter that this novel has to carry, I have chosen my chief individuals from among the sort of people who would be closest up to that matter. I have made one main figure a psychotherapeutist who as an intrusive outside lecturer carries on a feud with the academic traditions of

INTRODUCTION

Cambridge. He writes, he talks, he lectures, aggressively and destructively. Very much under his intellectual influence are my central "Babes", two keen young people, one a Newnham undergraduate and the other her lover, Gemini, an Oxford man, who writes and criticises in a "highbrow" weekly, talks abundantly and is in harsh conflict with his father, a London Police Magistrate, celebrated for his bitter utterances on the London bench, and constitutionally addicted to uttering judgments. The mother is a highly self-conscious writer of bright letters. The mental break-down of Gemini after some grim experiences in Poland and Finland, bring the methods of a leading psychoanalyst and modern psychosynthesis into the story. All these people talk, write and explain, by habit, profession and necessity. I could not devise a more favourable assemblage of personalities for a modern symposium, or I would have done so. The inexpert reader might imagine that nothing remained for the novelist to do but to report their conversations.

But that is by no means the case. Let us consider for example the long conversation between Stella and Gemini after they had received Uncle Hopkinshire's abusive threats. Everything reported of it, was actually said and understood, and to both interlocutors the chastened, edited, polished conversation given in that section would certainly be acceptable as a fair rendering of their intentions. Yet it is really as different from what they actually said to one another as clear, large print is from a note scribbled in faint pencil on crumpled scraps of paper. They talked a language that was sometimes a kind of shorthand to each other. They had been educated upon parallel lines; they had read the same books; they could say much of this that is set before you, with half the words and without ever finishing a sentence;

INTRODUCTION

all sorts of things could be assumed between them; they could pick up and finish each other's phrases; and if I were to write it all down verbatim you would find it, unless you were made to exactly the same pattern and belonged to the same generation, inconsecutive and incomprehensible to the extremest degree. And sometimes, when they entered upon unfamiliar territory, instead of shorthand they used a roundabout very elongated longhand, abounding in loops, digressions and corrections, while they felt their way to their meaning. Moreover, ever and again, it has been necessary, by a turn of the phrase or the neat insertion of a phrase, to interpose something that might be unknown to you, in order to get over the reality of what they said to you. Again and again, to do them justice, it has been necessary to clarify, condense, expand or underline their words. Nevertheless, what is given here is what they imagined they were saying, and what indeed they meant. And I do not know of any way of writing the novel of ideas that can dispense with such magnified and crystallised conversations and meditations...

That magnification and clarification applies in a greater or lesser degree to nearly all the talk in every novel of ideas. It is the exact opposite of that "flow of consciousness" technique, with which Mrs Virginia Woolf, following in the footsteps of Miss Dorothy Richardson, has experimented, more or less successfully. Thereby personalities are supposed to be stippled out by dabs of response – which after all have to be verbalised. Uncle Robert, when he discourses on a University Education, tells Stella a score of things that as a matter of fact he knew she knew. Later on he and Gemini perform a sort of duet of mutual information. They explain the whole gist and bearing of the new and entirely revolutionary philosophy of behaviourism to one another,

Introduction

cheerfully, uncivilly and without embarrassment. I know of no better way of setting out this new way of thinking. To the best of my ability I contrive a situation that makes their talk as plausible as possible, and I keep rigorously true to their mental characters. In this fashion I may manage to get away with the understanding reader. But against the carping realist who objects that people do not talk like this, there is no reply, except that people know what they mean much better than they say it, and that the most unrighteous thing a reporter can do to a speaker or lecturer is to report him verbatim. So I put this dialogue novel of contemporary ideas before you with characters I claim to be none the less living because through my lens you see them larger and clearer than life.

Book One
The Easy-going Cottage

Chapter One

Unrevealed World

And now what?

A girl still just short of twenty walked very gravely, lightly and happily beside her lover, a youngster of twenty-four, along an overgrown, sunken, sun-flecked lane in Suffolk. The lane ran sometimes between fields and sometimes along the boundaries of pleasant residences, and it led from the village green at the centre of all things to the cottage they occupied. It was early in June. Lilac was dropping but the may was at its last and best; and countless constellations of stitchwort, clusters and nebulae, celebrated a brief ascendancy over the promiscuous profusion of the hedge-banks.

"Stellaria!" said he, "it's just chickweed, which proves that Stella is a chick – a downy little chick."

"We won't always talk nonsense," said Stella.

"When one is drunk with happiness, what else can one talk?"

"Well," she considered...

They bumped themselves against each other, summer-drunk, love-drunk, smiled into each other's eyes, and he ran an impudent, appreciative hand over her bare shoulder. She shrank a little from that before she remembered not to shrink. His hand dropped to his side and they walked on, a little apart and with grave, preoccupied faces.

"Things that aren't nonsense are so hard to express," he said presently, and lapsed into another silence.

She was slight and lithe and sunburnt, with sun-bleached hair and intelligent, dark-blue eyes. She had finely modelled brows, with a faintly humorous crinkle in the broad forehead, and enough mouth for a variety of expressions; a wide mouth it was that could flash into a vivid smile or shut with considerable deliberation, which could kiss, as he knew, very delightfully, but was by no means specialised for that purpose. She was wearing an exiguous pale-green vest which emphasised rather than hid the points of her pretty body, a pair of grey flannel trousers, in which she evidently carried a lot of small possessions as well as her dirty little hands, and brown canvas shoes. Her third finger in her left-hand pocket bore a wedding ring that would not have deceived a rabbit. A bright patterned green and gold silk handkerchief round her slim but sufficient waist completed her costume.

Her companion was perhaps four of five inches taller, and darker in complexion. He was something of a pug about the face, with disarming brown eyes, a lot of forehead and a resolute mouth. His rather crisp brown hair seemed to grow anyhow and had apparently been cut *en brosse* by an impatient and easily discouraged barber. This young man also wore grey slacks and canvas shoes, with a white cotton shirt that had once no doubt possessed as many buttons as any shirt, but which was now buttoned only at the right wrist. He was carrying a spike of bananas still attached to their parent stem in his left (off) hand.

It was only as he walked that it became apparent that he was extremely lame.

The least worldly of people meeting this young couple would have known at once, if only by the challenging pride in their faces, that they were living in sin together, that they had been doing so for five or six days at the outside, and that they had never done anything of the sort before. But old Mrs Greedle, who did for them in Mary Clarkson's borrowed weekend cottage, never betrayed a shadow of doubt about that very loosely fitting wedding ring. She consulted Stella upon all sorts of matronly questions and prompted her with the right answer whenever there was the least sign of hesitation...

But of Mrs Greedle more later...

"It is just because we are so happy," he said, trying again.

"I know," she agreed.

"Has anyone any *right* to be happy in a world like this?"

"We were foolish to get those newspapers and letters."

"Sooner or later that had to come."

"They had to come. And anyhow it's been a lovely time. Such a lovely time. Such a very lovely time. Anyhow."

"But all those other fellows all over the world..."

"We've only stolen a week."

"And no one can ever take it away from us. Whatever happens. There's something unfair about our luck. Think of the ones who would – and can't. Down here – or wherever there's working people or out-of-works or gipsies or such – I look at them and feel a sort of thief. As though I'd stolen it from them. What right have we to our education, to the freedom in our minds, to the time and money, that makes all this possible? And our *health!* If *we* haven't stolen, our blessed progenitors did. We are Receivers of stolen goods."

"In a way it's getting less and less unfair. The Evil Thing is going to catch us all sooner or later. Why shouldn't we snatch this? At the eleventh hour?"

"To think that it's an advantage to have had a foot crushed between a motor-bike and a tram! *Luck* to be a cripple! No obligation to join up. One of the exempted. The last of the free. We shall catch it with the other civilians but anyhow we're not under orders."

"Not so much of a cripple," she reflected. "Anyhow I'm a woman now and grown-up and ready to look at what's coming to us."

"And what *is* coming to us?"

"It isn't fair. Life didn't come after our grandfathers and grandmothers and trim them up for slaughter. They had a breathing space."

"Much good they did with it."

"Romeo and Juliet weren't called on for national service."

"*They* didn't get away with so very much either."

"Just accidents and misunderstandings in their case, Gemini; they had bad luck, their people were awful people, worse than ours, and there were those mixed philtres, pure accident, and that was all there was the matter with them. But now everyone, all over the world, is being threatened, compelled, driven. Like a great hand feeling for us, catching more and more of us. It's only God's mercy that there isn't some siren howling after us, or some loud-speaker bellowing ARP instructions, here and now. It got us at the post office; it's waiting for us at the cottage... But I'm talking worse than you do, Gemini."

"And saying what everyone is saying. All the same we two *are* the world's pets. We've had education, art, literature, travel, while most of those others have been marched off long ago, trained to drudge, to obey, to trust the nice ruling classes. Ideas kept from them. Books hard to get at. What's the good of pretending that you and I are not the new ruling-class generation? We are. We've shared the loot. And what are we doing by way of thank-you for the education and the art and the literature and the travel we've had? Trying not to care a damn. Having as good a time as we can manage until something hits us... It's all the damned radio and the rest of it that does it. Why should I be worried because Chinese kids are being raped and disembowelled for fun by the Japs in Shanghai? Why should I be worried because they are being sold to the brothels and given syphilis and driven to death and all that, under the approving noses of our own blessed Pukka Sahibs in Hong Kong? Lousy Pukka Sahibs! Dirty old Blimps!... This, that and the other horror, up and down the world. That concentration camp stuff... And all hammering down on our poor little brains. All the time now. All hammering down on *us*. Things like that have always been going on, but they didn't worry grandfather when he walked in the lanes with grandmamma. They didn't come after them as they come after us."

"And they didn't say *You next*."

"Gods! Stella, and are we as bad as that? Maybe we are. Did it have to be bombs over London before any of our lot worried?"

She puckered her brows and weighed the question. She stuck her hands deeper in her trouser pockets as though that helped her thinking. "It wasn't in the same world then," she decided.

"Now it is. 'Ye ken the noo', as the Calvinist's God said."

"We ken. And what are we going to do about it, Gemini? Playing bright kids won't save us. If our sort can't think of something, nobody will think of anything. *We* have to do something about it. *We!* You and me! And what can we do?..."

"What can we do?" he echoed. "Oh hell! Stella, what can we do? Being a Communist! *What's* being a Communist? What good is it? Trotsky and Stalin don't matter a dam to me. Conscientious objectors – objectors to being alive, I suppose. This, this muddle, *is* life. How can we stand out of it?... Anti-Fascist?... What party is there to work with; what leader can one follow? Saying No, *No*, NO to everything isn't being alive. Why haven't we leaders to lead us *somewhere?* I forgot things for a bit, this last week, but that emetic speech of the Prime Minister's friend – what was his name? Lindsey – Jump-in-the-Snow Lindsey, they call him – and that story of those Jews in No Man's Land and that quotation from that book of Timperley's about those Japanese atrocities... It's all come back to me, and the helplessness of it. And the sun, old fool, goes on shining. You poor old fool up there! Why don't you go out and finish us up?"

"And none of the old religions are any good?"

"It's the old religions and faiths and patriotisms that have brought us to just exactly where we are. Manifestly."

"No good going back to *them* again."

"No good going back to anything again. But how to get on?"

"She confronted him. "Gemini," she said, "have you *no* ideas?"

"Oh! the shadows of the ghosts of ideas. And a sound of claptrap in the distance."

"Gemini Jimmini – that is to say Mr James Twain – listen to me. I love you. Always have done; long before you thought of it.

I am your true love. Haven't I proved it? And also, as I warned you, I am a prig."

"Don't I know it? Could I love you otherwise? Go on."

"I warn you I am going to talk like a prig. Almost like warning you I'm going to be sick. I've felt it coming on. Gemini, I *must* say it."

"Out with it, as they say on the excursion steamboats. Sorry! Oh – out with it, Stella!"

"Well, we two are individuals of outstanding intelligence. Outstanding intelligence. Young of course, silly in a way because we are young, but really damned intelligent. That's generally admitted by our friends and relations. Even Aunt Ruby said that. We *are* bright. In the privacy of this Lovers' Lane, need we hesitate to say as much to one another? We are. Yes. And I'm for getting on with it. You listen. For all practical purposes, about the conduct of our lives, about the conduct of life, we don't know a blessed thing. Not a blessed *real* thing. You as well as me. They haven't told us anything worth knowing. We are just bright enough to realise that. The religion and morals they fed us are exploded old rubbish. That much we've found out. The unbelieving way they taught it us was enough to show that. Blank. Yet we've got to devote ourselves to *something*, Gemini, all the same. We're made that way. We've got to do whatever is in us, to save ourselves and the world. Maybe we'll do something. Maybe we'll do nothing at all. But we've *got* to make the effort. In a war hundreds of people have to be killed or messed-up. Even if their side is winning. Some get in the way of their own side and get done in like that. Trying to do their best. All sorts go into the boiling. But they've *got* to join up, they've *got* to try. It doesn't matter so long as they don't slack or hide... We're slacking, Gemini..."

She was dismayed at herself.

"I can't go on. It's the very life of me I'm telling you, and it sounds – rot...preachment... Salvation indeed!... Salvation Army... If only I hadn't begun. I've never talked this way... I *must* – with you. I'm not just talking."

She was weeping.

"Darling," he said, and kissed and embraced her.

"No need to say any of this again," she sobbed, clinging to him...

"Can I borrow your snitch-rag, Gemini?" she said presently. "I left mine at home."

"We'll have to talk about things," he reflected. "I *will*. But – it's awful hard. We get this stuff out of books. We think of it bookishly. We have to at first. When we talk about it, it's like bringing up partly digested print. We've got to talk bookish. What natural words *are* there? Slang, love-making, smut, games, gossip, 'pass the mustard', one can talk about in a sort of natural unprintable way, but ideas... We're abashed. We've been trained to be abashed. My old nurse began it. 'Don't you talk like a book, Mr Jimmy', she said. 'Don't you go using long words'. But suppose the short words won't do it? You're so right, Stella. We've *got* to talk of these things. Of course we have. There's a sort of shyness they put upon us... Even between lovers..."

She nodded. "Worse than their damned decency," she said. She returned the handkerchief rolled into a ball.

Then she remarked, apropos of nothing: "This morning I saw a big bird flying across the garden and it cuckooed as it flew.

Always before, I thought they sat and did it. Did you know, Gemini, they cuckooed as they flew?"

"And sitting also. I've seen 'em perched on branches and doing it..."

But he did not seem to be thinking about cuckoos.

Neither of them was thinking with any particular intensity about cuckoos. And the sun, the old fool, went on shining upon them.

2

Block of Alabaster

One side of the deep lane changed its character and became highly respectable as a tall, well-trimmed hedge of yew. Presently that hedge had a lapse, where something had devoured or destroyed it and left only a stretch of oak palings to carry on in its place.

Our young people cast off the cares of the world abruptly and became gaminesque. Simultaneously they had one and the same idea. "Let's peek at old Kalikov's lump," she said. "Just once more. That lovely lump."

"Marble it is," he said.

"Alabaster, I tell you. I *know*."

"Marble. You never *get* alabaster in 'normous lumps like that. Alabaster's semi-precious or something of that sort. Just little bits."

"Who ever saw marble all bloodshot?"

"Obstinate. Alabaster *is* marble."

"Ignorance. It's gypsum."

"That G is hard. It's Greek."

"Even there you are wrong. It's English and soft. Naturalised ages ago."

She put out her tongue at him. That was that...

In the most perfect accord they crept up to the gap in the hedge and looked over. There, amidst thick grass and tall wild hemlock, was a big piece of Derbyshire alabaster, twelve feet high at least.

"See that sort of dirty pink vein," she began...

He laid a hand on her arm. "Sh," he said very softly. "*He's* there... There!"

They became as still and observant as startled fawns.

Kalikov, a great lump of a man, with a frizzy, non-Aryan coiffure and ears that you would have thought any sensitive sculptor would have cut off or improved upon years ago, was sitting on a garden seat in the shade of a mulberry tree, brooding over this huge, clumsy block of material. There was a flavour almost of blood-relationship between him and it. He was still as death and intensely wide awake. When at last he stirred it was as eventful as if the block had stirred. He put out his hand. He moved it slowly in a curving path. Then it came to rest, extended.

He shook his head disapprovingly. He repeated his gesture. This time it passed muster. He drew it back along an invisible lower path, carefully, mystically. It was as if he caressed the invisible. It was as if he was trying to hypnotise the inanimate. Then his hand went back into his pocket and he became still again, scheming, dreaming.

The two young people looked at one another and then dropped back noiselessly into the lane.

"Like that," she whispered.

"Then one day he will get his chisels and hammers and things and begin to hew it out," she expanded.

"No clay model?" he queried.

"Not for him." She was sure.

Some paces further he spoke with a note of intense surprise. "But that's exactly how we have to do it. Exactly. Exactly what has been trying to get into my mind for weeks."

She made an interrogative noise.

"That," he said, with a backward toss of the head. "That behind there. It's just exactly how I feel about things."

"Meaning?"

"Something completely hidden. *Which is there.*"

"Yeah?"

"Clumsy block of a world, monstrous, crushing the grass, bloodshot, and yet in it there is a world to be found, a real world, a great world."

"Which *he* may find?"

"Which *we* may find – our sort of people – in this block of a world today."

She stood regarding him with her legs wide apart, her arms akimbo and her head a little on one side.

"Gemini, you're saying something. You talk like an evangelist tract but you're saying something considerable. It's a new sort of approach."

"I've said something that's been in my mind in a state of helpless solution for ever so long. *That*, somehow, has crystallised it. The proper religion, the proper way of life, it isn't all this everlasting squabbling of anti-this and anti-that. Newspapers, politics, churches; the whole bloody jumble. Everybody wrong and nobody right. Our sort of people and more of us and more, have been astray, getting into disputes that don't matter a dam, blundering away at negations. That isn't the job for us. *Our* job is to realise the shape in the block, to get the vision of it clearer and clearer in our heads and then to set about carving it out. Am I saying something at last?"

"Sounds to me something quite considerable."

She reflected.

"I'll have a thousand criticisms presently," she said, "but you *are* saying something, Gemini. Something we can talk about for days."

"Leave it now then for a bit," said he, "for I'm hungry. Down here, what with the air and this love-making, I seem to be *always* hungry. Come on. Get to your kitchen, woman, for old mother Greedle is more of a talking heart than a head. See to things."

And he waved his bunch of bananas towards the cottage ahead of them, and went limping in front of her.

"It's such a consolidating idea," she said to his back.

"It *is* a consolidating idea. It's *the* consolidating idea. It's *the* consolidating idea. The unrevealed statue. The unrevealed new world. The *right* world... I wonder if we shall find the unquenchable Balch on the doorstep... So soon as he scents a meal afoot... I'll try this notion out on him."

3

Balchification

The unquenchable Balch, true to form, did not appear until the meal was ready. They went through the front room with its big open fireplace and its incongruous array of rugs, miscellaneous chairs, stools, ornaments, allusive and entirely irrational objects and artistic impedimenta – there were two inactive grandfather clocks, two brass panoplies for cart-horses, a powder horn, but only one copper warming-pan – towards the kitchen scullery at the back. They went calling "Hullo, Mrs Greedle, what have you got to eat?" and "Mrs Greedle, *is* there anything to eat?"

"Bubble and squeak, you said you liked, Mrs Twain," said Mrs Greedle. "The cabbage is all chopped. You left some bits of bacon; I can't think 'ow. With a bit of 'am and a hegg or so and a nunion for taste; not ten minutes it won't take, to 'ave it nice and spluttering, and there's them sardines to begin upon for an Orderove and that nice fruit cake Miss Clarkson sent you down, and a nice tomato cocktail and the siphons 'ave come."

"*Nice* siphons," whispered Gemini.

"With coffee to follow," said the temporary Mrs Twain, hitherto known to us as Stella.

"Yes, Ma'am, nice black coffee in them little cups. As usual. Nice and 'ot."

"On with the frying!" cried Gemini. "We'll eat it here. Ten minutes! I'm damned if I don't wash my hands."

"Me too," said Stella. "See what a good example does!"

"How's the whiskey?" said Gemini.

"S'in the Tantalus in the front room," said Mrs Greedle. "I didn't think to look 'ow much. I do 'ope..."

Gemini had a moment of apprehension, but he found the Tantalus, which ages ago had lost its key and ceased to tantalise, still resourceful, even if Balch dropped in. "I ordered two bottles from the grocer," said Gemini, "in case," but Mrs Greedle seemed too preoccupied with the appetising mess in her frying pan to hear.

They were busy with the sardines when Balch became audible as a copious throaty voice in the front room.

"Hoy Hoy!" it said. "*What* a reek of onions, and food at large! You children seem always to be eating."

"Bubble and squeak, Balch. You're just in time. Come and join us."

A large buff face with an enormous loose mouth, large grey eyes with a slight cast, and quantities of iron-grey hair, not only on the scalp but bursting generously from brows and ears, appeared in the doorway. The loose mouth was drawn down at the corners with a misleading effect of hauteur, and there was not so much a chin as a series of chin tentatives which finally gave it up and became a neck. The face radiated a sort of anxious benevolence, as though it was relieved to find things no worse than they were. It was closely followed by a body clad loosely in what was still technically a white linen suit, from the breast pocket of which bristled a number of fountain pens, several copying-ink pencils, a spectacle-case and a large red carpenter's pencil, proclaiming an alert, various and fecund literary worker. He looked like a ham actor; he looked like an unsuccessful playwright; he looked exactly what he was – a freelance journalist in the early fifties; the sort of man who is always getting on tremendously and volubly and never by any chance getting anywhere.

"If ever I hit this cottage between meals," he said, "I shall put it in my diary as a notable event."

"Join us," said Gemini, putting out the rest of the sardines for him upon a Woolworth plate. (All the plates in the house, except the wall decorations, were Woolworth plates and all the glasses Woolworth glasses.)

"I *ought* not," said Balch, and then relenting: "Just to save your greedy little faces, I *will*."

He did.

Mrs Greedle surveyed the consumption of her bubble-and-squeak with bland benevolence and felt that whatever criticisms might be passed upon her fancy dishes, her soofles, crimes, mooses, kickshaws, glasses, gallant tins, soup-raims, rag-whos?, consommers and debauches – tomato soup the latter is, with a bit of cream on the top – her arlar thises and her arlar thats – nevertheless at good old village cooking, at your bubble-and-squeak or your nice onion stew or your hot-pot or what not, she knew her business to a T. And in her heart she hoped that in the end the young gentleman would marry the young lady, for a nicer young lady she had never set eyes on in all her born days, speaking clearly like a lady and look you nicely in the eyes, and never getting drunk and not keeping it down like a lady should, and the mess and all of it, like so many young ladies of the best families seemed to make almost a point of doing nowadays...

The nice hot coffee was served on an Indian brass tray on a lacquered Moorish table in the front room, and the voice of the unquenchable Balch, released from degustation, began to play about the world of fact and fancy in a free and fearless fashion.

He was in the habit of calling his host and hostess "The ultimate generation, the last and so far the best". They were, he said, his "*Wunderkinds*". He combined an undisguised admiration for their youth, boldness, directness and intelligence with an air of immense helpfulness and patronage and tutorial responsibility. And also there was a note of sadness because this world would surely be too much for them. "You two ought to *write* while you are fresh and young and new. And still alive. Use your baby language – for I know you have one, mum though you keep about it – and any little Joycery that comes into your heads. Write! Tell me about it, show it to me. Anything you do. I know things. I know people. If you have any ideas. I might save you endless experimenting..."

Now over the coffee Gemini unfolded his idea, and Balch interrupted, commented and expanded, and Stella sat on the settle with her chin between her fists and her elbows on the old polished cask, resolved to let no nonsense get past her.

"We're the heirs of a bankrupt world," said Gemini. "The religions, the patriotisms, have all killed one another. This war, this war that is going to drink us all up, will be a war about nothing, because the sense has gone out of everything. Worse than the War to End War. Whichever way it goes, things after it will be worse than ever. One thing's as rotten as another, and there's nothing we can join on to. Nothing. See? Nothing. Nothing by way of a going concern. And that's where the great idea comes in..."

"Come to the great idea," said Balch, waving aside the preamble.

"The thing we have to serve isn't divinity or a church or a country or an empire or a class or a party. None of them is worthwhile now. None. It's something greater."

Balch opened his mouth to speak.

"Listen, Balch! It's a possibility we have to serve."

He went on, holding up a hand like a traffic policeman to restrain Balch, while he told of their glimpse of Kalikov brooding in his garden. "There's this great block, the world, and there's the human imagination gradually realising what it can do with it... Now you have your say, Balch."

BABES IN THE DARKLING WOOD

At first he was not appreciative. "This is Utopianism, my dear chap," he protested, "just Utopianism."

"No. Utopia is nowhere, but the Unrevealed World is here and now. Smothered up. Embedded. It's not a dream. It's the possibility, close at hand, which is something quite different."

"Your possibility isn't everybody's possibility," said Balch.

"Gemini, grapple with that," said Stella.

"I've thought of that. Already I've thought of that. While I was washing my hands. First, let me ask you a question. First, Balch, do you think that Kalikov could make anything he pleases out of that block he has? *Anything?*"

"Within certain limits."

"You don't think that?"

"But I *do*."

"Then why does he sit and brood over it? Tell me that. He can make all sorts of messes of it, I admit, chip it to bits, spoil it and waste it, but there's only one supreme thing waiting for him there. That's what he has to get out of it. That's why he broods. Everything else, everything else, will be failure."

"Something in that," said Balch. "Something in that. I give you old Kalikov. Leave him. But who's going to imagine the hidden world in *our* world? You?"

"M'm?" said Stella.

"I think there is an answer to that too. The artist in front of our world is the human imagination. No! Don't tell me human imaginations can imagine anything. I've had a brain-wave about that. They can't. Any more than Kalikov can. They may go astray. I guess Kalikov has his wandering fancies which he has to dismiss. But – here's my second great idea – the human imagination is like the human blood corpuscle; it's the same everywhere. Fundamentally. We aren't all at sixes and sevens. We seem to be, but fundamentally we are not. See?"

"I don't see," said Balch. "No. What are you driving at?"

"This. All over the world the mass of human beings want peace. Don't they? But their minds are confused. They are misled, miseducated. They don't see the shape of it as a world organisation. They don't give it a form. All over the world they are staring at this great lump of a world – all this war, all this hatred – blood-red streaks and stains – and yet with a loveliness – like Kalikov. See? But gradually, quickly or not, they will begin to realise – what is practically the same idea – the idea of a whole world in one active order..."

"H'm." Balch weighed it profoundly. "Differences of race," he said. "Differences of culture. Differences of tradition. Differences of colour."

"Streaks in the alabaster," said Stella softly.

Gemini was fairly launched upon his second great idea, and he did not mean to have it set aside.

"The human brain," he declared, "is more alike everywhere than anything else in the human make-up. I can assure you it is. A little heavier or a little lighter. You can tell the race, the sex, of a finger or a hair, but you couldn't tell anything about a human brain in pickle except that it was a human brain."

"And is that so?" said Balch.

"Common knowledge," said Gemini stoutly. "Human minds, I tell you, are more alike than human bodies. Make them think; put the same problem before them, and the harder they think the nearer they'll come to the same answer. There's a Common Human Imagination, waiting to be awakened..."

Balch shut his extensive mouth hard, put his head on one side, and regarded the timbered ceiling. "Now that's a large proposition," he considered, rallying his mind, and was glad to defer to Stella, who was preparing to point her remarks with an extended finger.

"This idea of yours, Gemini, sounded so good at first," she said. "But is it after all even a good analogy? There's Kalikov there with his block of alabaster – because you know, Gemini, it *is* alabaster – and it's fixed. It won't do a thing until Kalikov makes up his mind. It squats there in the grass and waits. He can go away for a holiday and forget about it, and when he comes back there it is just the same. But *our* block of alabaster isn't fixed."

"M'm," said Twain, as if he was beginning something.

"It isn't the least bit fixed," she said, raising her voice by way of a protest against a possible interruption. "*Our* lump, our world, hangs over us, keeps heeling over us. It is moving, like a mountain moving down to crush a Swiss village. It won't wait for anything. Kalikov can brood over his lump for a year. But our imaginations – "

"The common human imagination," said Gemini, sticking to his second great idea.

"Of which ours are the only samples now in court. Our imaginations have no time for that sort of thing. Our mass of a world may do anything to us now. The one thing we can be sure of is that it won't leave us alone. *We* carve it; it's much more likely to carve us. It may blow us to bloody rags; it may smash us underfoot, flat as squashed ants. Kalikov can afford to say 'I will sleep on it. I will do it tomorrow', but for our block, which is in front of us and behind us and over us and under us – the word is *now*."

"Yes," she added, as rapidly as possible because Balch was making the sort of noises that preluded an eruption. "And about human imaginations being all alike. If only they were. If only they were. But what sort of proof – ? They don't even begin to get together... The imaginations of man's heart are only evil continually..."

But now Balch was rising to his occasion.

He began to wave his hand about like a hovering wasp while Stella was speaking. "Wup," he said. "Mur. Waur. Oom." He pounced on her first pause for breath. "Very good," he said, "very good, Madam Stella. True and penetrating. But it doesn't alter the proposition in any essential respect. Let me explain. Let me speak. The essential thing is the challenge of the block. There's the lump you have to carve life out of. Whether it keeps still or whether it keeps sliding after you, is secondary. Secondary. Still – . Sculptor chased by a block of alabaster. Ugh? *Idea* in that. Short story perhaps. But it doesn't abolish the sculpture idea. Twain, I apologise for calling this notion of yours Utopian. I do indeed. I begin to see your drift. It isn't Utopian. Far from it. It's immensely common-sense. I didn't get your drift at first. I didn't expect it from you. I wonder if *you* even begin to realise the importance of what you have said. The Universality! It's an Enormous Idea. E-normous. You've hit on something... Now I begin to think of it... I wonder I never thought of it myself. It's all very well for you to call it down, young lady, and criticise it, but don't let her discourage you, Twain. Your mind is building better than you know."

"I didn't," began Stella...

"I don't think I implied," began Gemini...

But Balch was now under way and he raised his voice, at once powerful and plaintive, so as to take complete possession of the air.

"There is a great world order here and now, hidden in our circumstances and in men's minds. True! And you can prove it by the universal similarity of brains and cells. Good! Excellent! *That's* your idea. A biological assertion of human brotherhood. Don't you see that that is what you are saying?"

"*Saying* it," protested Gemini unavailingly...

"Don't you see that this gives the preliminary concept for a new and hopeful – as far as anything can be hopeful nowadays – a new and hopeful attack on life? At the eleventh hour. It's – it's as fundamental... It's a new, a creative restatement of religion. It calls together everything that is progressive and constructive in life. Think what it says! Never mind what *is*, it says. That's the essence of it. To hell with what is. Whatever is, is just material, stuff to be used or stuff to be thrown away. You get together sooner or later with all the other imaginations in the world that have got lit up. And the What Is, vanishes." His arm swept the World that Is away. "It melts into the World of Heart's Desire. What is, meanwhile can do its damnedest. It has no claim on you. The only thing that has a claim on you is this non-existent world hidden in the alabaster. Oh! A great idea. The only thing that has a hold upon you is your own free thought and free imagination about that. You are the Free Man looking for his world, the world that has to be, in the world that's been put over you. If they clap you into a uniform and put a rifle in your hand, you owe them no obedience. None. If they put an oath into your mouth it doesn't matter. No oath can hold you that you don't make of your own free accord. Whether you let fly at the man in front of you, or your officer, or the ammunition dump or into the air or try potting the War Boss himself, depends upon just what you think will help most to release the Unrevealed World...

"Phew!" Evidently he would have liked a breathing space, but plainly he felt that Gemini or Stella might cut in if he stopped. So he just let loose a howling, tenoring sound – "Warrow. Ugh. Warrow" – until he could begin his next paragraph.

"*Such* an idea! Oh such an idea! The Unrevealed World! You can state it in general terms now. It forms itself in people's minds all over the world. Peace from pole to pole. Don't we all want it? But we're held up by How? *How's* a mouthful. *How's* the giant in the path. That's not going to hold us up for ever. What are brains for? The service of the human spirit. All over the world people are working their brains like hell to get a practical answer to *How?* To conceive it and behold it. Kalikovs all. You young people may think you are the only people on earth who've glimpsed this idea, but I tell you there are thousands of you; there will be *millions* of you. Not seeing it so clearly perhaps, but feeling it, urged by it. Maybe you exaggerate the possibility of a common human imagination, Twain; maybe you do. But that is merely an exaggeration. The common human imagination *is* there. Ready to be lit. And it can and it shall be lit. It shall be discovered and lit. What you are proposing is a Great Possibility."

"I *said* that," Gemini half whispered.

"The Great Possibility in the Human Imagination the Human Heart; Various, I admit, Madam, and yet the Same throughout the World. *He* sees sameness; *you* may see variety. What *I* see is sameness in variety. That was the discovery of all the great propagandist religions of the world. They saw it even if they lost sight of it again. Think what we mean when we say all men are Brothers. Who said that first? What anonymous Seer? But what a Leap into the Light! The awakening idea of one kingdom of heaven on earth; that step by step realises itself and becomes the Great Human Reality. Ugh! Wur! I've been watching it grow upon people in these years we've lived through. For I too – *I* am a Kalikov. *You* are Kalikovs, yes; but I've been in this thing longer than you. I've *watched* this dream – of world unity, world justice. Not here; not there; but everywhere. World co-operation in giant undertakings, becoming real almost day by day. Why! in 1900, it was a dream, thinner than a dream, the shadow of a dream. People were too far away from one another. Now there are schemes of federalisms, schemes of alliances by the score, – that book you lent me the other day, *Union Now* – just one sample. Everyone making schemes and plans for it, more and more practicable, closer and closer to actuality. Up and down the scale. Internationalism! The Oxford Movement. All touched by the spirit of it. Why! there's even a sort of Cosmopolis in the Rotary Clubs. This has been going on for ages. In a sense, that is, it has been going on for ages. Dumbly. Blindly. Getting clearer – more definite. Never so swiftly. That is what Christ meant by his Kingdom. Buddha was after this! Prophets and teachers. Confucius. *All* of 'em! Pisgah! Feeling for a way out from the Thing that is... Seekers all."

He extended a waving hand and twiddled his fingers to express a great multitude of active seekers.

"Like an immense crowd feeling about in the dark, jostling against each other – but with the dawn breaking. Humanity! Dawn! Darkest hour before the Dawn! Hitler? What's Hitler? The ultimate Cain? The last parricide? Can he prevail? Don't tell me. Japan? A final black-out? The end of all things? No! A thousand times, No! Nerve storms. Fits of evil temper. I tell you the dawn's breaking. Then comes this conception of the Unrevealed World. Nobody is a winner and all win. Don't go on with anything in particular. Carve it out of everything in particular. But everywhere. The Unrevealed World! Shinning darkly through governments, through religions. But plainer now than it was. To think it's got hold of *you!* And so clearly that you even make it plainer to me. You *brilliant* kids! When I hear you saying it clear and definite, Twain, I want to get up and shout and march about..."

Never had this unquenchable Balch been quite so unquenchable. It was just his excessiveness that made him want to shout even more than he was doing. He was already definitely shouting. He was already bumping up and down in his seat. He was like a large boy who has pounced on a small boy's new bicycle. He went on riding it round and round even when he was out of breath. They could not get in a word of their own nice clear thoughts edgeways.

Stella, silenced, regarded him grimly. She had several fine points to make. Every moment she was feeling more clearly that Gemini had jumped too confidently at that "common human imagination" of his. That had to be cleared up. But how could she collect her thoughts, much less say anything, under all this Balchery?

Gemini fretted under the torrent. Hitherto he had thought Balch a joke, a joke with a vulture's scent for distant nourishment, but this was almost too much. "He takes anything," thought Gemini; "it doesn't matter how fine and good it is, he swallows it down and he brings it up, and he turns it into this sort of spew. All the same my idea is a great one. All the same I stick to it and will look at it presently, Balchify though you will."

"Waur! Let us think for a moment of the implication of this great movement which is a old as the hills and as new as sunrise! To which you in your turn have come. In your turn. Such a lot of people have felt it and thought it, and yet it's only now we see clearly what it is that we have felt and thought. Citizens of a state that hasn't arrived; advance agents of a government yet to be. All the roads and railways and mines and factories, all the arsenals, barracks, warships, all the aeroplanes and aerodromes, from end to end of the earth, are the property of our unrevealed government, are *ours*, but mark you, in the hands of usurpers. *Our* heritage – not handed over to us. Every actual government in the world, either a usurpation or a trust. Its end is to hand over or get out. All the Universities and schools, all the churches and religions, are just the germs of *our* One Great World Teaching. Squabbling with one another, keeping us in the dark and failing to unite and develop. Slash and hammer and we clear the alabaster, dig out the shape in it. Hand over, you there, get on, or get out. Kings, Presidents, officials, Ministers, every sort of leader, hand over – get ready to hand over – or get out. Get on to the revelation of Cosmopolis or get off the earth! Some slogan that, eh? Gods! If only I could touch someone for money I'd start a newspaper, I'd start a movement, I'd start a campaign tomorrow. Right on this idea. This is what the Anarchists have been feeling their way towards. Shelley, Kropotkin... If you can call Shelley an Anarchist. He used, I admit, to call the actual governments, Anarchs. Yess. Never mind. Mere matter of phraseology. He meant what I do. What we all do. He would have been with us. Your method must be so far anarchism, that it uses all governments and respects none of them."

"There can be no idea of anarchy in a world of reasonable men," said Gemini's submerged voice.

"We begin to realise at last what it implied in that good old phrase, a Citizen of the World. He is the heir to the future, seeking his divided and mismanaged estate, resolved to unify it now for good and all... I'm talking, I know. Too much perhaps. I can't help talking because the more I think of this phrase of yours – a great phrase it is – the Unrevealed World, I realise that it releases all that has been accumulating in me – for years. I feel as though at last I was being born again. After a sacrament of bubble-and-squeak. We are all being born again here and now. We are not the people we were yesterday. We slot into the new order. Now...

"Think of the new behaviour our great idea demands. Because we new people are the real kings, the rightful owners, and our bearing must be masterly. *Masterly,*" he repeated, as though the timbered ceiling had contradicted him. "Just in so far as we hold to our relentless aim, just so far are we living rightly. Complaisant to all that is decent and creative in the world, but inflexible to whatever is treason to one universal citizenship. Then we must resist; then we must withstand, not seeking martyrdom but facing it calmly, daring to say 'I disbelieve in your encumbering, separating faiths, I disavow your irrational loyalties...' So!"

He paused with hand extended, breathing deeply, his great face aflame with leadership and defiance.

Then he started like a man stung.

Babes in the Darkling Wood

It was a minute mechanical sound that startled him. It was the click of the latch of the garden gate. He turned, extended his neck, and stared through the half open door. An expression of consternation spread swiftly over his countenance.

"Gee-whizz, here's the plurry parson coming up the path!" he said, clawing at the air, and vanished by way of the kitchen as they turned their heads.

It was almost incredible that so much sound and substance could be so completely and instantaneously annihilated. It was like the bursting of some vast, sonorous soap bubble.

Stella and Gemini found themselves staring across the littered room at one another in empty silence, a silence which nevertheless seemed to reverberate with inaudible echoes of Balch's phrases.

"I can't tell lies," said Stella, suddenly and simply. "I can't tell any more lies."

"*What?*" cried Gemini.

"I won't. It's sucking up to the Old World. See?"

"But it's still the old world," said Gemini, aghast. "Go easy, Stella."

The clergyman called attention to his arrival by a neat rat-rat of his knuckles on the front door.

"Come in," said Gemini, standing up politely.

"No lies, mind you," said Stella, sitting tight and clenching her little fists. That wedding ring pinched her. "Damn you!" she whispered to it, but there was no time to fumble it off.

The clergyman, stooping slightly under the six foot door, came in, quite unaware that the world he lived in had just been warned to get itself born again or go.

Chapter Two

Church Militant?

Fine Point in Ethics

He was partly camouflaged as a layman. He wore a light-grey flannel suit and he was holding a Panama hat in his hand, but an unbroken line of collar round his neck reminded one that he was not quite of this world. He was tall and thin, with a bony, aquiline, ascetic face, and the natural earnestness of his countenance had evidently been subjected to intensive cultivation. He might have been of any age between thirty-five and fifty.

"I don't intrude, I hope," he said. "I do hope I don't intrude."

"Won't you sit down?" said Stella with a gesture that indicated most of the wide range of Mary Clarkson's sitting apparatus available in the room.

He ignored her invitation and remained standing.

"Charming room, this of Miss Clarkson's," he said. "Quite charming. Old-world *and* at the same time modern. Such a delightful contrast to – to houses in a different style. Quite... I'm told you've been here a week or more."

"Yesterday week," said Stella.

"And beautiful weather it *has* been, Mrs Twain."

"My name," said Stella, leaning back on the settle, avoiding Gemini's probably horrified eye, sticking the offending wedding ring to the very bottom of her trouser pocket and trying to get it off, "is Miss Stella Kentlake."

She realised suddenly that she had lost her breath and took a large gulp. She felt exactly as though she was playing in a charade and that if she lost her nerve for a moment it would go altogether.

The clergyman altered the angle of his face slightly, so as to seem just a trifle more austere. "I understood," said he, "you were a young married couple."

"No relationship whatever," said Stella. "Just friends. *He's* Twain."

She nodded her head to indicate Gemini.

"Well, well," said the good man. He had heard of the wedding ring and was a little taken aback by her frankness. He had come all prepared to accept wedding ring conventions. "Customs change," he said. "In my grandmother's time you young people might have been considered a trifle indiscreet, you know. But now – . *Honi soit qui mal y pense*, I hope?"

"Exactly what I was going to suggest," said Stella, getting clear of the ring at last, sitting up briskly and behaving as much like a respectable hostess of forty as she knew how. "And now Mr —?"

"Morton Richardson."

"Won't you sit down? We've had a perfectly lovely week down here, loving sunshine and everything, and we'd love to hear something about its parochial life. And all that. We'd love to. My hus– , Mr Twain, I mean, is beginning to write and so on. That sort of young man..."

BABES IN THE DARKLING WOOD

She glanced commandingly at Gemini, who was watching her with undisguised admiration and making no effort at all to assist. He took up his cue with a start.

"Unperformed dramatist, Sir, mute poet, indispensable clerk in the Penguin Press organisation, reserve literary worker for the Propaganda Department. Too lame for military service – leg crushed some years ago. But do please sit down. This rather large chair here has never failed anyone."

"Certainly. Certainly. Though I can't promise to stay very long, you know."

"A little coffee perhaps? There's some in the kitchen. Mrs Greedle. Mrs *Gree*-dle."

Mrs Greedle appeared promptly and curtsied intimately to Mr Morton Richardson.

"Aah! Mrs Greedle, and how are *we* nowadays?"

"Never so well, Sir. I'm a patent for our new doctor. Them charcoal biscuits E gave me, they worked a miracle. Indeed they did, Sir. For the last three weeks I haven't know what gas was. It's gone. B'sorbed completely. Shall I bring fresh coffee, Mrs Twain, nice and hot?"

She disappeared.

"*Mrs* Twain," said the clergyman, as he lowered himself carefully into the large chair and extended his legs towards the open fireplace. "I'm glad that you didn't – . That you have been tender with her possible feelings. About the – er – the situation."

"*Well*," said Stella. "It's rather on my conscience. I'd be glad of your advice. Don't you think perhaps we ought to break it to her? After all, this calling myself 'Mrs', it is, you know, *lying*."

The Reverend Morton Richardson became gravely thoughtful. He put his two long fine hands into an attitude of prayer and rotated them gently against each other. "I would do nothing precipitate," he said. "The situation so far as she is concerned has already been created. With me you have been charmingly frank – charmingly. I take it as a compliment. But – "

Mrs Greedle came back with the coffee and in the pause caused by her presence Gemini poured out for the vicar. "I'm interested in your view, Sir," said the young man, handing the little cup.

"I should do nothing precipitate," the clergyman repeated, when he had assured himself that the door of the kitchen had closed again on Mrs Greedle. "And on the whole if you don't mind I would rather she did not know that *I* know of the exact nature of this – er – Platonic experiment of yours. Because you see that would make me a party, so to speak, in the – I think of the whole justifiable deception..."

At the word "Platonic" Gemini had raised his eyebrows slightly at Stella. But Stella remained modestly expressionless.

"But it *is* a lie, Sir," said Gemini.

"Probably it all began with your charming hostess. Before you came here at all. She may have used some expression... She may have said 'a young couple' is coming down. That makes it a misapprehension rather than a deception. Mrs Greedle, I know, is apt to jump to conclusions. Almost too apt. If you try to clear things up with her now you may sow the seeds of distrust... Suppose we let it rest at that. For the present at any rate..."

"You couldn't say fairer," said Mrs Greedle, ceasing to listen at the kitchen door. "So that's that."

She returned to her gas stove to make a reassuring clatter there. "Seeds of distruss, my eye! Charming 'ostess! As though I didn't know 'er. Through *and* through!... The things I've seen! Crikey! Seeds of distruss! If I tole him One Tenth!..."

A brilliant, rollicking but extremely improper thought came into Mrs Greedle's busy brain. She chuckled confidentially to the plate-rack. "But you can't say things like that to a parson, you know," said Mrs Greedle archly, putting a rinsed plate to dry. "They've an innocence... Even babies 'ave a knowingness. Dirty little darlins. But *parsons* – . Oh *parsons!* Don't even wet themselves. It isn't as though they was natural white paper; it's as though they'd been washed out. Sort of bleached... *Ne-o-o-w.*"

Mrs Greedle, featuring a distaste for a secondary and acquired innocence by a grimace of concentrated scorn and a haughty backward movement of the head, came within an inch of breaking a plate.

2

Sheep Astray

By that time the party in the living-room were well away upon other topics.

"Did I," said the vicar, "did I hear you say your name was Kentlake? Have you any relationship, by any chance, to the – rather – well – conspicuous – well-known – "

"The philosophical psychologist," said Stella. "He's my favourite uncle. It was he, had me sent to Cambridge."

"Cambridge?"

"Newnham."

"*I* was a Trinity man," said the vicar. "But long before your time. Dear me. How the year slip by! Just in time to be a padre. But you, you can't have taken your degree yet?"

"Second year. Whether I take the tripos now, depends... It depends on all sorts of things... Obviously."

"Obviously. Now. Forgive me for saying it but don't you think you should have thought of that before," said the vicar. "If people, if the authorities at Newnham, chose to put an uncharitable interpretation upon this — this little adventure of yours — it might interfere rather seriously — "

"You can't always think of a situation until you've made it," said the young lady, with a faint touch of defensive acidity. "You were speaking of my uncle."

"I was thinking of his ideas," said the vicar, regarding the dogs and logs in the fireplace with an unworldly, kindly expression and beginning to triturate his hands again.

"He's always so *Right*," said Stella.

"You say he sent you to Cambridge. Forgive my curiosity, but *why* was it he sent you?"

"My mother wasn't in a position to send me. But need we go into that?"

"Certainly not. Not unless you wish it. If I were asked to advise...mediate... I was only thinking — . So many issues..."

"You were thinking, you said, of my uncle's ideas. I warn you we're full of them, both of us. It's that brought us together. And rather encouraged us. We believe in him solidly. Almost solidly."

"You must forgive me if my admiration is more — *critical*. In this world there has of course to be variety — variety of standpoints — variety of opinions. Different aspects."

"We both feel that acutely," said Gemini. "Of course we of the younger generation, in these urgent times, find the variety of opinions rather perplexing. It's we who have to decide among them and we don't seem to have so very much time. Not so easy, Sir. We'd like any criticism of Doctor Kentlake and his sort of thinking, if you could give it us, above all things. Sometimes I feel when I'm reading him that he's so completely convincing, as far as he goes, that there must be a trick in it somewhere. His literary style may carry one over things…"

"A very very good comment," said the vicar. "A very penetrating comment."

"Yes, Sir," said Gemini and stopped attentively.

"I must confess," said the vicar, smiling faintly, "that, come to think of it, I find an impromptu critique of the writings and philosophy of Doctor Kentlake rather a large order. On the spur of the moment. Don't you think?"

"Not from you, Sir. Isn't it after all your particular business – ?"

"Literary criticism?"

"No, Sir. The teaching of the Church which Doctor Kentlake flouts and attacks. If he is right; then, Sir, forgive me, you have no justification for being what you are?"

"Yes. Yes. Perhaps so."

"We *expect* it from you, Sir," said Gemini, with the shadow of a grin in his voice. "For what else are you for? You are here to embody the real truth and the right way. A sort of sanitary inspector of conduct and ideas. Just as you were able to tell us just now *when* the truth ought to be handled – well – with gloves on – ."

"That wasn't *quite* how we settled it; was it?" said the vicar.

"Anyhow, now, you ought to give us at least an idea of the reply, the orthodox right reply, to what Doctor Kentlake says about orthodox religion and morals. And I can assure you, Sir, from the things I've heard Stella say and the things she's heard me say, you don't come any too soon here..."

The vicar made that noise which is usually indicated in print by "Chirm". He grasped the arms of his chair firmly, sat a little lower and longer in it, and regarded the fireplace now with a certain mournful sternness. "Of course," he said, "you must not regard me as a compendium of theological controversy."

"Still, Sir, you must admit; it's your job," said Gemini.

"Well, among other things."

"Surely, Sir, *above* other things. The faith must be maintained. Our generation is drifting away. You come just in the nick of time. I hesitate to tell you how far out to sea *we* are. We hardly believe a thing you believe, according to your creeds. We just don't take the Bible story. And people who give serious thought to life, they are reading these sceptical writers, Kentlake and Shaw and Bertrand Russell and Joad, the two Huxleys, Hogben, Levy, J B S Haldane – in preference to any orthodox authorities. Even when it comes to belief they seem to prefer mathematicians – mystical mathematicians – Jeans and Eddington for example, Captain Dunne and Whitehead – to people like Cosmo Gordon Lang and Temple. They'd almost rather have Uspensky than a bishop. And can you wonder at it? Such a lot of the Anglican Church seems to be deliberate talking beside the mark. That fat book, *The Study of Theology*, the other day. I got it and read it. That shows I'm up-to-date. Published quite recently and I – well I saw a review of it. You may have missed it, Sir... It isn't exposition, Sir; it isn't any sort of fundamental discussion; it's stuff got up to look like exposition and discussion. The Catholics put up a better sort of fight. There's Belloc with his impudent assertiveness; he has the creative gift, he makes his own biology as he goes along; and there's this Professor Karl Adam coming up. Have you read Professor Karl Adam at all, Sir? There's a boldness about him...

"I can tell you, Sir, that making up our minds about – about what is truth and what are the right principles of living for us –; it's a *frightful* task. The ideas we are expected to know about. The stuff we have to read. The stuff we have to keep up with. And whatever of it is right, makes all the rest wrong. Somebody must be right. Nobody grips it and holds it still and digests it all for us. And the Church, they tell me, goes on. Empty pews, silent pulpits – sermons cut to nothing. Yet preventing anything else from taking its place. Why *is* it, Sir? Why does the Church have nothing definite to say for itself? We sheep are all astray. We – the young. It isn't for nothing that a bishop carries a pastoral crook, surely? But does he try to use it? Have I ever felt a bishop pulling my leg, Sir? Never. Sorry to seem so critical, Sir. I'm garrulous. My ideas run away with me."

"Little you know of a parson's duties," said the vicar, "to demand this of him. Births, marriages and deaths. The coal club, the rummage sale, the choir, the bell-ringers, the charities, the school treat and the churchwardens. The constant calls for advice, temporal as well as spiritual. The sick and dying in need of consolation..."

"But what do you tell them, Sir? What *is* the consolation?"

"Simple things. The restoration of faith."

"But what faith, sir? What *is* the faith? That's the question."

The vicar was evidently doing his best to be frank and honest. He continued to stare into the fireplace and there was a flavour of soliloquy in his voice.

"In the case of the sick and dying, I will make no bones about it, and I am speaking as an experienced priest, you have to use the faith you find there already. Whatever it is. You must. To help, and I assure you I want to help, I make myself all things to all men, to all failing and dying souls... You would too."... He stopped short and resumed more briskly. "Well, all these things keep one busy. So that when you pull me back to theology... I admit it is what you call my job — but don't expect me to be a specialist. I'll answer to the best of my ability."

He paused.

"All these other things are frightfully important things," said Stella. "But as my — as Twain, there, says, they aren't the essential jobs of the Church. Surely. Some of that is civil administration; some might be better done by a medical or psychic or educational adviser — or a parish clerk. Or a glorified community schoolmaster. As my uncle is always saying. But the essential claim of the Church is its religion, its belief that is, the right theory and the right practice of living. If that is wrong, then what is its authority?"

"If," said the inexorable Gemini, "if you have to — well, Sir, not to put too fine a point on it — prevaricate, to the distressed and sick and dying, isn't that because you haven't established — how is it Kentlake puts it? — a high right-mindedness in them, when they were well?"

"You put me on the defensive, young people... I stand by my creed."

Babes in the Darkling Wood

"It is your Church, Sir, that is on the defensive. We *have* to ask you. What are the sure and irreducible verities that justify your practical control of social conduct? You do control it a lot, you know. You interfere a lot. Practical morals. Judgments on people. Education. The Abdication. You stand for all that, and this country is largely what you have made it. Isn't an uneducated country now, but it's about as badly educated as it can be. So Kentlake says. At the back of it all surely there has to be a creed, a fundamental statement, put in language that does not jar with every reality we know about the world. We don't want to be put off with serpents and fig-leaves and sacrificial lambs. We want a creed in modern English, Sir. And we can't find it. You *must* have a foundation or you would resign. Mr Gladstone wrote of the Impregnable Rock of Holy Scriptures. But it isn't quite like that, Sir, now, is it? The Rock's all at sea. Still – there ought to be some sort of rock bottom…?"

For the better part of a minute the vicar said nothing and the two young people remained in a state of mercilessly silent expectation. Gemini studied the ascetic face before him with a vivid, new-born curiosity. He seemed to be seeing something that had always been under his eyes but which he had never clearly observed before. His brain was already acquiring many of the habitual vices of a writer's. A riot of stereotyped phrases ran through his mind and were rejected – "wily ecclesiastic", "priestly domination", "professional churchman" for example. He pushed these confusing suggestions aside in his determination to see for himself. This face, he realised, was neither a good face nor a bad face, neither a saint's nor a sinner's but it was at one and the same time an extremely usual face and also a profoundly unreal one. It was a made and disciplined face. It betrayed nothing inadvertently. It expressed what it was intended to express.

It had never struck Gemini before but now it came to him as something very important that this was the case with almost all the cases he had encountered of teachers, professors, doctors, magistrates and all those set in authority over their fellow-men, they were all definitely determined façades, façades not assumed to deceive but to maintain a definite line under difficulties and to suppress and conceal as completely as possible whatever complex inconsistencies might still be stirring within. It seemed to him now that he was apprehending for the first time how high and deep and far-reaching and necessary (necessary?) is the artificiality of social life...

When at last the vicar spoke he went off at a tangent. He attempted no statement of his creed in modern terms. "My main objection to Doctor Kentlake's views," he began, "is his one-sided materialism, his deliberate disregard of any spiritual values whatever..."

This led to a complicated metaphysical digression that began badly and degenerated towards the end.

3

Metaphysical-Theological

All unwittingly, you see, the vicar had detonated a mine of newly digested discussion that had been floating ready in Gemini's mind.

"I'm sorry to cut in, Sir," said the young man eagerly.

"Ask me any question."

"You say material. You say spiritual. You seem to be assuming that there is a sort of primary two-sidedness in things. Most of us, I admit, have been brought up on that assumption. Language is soaked with it. But a lot of us have come to believe that it is an almost fundamental error in human thought."

"But surely you attach some meaning to – when I say 'spiritual values'?"

"No, Sir. For me, for us, no. We know the sort of thing that attaches, that has attached, to that phrase. But for us, when we are talking of reality, that sort of association has got quite loose."

"But then. Are you so old-fashioned as to be materialistic?"

"Is that 'old-fashioned' quite fair? Anyhow it is easy to say *tu quoque* and leave it at that." And Gemini proceeded to argue, with all the confidence and ready fullness of a brilliant student fresh from his preparation, that the false fundamental dichotomy implied in the opposition of material and spiritual was being kept alive by the organised religions in despite of advancing human thought, that it encumbered that advance, and this was the chief cause of the stupefaction of civilisation in the present crisis.

"Fundamental dichotomy," repeated the vicar almost inaudibly. "Chirm – "

Doctor Kentlake, pursued Gemini, allowing no intervention, treated the universe as being of one nature throughout, would have nothing to do with that ancient primary opposition. You couldn't call him materialist; you couldn't call him spiritualist, "Monist" was a better word. Doctor Kentlake had merely given a philosophical form to what was the established practice of the scientific worker. The practical scientific worker thought in the same way even if he did not formulate it very clearly. He might be pluralist or he might be monist, consciously or implicitly, but he was never in practice dualist. Essentially he was a pragmatist. He threw terms over reality rather like a flyfisher making a cast, Sir, and found out what they hooked for him. Matter, force, rhythm, electricity and so on were terms invented by the human mind in its struggle to apprehend the world, they were all in reality "partial, tentative terms". They were bait, so to speak, to catch the unknown. So were such words as imagination or beauty or belief...

The vicar opened and shut his mouth.

"Where has Gemini got all this?" Stella asked herself. "He must have been reviewing some book. He can't simply have read it up. He must have been writing it down. He's glib. That Oxford glibness of his! He's got it at his fingers' ends."

Intelligent people nowadays, Gemini went on remorselessly; intelligent people were ceasing to consider any of the terms they used as finalities. Formerly they did so, but now they were more penetrating. Meaning, they were discovering, was elusive, it was the final wisdom towards which the mind moved; it did not leap into existence with a word and a definition. They knew the terms they employed never did quite "get it". Our naïve forefathers thought they "got it" completely and that "it" could be defined exactly and completely. You defined your term, you put it through the logical machines and there you were with your conclusion neatly extracted. Such word-worship was coming to an end. Semantics had changed all that. Semantics – or Significs if you preferred the older term. It was just as unreasonable to say the world was all matter, as it was to say it was all movement, or all electricity or all rhythm or all beauty or all imagination.

"Shakespeare! Imagination all compact!" interjected the vicar with an air of scoring an unexpected point. "We are such things as dreams are made on."

"And also, Sir, we are creatures who can eat potatoes, get drunk and suffer from rheumatic fever. We are such stuff as crowds and concentration camps are made on. We are such stuff as operating theatres deal with. All that and more. The universe won't simplify out to oblige us, Sir."

Gemini had warmed up steadily as his argument had unfolded. He spoke now with all the precocious maturity of the Ex-Union President. His was a compendium of lecturers' styles and debaters' expositions. A great dominating organisation like the Anglican or Roman Church had no right, he asserted, to carry on nowadays with "this old, this superseded and misleading bilateralism". It ought to speak the language of the new period. But Christianity had planted itself in the way of the modernisation of thinking, just as, by its Creationism, it still blocked the way to a clear biological vision of life. That was one of the chief reasons why we were all now at sixes and sevens and so desperately out of touch with reality – in the face of catastrophe. "To which our generation seems likely to be pretty completely sacrificed, Sir. Far worse than 1914. You must forgive us if we get a little shrill about it."

"H'm," said Stella, manifestly approving, and she turned like a chairman to the vicar. She had not suspected Gemini of any of this metaphysical precision. He had it all so well packed and so ready to hand. Certainly he must have been summarising something or editing something very very recently indeed. Queer quick mind he had! Better than hers!

The vicar sat with his extended hands together, finger tips to finger tips. As Gemini had talked he had, to begin with, nodded his head gravely and encouragingly, listening as a doctor might listen to the symptoms of a patient. In that phase he had a faintly irritating air of having expected all that Gemini had to say. He had nodded less frequently as the spate had proceeded. "Fundamental dichotomy" had definitely ended the nodding phase, and a mood of apprehensive listening had followed, as who should say, What next? His pose was failing him. At "semantics" he had quailed visibly. Had he heard that strange word before, she asked herself? No. Evidently not. Now he took a deep breath almost like a sigh before he spoke.

"I admit," said he. "I grant you there has been much vigorous thinking about fundamentals in the – shall we say? scientific world in the last half century. Yes. I should be the last to quarrel with these modern ideas. Nevertheless – ."

He began to argue that perhaps it was unreasonable to treat spirit and matter as things *diametrically* opposed. Not *diametrically*. He would meet them there. He stressed the word. He adopted a tone of reluctantly using an alien and subtly unsatisfactory terminology for the benefit of his hearers. "Let us agree upon that." Nevertheless there were *grades* of value, things one could call *higher* and things one would call *lower*. Were not those higher things, the things of the spirit? Possibly one might find a more exact and more technical word nowadays, some phrase from Pavlov or Freud or one of those people might please Gemini better, but "spirit" was still the old, customary, established word. It was still the "*normal*" language. "If you will forgive my reverting to normal language", he said with a tentative smile.

Gemini answered this warily, rather more in debating society fashion and rather less professionally. The grades of value, he said, did not run on those lines the vicar was suggesting. It was not a question of moral quality; it was a question of scope. Yes, scope. Stella perceived his main attack was over. He went on talking, but now he was getting away from the substance of that book review and his exposition was less lucid and assured. The vicar seemed to be rallying his evasiveness. Stella noted the change of phase with the impartiality of a boxing referee. The fine precise sparring was over. The disputants were getting winded.

They were soon embarked upon a manifestly futile wrangle; they were playing now for points in the air; their terms and phrases were failing to mesh; were swinging about without any attempt to mesh; it was becoming an argey-bargey. Stella listened with growing impatience. They were saying nothing now of any significance whatever to her. She broke in at last with "But what has this to do with my uncle having no spirituality?"

"We have rather got away from that," said the vicar. "I may, I admit, have formed false conclusions about your uncle's line of thought. After all, you know, in this busy parochial life of mine one is apt to get one's ideas about things from reports and reviews and secondary sources. One has to carry on. I would be the last person to take a rigid line about him. Without further enquiries... But fundamentally you know... Fundamentally..."

He looked at his wrist watch. "I must go very soon. Always I seem to be going on and going away. But before I go I'd like to say something that has been coming up in my mind as we have been arguing here."

"But first of all, Sir"; Gemini pressed; "I must say a word or so more. I do want to put our case to you, Sir. I presume that you stand by the literal statement of your creeds and the story in the New Testament, even if you find some of the Old rather coloured by – well, – primitive oriental symbolism. What we want you to know is that it isn't simply a question of metaphysics with us; it's a question of fact. We do not believe in your creeds. We find your Trinity — whatever it meant to the Greeks and Egyptians — entirely inconceivable. We do not believe in your simple Bible story. From the paternity by the Holy Ghost right up to Pentecost, Sir, it all seems to us mythology, absurdity, with no relation to any living human reality at all. That's what we tell you. And there's a whole lot like us. What have you to say to that?"

"What I have to say will seem a paradox to you," said the vicar. "When I was a child I believed in all those thing as simply as one believes at that age in brightly painted pictures on a wall. Since then, I have not been impervious to modern doubt. No. Some of those pictures, I admit, have faded out, others have become transparent. I have had struggles. I have had to wrestle with many perplexities. But always afterwards I have won my way back to a profounder, more subtle and satisfying interpretation. Always. Always, I assure you. The deeper I go, the more certainly I believe. But as concerns many of the factual elements in the story, as crude facts, the Miracle of the Loaves and Fishes for example, or the swallowing and disgorging of Jonah, I refuse to argue that it happened precisely so, or indeed that it actually happened at all... No."

"And you cannot impart these deeper meanings?"

"No. Frankly no. Not in an atmosphere of factual scepticism. Not without conviction of sin and prayer. That is why the Church never really comes into the Debating Society, stark and unreservedly, as your scientific theories do. Let us recognise that. In the last resort the Church relies upon something that science excludes, if only on the score that repetition and verification are impossible; it relies upon religious experience. Naturally, necessarily, religion rests on religious experience and on nothing else. If you do not know what that is from having undergone it, you do not know what it is."

"But you can describe – ?"

"One can describe. Yes. Yes, I think one can describe. First then there is a deepening and at last insupportable sense of Sin. Self-disgust."

"But we do not believe in sin. Are you sure you do not mean just a fear of life?"

"A fear of God and his righteousness."

"There again we are not equipped with the necessary belief. I can understand a fear that life may be too much for one. But that is not self-disgust."

"Well, grant me that. And then comes an intense hunger for reconciliation to God – ."

"That is how you phrase it."

"And then conversion. Suddenly. An unutterable sense of concentration, oneness and completion. The peace of God that passeth understanding."

"Or a return of courage. Don't you think, Sir, one may go through all these phases without the slightest reference to theology? You feel reconciled to something, but how does that establish a belief on the Virgin Birth, or the raising of Lazarus, or the story that God created the world in, as Huxley had to explain to Mr Gladstone, a non-evolutionary sequence? And what will you say if an out-and-out atheist tells you he has had much the same experience, the depression, the self-disgust, the sense of an urgent need for a change, and then release suddenly to a feeling of Rightness and Oneness, and that he attaches no religious significance whatever to it all? This sequence of moods, Sir, has, I assure you, no special relation to Christianity. It's in all the text-books. William James gives instances from a dozen creeds. Moslem mystics have it. Rabindranath Tagore related the whole experience as the achievement of a sense of Oneness with the universe. It's a way the mind has of recoiling and changing phase. William James tells of an avaricious man who felt conviction of sin; it was the sin of extravagance in his case; and found concentration and salvation in becoming a strict miser."

The vicar made no answer for a moment. Then he answered with an evasion of the question so complex as to take away Gemini's controversial wind altogether. "Faith may realise itself under many Formulae. Nevertheless it remains Faith."

What could one say to that?

The vicar ceased to lounge and sat up. He simply abandoned the argument. "I must go," he said. "What I had in mind to say was this, a point very urgent nowadays. Suppose – . Suppose the Christian religion *is* based on a fundamental error in what you call this assumption of the dualism of matter and spirit. Suppose it is. For the purposes of argument, let us suppose even that. None the less, that assumption has interwoven with human thought and language for thousand of years. Suppose its myth, as you would term it, the Fall and the Redemption, has no factual reality. Suppose what we call the beliefs, the prayers and ceremonies on which the Christian life is based, incorporate a whole tangle of inaccuracies and errors. Suppose they do. Nevertheless that system of living, morality, civilisation, the most successful civilisation the world has ever known, rests upon those same foundations. What happens if you pull them away? They are the sustaining skeleton of the present social order.

Babes in the Darkling Wood

Man's skeleton, I am told, is mechanically imperfect; we could have bigger heads and better brains if what they call the pelvis was larger or the skull sutures didn't close so early. But that doesn't justify an attempt to remove the skeleton and put in steel rods. I tell you that – when everything has been said and done – still from the practical point of view only, and disregarding everything else, the Christian religion is well worth the effort of believing."

"It *is* an effort," said Gemini.

"Certainly," said the vicar. "There is nothing good in this life that you do not have to hold on to with both hands."

"It is an effort for you, Sir? If you lost your grip – ?"

"I do not intend to lose my grip."

He stood up.

"Now I think we see you better," said Gemini. "I wish we could go on with this talk. I am sorry you have to go. It was very kind and friendly of you to call, and I am afraid we have put you through it, rather"

"Good for me too," said the vicar civilly. "And let me repeat my question why, until you can see your way to another social system *better* than this we live in, you should abandon the worn old serviceable working creed?"

"But we question that, Sir. We must make it clear we disagree with that. We two – in all honesty – brought up in a Christian country – do sincerely believe that Christianity, in itself, and apart from other humanising influences, has been an evil rather that a good thing in human life, and that for the past century or more in particular it has been a barrier to human enlightenment. We want you to understand clearly that we have no sort of religious belief at all, in Providence, in a Supreme Being or in anything of the sort. We two are Atheists right out, and to us you, with your religion, seem like a man who has been squeezed into antiquated and quite useless armour that does nothing but impede the freedom of his life and mind."

"You are franker and franker," said the vicar. "Indeed you are almost needlessly frank. But you are young yet. I thank God for that ancient armour, into which I have been as you say squeezed, daily, hourly. I thank Him. Why should I complain of a loss of freedom? Where should I be without it?"

He glanced again at his watch.

For a moment the three stood still.

"We haven't been outrageous with our arguments, I hope," said Gemini. "You see life presses on us. Things are very urgent with all us young people just now. The shadow of war – "

"At any moment," said the vicar, as though he forced himself to say it, "you may have a realisation of Sin."

"We have about as much conviction of sin," said Gemini, with a faint distaste for the Balch touch in the phrasing that had come into his mind, "as lambs in a slaughter house. We may feel frightened presently... That is different..."

"I *must* go," said the vicar for the third time.

He liked them, they liked him and he knew they both liked him. But disapproval and entire detachment was his duty. He bowed gravely to Stella as though she was the accomplished hostess she had been impersonating. Then he went to the door and stood for a moment on the threshold.

"Anyway we've not humbugged you in any way," said Gemini.

"Not at all. I shall have much to think about. There is more in all this than mere argument."

"You won't invoke the prayers of the congregation, Sir?"

Stella flashed a silent reproof at Gemini.

"I may pray for you myself," said the vicar. "I don't know. You are so wrong about all this – and so well-meaning."

But Gemini was still out of hand. Stella's sudden decision to fling deception to the winds, had infected him. He pressed his defeated antagonist. "I'm afraid, too, that we ought to tell you that we're living in what you would call Sin, Sir. We don't want to deceive you in any way."

The vicar winced.

"I can't countenance that. I'm so sorry. I am sorry to hear you say it. No good was ever done by *open* lawlessness, even when the law was wrong. No. And why *tell* me? Why have you told me? I wonder. Defiance only makes things more awkward."

He turned at the gate and looked back at them for a whole second perhaps. Again there was an air of hesitation about him. "No," he said, almost as much to himself as to them.

He passed out of sight behind the hedge.

"Patriotism is a vice," said Gemini, still glowing with self-approval from his dialectical display and his ultimate lapse into sincerity. "But in this mild sunshine, this green privacy, this picturesque, unobtrusive go-as-you-please – . To the sound of church bells. Dear, mellow, humbugging, tolerant old England!... Tolerant... And now how about breaking it to Mrs Greedle?"

"That," said Stella, "would not be honesty. It would be indelicacy. The essence of indecency is insisting upon things that everybody knows are there..."

"Stella," said Gemini, still pleased with himself and the encounter; "there was something infectious about that parson. That was absolutely in his line of thought."

Chapter Three

The World's Harsh Voice, is Heard Off

Advent of Uncle Hopkinshire

They were aware of Mrs Greedle's voice behind them.

"The postman came," she said, "but I thought I wouldn't disturve that nice talk you was 'aving. E's a nice gentleman the vicar. 'Armless and kind. Never forgets to ask after anyone when he sees them. He'll ask three times a day sometimes. Nice *'abits* he has…"

Gemini took the letter and examined it. It bore the Bristol postmark. It was addressed in an unfamiliar hand-writing to James Twain. Originally it had been addressed to James Twain, Esquire. Then apparently the sender had thought better of the "Esquire" and had scratched it out carefully with a penknife. That was odd. He opened the letter and read it. "Golly!" he said, and re-read.

He looked at Stella's interrogative face.

"They know," he said compactly.

"How?"

He hesitated and then handed her the letter silently.

She read in a largish sprawling handwriting with various erasures and corrections: "You dirty young Blackguard, it is only now that I have learnt where you are and what you have been up to. Her mother is broken-hearted. What that woman Clarkson can be about, making her cottage into a common" – "convenience" erased, "brothel" substituted, and this again had been changed to "disorderly house". "She ought to be prosecuted. Or does she know? I don't know if you realise the seriousness of your offence. You must know that Stella, poor child, and I have nothing but pity for her, is a minor, under age. Maybe it may not be too late to save her. If not, so much the worse for you. At any rate she must come home at once. What you have done is an indictable offence. I shall come by the first train tomorrow. At considerable inconvenience to myself. I give you fair warning to clear out before I come to fetch her home. I may not be able to keep my hands off you. That's all. Clear out of my way before I get hold of you. Best for all parties. I may see red. Horse-whipping is too good for you, you filthy young hound."

Indecision over signature and what sort of "Yours" it ought to be, and then a bare "Hubert Polydore Hopkinshire."

She read and handed it back to Gemini.

"That," she said, "is Uncle."

Pause for reflection.

"Sounds choleric."

"He was a Black and Tan and he's never got over it."

"I don't like it."

"No," she agreed.

"*This*," he said, and failed to complete his sentence.

He tried again. "It's unreasonable to feel as I do; but this seems suddenly to alter everything. It's a point of view we've been forgetting. It's – as though something had happened to the sky – gone bleak and beastly."

"Yes."

"All that we find lovely, the loveliest thing in the world, he finds disgraceful, disgusting, dirty, criminal."

She shrugged her shoulders.

"It's like some gas being released unexpectedly, a stink-bomb, in Paradise."

Stella was still speechless.

"It's the ugly side of life coming up. Or the real side? But how did he know? How did he come to know?... And your mother?"

"She must have known first and written to him. Or told him. Someone must have told her."

"Where is she?"

"She was staying with the Battiscombes."

"Battiscombes mean nothing to me."

"Cousins at Weston-super-Mare. They keep a sort of hydro and this Uncle Hubert has a riding-school ten or twelve miles away. Somewhere near Clifton."

"A hydropath?"

"Of sorts."

"But anyone may have gone there and let things out. If Mary talked. But she always talks..."

Gemini reconsidered the letter. "He reads perfectly honest. He means every word of this."

"He *is* perfectly honest. It wouldn't hurt us a bit – if he wasn't perfectly honest. It's just that he does mean it. *That's* how he and half the world are going to see all this. That's what we're up against, Gemini."

"Why doesn't he go and hoot at *Romeo and Juliet?*"

"He would, but he's never thought of doing it. No! Come to think of it, *they* were married, Gemini. Irregularly, but they *were* married... And besides, the Bible and Shakespeare are above suspicion."

"Curious thing. We'd like the whole world to approve of us, and it's a smack in the face for us when we get it straight that quite a lot of people whey they know of our week here won't. They won't. Approve of us! They won't stand us."

"Evidently *he* won't," said Stella.

"That parson did. That parson had an effect of standing us."

"Yes. I think he did. There was something about him, Gemini... We attracted him and we frightened him. Of course he knew all about it before he called. He was attracted, he was excited by us and then – we were too frank for him. And he didn't expect we'd cross-examine him as you did. And your philosophy and theology carried him off his feet. *How* you talked! How was he to know he was running up against the most industrious mugger on the *New Spectator* staff? That parson put us above ourselves. He was really one of *us*. Of course you got no *admissions* out of him. You couldn't expect it. He has made up his mind and he keeps it made up. He has to. What would become of him if he didn't? Where could he go? What could he do? I remember Uncle Robert saying, 'What refuge is there in the world for a common priest or a common parson when his faith falls away from him? None. The less he believes it the more firmly he must cling to it'. It's like that bathing-gown of mine that has lost all its buttons. He daren't leave go for a moment.

And the Churches can't leave go. But Uncle Hopkinshire is different. He's the hairy cave-man, all out and himself. No softness about him. He's the natural man. Creeds may come and creeds may go, but Uncle Hopkinshire goes on for ever."

"We've taken on a lot, Stella, in coming here."

"We've taken on more than we realised."

"We have."

"Sorry?"

"No. But what are we going to do?"

"Nothing until he comes. Sufficiently unto the day is the evil thereof. We still have hours and hours, Gemini, in this dear cottage, in this dear garden, before the storm breaks."

"Yes. But – . It's well, as the posters say, to be prepared. I shall stay for him here."

"Obviously."

"And what is the quality of this – this raucous individual? What does he amount to? You've seen him? You know him? So high is he? Or *so* high? What do these threats of violence amount to?"

"I've only seen him with what he'd call his womankind. Mother, in fact. He's distinctly anti-feminist. Married his cook and she died – and it seems to have annoyed him. Put him to a lot of trouble. Hard to describe him. Blue-black moustache. Dyed we think. Stocky. Bandyish. Hair on his hands. Still I suppose, Gemini, you can take care of yourself?"

"I'm not so bad if it comes to a scrap. Footwork poor, but I know how to punch if it comes to that. I've got some reach and I've got some weight. If I hit 'em fair, they are apt to go down. That's all right. But is he likely to try anything that may lead to a scuffle? Is he likely to produce something in the nature of a horsewhip? If so, I suppose I shall have to take it away from him. Or try to. I don't see how we can avoid that."

Stella reconsidered the letter. "He probably thinks that you are what he would call a long-haired Bolshie, rather on the weedy side. And that you'll make off at this whiff of virility. I think he hopes that."

"Hopes what?"

"That you'll clear out."

"And if I don't go?"

"Then he'll rant and shout. But if you keep your eye on him, nothing will happen. That's my impression of him. Keep your eye on him and speak to him with a quiet voice. There won't be any horsewhip – where does one by a horsewhip nowadays? But he'll probably turn up in breeches – he loves riding-breeches when he's about at home – and if so he'll bring a riding-crop to flourish under your nose."

"Very well. And what shall we argue about?"

"Why anticipate?"

"I want to know. That is exactly what I want to know."

"Why spoil the time that is left to us?"

"Yes. When you say that, I want to know more than ever."

She reflected, arms akimbo. "Let's walk up the lane a bit. I can feel Mother Greedle at the kitchen window listening with all her eyes."

They walked a hundred feet in silence.

"Uncle Hopkinshire," said Stella, "is coming to take me back to my mother, who has probably been weeping... Never mind about my mother... What else can I do? I shall have to go back."

"Stella, I want to keep you."

"We said ten happy days."

"But now it's different."

"We jumped into this, Gemini. Don't let's put it too high and mighty. If we hadn't had the chance of Mary Clarkson's cottage and that – that – well how you kissed me after the Winchcombe's dance, and your saying 'Oh Hell! this is just half and half'."

"And I could get a fortnight off and you managed to vanish… You must have told your mother some fibs, Stella! I never thought of that."

"One fib, Gemini. Just one little one. Hardly a fib. I'm sorry. You see… I pronounced your name Jemima. As the parson would put it, that makes it a misunderstanding rather than a deception…"

"Somebody who knows about Mary Clarkson," he considered. "Or Mary herself talking to astonish and appal. As she does at times. Or someone who saw a chance of making mischief… And so, what are we going to do?"

"As I say. What else is there to do? We've had a lovely time. And now it is almost over."

"I can't drop it like that. I can't give you up. I feel as if I'd hardly tasted you. Damnation, Stella, let's get married?"

"We agreed we didn't believe in marriage. At least we agreed before we came. And also who's going to let us? My mother can say No. She – for some reason – has a horror of sex. Your – father…?"

"He thinks I ought to wait until I'm five and thirty and then marry money. But with us – now?"

"I still don't believe in marriage. I don't know. I don't. Even if I did, I'm a minor. Not for a whole year and a half can we do that. They'll say wait, wait, and wait. Nineteen long months! We've been into all that. Wait while the world has fallen to pieces altogether. They can spoil it for us, all that time, and from what I know of Uncle Hubert and Mother, they'll make things as nasty as they can."

"Let's bolt to France."

"Chucking your work, stopping mine? What could one do in France?"

"Aren't we lovers?"

She made no answer.

"Do you really *want* this separation, this surrender?"

"Gemini, darling, I'm in love with you so much, and I'm in love with love so much, that I can hardly reason about it. I've just had one little week of love. I'm being calm and collected because otherwise I might scream and throw myself about. I *did* count on ten days. Three days less! It's a damned shame. All the same I know that we have to part tomorrow. I won't face it now. I won't think about it until tomorrow comes. Gemini, we still have two-thirds of a day and night."

"Yes," he said, "but – "

Pause for consideration.

2

Rally or Stampede

"The whole universe aches," said Gemini.

"Oh! It aches right enough," said Stella. "Forget about it now. There is just this time left to us, to talk of everything that matters. And kiss Good-bye."

"After all. This is just one single scribbled letter, and it has shattered us. All our self-satisfaction."

"Has it shattered us? I don't thing so, Gemini. We're kids yet. Rather helpless. We've jumped into what suddenly looks like an impossible situation. We *are* kids, you know. All the same, the things we have thought and said this last week; they hold good, Gemini?"

"Sound enough. But this brutality; this bawling vulgarity..."

"But that is what we have know we were up against all along. We – we stand for life. Haven't we said that over and over again? We stand for the free, abundant, life. We are against compulsion, against uncriticised direction, against war. We've been talking all the time about war and how we had to put an end to it. Our sort of people. We – we were going to carve a new world out of this clumsy landslide of an old world. A whole new world, Gemini! That was to be our ruling idea, our religion."

"All that holds," said Gemini, "That *is* our religion."

"And people were to live without all the nervous stresses of sexual compulsion. That was a part of it. We said that. A wholesome free life. Well, we mean to do that to the best of our ability. You've forgotten that side of it. For our own sakes, we said. For the sakes of everybody. To make a world without ugly repressions, hates, morbidities... We've made our protest. Marriage is compulsion, obligation. It turns a happy companionship into a semi-legal obligation."

Gemini did not seem so sure of that.

She considered his face for a moment.

"How did we put it the other day, Gemini? Organised economic freedom throughout the world, education for everyone as much as they can stand, universally accessible knowledge, freedom of movement about the world, the maximum of private ownership in one's own body and mind... I'm only quoting you,

Gemini. When we said these things we were exalted. We felt fine and large about them. It was like ordering the world about. Now comes the chill, the reminder. We are living in a world where the craving for power and compulsion seems to be the only effective human passion. The only serious people in the world are the brutes and bullies. And the abject. Everyone is barking commands or saluting or doing both. We suddenly realise we are small. Ever so small. But does that matter? Haven't we got to resist all the same? Begin with ourselves. The world *is* ourselves – multiplied by a thousand million. Why should we cower? Why tell lies?"

"But if telling the truth means separation?"

"After all, we should still be alive, Gemini. We shall still be in the same world."

"That's no great consolation. I like *talking* to you. In your physical presence everything is different. And I can't write long letters. I can't. I write all day as it is. I want you."

"I'll read all you print, trust me. I'll keep you posted where I am. Nothing they can do to us can keep us from communicating. Love letters? I wonder how it feels to write a love letter. I've never sent you anything but notes… By 1940 there will be nothing to keep us apart if we still want to live together. Married or not…"

"What if we have a chance of meeting before the time is up?"

"Need you ask, Gemini?"

"That's not so bad. We might manage…"

"We'll see about that. I may be rusticated in Somerset. I don't know. There's Uncle Robert… But the chances are I shall live the life of a penitent with my mother at Barnes. All sorts of things may happen. They've not beaten us yet. You will go on living in London…"

"I wonder," said Gemini.

"*Eh?*"

"I wonder if this business will get round to my father. After all, he's something of the Roman father. Well, don't let's complicate the problem with him now."

It was only too manifest in his candid face that he was complicating the problem with fresh and none too agreeable considerations. She remembered that Gemini still lived mainly on an allowance from his father. His literary earnings and so forth were casual and made up no great income. Yes, and she remembered that there had been threats already to force Gemini into a profession.

"Shall we turn now?" said Stella. "The next bend and we'll be seeing the village green."

"I don't want to run against Balch. We don't want Balch to know about all this. We don't want any of these last hours Balchified. But I doubt if we'll see him again. He got a bellyful at lunch and the parson frightened him. He must have felt rather a fool, bolting as he did. He'll be in the pub playing darts at the top of his voice and being ever so witty and playful and appreciative and proletarian about it. Darts! All his sort play darts. And in a year or so they'll all be ashamed of dart-cant. So stale it will be. They'll have some new playfulness. Still there's no need to run risks."

"Let's go up through the pinewoods and sit there until twilight and come down to the cottage at the back."

They did that…

Gemini laughed suddenly. "We're so deflated!" he said.

"Deflated?" said Stella, sitting astride a felled tree trunk and considering the word. "Strange things you say at times, Gemini! Deflated! I feel as if I was just beginning to live. I don't know what this week has done for you, Gemini, but it's made me a woman. There's no going back on that. I've discovered myself. I've discovered my body and I am in love with it. I stood before the bathroom mirror yesterday loving every bit of it, loving all its loveliness. And talking to you and being in love with you, has made me a soul. I'm twice the thing I was. Yes, I know, that old dualism is wrong, but how else can I say it? Body and soul I'm lit up, and you've done it very nicely, thank you, Gemini, and here we are! We've decided we're going to carve a new world out of the old; haven't we? You weren't just talking were you, Gemini, when you, when you impregnated me with that? That Unrevealed World! Think it out and carve it out. That's what we're going to do, if the whole of the rest of the world is against us. It can come down on us, hurt us, weary us, trick us, mock us, frustrate us, defeat us, kill us. Gemini, that's all detail. That's in the chapter of accidents. But it isn't going to make us give up our – our great conception…"

Gemini regarded her with admiration and desire. He was sitting side-saddle, so to speak, on the tree, with his arms folded.

"And you don't think it's possible for two young people to take themselves too seriously?" he said.

"No. Not in their private thoughts. Not when they have to talk as we are talking. Talking like this to anyone else would be preposterous, but to ourselves… The whole world, you said, is our inheritance so far as we can carve it out. Was that serious or was it not? Did we say that or did we not? What has come over you, Gemini? Either we are the heirs and gods and Garsteins of this rebellious lump of a world or we've just been Balching about it, and it would become us better to be saying Heil Hitler! or kneeling in a confessional for instruction. Crawling somehow. To hell with all that! We *can't* take ourselves too seriously. We *can't* have too much backbone. No."

"Gods, but I love you, Stella."

She stared at him and for the first time in their relationship it seemed to him that she was staring through him at something else. When she spoke again, she spoke tentatively.

"Maybe they'll break us in, but I mean us to be as serious a proposition to ourselves as Adam and Eve. We are *our* Adam and Eve. Gemini, this life is all the life we're ever going to have. The world is all before us – . Ours. The death of us or the life of us. That may be being a prig. What are the alternatives to being a prig? A self-pitying, shirking slouch, a cocktail boozer, a humorist, a games lout, a charming borrower, a Catholic convert with a taste for ceremony and an inclination to sodomy, a tough guy, an all-round stinker? Look at the vermin who aren't prigs! Look at them, Gemini! Look at Mary Clarkson's midnight crowd! You can put names to all I have been saying. Tick 'em off on your fingers. I've had my eyes open. Mary's other name is Circe. Circe of Bloomsbury. She brings out the worst in them."

"Don't be ungrateful, Stella. She lent us the cottage."

"She lent *you* the cottage."

"She lent the cottage."

"I don't see that that alters the quality of her friends. They're – what is the word – escapists. Drunkards and whimsies. I'm talking fact. Give me a prig all the time. Absurd? *Take* myself too seriously? Better be absurd than disgusting. If there were only we two of our sort in the world, I'd still be all for this new-world business. Our world or theirs. But we're not such exceptions as all that. There must be thousands thinking like us – or just not daring to think like us. There may be hundreds of thousands. So much the better. But that doesn't excuse us from behaving as though it all rested on us alone. Saying 'Oh someone else will do that. Have a drink, old boy! Don't worry!' Oh Gemini, this *damned* modesty! this *damned* sense of humour! this *damned* common sense! We've just got this one life to live, Gemini, and I mean to live it – up to the hilt – without drugs. I mean to live in the middle of things, not get into a corner and snigger life away. I – . I – !"

She had stopped looking through him and she was looking straight at him, as though she had suddenly recalled his existence.

"I can't do without you, Gemini. Everything I say is an echo of something you have said. You can reason out these things and say them. And then I believe them. But do *you* believe them?"

"When I have you, Stella. When I've got you."

She repeated, "When you've got me..."

She looked about her. She clenched her fists and held them up on either side of her glowing face. "This being alive," she cried. "It's Hell! It's Heaven! I can't live it enough."

She stood up, one knee on the fallen tree.

"The loveliness of it. This soft afternoon sunshine. This faint smell of resin. Soft moss and turf. It's ours. I swear – . Swear with me, Gemini. I swear to extract this lovely world of might-be out of the hands of the beasts and the bullies and the blockheads..." She lifted up her pretty bare arm. "No other way of living."

He stood up too and echoed her absurdly grave attitude and her absurd words. He swore to extract this lovely world of might-be out of the hands of the beasts and bullies and blockheads. "No other way of living, Stella," he concluded.

Never, he thought, had he seen anyone so earnestly alive.

She changed. The declaration had been made. She lowered her arm slowly, with her hands extended at her sides like a surrender, smiling faintly at him. "Well?" she said.

He trembled for a moment and then caught her in his arms.

Sunshine, stillness, warmth, the mossy ground between the felled trees and the faint smell of resin. It was all of a piece and yet – was it not also – the thought was like being stung by a gnat and yet it came to him there – fantastically inconsecutive?

3

Evensong

"What a day!" said Gemini, first in bed.

"We've done some thinking anyhow," said Stella, and came and sat on the counterpane. She was in her pyjamas, and was still combing her shock of hair unnecessarily after it had long since been fully and properly combed. At last she stopped and shook the comb at him.

"Look here, Gemini," she said, "this stuff of yours about everybody having ultimately – ultimately? or fundamentally is it? – ultimately the same imagination if they think hard enough! It sticks in my mind. I've been thinking about it all day. It doesn't wash. Things aren't as simple as that. See?"

"Nothing is perfectly simple," said Gemini.

"Yes, but – . I must talk for a bit, my dear. I've got such a lot to say to you. Heaven knows when we two will talk again. If I knew how Joshua did it I'd hold this day for an eternity or so. It slips away so fast. But I want this clear. Ever since we talked in the lane and went through that Balch deluge I have been turning over that notion of yours of people being fundamentally alike. You say that if everyone had full knowledge and thought everything out and all that, everyone would come out at last to the same idea of the kind of civilised world there ought to be. That came into your head suddenly, as things do come into that queer head of yours; and then you heard what Balch made of it. That shook you up a little. But still you stuck to it. One common universal imagination! That makes things out to be pretty easy. All one needs to do is to tell the world. Just a war of ideas for a generation or so and the thing is done. Just a little teaching and persuasion. Then they'll know for certain what they always thought. Dearest, it isn't nearly so simple as that. That's all wrong. That common human imagination of yours – why! it's the lie behind all these religions that have failed us. Human brains are just as various as human legs or skins and – anything. More so perhaps. That idea of yours doesn't *begin* to be true."

Gemini regarded her thoughtfully, and with that faint sulkiness he sometimes betrayed when she contradicted him too flatly. "Anyhow human imaginations have to be got upon a common basis. There has to be a sort of propaganda education of all the world to this one world idea. Even if they aren't all honestly *for* it; they can be got to know about it clearly. They have to be got to behave like brothers. Or anyhow feel the obligation of brotherhood. And then at last they may begin to feel like brothers."

"Yes. But first, a great lot of people won't *want* this world civilisation in any form, at any price. They just won't. Educate them as much as you like; they won't. It doesn't matter how rotten the world is; they'll be against a better one. They've impulses to triumph, revenge, hate and cruel self-assertion that they know a better world would never allow. And a still greater multitude will bar every effort you make to spread this great idea of yours, out of fear. It seems so clear, sweet and reasonable to us, but the very first movement towards it will seem to them weird, horrible, wicked. *You* may begin presently to see the shape in the alabaster, but will they? Will they even try to see it? Will they ever believe there is a shape in the alabaster? It's no use our thinking the whole world is just waiting to go our way – just a little vehement Balchification and off we go on the new road. Don't you believe anything of the sort, Gemini. Our millennium idea will always be unpopular, damned unpopular.

"There's Uncle Hubert – there's more Uncle Huberts than us in the world – and you'll no more get him to stop being patriotic, virile about women and all that, than you'll teach a dog to stop yapping. You *can't* teach him different. He won't learn. He isn't made that way. Establish our world state if you like. He'll contrive somehow to make it a kennel. Whips and dog-fights. You try him tomorrow. I'll be watching you, Gemini.

"And consider that parson again. Very sympathetic and all that, but do you think he'll let our sort get hold of the schools, or alter the code of orthodox morality? Wherever the world goes and whatever is done, he will insist on having restraints and pretences. He will want to sit tight wherever he is. He is an honest man really, though you think him an old humbug. No, Gemini, why make a face at him? He's as honest as you are. The other way round. He's so honest, you see, that he dare not risk letting his impulses escape from his principles, and you, you are so honest that you dare not let any principles suppress your impulses. Two honest men together. But he's a more ordinary man than you are, Gemini. He's more the stuff that makes stable nations, creeds and businesses. He's what they call trustworthy. He'll think as agreed – even if he doesn't really think so. He's the perfect man of character... And you, I realise, aren't."

She had come to the end of her matter, but she felt she had not arrived at any conclusion. "Like that," she said, and combed a stroke.

Gemini had been considering her speech and doing his honest best to ignore the fact that when Stella was most lucid and in earnest she was apt to be most lovely and desirable.

"I think I see what you are driving at," he said, holding his mind resolutely to the question under discussion. "You are right and I am right. You are wrong and I am wrong. Let me try and de-Balch this business. First I admit that the majority of the sort of human beings we deal with today are either so primitive – like your Uncle Hubert – that they will always behave like dogs or bulls or wolves – 'seeing red', *wanting* to see red – or so practical-minded and timid and unbelieving that they will always be obstructively conservative of the thing that is. Man, generally, is going to remain at those levels for quite a time yet. The real job in human affairs will have to be done by a minority of people who, like you, will only consent to think of existence as its heirs and its owners – "

"And you, Gemini?"

"*We*. Yes – don't draw me away from my argument... Heirs and owners. *But* – it does not follow that dogs cannot be turned into sheep dogs. All dogs don't hunt in packs and fly at strangers. Or that the born conformist will not steady a reconstructed progressive society and hold it together. You can make him face forward, or mark for the company to wheel, even though he himself doesn't budge."

She considered that. "So far as that isn't to be twisted, so as to exonerate every intelligent human being from complete, separate responsibility... And though that's all very well when we have got this propaganda education of the new world, over; until we, our sort, get that done, for a generation or a hundred generations, none of these others are coming half-way to meet us or anything of that sort... You see what I want to say. That's what I want to be clear about. The whole thing is still up to us. It's up to you and me. Just as though we were alone in the presence of God."

"In the absence of God," said Gemini.

"Which leaves things even more completely to us."

Pause.

"Well," said Gemini," and since we are trying to have everything out while there is still time for it, I want a few words – funny to say them now here as we are – about sex. I've had them on my mind and I've been keeping them under. I am head over heels in love with you, I have been making love to you for a week, I am going to make love to you again just as soon as you stop pretending to comb your hair, and all the time I have been thinking things behind your back, so to speak, and you – you have been doing the same to me. You'd hardly guess when it came into my head today. Something puzzling us both. Me anyhow. Something very puzzling. This time we've had here; it's the crowning thing in life for us, so bright, so intense and – .

What's it got to do with *anything*, Stella? What's it got to do with the rest of life?"

She stopped combing, grave and attentive.

"You say things, Gemini... You say things that one seems to have been on the verve of thinking all one's life. It's your way of saying them. But this time again; aren't you wrong? I think you are wrong. Of course sex has *everything* to do with the rest of life. Yet I've had that thought that it hasn't, creeping into my mind. But I've sent it packing... But *why* did I send it packing? I ought to have an answer. What, after all, *has* this love-making got to do with the rest of life? What's in your head, Gemini?"

"The excuse we lovers make is that it animates everything. Is that true? We two would make love anyhow, whether it animated things or not. Even if it took the life out of us. You daren't deny it. That's the point. Listen, Stella; while you squat there pretending to comb, I shall lie here and improve your mind. Your mind or my own.

"Before I came down here I was reading a book, more or less, off and on, for review. It's at home. That's what put this idea into my head. What is it called? *The Expansion of Sex*. The idea of it is this; that man is an animal with a tremendously developed cerebrum, memory, mental flexibility and all that. It has made him in his savage and destructive way lord of the earth. So far good. The big brain wins, but side by side with that, or even perhaps connected with it inseparably, there has been a monstrous, useless, troublesome exaggeration and elaboration of man's sexual interest and urgency. So he says. The sex in human mentality, he says, is a superfluous overgrowth – like those vast horns a deer has to produce every year. No other creature is so sexual as man, unless it is some of the monkeys. The brain expanded in response to practical needs, produced energy, imagination, fantasy, and then sex stole it. To a large extent. So far as the continuation of the race goes, all that is necessary is at most a month or so of sex consciousness in the year. For the rest of the time complete indifference to any sex difference, sexual indulgence, beauty, would be a clear advantage for survival. No! – hold on for a moment, I am quoting this man. That is the way with most animals. They have a rutting season and then it's all over. For the rest of the time we should do our work, make our machines, subdue the earth to our needs, in sexless tranquillity."

"Only it isn't like that."

"Only it isn't like that. And this man – I'll remember his name in a moment – he's an American naturalist – quite well known – he goes on to argue that you could write a sort of human history entirely as the story of the Sex Problem through the ages. It has always been getting in the way, that was how he put it, getting in the way, and three-quarters of religion and custom are methods of getting it out of the way. And so far the problem has never been solved. Sometimes the trend is all to hold it in, hold it back, suppress. 'Oh no, we never think of it!' That was the way of the Victorian age. And it failed. It developed repressions and morbid states. It festered in the subconscious. The generations before the war cleared up all that. The war finished the release. They abandoned all restriction on speech, they took off their clothes, they took off their morals, they let sex rip. But – I'm quoting my authority – when you let sex go, it proliferates. It asks for more. Indulgence is no remedy. It becomes sensuality. That's his case. Sex grows by what it feeds on. Sex – not love. It ousts love. It begins mixed up with love – and then ousts it. And then sensuality ousts sex and you get exaggerations and perversions. It takes possession of more and more of your life. It becomes an overpowering obsession. You are urged to do more and more sexual things. You talk about it. Boast about it. It ekes itself out with melodrama. It insists on extravaganza. Mysticism. Somewhere in between these two extremes there's got to be adjustment, that is to say morals, a code of permissible and forbidden things. And the rest of this chap's book is a survey of morals, a sort of Variety of Moral Experiences."

"And what are his conclusions?"

"He comes to no definite conclusions. It is a scientific treatise."

"I thought so."

"Of course he points out the social and biological consequences of various codes. His line is, take them or leave them."

"I don't believe very much in your great American naturalist," said Stella. "No. His attitude, Gemini, is a common male attitude. The attitude of a middle-aged bachelor who goes round the corner to a brothel and then regrets the risk and expense and waste of time, and wishes it didn't have to happen. The man pretending he's a mighty inventor, genius, administrator and all that, and that sex is a terrible interruption. If only the women would leave him alone!"

"Not *quite* like that."

"That's the spirit of it. If only sex would leave him alone!"

"You're not being just to him. He says sex is as big a nuisance to women as to men. More so."

"I don't *like* him," she said, "He's – Gemini, he's a sex-shirker."

At the moment her judgement seemed decisive.

Babes in the Darkling Wood

"Well, how do you see it, Stella?"

"Turning it over in my mind... How do I see it? What has this love-making to do with anything else, you ask. Well – *everything*. Sex is *not* irrelevant to the other side of life. It's like the other side of a coin. Love, love-making, is as important as hunting, shooting, ploughing, making things, and it's nearer to vital reality. See? Nearer. More than the other side of a coin. Of *course* it is nearer and closer! Society is built upon sex – more than it is built on any economic or practical necessity. If that is the left hand, sex is the right. The first societies were families and then tribes, the Children of Israel and so on. They were not plantation gangs or trade unions. Sex uppermost; sex first. How does that sound to you?"

"If," said Gemini, "you use the word sex for every sort of personal relationship that has an element of physical feeling in it, what you say is largely true."

"*Largely* true?"

"True."

"Well, you know best, Gemini. Can you draw a line between all these liking feelings, between friendship, preference, affection, love, intimacies, caresses? Can you? Is there really even a homosexual limit? You might expect that, if it was all just a question of reproduction. But is there?"

"No. You can have all that."

"Then the real evil about sex is not that it pervades human life, because it wouldn't be human life without it. Its attractions and preferences are the web to hold together the whole species. The trouble is that it *can* be isolated from the rest of life, made a special thing of, be inflamed and exaggerated, so that instead of linking people it cuts them off either by an obsession through suppression or an obsession through excess. As your professor has it, love becomes love-making, love-making becomes sex, sex becomes sensuality. That's no condemnation of any of them so long as they keep in a bundle together. It is stupid to run down sex because of that. The more I think over that sex-shirking professor of yours the less I like him. Irrelevance! I hug your mind when I hug your body. It all belongs together."

"I think it does. I give you *The Expansion of Sex*. When I write that review I will slate it. You shall see. The man's a dismal misogynist. Cottenham Bower. That's his name. Cottenham C Bower. Radnor Smith University. In the south. But now may I ask what the code, our code, ought to be?"

"Freedom," she said.

"Free love, is that?"

"In love one gives. How can one give under a bond?"

"Shelley and your uncle, my dear. But still we must have a code. If my professor was right about anything, it is that sex without rule or restriction eats up the rest of life. He makes a good case for that. There must be *some* behaviour pattern."

"It's religion and politics over again."

"I don't understand you."

"I mean we told that parson how we young people were lost in such a medley of religions and politics and suggestions, that we didn't know how to choose and what values to take – and life pressed upon us..."

"Good, Stella."

"It's the same sort of confusion about sex. We don't know what to do about it, day by day. Look at the novels, the romances, the plays and poems, the pictures and the statuary all telling a thousand varieties of values, saying this is splendid, this is noble, this is decay, this is vile, making this romantic and that atrocious. No sort of agreement at all. Every sort of interpretation and no guide. Scores of patterns of behaviour and which is it to be? Life won't wait. What are we to do about it? What are we to do? Here's your lover. Well? Here's your lover and you may be dead tomorrow. Maybe there are vast differences between people, and what is fine for one, is ugly for another. Some may hesitate and regret it. Some may snatch and be sorry. Perhaps these things are more personal and secret than religious and political things, but the need for decisions is none the less urgent. All over it's the same question: 'What about it *now?*' "

"That's good, Stella. Yes. That's sound. But since it's so various a thing, we can't have a common pattern for everyone – except a framework of tolerance. Suppose there are a lot of possible patterns. We don't know much about life yet. Suppose there are a lot of patterns, and suppose that so long as they don't destroy social life they are all equally permissible. Some people may be really and properly promiscuous, radiating contacts. Others may have an innate bias for particular reactions. And we may vary in different phases of our lives. Have you thought of that?... We may find things when we are in the mood for them and disgusting when we are not. Manifestly we must have decency... But also freedom, privacy and charity. Everybody is not to be linked in the same way. So I reason it out. There will still have to be things that are never done anyhow. Things that are cruel for example. Things that destroy. But Stella, let us drop all this high theorising for a moment. How do things stand with us two? That's what I want to have clear."

"Well, I'm in love. I'm very much in love. That doesn't conduce to a broad view of things. I'm in love with you, Gemini, and I want you for keeps. I want to be woman to my own, my very own, man. That's *my* pattern now. Perhaps I had other ideas before we came down here but that's how I want it now. I'm going to quote you something from that old prayer book I was reading downstairs. How does it go? 'To have and to hold from this day forward, for better, for worse, for richer, for poorer, in sickness and in health, to love and to cherish, till death do us part.' There's something fine there. That's a damned good pattern for love, Gemini, and it's stood some wear in its time. Don't you feel it's real human stuff? Promiscuity – infidelity – I don't care what you call it, seems to me to be something soiling after that. I speak for myself and how I feel now. It would be – . I don't think I could look at myself in the mirror again. I think I should feel dispersed – dirty. But who am I to judge? I've only just come into existence. Anyhow, everyone ought to be free. Even if there is a natural pairing, a natural marriage, to have and to hold, there should be no marriage bond. No bond. This feeling for monogamy – to love and to cherish – this is a matter of personal quality. But one must always be giving. To love is to give. No bond. That's how I feel now. Don't you?"

"Question of children?"

She reflected.

"That's justifies a ten-year responsibility perhaps. George Meredith suggested that. Or longer. The psychologists say that every child ought to *own* two parents, and won't be completely happy and normal without them... Is there any religious bias in that belief? I suspect there is... So far we have been thinking chiefly of love, before the children come in. Maybe people can love and forget and begin again. You have, Gemini, lots of times."

BABES IN THE DARKLING WOOD

"How do you *know*, Stella? Not lots of times. Still – . I have. How do you know?"

"I just know. I don't want to dig up your memories. Maybe love is something different for a man. Maybe the world is made up not of males and females but of rakes and – serious people who play for keeps. Maybe – all sorts of things. What do we know about it? We've hardly begun. Four years ago I was a flapper in love with Clark Gable. And you – what were you at fifteen? You've forgotten. Eh? You've seen fit to forget. We know only how we feel now. How can we guess at the physical and moral needs of men and women of thirty and fifty? I suppose they still have them. We can only decide for ourselves. I feel now that I've got a life sentence and I love it. Suppose I am wrong? How can I tell I am wrong?"

"Now listen, Stella. I want to marry you."

"But we can't."

"I want to marry you here and now, so to speak, and to live in the hope of really and lawfully marrying you as soon as ever we can."

"But I have told you – "

"About freedom and all that?"

"Yes."

"Stella, we've planned a very considerable fight with this old world. I submit that our sexual status is not the proper battleground to begin upon. That means a narrow close struggle. It means trouble with servants. Telling white lies to Mrs Greedle. Quarrels with neighbours. Waste of force on what is after all a personal and minor issue. It isn't there that I want to give battle."

"Now that's a point of view. And you really want me, Gemini, for good and keeps? Really and truly? As I do you?"

"Yes."

"Say it, Gemini. Say it again. On our last night together. Make me your offer of marriage."

"I will... I want you – all of you. I want you, Stella, from the top squeak of your voice down to that thin fine leathery sole of your foot I tickled yesterday, and every bit of your body in between, and if there wasn't a sound or a sight of you I'd still want you to talk these thoughts of mine into you until they come alive. So much for parting and promiscuity. I'm yours. You're mine. Can't you put that comb away now and come to bed? We've been talking for half an hour or more."

"Are you so sure of that, Gemini? Are you really so sure of that? Of loving me for ever and ever?"

"Absolutely sure."

"I wonder. Will you say it over again, Gemini?"

"Put that comb away," said Gemini.

She made no sign of doing so.

"There are moments when I doubt your intellectual integrity profoundly," she considered.

"If you don't put that comb away I'll make you."

A freak of desire took possession of her. "Very well," she said, gripping the comb firmly and locking her hands round her knees; "*make* me."

Chapter Four

Conference of the Powers

Before Zero Hour

A feeling of tension increased as the hour for Uncle Hubert's arrival approached. The spree of getting up together, the wet sponge throwing, the snatches of improvised doggerel, had lost their sparkle. They were both preoccupied, rehearsing scraps of anticipatory dialogue in their minds.

Gemini tried to relieve the strain by chanting an improvised oratorio. "Strong Bulls of Bashan have compassed me about, Strong Bulls have compassed me, have compassed me about, have com-passed me a-bout. Be not far from me O Lord my Strength, O Lord my Strength, hasten thou to help me and deliver my darling, my darling, my own darling, my darling Stella, O deliver her, deliver her from the power of the dog, from Polydore the clumsy unicorn and Hubert's horrid mouth. From Hu-bert's hor-rid mouth…"

"Oh *shut* it," said Stella.

Gemini, as reproachful as a cocker spaniel, retired silenced to the bathroom.

When he returned he found Stella before the looking-glass considering an important question of tactics. "If I wear my trousers," she said, "it will increase the general effect of depravity, but it will absolutely prevent my being carried off, until I have changed and packed... Gemini, I shall wear my trousers."

"What *I* wear does not matter. I am not going to be carried off anyhow. Golly! I never thought of that. I can't stay here tonight alone... I have made no plans..."

It was manifest at breakfast that Mrs Greedle was acutely aware that something was wrong, although every precaution had been taken against her seeing Uncle Hubert's letter. "You're not eating so hearty this morning," she said. "And such a nice morning too. You're wanting the ABC? Not thinking of going, I 'ope. There's no ABC but here's the local time-table on the dresser."

"We're expecting a friend by the morning train," said Gemini.

"The ten seven, I expect," said Mrs Greedle. "And will it be a lady or a gentleman, Sir?"

"A gentleman," said Gemini.

"He'll be staying to lunch then," said Mrs Greedle. "You'll like something nice for him."

"I'm not quite sure whether he will stay to lunch. No. He may have to go on."

"Just a call like?" said Mrs Greedle and received no answer. No sound for a time but munching. Mrs Greedle said nothing audible, but her face said "Hoity toity."

"Let's go up the hill at the back to the pines, Stella," said Gemini, breaking an unusual, uncomfortable silence, and standing up.

"Right O," said Stella, also standing.

"And lunch, m'am?" asked Mrs Greedle.

"The usual sort of thing," said Stella, with a novel indifference.

"If the gentleman should come before we return," said Gemini, "will you show him the tantalus and ask him to sit down?"...

"It might be good tactics if we let him cool off in the cottage for a bit before we come in," he explained as they went out by the back way.

"Not Uncle Hubert, not with the tantalus," said Stella. "We must be back there first..."

They were back by ten minutes past ten. They reckoned Uncle Hubert would find his way from the station to the cottage in another ten minutes. They had steadied their nerves by fragmentary talk and silences, and accustomed themselves to the advent of Uncle Hubert until it had become as it were the normal state of affairs. Stella had developed the taciturnity of one who has exhausted a subject, but a combatant liveliness was growing upon Gemini. She walked with her hands deeper and deeper in her trouser pockets.

His hands flitted from patting her shoulder to rest jauntily on his hips. They made sudden rhetorical flourishes in the air. His mind had escaped from the theme of love and separation and was playing about with the details of the encounter. "Hubert Polydore," he said. "Why on earth was he called Polydore? Who *was* Polydore? What is a Polydore? Polydore! A thing that grows in your nose? No. That's a polypus. If I had a name like that, I'd hush it up. Particularly in a quarrel."

The approaching interview was profoundly important and all that, but at the same time it was going to be, in its terrific way, *inter alia*, rather a lark.

At last they heard the station cab stop at the end of the lane, and voices. "You can't mistake it," they heard old Crump the cab-driver. They peered through the scented screen of Mary Clarkson's geraniums on the window sill. He squeezed Stella's hand as if for a last farewell.

"Gemini," whispered Stella in a faint voice and her grip relaxed. "There's *two* of them! He must have brought a lawyer or something."

Gemini's ear and cheek pushed her face aside. "Lawyer!" he said. "Something! Any old something! *It's my father!*"

2

Overture of the Conference

"My revered parent," said Gemini, between dismay and exaltation, standing back from the window. "This is unexpected. Oh! this puts a new complexion on things...

"Polypus has got hold of my father. My Roman father! The Cadi of Clarges Street! The two of them together! Oh courage, Gemini, my boy. Courage! I suggest, Stella, you slip away upstairs and come down in about five minutes, – singing happily... I'd rather. Please. No time to argue. Skip it, Stella."

The latch of the garden gate clicked. "And now into the imminent deadly breach," said Gemini.

He went to the door and opened it and stood, trying to look normal and surprised and slightly inhospitable. The staircase door slammed behind Stella.

He became aware of an unobtrusive observer in the background. "Do you mind shutting that kitchen door completely, Mrs Greedle? There's a draught... Now then, the two of you."

It was in the temperament of Gemini to be elated by sudden difficult situations. The more serious the challenge the less serious he became. An essential flippancy was released. Now he floated above himself, arms akimbo and chin up.

Physically he found there was nothing to be anxious about. He was, he realised, a good three inches taller than the approaching Uncle Hubert, and the doorstep gave him perhaps a couple of inches more. Uncle Hubert, in a pale bowler that, a bright checked suit, and exaggerated coat-tails and hams, looked extraordinary pseudo-equestrian, squat and unpleasant rather than a formidable horse-whipper; most of his face had been sacrificed to an immense moustache and an oblique expression of scrutinising determination which was now probably second nature. Gemini suppressed an impulse to say "So this is Uncle Polypus!"

It wasn't as though Uncle Hubert was alone. Close behind came the more urbane and dignified figure of Mr Twain, face and movement eloquent, as Gemini felt, of that sustained and controlled hate which only an acutely estranged father can feel. He was cast rather in Gemini's mould physically, but he was not quite so loose and tall. He had the same broad brows and the same pug nose, but he had orderly hair, deep-set eyes, a stiffer backbone and a severely pursed mouth; he walked with a well-rolled, important umbrella, and he was wearing a grey lounge suit and a soft black felt hat. There was something in his face that seemed to intimate that Uncle Hubert stank. The conversation in the train must have been interesting. He seemed to be trying to look as though Uncle Hubert was not walking in front of him, was in fact not there. Something about Uncle Hubert on the other hand suggested that he considered Mr Twain to be there at his initiative in the capacity of a subordinate, yes-man or stooge but that he was not quite certain about it.

"How do, Father?" said Gemini, filling the entrance. "Didn't except to see you. Who's your friend?"

"Get-*tout* of the way," growled Uncle Hubert, as one who speaks to a dog. "Where's my niece?"

Gemini smiled genially at him and continued to fill the entrance. "Are you the Mr – what was it? – Hubert Polydore Hopkinshire, who wrote me a sort of letter? Rather a rude letter."

"Get out of my way I tell you. I didn't come to bandy words with you. Get *out* of the way."

"*No*," said Gemini and stood tense.

No immediate action followed.

"One moment," said Mr Twain, and put out a restraining hand. "We want no violence. We have come down – "

That restraining hand absolved Uncle Hubert from immediate action.

"I tell you, Sir, *get out of the way!*" he shouted, giving the riding-whip a minor flourish but accepting the postponement of his purpose.

"Sssh!" said Gemini, like a sudden steam jet, to the Major's great surprise. "You were saying, Father – ?"

The Major allowed himself to be pushed a little aside by Mr Twain. "We have come down to discuss" ("*Discuss!*" in tones of scorn from the Major) "this situation you two foolish young people have created. It is surely not a matter to be debated at the tops of our voices on the doorstep – particularly as your end window is open and your domestic appears to be listening – "

"Come in and sit down," said Gemini, and stood aside so that the Major had to brush against him as he came in. He followed him into the room. "That's a good chair, Major, and you can put your hat and crop on the little table behind. We can't talk until we sit down."

Neither of his visitors sat down. Uncle Hubert felt he could express himself best by walking up and down with his hat on and his whip gripped behind him. Mr Twain put his hat very carefully so as to extinguish a potful of window geraniums, laid his umbrella on the sill and as if by right took up a magisterial position before the fireplace. Gemini seated himself on the arm of the big chair. "I want to see that girl," Uncle Hubert insisted, coming up to him. "And I want to see her now."

"Miss Kentlake will be down very soon. She did not expect visitors. She asked us to – er – *begin*. Doesn't that hat of yours come off? As you will, but you'd be better without it in this close, low room. Thins the hair. You were saying something, Father – ?"

"Your share in this affair is unforgivable. That is chiefly what I have come to say. I have come down to deal with *you*. Clear things up with *you*."

"Now look here," said Uncle Hubert, "we don't want a lot more palaver. I told you what I thought of things in the train. I imagine I made myself clear. You take your blessed son off out of this. That's what you've got to do. Or I shall deal with him. I want to see my niece. Now."

Gemini saw his father's face harden and realised something of the mutual exasperation of the journey down. He addressed himself to Uncle Hubert. "You *can't* see Miss Kentlake, you know, for the next five minutes, unless you are prepared to break down the bathroom door and drag her out screaming – regardless of decency and morality. You may just as well hear what my father has to say about it."

"Well. This is no occasion for talking. Still, talk if you want to – ."

Uncle Hubert went to the window and stood with his back to the room, easing his legs alternately.

Gemini turned hopefully to the grim resolution of the parental visage.

"Mr Hopkinshire," said the magistrate, "or Major as you call yourself – "

This swung the Major round.

"You have obliged me to come down here by threats of violence, exposure and scandal as discreditable and undesirable to your family – if you really have any family – as they are to me and mine. I have come, in your company, and I will confess I have known pleasanter company, to deal with this painful business, sanely, justly, decently and, I must add, James, sternly. And now I am here I insist upon having the whole affair handled in that manner. I insist, Sir. You cannot have it all your own way. And to begin with, accustomed as I am to the decorum of a court of law, I must ask you, please, as you are indoors and in conference, in what is practically a legal conference, to oblige me by removing that hat... No? Of course if it is irremovable, if for some reason, some hideous and shameful disfigurement, some tumour or suchlike morbid and offensive growth, you cannot take it off, then of course we will set aside the ordinary usages of decent society..."

"Damn the *bloody* hat!" said Uncle Hubert. "Making a red herring of my hat!" He tore it off and pitched it into a corner of the room. "There! Now let's have it."

Gemini's eye followed the hat with an inward prayer that sooner or later he would get a chance of treading on it. Then they returned to the slightly ameliorated severity of his father's countenance.

"That's better," said the magistrate. "That's much better. And if also you would sit down I would feel more in control – of myself and everybody. To me the very first consideration in this affair is to avoid any unmannerly uproar about it. What are the facts of the case? My son, like so many young men, has – given way to incontinence. Grossly. That in itself shows a discreditable want of self-control but – in itself – it is not a matter – . Its importance can be exaggerated. But that is not all. What you object to and what I also object to is not that. It is the way in which he has seen fit to gratify these urgencies. Instead of availing himself of the – er – ordinary reliefs tolerated, under protest of course, by society, he has deliberately set himself to the plan and scheme – so far as I understand your charges – the seduction of a previously innocent girl. Previously innocent. That remains to the proved. Until I actually see the young woman in question, I do not see how far I can apportion the exact degree of culpability – ."

"Oh damn it, Father," said Gemini, "steady on. Stella's as right as rain."

Which released Uncle Hubert. He was still keeping the centre of the room. He pointed his remarks with his riding-crop. His voice rose steadily to a shout.

"If you two blaggards mean to suggest that my niece did the seducing – . But I've had enough of this. She's upstairs. Well where's upstairs? The sooner I take her out of this the better, bathroom or not. Bathroom be damned! It's another dodge. Stella! Where *are* you? They're calling you a bitch. They're saying you're no better than a blasted little tart. Where the devil have they hidden you? *Stella!*"

The cupboard-like door leading to the staircase opened almost noiselessly.

"Did I hear you shouting something about me, Uncle Hubert?" said Stella's clear voice. "*Oh!*"

It was Stella's voice but in some subtle way clarified and refined. Gemini heard it and admired it; he loved Stella's voice always, and always its crystalline charm came freshly to him; but he was too intent on his father's reactions to turn round. He has expected and feared scandalised horror at the flimsy vest and the trousers. Instead he discovered a certain surprise, an expression of restrained and reluctant respect. He turned hastily and discovered a new Stella, a very dignified figure indeed, white and slender and more than ever blue-eyed.

She seemed to be slightly taller than the Stella he had known. She was wearing a very simple summer dress of muslin with a clasp of silver at the neck, and her sun-bleached hair, almost incredibly smoothed, was restrained by a fillet of black velvet that bore a small cut steel star in the centre, a fillet which he last remembered her wearing, practically alone, as a garter. There was something about her now virginal and faintly pre-Raphaelite. She might have been a handmaiden of the Queen of Heaven in some picture by Holman Hunt or Madox Brown. The little brown hand that seemed to restrain the apprehension of her heart was punctiliously clean.

"Mr Twain? I knew you at once. You are so like him... How kind of you to come down to us in – our perplexities. Gem – your son is always talking about you."

There was a decided grimness about the tall figure on the hearthrug. She overcame a qualm of terror and an impulse to yell "I can't," and bolt upstairs again, and advanced with an outstretched hand, pink side up, that, thank Heaven! did not tremble. The great man relaxed slightly, touched it and bowed. Again thank Heaven!

Her courage mounted. She found she was not going to lose her breath. Her heart was beating fast but not too fast. She would be able to talk. Thank Heaven and again thank Heaven! Heaven was behaving beautifully to her and she was going to carry things off. She spoke meekly but firmly and her voice was all right.

"May I listen to what you are saying?" she said. "Please. I know – . We have been rash. And perhaps our ideas are not quite your ideas. But do please treat us as reasonable people. And not just shout and bawl disgusting words at us." She looked at the Major; she, the magistrate and Gemini, all looked at the Major. "Don't stand, Uncle," she said.

She seated herself in the corner of the settle and made as if to listen.

But Uncle Hubert was not so easily silenced. He remained at the centre of the room. He spoke in what he considered to be a low grave tone. His voice vibrated.

"Your mother," he said, "is broken-hearted. Bro-ken-hearted. That poor woman! The cruelty of it all. Don't you understand, Stella, what you have done to her?"

"It's dreadful."

"Well? What did you expect? Dreadful! And you can say it!"

"It's dreadful, I mean, that anyone should have told her but myself. I could have explained it all to her. Perfectly. She would have understood. I am sure she would have understood. I did not know she knew *anything* about this. Who told her? Not *you*, Uncle?"

"Never mind who told her or how she came to know. The thing is she's broken-hearted with the sin and the shame of it, that she's in a state – . *Weeping!* She weeps and she weeps."

"She *would*," said Stella, with a momentary, almost imperceptible lapse from her modest sweetness. "Of course I must go to her. I didn't imagine – "

"You cannot imagine – "

"Yes I can, Uncle."

"Her distress. The ruin of all her hopes in you. Her one child! Her ewe lamb! The apple of her eye! Broken-hearted she is at your deception. Broken, she is; *ill*. Physically ill... Have you no *moral* understanding?... You must come back with me now."

"That's *settled* already, Uncle. Of course I must come back. Poor Mother! I suppose you have talked to her about it quite a lot. Poor *little* mother! There are plenty of trains. We can be in Barnes by six or seven. Easily. But don't you realise we must hear what Mr Twain has to say about it, before we go? I think he's being very patient with us. He's a very great lawyer and he's come down here... Why – *you* must have asked him to come down here! Who else?"

"When's the next train back?" asked Uncle Hubert. "Has no one a time-table?"

Silence.

"Hasn't this damned cottage got such a thing as a railway time-table?"

No reply.

No one apparently had a time-table and no one displayed the slightest interest in his demand. His air of masterful expectation evaporated and with a grunt he sat down in the chair Gemini had placed for him, sprawling out arms and legs in a manner suggestive of protest, impatience and obduracy.

Stella looked up for the magistrate to begin. She had lost any disposition to panic now. She was no longer acting self-possession. She was in complete possession of herself. She was intelligently interested in the situation. She had dressed and acted her part with such good fortune that now there was no need for further acting. She could put herself away and forget herself.

From the moment of her entry she had never once met the eye of her fellow-sinner. In some extraordinary way she had banished their intimacy from the agenda. She made them all feel that the sort of thing that had to be said was just the sort of thing that could only be talked about in her presence with the utmost delicacy and restraint.

The Cadi of Clarges Street cleared his throat. His expression remained stern, unbending, resolute. After one brief ambiguous glance at the self-possessed and entirely modest-looking young lady on the settle, who was evidently quite unlike anything he had anticipated, he kept his eye upon the slightly unconvincing candour, the restrained, qualified and uncertain dutifulness, of his son. The scene became a duologue, with Uncle Hubert as a restless and ineffective commentator.

3

The Cadi of Clarges Street

From the outset it was plain to Stella that Mr Twain Senior was something much harder and more formidable than anything she and Gemini had encountered hitherto. He had a drive in him. It was something that made his behaviour different in kind from that of Balch or Uncle Hubert or the vicar. They had a conception of themselves, they behaved accordingly and played their parts as parts, conscious of the effect they created. But this brown-faced old man was not thinking of his effect at all; he had an objective in view and he was pressing towards it, regardless of appearances. He had squashed Uncle Hubert because he wanted him squashed, just as he was accustomed to squash interruptions and impertinences in his court, and now he was preparing to deal with Gemini, if he could, with the same self-forgetful hardness. His voice and intonations, she noted, were absurdly like Gemini's, but it was as if they had been dried and sharpened to a point.

He was like Gemini not only in complexion, voice and build but in this forgetfulness of his audience. When an idea bolted with Gemini, he ceased to be conscious of himself and his effect. He too was bracing himself now for the encounter. He was half-seated on a chair-arm, and half standing so that his father could not talk down to him, and he had about him something of the quiet insolence of a confident but not over-confident fencer. "Come on," he seemed to say. Stella and Uncle Hubert might have been a thousand miles away for any reaction he betrayed to their presence. "Hard father, hard son," thought Stella. "But there's laugher in Gemini. Was there ever laughter in the Cadi?"

"Well, James," the father was saying, as though he liked saying it, "this does at last bring matters to a head between us."

Gemini answered gravely: "Apparently. It is how you choose to see it."

The old man was ready with his retort. "Choose to see it!" he retorted. "That is how things are. Let me remind you, Sir – "

He began to speak quietly, clearly and incisively. He spoke with the swift lucidity of a long meditated indictment. "I want to have things out with you," he said and he had them out with a vengeance. It was the whole story of a relationship. He reminded Gemini of this; he reminded him of that. It was not merely the present situation he had in mind, he said. That, it seemed, was only the culmination of a long accumulation of grievances. The way he set about stating his case was extraordinarily like Gemini's method of attacking a subject, the other way round. He charged Gemini with setting himself deliberately to thwart and defeat the parental benevolence, humble the parental pride. At Oxford –

"The degree I took wasn't so bad, Sir," protested Gemini.

"But the other things! Your extravagances in the Union. Bolshevism, Republicanism, Atheism. All very bright and witty no doubt and all completely silly."

"I believed in these things."

"*Believed!*"

There was no answering that. He passed to Gemini's life in London. "Idleness," he said. "Discursiveness. Ill-chosen friends. I know more than you suppose of the life you have led. I know of the parties you have attended, the hours you have kept. Studios, cocktail parties, night boozing with artists, actors, actresses and models, loose women, fantastic meetings and fights in the East End, that Mass Observation nonsense, living as a sham out-of-work in a Cardiff slum. Then this cheap book publishing. Trashy-looking little books in paper covers that people throw away when they have read them. If not before. Oh yes, I know. Your mother has done her best to shield you, but I know quite enough. 'Wait,' she said. 'Give him a chance.' I have, I realise, waited all too long.

"I saw you wasting those years of vital opportunity but I still clung to the desperate idea that you would do nothing dishonourable. Nothing to disgrace the name you bore and exile you from the company of honourable men. Your wits might be flighty, but surely your character was sound. And here we are! I find you denounced and justly denounced by this, this, indignant – *gentleman* – as a vulgar seducer – outraging the sanctity of a good upbringing and destroying the happiness of a decent home. With no extenuation. No extenuation whatever."

Stella was on the point of speaking, and checked herself. She realised that the less she attempted to supplement Gemini the less she would cramp his style.

"Heaven knows what idea you had in bringing this poor girl – evidently, as I realise, a very simple and trustful girl – a mere child indeed – to this disreputable haunt of a disreputable woman."

"Is this going on *long?*" said Uncle Hubert, and began to redistribute his limbs into fresh poses of unrest.

Nobody heeded him.

The Cadi warmed up against Mary Clarkson. "In the decent past a woman who kept a house of this sort would have been hounded out of the village... Rough music... Marrow-bones and cleavers..."

BABES IN THE DARKLING WOOD

Stella was moved to defend Mary but exercised self-control. The tirade broadened and deepened. The precise voice went on, very distinct and deliberate, with a note of satisfaction at the phrasing and point of its utterance.

She scrutinised his intent face, and slowly and reluctantly she realised the quality of its expression. It was cold and steadfast hate. The drive in him was white hate. He hated Gemini. He was working himself up against him now. He was giving rein to a long-accumulated passion. This was his crowing opportunity.

She looked at Gemini. He too was combatant. Was he too hating? He was looking his father in the face, wary, with a faintly contemptuous and altogether pitiless expression. In his childhood, she knew, he had gone in great fear of his father, and hidden from him and sheltered behind his mother. He had told Stella how he had learnt from his schoolfellows and the newspaper paragraphs they showed him, that Clarges Street was famous for the bullying of witnesses and the heavy sentences and blistering comments of the presiding magistrate. It was only in the last year or so that he had dared to stand up to this autocracy, even in minor matters. She had read about such hatreds of the old for the young and between fathers and sons, in books about psychology, but what one reads about in books is never more than half real; here was the living thing visible and audible, the primordial triangle of Atkinson's Old Man, his envy and jealousy of his son and of the son's possession of a woman. It had suddenly walked out of anthropology into this cottage and planted itself upon the hearthrug.

The Old Man and the Son! She had read about it as an old far-away tale of social beginnings. Was it something that was still going on now, something woven into the whole social process?

Was it, as her Uncle Robert had written in a review of Freud's last book, a contemporary structural reality? Queer fragments of these speculations spun in a wild eddy through Stella's brain and imposed strange generalisations upon the scene before her. What was he saying? He could be patient with his son no longer, he said. He wanted – what was it he said he wanted?

"I want Mr – Major Hopkinshire here to know exactly what I feel and intend towards you, because I trust that then we shall have complete co-operation from his side. Natural affection I still bear you, but to be weak with you now would be cruel." He paused for a moment with tightening lips. "This income of yours must cease, both what comes from your mother's estate and the allowance she persuaded me to add to it. It must cease absolutely. It must be cut off altogether. It is simply subsidising idleness and depravity. You will have to leave London. I shall arrange for you to go abroad, preferably to some country where the atmosphere is manly and clean, and where you will not be exposed to gross temptation, to High Germany perhaps, where you can at least master a language, harden your character, and have time to reflect upon your outlook. Money will be paid you in sufficient amounts at regular intervals to sustain you – upon certain definite conditions. You must get right out of my life and my circle altogether. You must cut your connections with your Bohemian friends. You must correspond with your mother only with my knowledge and my consent. There must be no further communication, no communication at all, between you and this – this, well – young lady. You must give an undertaking to that effect."

"May I interrupt for a moment, Sir?" said Gemini.

"Well?"

"Neither of us agree that we have done anything wrong at all. And – I shall go on with my work in London."

"You will disobey me – flatly?"

"I am of age, Sir."

The old man reconstructed his attack promptly. If he felt countered by this defiance, he did not betray it. "Then you will leave my house forthwith," he said.

"Evidently! Good Lord! Imagine the breakfast table!... I'll come back and pack. It's all right, Sir, don't be alarmed, we won't travel together. I shall travel third. The third-class people are more human. And I can go by a different train. I'll turn out willingly enough. I think I can rub along in London all right. What with one thing and another. And so – ?"

Stella felt called upon for a declaration at this stage. "I am going to my mother because she says she is ill – and for no other reason at all," she said, staring calmly in front of her. For one instant her hands sought those abandoned trouser pockets and then returned to their ladylike pose on her lap. "We do not consider we have done anything wrong."

"Then you don't know what you are talking about, either of you," said Mr Twain. "You don't know the meaning of right and wrong. It is hard to stigmatise your conduct without the use of words that may sound harshly" – he half turned to Stella – "in your ears."

"I've read the Bible," reflected Stella. "And of course there's Uncle."

As soon as she said that she knew she had been gratingly flippant. The Cadi was manifestly shocked. When next he spoke to her it was in a tone of deep reproach.

"Do incontinence, fornication, deception, disobedience, then, mean nothing to you? Have you never heard of fallen women? You are living in a Christian country under a definitely Christian moral code and my son there" – he pointed – "has persuaded you to outrage it. And you have done so. Don't you begin to realise your present position? Do you know nothing of the social penalties – ?"

"We are *not* Christians," said Gemini.

"Don't imagine that. You are."

"But surely we know our own minds!"

"What have your fancies about your own minds got to do with it? You are Christians, just as you are English. You can no more escape from the one thing than the other. You were born and baptised Christian. You were clothed and fed and housed Christian, the law and order about you is Christian, the education is Christian, this country is a Christian country with a State Church, ruled by a Christian monarch. You are Christian just as much as you are Twain and Kentlake. You can't alter facts like that by your mere say-so. You can't contract out of your born religion any more than you can contract out of your born nationality."

"But we do not believe a word of your creed, Sir. Not a word of it."

"That is as may be. It is quite a minor point what amount of concrete reality you may attach to the statements in the creed, or in the Bible or in the articles of religion. Quite a minor point. The important thing is that the whole fabric of social life, conduct, law, property, confidence, is built upon this Christian system of ideas. It is too late, even if it were desirable, to alter that now. We can't have everything upset because of some discordant oddity about a chance skull or a fossil reptile or a bit of archaeology or something of that sort. Have you no sense of proportion? What practical formula of denial, may I ask, do you young people affect? How do you put this – something that isn't Christianity? On which apparently you propose to base something which isn't morality, and found something which will certainly not be a new social order?"

"I do not believe in a personal God," said Gemini. "If you really want to know. In plain language I suppose that is Atheism. The word, as people say, is in bad odour, but it means what it says."

"And what ultimate wisdom, may I ask, have *you* attained, young lady, in the course of your eighteen or nineteen years?"

Stella kept her temper and weighed her words. Her tone was almost apologetic.

"I cannot find any reality in the Christian God or anything particularly compelling in what you call Christian morality. I am sorry, Mr Twain, but I don't. I doubt if many Christians do. From the Christian point of view, anyhow, that ought to be called Atheism. I should be quibbling to call it anything else."

Now that wasn't flippant anyhow.

The Cadi launched himself upon one of those Obiter Dicta for which he hand made Clarges Street famous.

"And so you emerge with your Nothing, your Atheos. And that is all you have. But this Christianity which so many of you young people are accustomed to dispose of so glibly, so impertinently, carries with it a vast complex of guidance, support, tested reactions, certitudes of understanding, obligations, duties, honour and consolations, which we call the Christian life. All interwoven and inseparable. It is the greatest, most comprehensive complex of controls, protections, guidance that humanity has ever evolved. It all follows on the creeds. What follows upon your Atheos – your Nothing? Tell me that."

Gemini felt the old man had scored a point. He admitted it frankly. "The rational life has still to be worked out, carved out, from these disorders of today."

"It certainly has, And I should have imagined that a young man of your high intelligence – with more than all the usual omniscience of youth – would have known that the Christian life does not so much depend on its theology as justify it. It is odd you have never discovered that. It is this ultimate practical consistency of life and formula, that all you young – intelligentsia I think you call ourselves, seem to miss. It recalls that excellent old story, which has rather dropped out of attention nowadays, of the headmaster's repartee. A certain young gentleman from the lower sixth came to him one day and announced himself, with great dignity, an Atheist. Probably Shelley-bitten. Whereupon the schoolmaster without further parley took down the lad's trousers and administered a sound thrashing."

"Good business!" exclaimed Uncle Hubert, with only too evident a reference to Gemini. "Serve the cocky little bastard right. Did it cure him?"

"I believe," said the magistrate, "that ultimately that particular young gentlemen died a bishop, but the essence of the story is the way in which it puts the creed, the formula, in its place, as a mere part or aspect of the integral reality of its place, as a mere part or aspect of the integral reality of religion. The Christian creed fits because it has grown to fit the social needs it satisfies. Every day this sort of ignorance of the essential nature of religion – on the part of – of samples of the so-called educated classes – crops up in my court. What I am saying I have said a dozen times at Clarges Street. There was that case of Ripper the bookseller whom I committed to prison without the option of a fine. I stated the case very clearly. There's a verbatim report. Atheism is not really a matter of belief; it is a preliminary to bad conduct. It is a formula of sedition. My decision was reversed for political reasons, but it was never disproved. Never. I make these remarks now by the way. I was led astray from our particular business by the foolishness of your words. Atheism! Bah! Let us return to the matter in hand. Of course you are Christian and if you are nothing else, you belong to the Church of England."

"Well, we don't," said Gemini rather feebly.

"You can't exist *in vacuo*. You are British; you are a subject of the King, you belong to the Church of England. That is your legal status. So please don't talk nonsense."

Now this in effect, Stella reflected, was very much what the vicar had said. Or half said. But he had said it apologetically and here it was stated outrageously.

"I don't agree," said Gemini. "Are you assuming a world as unalterable as the laws of the Medes and Persians? Because the world has altered; it alters; it will alter and it can be made to alter."

"I have assumed nothing of the sort," said his father. "Of course the world alters. What else is life but alteration? Our social world alters, but, sanely conceived, it alters in a broad, natural and progressive way and within limits. It pours on continually but it never leaps gaps. It remains a vast going concern. It remains the same thing essentially throughout the world – as a growing organism remains the same thing. It is no Phoenix. It does not fly off at a tangent. It may grow and ripen with the years. It cannot break off to give way to something else. If it ends, that will be the end of mankind. There have been ups and downs in the past; there may be wars and dark ages ahead."

"They may be very close ahead."

"They may. The human outlook may be altogether uncertain. How can we help that? I am no mechanical optimist. And what of that? I tell you again that whether we like it or not the development of human social life and usage is a slow and complex evolution – have you never heard that word 'evolution'? – and at present the whole growing fabric finds its best, most successful formulation in the Christian formulation. Which has grown and spread steadily for two thousand years. To which it is our privilege to belong by nature and necessity. It is the touchstone of method and right behaviour now all over the world. Far beyond its formal limits. You make your feeble defiance... For some freakish reason. Something wrong in the theology. It is like jumping off a liner in mid-Atlantic because you discover the captain has been cheating at cards... You merely destroy yourselves."

Gemini could only contradict flatly. "I believe there is no limit to the possibilities of reconstructing human life. That liner can be turned round, re-fitted, re-manned. You can land from it. Shift to another bottom. Never in the whole course of history were human affairs more plastic than they are today."

"You think that?" said the old man, and a gleam of destructive spite came into his face. "You think that?" Stella perceived that more or less completely he had realised that darling sustaining idea of theirs, and that he meant to kill it there and then if he could. It meant nothing to him except that it was something of Gemini's and hers that he might cheapen and break. In the same spirit she realised he might have set about killing some pet animal of his son's.

He attacked this idea of any reconstruction of human affairs because it was intolerable to him that anyone could contemplate a world different and better than the one that had given him his importance and framed the way of life to which he was accustomed, intolerable that there was conceivably a better world for his renegade offspring. "You've got this idea of a great new beginning in your head. I see. Manifestly. Well, you're doomed to some bitter experiences if that is your conception of life. Oh! Bitter disillusionment. Have you no sense at all of material realities? Do you think, do you really think, that you – your sort with your feeble wits and your feebler characters, squabbling and divided among yourselves, young and green, too clever by half and all that – do you imagine that you can stop the march of history now, just as you might hold out your hand to stop a bus, and go right back again to the beginning and start a new world?"

"That, Sir, is precisely what we think possible," said Gemini. "We are revolutionaries."

"It is precisely what you think possible! Precisely! Precisely think possible! And so you are revolutionaries! And the alternative? This new thing that is going to take the place of the old? Tell me about it. *You!* You Radicals! You Revolutionaries! You Atheists! What have you got to put against this current social order, this great growth of ages, in which we live? Are you going to destroy it by a few simple denials and outrages and defiances? I suppose this blackguardly seduction of yours is part of the new movement. You remind me of that other disreputable rascal, Hosea the prophet. Oh! Being a Christian doesn't blind me to the scandals of the Old Dispensation. Why should it? Why should a

Hebrew prophet be a gentleman? Gentleman is a Christian ideal. Where is this other world of yours which is going to be such a mighty improvement upon the wisdom of the ages and show up all your seniors for old fools? Why! you are not even beginning another world. Where are your atheist public schools? Where is your new social structure, even in embryo? Your new way of life? Show me what you have. A lot of ramshackle people all at sixes and sevens and mostly drunk and depraved... Agitators... Sabotage... Is that all?"

"Russia?" thought Stella, but she did not interrupt. This was Gemini's affair and he must handle it in his own way.

"But look at your own world, my dear father! This is pure romance of yours, this sort of Crown-and-Church-led world you are talking about, this large, stable, established order, going on from strength to strength. I never expected you of all people to indulge in romance. *Your* world now is just a dismal jumble of armaments and fear. It is breaking down everywhere into warfare and violence. The Cross over Guernica. Holy massacre in Burgos. And here? Scampering like hares and burrowing like rabbits. ARP."

"It can stand a lot of that. It has vast reserves to draw upon. Need for discipline there is, but no excuse yet for panic."

"You mean in effect that it will last your time and that is all you care for."

"I mean in effect it will last my time and your time and a lot of time still after that. Church bells will be ringing a hundred years from now. There will still be England and a British Empire and probably a regenerate France. Paris less *gay* perhaps, but happier... Understand me, James, I don't care in the least if Christianity and our social order doesn't stand to reason; no sensible Englishman does; that's for theologians; the proof of the pudding is in the eating, and our system *works*. It is a growth as sturdy and enduring as one of our British oaks."

"And you think that a hundred years from now, things will be going on – very much as they are going on today?"

"I do."

"The good old *Times* fresh every morning and always stale; Court Circular, Stock Exchange article, crossword puzzle – number 40,000 or so will it be?"

"I see no reason why any of these things should cease. A certain enlargement perhaps."

"And that is as far as your mind goes?"

"That is as far as my mind goes and that is all I care for. Because my mind and my demands on life are sane. There is no other possible world that I can imagine beyond this we live in. Even now, even if it shows some signs of age and stress, that does not alter the fact that there is no other possible world. If the present system, through some mysterious evaporation of faith, dies, human society, as I understand it, dies also."

"But, Sir, we do not think anything of that sort. That is where we of our generation differ from yours. We believe that there *is* a possible better world, profoundly different from the aimless bloodstained muddle you have brought us into. Yes, Sir, we believe *that*. We do not credit you with ultimate wisdom. We think this quasi-Christian civilisation of yours in particular, with all its piled-up political and social associations, its mulish insistence on the thing that is – yes, Sir, *mulish*. I must use the proper word – is what stands in the way of that possible better world. It is hanging on – like a wicked overgrown trustee who will not deliver. In Europe, in America, the vital centres of the world, it blocks education, it blocks social readjustments, it blocks the way to Cosmopolis."

"Cos-*mop*-olis," said Uncle Hubert in a sort of aside to God. Nobody heeded him. He might have been furniture.

"It is your only hope of what you call Cosmopolis," said the magistrate. "Because, you see, it is in possession of things. You can get your Cosmopolis only with its consent. Blocks the way! It blocks the way to headlong anarchy. The only possible united world now is a world Europeanised, completely Europeanised, and so far as outward forms go, Christianised, a natural steady development of tested usage. You twit me with my age – "

"Well, a father is naturally – "

"And I twit you with ignorance and inexperience. With flimsiness and flightiness. 'A father is naturally' – and what, Sir, is the son? A raw young fool, headstrong and obstinate. Can you give me credit for *no* intelligence? Do you think that I have not wrestled with those riddles of life in my time? For more than double the total of our years. Double! I have thought now, thought hard, for more than fifty years, and you could hardly read a dozen, well, fifteen, years ago. Do you imagine life began with you? You! Of all people!"

(They can insult each other like that, thought Stella, and neither of them raises his voice! Now Uncle Hubert would bellow and intone and play tunes. But how horrible these things they were saying would sound if they were shouted!)

Gemini was holding on to their argument in spite of this sudden lunge into personal abuse. "But this story of yours of reactionary Christianity spreading now all over the world – it's nonsense. Consider Russia – . There you have already something like a working system – based on modern ideas and owing nothing to Christianity. Repudiating it altogether. Has there been ever so complete a new start in all history as Russian Communism? And if such a new start is possible once, other new starts are possible. The Age of Revolution is only just beginning. Life has become Revolution."

Stella sat up and endorsed this congenial argument with a slight nod or so. She had wanted Gemini to say that before. What had the magistrate to say to that? She turned to him.

He hadn't very much to say. He bullied and he denied Gemini's statements. At the word "Russia" his countenance winced and changed and blind prejudice took the place of argument. Russia was an utter failure, a tragedy, a horror, not so much a sin as an insult in the face of God. Like so many men of his type and generation he had refused steadfastly to think about Russia from the October Revolution onward. It had been too much for them altogether. At the outset he had said the Soviet Republic would not last six months, and the longer this strange new abomination carried on, the angrier he became with it. Its failure, he insisted, was all the greater the longer it endured. A red rag for a bull was nothing to a red outlook for the Cadi... "Crew of murderers," he said... And now they were murdering one another and going back to a pure Oriental despotism. The contemptuous certitude of the *Obiter Dicta* vanished. There was a limit to the things one can argue about, he asserted. Then, as he saw Gemini prepared with some intolerable reply, he broke back to the personal issue.

He lapsed abruptly from scorn and derision to self-justification. He returned to the case in hand of Twain *v*. Twain. "Well, well," he said. "About this sort of thing one might argue for ever. None are so blind as those who will not see. Russia! You set Russia up against a rational Christianity! I'm ashamed of the brains I've begotten. We have wandered far from this business that brought me down here. Come back to that. When I hear you pour out this credulous commonplace rubbish about Russia, this cheap sedition of the lower classes, then it is I realise in its full bitterness how completely I have lost my son. Nothing too vile for him to seize upon to wound me! That is the business before us now. To that I return. I will not bandy politics with you. Some day perhaps you too may have a son and learn a little of what all this means to me. I had such hopes of you. Let me be plain and simple with you. Now that we are going to part. For part we must. Let me try and tell you things that may come back some day into your mind. They will mean nothing to you now but some day they will. My life has not always been a happy one. Through no fault of my own. I have had many disappointments, my affections have been ill requited... Perhaps I imagined and hoped for far too much from you. I imagined you making a career that might compensate me for my own comparative insuccess."

"Oh come! You haven't done so badly."

"Not so badly, you think? You think that?"

"Well. You *haven't* done so badly."

"I have not. In a sense – no. If leading a clean life and doing my duty, day in and day out, punctually, righteously, fearlessly and ungrudgingly, is doing well, I have done well. Yes. At least I can claim the satisfaction of a righteous self-applause. But for you I hoped for a career of wider scope and ampler recognition. If youth but knew! If you knew the toil, the self-control on my part in my young days, that made your easy beginnings possible! I stood beside your cot and said 'This boy shall have a better chance than I'. I sent you to Oxford – "

Babes in the Darkling Wood

"Mostly it was scholarships," Gemini interjected, "and I worked damned hard for them."

"You took all these hard-won opportunities I gave you, as a matter of course. You sneer at them. You sneer at the bare mention of a career for you...

"Don't deny it, Sir – I can *see* you sneer. I suppose you imagine *I* am some sort of careerist. If so you must think me a very unsuccessful careerist. Oh *very!* What sort of career have *I* had? I worked as a mere flimsy child for scholarships to get any foothold at all. I worked up to my present position. While less scrupulous men wriggled and flattered their way to success. I worked, I tell you. No one can say it was not good measure I gave them, filled up and running over. And what acknowledgment have I had? What honour has been given me for all my work? I have seen my contemporaries and my juniors advanced and rewarded, beribboned and decorated. I have been given nothing and I have disdained to ask. I have been passed over. With all the comings and goings of the last few years I have been passed over. I have devoted my utmost abilities to my job. I have sought to do justice according to my lights and exercise a restraining influence on the disorder under my jurisdiction. My reward, you should know as well as I do, has been a perpetual hostile press campaign, against my sentences, against the discipline in my courts. No man has ever sought more strenuously than I to administer an even-handed justice, but these journalists in their craving for sensational copy have picked upon me to represent me as a sort of sadistic monster. They have set themselves out to discredit and ruin me. I know. I see the papers. The Cadi of Clarges Street! Corrosive! Acid! Hard as nails! That legend of my hardness has affected my social life; it has even tainted my home. As you must know. Even you... That will not deter me – "

"I quite see that," said Gemini. "I can quite see how anyone in your position may even get his sense of injustice – how shall I say it? – inflamed. Haven't I had to listen to you at meals – telling my mother about it all? Your wrongs and your righteousness. But surely now there is a certain compensation to you, when you get into court, in – sticking to your guns and using your power. *There* at least you command respect. A little god within the limits of your jurisdiction. You can sting a witness and flay an offender. You can give it them hot, say what you like, and get square with yourself."

"That is how you see me, is it?"

"Yes, my father, that is how I see you. And since we are parting now, for good, I tell you plainly that is how I see you."

"No better than that?"

"No better than that."

The Cadi's discourse became almost a soliloquy. "I do not know what I have done to breed antagonism wherever I turn... There is a spirit even in my household... I know. I know. And at last my son, my only son, turns against me, defies me and prepares to leave me for ever with a grin of hate."

"I'm not grinning, Sir. You seem to forget you are turning me out-of-doors. Cutting me off without a shilling and all that. No grinning matter."

"Turning you out-of-doors! It is your own choice, James. All you have to do is to accept my terms. Even now..."

He stopped short and Stella realised how greatly a sudden repentance on Gemini's part would embarrass him.

BABES IN THE DARKLING WOOD

Gemini laughed contemptuously. "And so my life was to have made up for yours, was it? I was just to be a fresh start for you. You were to live my life for me and more successfully, instead of my living any life of my own. You wanted to brag – 'That boy of mine did this', 'That boy of mine did that'. Don't I know? So that's how fathers love their sons. Thank you, but I prefer living my own life."

An added note of viciousness came into the Cadi's voice "Live your own life. Live it! You talk like a lady novelist. *Live* your own life. Very well. But take care to keep out of Clarges Street Police Court."

"Manlius Torquatus – you see I know my Roman History – wouldn't be in it with you," jeered Gemini.

They were no longer discussing anything now. They were flinging bitter words at one another.

"I have nothing more to say to you. Nothing. I have done with you. You are no more my son... No more my son."

It was as if his voice died suddenly.

He had come down here to say that very thing, thought Stella, and now that he has discharged his hate he says it as if it had become an unmitigated tragedy for him. And it was. Nothing would have prevented him doing what he has done and now in the very moment of doing it, his gratification is changed to grief!

The old man did not so much shut his mouth at his last sentence of repudiation as slam it and stand lowering before the fireplace. Gemini shrugged his shoulders and turned towards Stella as though he had just remembered she was there.

She had been listening to it all, he realised. What had she made of it all? How did it look in her eyes?

"And now, Stella," said the Major, untwisting his limbs all at one coup like a conjuring trick, and standing up, "perhaps now that we have heard all this – this edifying row, and your – your young gentleman has been given the key of the street in a proper legal fashion, hats off in court and all that – perhaps *now* we shall be allowed to go back to your mother."

Stella was on her feet already and looking alternately at the obviously very miserable but quite implacable old man and then at Gemini's stiff rebelliousness. Didn't Gemini realise his father was practically an old man and bitterly disappointed, none the less bitterly because he had acted stupidly and unreasonably? If she could have worked a miracle, somehow she would have made them shake hands.

She wanted to say some solvent thing.

She said, "I'm sorry."

"Too late, my girl," said the old man. "Won't do now."

"I didn't mean it quite like that. But all this makes me sorry."

"Well," he said, and suddenly stepped forward and stood beside her patting her shoulder a little awkwardly. "Anyhow you're sorry. You at least have feeling and can say you are sorry."

He spoke, as it were, confidentially. It was as if he was obscurely moved to steal away some crumb at least of her youth and vitality from Gemini, even if it was no more than a touch of pity.

4

Mizpah

"So that's that," said Gemini. "I suppose, Stella, I must look up your train."

Now that the excitement of the row was over and everything was settled, a dark blue depression had descended upon and enveloped him. He felt nothing more about his father. That was over. They had done with each other. He felt nothing but the sheer misery of parting from Stella. He stood up almost noiselessly and moved a pace or so towards the kitchen.

He glanced at the Major's hat in the corner. He didn't even want to tread on it. So completely had the heart gone out of him. He opened the kitchen door suddenly and faced a startled Mrs Greedle on the other side. "I was just," she began.

"You were," he answered. "Mrs Greedle, I have to tell you, if you do not know already, that we are both going away. Mrs Twain's mother, you see, has been taken very seriously ill, very seriously ill indeed, and Mrs Twain has to go to her at once. My father will probably go by the same train. Yes, that gentleman in grey is my father. You think I take after him? Don't mention it. I shall stay to settle up and follow later. The other gentleman is – an uncle. He is Mrs Twain's uncle. No. Nobody takes after *him*. I don't know why. Give me that local time-table you have on the dresser, please... Thank you."

He limped back into the room with the pink leaflet in hand. "Twelve fifty-eight," he read. The Major stood holding out his hand for the time-table to assure himself that all was fair and above board. Gemini gave it to him. "We can telephone to have a cab here at twelve thirty-five," he said. "That leaves us about twenty-five minutes. Mrs Greedle, will you please put out some refreshments? Biscuits and things. No sherry! Mr Balch finished that, eh? But there's whiskey."

He looked at Stella. His expression was ambiguous. He turned to his father and hesitated. He became almost propitiatory. "We two can have ten minutes together? There is just a word or so..."

"That is a concession to ask of me," said the magistrate, after a moment's consideration. "It is a considerable concession." And then to Stella, to make it clear that he did it for her alone, a stern, evilly-entreated but gallant old gentleman: "Very well. You can have ten minutes."

"Not upstairs, mind you," said Uncle Hubert, loutish to the last.

"At the back. There's little path. Quite under observation, Major. Come, Stella."

They went down the garden until they felt they were well out of earshot. "Not much time to talk about it all," he said. "But I think we know now where we are. The old man *can* state a case. He can discourse." He spoke like a fellow expert. "I suppose they ought to have made him something better than a stipendiary. But he was born self-righteous and disagreeable. Is he right and are we just mad to think of re-shaping the world? Is the world – perhaps – the invincible lump he says? Started ages ago. Rolling sternly down to wars and disaster so that nothing can stop it?"

"I never felt so full of fight against all that as I do now," said Stella.

"I'd feel full of fight perhaps, if my heart wasn't aching at the loss of you. I'm *aching*, Stella."

"I ache. Likely I'll be at Barnes. I may go back to Newnham. If we can keep all this quiet. Yes. It's possible. And we'll learn, we'll study. Rather than live as *he* has lived, give me jails, give me trenches, give me hospital wards. He was plausible. In a way he was right. Our world may be the blind ship going nowhere, the aimless damned lie, he says it is. Stick in your comfortable cabin until the ship sinks because there is nothing else to be done. There may be no escape, no hope of a real renewal of the world. All the same, Gemini, what can we do but beat ourselves against it all?"

He did not answer for a moment.

"I wonder," said Gemini, "how much of that soured, inflexible, vindictive old man there is in me?"

"In *you!*"

"I seem to understand him so well. And see through him. The over-subtlety. That streak of self-pity that came up at last. It makes me afraid."

"There is something about his reasoning... But I'm not afraid for you, Gemini... For him I'm sorry."

"I'm much more sorry for Dione – for my mother – when he gets home to her. God! He'll run me down, inventing one evil thing about me after another, until he makes her cry or drives her – scared stiff, sniffing, but nose in the air – from the room... You've never seen him with her as I have. I've lived too much in that bitter comedy. Sorry for *him!* No."

They stood together in silence.

They wanted to say deep and intricate things and their words were unready. The bickering in the cottage was too fresh in their minds. They couldn't forget those missile repartees.

"So we dedicate ourselves," cried Gemini. "How shall I put it? We two will live all our lives working to release that free and fearless world-state we have dreamt about this happy week – free and fearless – release it from the world of all these people. Great and happy world of abundant living, hidden and buried now beneath the world of all these people. Which is *there*, Stella.

Which is *there*. Which we swear by every God is *there*. Does that say it?"

"That says it, I think," said Stella.

"Prigs we are and we don't care."

"Better prigs than rabbits. Better prigs than hogs. Better prigs than worms. Prigs is human, Gemini, and the rest is grunting snorting snapping crawling beasts. Stiff prigs."

"Great apes we might be."

"Little apes is all men could rise to be in the animal line. They'll never get back now to the big black gorilla. I am human. I am self-conscious. I insist I am a prig."

"And now before it is too late, let us check addresses and telephone numbers and things, so that we shall make no slips..."

They became very business-like.

They came back into the garden. His wrist-watch seemed to have raced.

"Here we are. Good bye, Stella."

"Good bye, Gemini."

"It's for keeps, all this."

"Keeps for me. And you, Gemini?"

"Keeps."

"Mizpah, as they say inside the engagement rings. We're engaged, Gemini. Adam Prig and Eve Prig just turned out of Paradise."

The word seemed to strike her as she said it. She stopped short for a moment and stared at the cottage. "Oh dear, *dear* Paradise!" She swallowed a sob. "Shall we hold on to all this, or is it just nonsense? Anyhow, Gemini, Mizpah! I'm not crying. No... Mizpah. The Lord watch between me and thee..."

"Mizpah," he responded.

Like most English people they thought that was a pledge between two young lovers. They said it in that spirit.

They went back into the house and found his father and her uncle waiting in an estranged silence.

Book Two

Stella has Time to Think Things Over

Chapter One

Experimentalist in Moeurs

Declaration of Faith

Two days later Gemini sat on a bedroom chair at a small, bare, ill-balanced writing-table, writing a letter to Stella. He had propped up one table-leg with a wad of folded paper, but the table still wobbled a little. The room he occupied was a mean apartment looking out upon a mean street of small hopeless shops; oil and colour merchants, undertakers' accessories, bird stuffers, jobbing tailors and the like. It was one of those Victorian London back streets that have survived the rebuilding energy of recent years. The rickety, untidy table and a wicker wastepaper basket with one ear torn had been a matter for special negotiation when he had taken this room. There was a capacious chest of drawers with wooden handles made of some red wood and obviously second-hand, on which he had piled a number of books to read and review, and the three valises with which he had left the parental roof still waited on the floor to be unpacked. Beside them was his typewriter, also as yet unpacked.

There was a wash-hand-stand with ewer, basin and so forth nakedly displayed, and a small night table bore his shaving things and brush and comb. Over the wash-hand-stand was a square mirror, slightly blotched, and the walls were papered with a striped paper which did not even pretend to be brighter than it was. The bedstead was iron and brass-knobbed and the bed had a firm simplicity. Two engravings, one of a naked, unappetising but expectant Odalisque and the other of Etty's Bather Surprised, hinted at a tolerant moral outlook on the part of the management. You paid your money and you used your room as you liked, provided you did not give trouble. There was a brown spring blind with a wooden acorn-pull, and a red wooden curtain pole with wooden rings carried green and dust-coloured curtains.

Two white-shaded electric lights, one on the writing-table and the other in the centre of the room, provided illumination. There was no telephone in the apartment, but there was, he knew, a semi-public twopence-in-the-slot machine on the landing outside.

He was composing a letter to Stella. He was writing in pencil on a pad of manuscript paper, because he felt that typescript was unsuitable for a lover, and his fountain pen had, as usual, run dry. He had found it a little difficult to begin. He had written, "My dear and lovely Stella", and then he had disliked that. It had sounded formal and clumsy. The worst of having literary preoccupations and sensibilities, he reflected, was that they robbed this sort of thing of any spontaneity. He would have liked an uncontrolled effusion of beautiful words, something with the quasi-natural conventionality of a Restoration lover, "My sweete dear Wyfe..."

BABES IN THE DARKLING WOOD

He wrote on a second sheet: "My sweet dear Stella, Do you remember how those starry white flowers boiled along the hedge in the lane?..."

He reflected. Just how would she look when she read that?

He changed the key. "I said I would write no love letters, and this is nothing of the sort. It is a memorandum, and as soon as I get a safe address from you I shall post it, I want to set down clearly what we said and agreed about while our talks are still clear in my mind.

"My news is very simple. I have been duly turned out-of-doors, and I am installed in a shabby apartment in Duluth Crescent near St Pancras Station. It is not very nice, I find, and I do not intend to stay on here after the week for which I took it, is out. The landlady has a hostile manner and a squint, and a man with beak and eyes like a cuttlefish sits in the room below her and scrutinises you as you come in and picks his teeth with one of his tentacles. My best address therefore will be the Maston Street Labour Club where I do most of my work, or better perhaps, the publishing office, as I told you. I am most likely to be at Maston Street on Saturday and Sunday, but for the rest of the week the office is likeliest.

"This place is a mistake. It's too cheap. It's absurdly uncomfortable. I am ashamed of myself to be lodged so dingily. I took it late on Thursday night because I was tired out and a bit masochist, dramatising myself as an outcast. I thought it became a revolutionist to lodge cramped and slummy. I thought of Lenin in his bed-sitting-room in Geneva. You see, in reality I have still lots of money to carry on with and all that. And resources. Dione M'am, that is to say my mother, smuggled what is called a 'useful tenner' into my bag, pretending it was a forgotten pair of socks.

Very like her. I don't really need it, but it expressed her feelings. About me and about my father. You'll love my dear and disingenuous Dione M'am when you meet her. There's no describing her.

"But to our memorandum."

He reflected, and the growing politico-social journalist in his make-up took possession of him. Stella became the "dear reader" and ceased to be a desired presence.

"MEMORANDUM

"We have agreed upon certain fundamental things. They are to be our religion and our way of life.

"*Firstly*, we have agreed that it is not true, as my father believes, as the parson believes, as Uncle Hubert believes, as Balch at the bottom of his rhetoric believes, that the present moral, religious, political and social system is an inevitable, irreplaceable growth, in which the best thing to do politically is to manœuvre about with treaties, leagues, Acts of Parliament and so forth, muddling along, staving things off. They all believe the present system is Necessity and Destiny. It is, they believe (and by this belief they are damned), the unavoidable Course of Events; the inevitable Thing that is; the moving, rolling block of alabaster in front of which we had better dodge about as well as we can, since it cannot now undergo any fundamental alterations in its movement and structure. We deny all that. We refuse to take life at that, even if we are destroyed altogether for our refusal.

"*Secondly*, we have agreed that in this gross, confused, moving and dangerous mass of a world as it is, there is hidden the possibility of a human existence of so general a happiness, such

BABES IN THE DARKLING WOOD

liveliness of interest and such abundance as no living species has ever yet known. Look at flowers, light in a thousand refractions, in sunsets, crystals, ripples, look at beautiful bodies, think of music, art, poetry – these are the mere first intimations of the possibility of life as man might shape it. We believe that by a strenuous readjustment of mental and social life, a good, lovely and continually progressive world could be carved out of this enormous dreadful world of today, as a sculptor carves loveliness out of his block.

"This means that you and I are revolutionaries, to the fullest meaning of the word. That is to say we propose the abolition, supersession or reconstruction of every government, every social institution, every organisation in the world which keeps mankind divided and contentious, in favour of a single, rational and steadfastly progressive world system. Our world system includes not only governments but religion and, above all – education. We are against all these rulers and teachers as they exist, we are against them for the sake of our invincible belief in that possible new world. (And here, mark you, Stella, I am putting in more than we said, and dotting i's and crossing t's we left undotted and uncrossed.) We want to destroy nothing that can be made over into a new world. Much of the industrial life of the world, most production, can carry on, with a steady rationalisation, an increasing saturation of interest, efficiency and happiness. We simply want to change the spirit of the producer to a spirit of contented and interested world-citizenship.

"For example we do not want to destroy schools and teaching and the intelligence services of the world, press, colleges, research institutions, etc., etc., but we want to expand, regenerate and invigorate them beyond measure, to give all these things concerned in mind-making, enormously greater powers and a vaster responsibility. Nor do we want, for example, to destroy the transport system of the world but to inject it with a broader conception of service. Here, Stella, I economise energy by writing 'and so forth and so on'. Think of every social process in the world, purged of national, sectarian, class or race feeling and say: 'We do not want to destroy... But – '. The great idea that has seized upon us can come to nothing unless it is an infectious idea and unless we contemplate new-world mechanical workers, new-world planters and plantation workers, new-world seamen and aviators, new-world medical services, etc. etc., all educated and accustomed to regard themselves primarily as owner-co-operators of the collective community. Their pride and their glory must be in their function. They must not attempt either to monopolise or possess. (Sez we.)

"The fundamental social crime (this is a new extension of our idea) is *interception or appropriation* in *any* form. In *any* form whatever. It is a limited view that makes private property in matters of common interest, and the 'capitalist system' the only social evils. There are many other conceivable forms of interception and monopolisation. Class privilege or party rule or official authority or race discrimination can intercept as badly or worse. The subtle variations of interception or appropriation can be detected and controlled only by the constant vigilance of an alert world public opinion. Fixing upon the 'Capitalist System' as the central evil in human affairs, was one of the primary blunders of that purblind old pedant Marx. It was merely the current form of interception and appropriation in the nineteenth century. Uncle Robert has cleaned up all that. Thank heaven for Uncle Robert! No doubt there's something to be said for old Marx, but not now. Not until people have escaped from him.

"The inconclusiveness of the French (There was only one real Revolution in France.) and the Russian Revolutions, was due, in each case, to too narrow a view of what constituted interception. The French thought it was land-owning and aristocratic privilege; the Russians that it was property. But these are only two forms of what is really a protean enemy. Only an incessantly vigilant, scientific criticism, a penetrating social psychology and unlimited publicity can restrain the universal impulse in man to get the better of his fellow man. (All this is new so far as we are concerned, but it follows logically upon what we said.) Moreover, there is no reason to believe that revolutions are futile because those two pioneer modern revolutions did not renew the world entirely. Revolution is a collective art that has to be learnt by experiment. Revolution is just like science; it progresses by a succession of experimental failures, each of which brings it nearer success. (So far Uncle Robert and ourselves in independent agreement.)

"Now *we* come in – where do we two come in? To begin with we come in as devotees and learners, trying out this great idea that has seized upon us, bending it this way and that, making sure of it, making it as simple and communicable as possible. And (new again) we have to avoid the common pitfall of all revolutionaries who are a little aloof from practical experience, which is to over-emphasise some particular slogan or formula, get touchily defensive about its exactness or comprehensiveness and so become doctrinaire. The more rigid a law is, the more it lends itself to systematic and organised distortion and abusive application. In thought, in practical life, just as in law, the letter of the law must be tempered by a vital equity. We must be continually restating our great idea in new phrases and images adapted to the varying circumstances of different types and occupations. Communism, in the West especially, has been largely sterilised by the ossification of its formulae. Our renascent Revolution (1939 pattern) has to keep statement alive and flexible. Ours is a new pattern of revolution. It is Post-Communism.

"*Our* particular line of work seems to be variation and dissemination. We two are earmarked by our mental qualities and characters to become professional revolutionaries. The general mass of the world will ultimately be in revolution, but our sort has to supply the guides and markers of the movement. That is the life before us, Stella, if what we said meant anything. We have to go about finding other people parallel with or identifiable with ourselves. We have to evoke, parallelise and converge upon whatever disposition to service and co-operation lies in them.

"This is not the same thing as converting everyone to one single creed. The meaning of words and phrases is very elusive, and what is sense to one is verbiage to another. The thing in common is the world in common, *mankind co-operative in variety*, under a common protective law and order.

"We have to play over again the part played by the revolutionary students in the Russia of Czarist days when they set about putting ideas into the heads of the workers and peasants, but we of the 1939 class have to play that part better and on a larger and more varied field. That is our part of the 'Kalikov' job. We have to be, as the Bible puts it, grains of mustard seed, inconsiderable today but growing into a vast tree of sustenance and shelter. (My own experience with mustard seed as a small boy was different to that, it grew into a little, low, hot weed, suitable for sandwiches, but I suppose the Holy Land mustard tree is different.) It is the legendary, the parable mustard seed, not the actual stuff sold in packets to the young, that I have in mind, the one that grows into a vast tree that shelters the birds of the air and the beasts of the field. And there are not only our two selves, but presently there will be quite a rush of other sowers of mustard seed, and together we may produce a mighty continuous forest, quite possibly a mixed-looking forest – to harbour and cover the whole world of mankind.

"I perceive that this new and vaster revolutionary idea of ours is going to produce not stereotyped phrases and formulae, which have been the curse of all revolutionary movements in the past, but whole crops of interesting and stimulating images. Alabaster. Mustard seed. The new type of Revolution is Flexible Revolution. We have produced the metaphor of the sculptor working upon the block of alabaster, and we have expanded that block of alabaster into an obstinately malignant Thing-that-Is, which will pursue and kill us and everything we care for if we do not up and tackle it. That is our Idea Number One. Our revised and rallied World Revolution is to be, in the first place, a tremendous sowing of mustard seeds. Until presently we find the New World has overgrown the old and that the thorns and nettles we hated are dead. Something of the jungle has got into my metaphors. But you will understand – and I want to get on to 'Thirdly' before this greasy light fails.

"*Thirdly*, last and culminating article in the memorandum, we two agreed between ourselves that we love each other exclusively..."

His flow of words ceased abruptly. He pushed the paper-block back and began writing on the blotting-paper before him, "exclusively. Exclusively." That surely was not all he had to say about love. But what came next?

He tried to recall that last conversation he had had with Stella in the bedroom of the cottage. How lovely she had been, perched upon the bed, whimsical and defiant! "Make me!" she had said. He had made her... But no! Do not think of that. What had they talked about? They had gone over the relationship of sex to political life very thoroughly, he thought, *apropos* of Cottenham C Bower's *Expansion of Sex*, which now surmounted a pile of books for reviewing on the top of the clumsy chest of drawers. What exactly was the conclusion at which they had arrived?

He remembered now. They had come to no general conclusion at all. They had left the rules for general sexual behaviour quite open and simply made a declaration for themselves, and then lapsed into wrestling and love-making.

But also, he remembered, he had promised to slate The *Expansion of Sex* and show this Cottenham C Bower no mercy. Why had he promised that? How did that fit in? Because, after all, the man had a case for his general theory. But somehow the mere suggestion of his idea had aroused Stella's resentment. She had evoked an imaginary "sex-shirking" Cottenham C Bower... Without the slightest justification in the book, which was, to tell the truth, a good, deliberate assemblage and criticism of fact. A very good assemblage. And something more than that. The book was written with the assumption of a certain underlying philosophy which Gemini was beginning to find novel and interesting. It was, according to his phraseology, *"ultra behaviouristic"*. Cottenham C Bower was like a window opening upon a Transatlantic vista whose existence had still to be apprehended in Britain. The man was treating sexual conduct from the standpoint of the conditioned reflex, and making a very good case for what he had to say…

Gemini realised he couldn't slate this piece of work, if only for the sake of his own good name. But if he didn't slate it, he would have to make his review justify his broken promise to her. She would understand that. At the time she had just carried him off his feet.

Queer how she could stand up to him, contradict him and carry him off his feet by something which was not so much reasoning as strength of feeling and the compelling steadiness of her mind.

No sex-shirking about Stella, he thought. He recalled her, supple and vivid, her eyes alight and her cheeks aflame, squatting up at the foot of Mary Clarkson's ample bed and punctuating her remarks with that comb. What vigour she had in her swift, unhesitating convictions!

Right or wrong!

She was the best thing in life he had ever encountered. She was better than all the rest of life together.

He ceased to struggle against reminiscence. He sat invoking one lovely memory after another from the beginning of their week together until the moment when, valiant to the last, she had turned round as Uncle Hubert stood aside for her to climb into old Crump's cab and kissed her hand defiantly, calling "Goodbye, my dear!" And then they had carried her off. For how long?

A vast sense of deprivation overwhelmed Gemini at the immensity and insecurities of this separation. He would certainly never see her for weeks and months yet, and he was all alive at the bare thought of her. He wanted her now. He wanted her most damnably now.

He was going to want most damnably any number of times before ever he set eyes on her again. He would think of her by day; he would dream of her by night.

"Damn!" said Gemini, and tried to pace about the room. But the size of the room and the litter on the floor did not admit of passionate pacing. He had to pick his way.

"Damn!" he said, and sat down in the chair again.

He assembled the sheets of manuscript before him and numbered them and pinned them together. Queer stuff, he thought, to write to a young woman you were dying to hug. He had written it at her command. But not bad stuff. It expressed newish ideas with a certain freshness... But what he ought to be writing about to her was love.

Anyhow this unruly stir in his blood surely gave him the material for the continuation of his letter. Since he was thinking of love-making, he might as well make love by letter. He scribbled out from "Thirdly, last and culminating article in this memorandum" to the end, and wrote instead, "Thirdly, I love you and I want you and I want you here now, body and soul..."

And then again he pulled up. That again seemed to be all he had in his mind. He sat back, harder and harder, until the bedroom chair suddenly expressed a disposition to break under him by an explosive creak. Then he sat forward and rested his chin between his knuckles.

He seemed now to have in mind two different themes struggling against each other. They were part of one original theme but they had split. One strand concerned this review he was going to write about Cottenham C Bower. He had got an outrageously pedantic phrase in his head upon which he wanted to base his critique. He thought it would be clever to declare that the "living nexus" of human society was a "continually complicating sub-sexual syncytium of originally separate cells", and it did not occur to him that nobody but a cellular pathologist could ever guess what he was driving at, that anyone who did guess what he was driving at would probably disagree with him, and that finally, if it came to a scrutiny, his use of the word "syncytium" was loose to the point of inaccuracy. He had, he knew, this trick of becoming abstruse at times, to the great annoyance of his editors and the irritation of their readers; he had been warned; but when he got launched upon a speculation he found it very difficult to restrain himself. He turned his back on his possible reader and played amusing conjuring tricks with words and phrases and suggestions. It was sort of levity of erudition with him. A private lark. A form of wit.

He really wanted to assert that human society was a vast and intricate family, knit together mainly by mitigated, extended and sublimated sexual feeling. And by sexual feeling he was meaning almost any strong feeling of attraction or repulsion that one living individual could have for another. He was including not only paternal and maternal feelings but even sadistic and cannibalistic impulses. What he wanted to deny and replace, was the idea that human society was a rational complex of enlightened self-interest held together by an implicit social contract. In thus restoring sexuality to its priority, he felt he was traversing Bower's argument and getting into a sort of agreement with Stella. His intelligence and her insistence alike, were leading him to a sociology and economics of feelings rather than a sociology and economics of facts and figures.

But then came a gap in his reasoning, and he found it absolutely impossible to recall how it was that he and Stella had got to that very simple and important declaration of their mutual devotion. This "Thirdly" of his was to have been the third arch of the bridge between them, and somehow, when it came to writing it down, it came to pieces. There was indeed no arch there but a space he had jumped.

Now why?

In this elaborate, careful, unavoidably rather pompous memorandum, he was doing his best, he told himself, to meet Stella's wish to have a clearly stated framework of convictions by which they could live. He was not doing it of his own initiative, he was doing it to meet the demand she made upon him. Clearly it was the right thing to do. Everybody ought to do this sort of thing, everyone above the level of the Balches and bawlers and Uncle Huberts. Everybody ought to set down his creed, whether it was new and home-made or old and established, ought to examine it for ambiguous phrases and make sure that every word of it and every word of elucidation meant something definite to him. He had not only reviewed Stuart Chase's *Tyranny of Words*, he had read it and stood by it firmly. It was a good, chastening, primary book. Yet until he had encountered Stella's insistence upon clear consistency, he had never attempted anything of the sort for himself. "I admit the need of being definitive," he told himself, "but I like to keep a free mind. She has more character, more strength of character than I. She holds me to what I say."

He repeated: "She holds me to what I say."

He turned that over in his mind.

The light was failing. Should he knock off now and finish this tomorrow? He had been thinking too hard and working too long.

Any further work he did now would be against an internal resistance. He had been at this memorandum since half-past two and he had had no tea. How did one get tea in this confounded place? He would have to go out for tea to an ABC if he wanted tea. Bed and breakfast, breakfast brought up to his room on a tray, was all his contract covered, and he had to turn out before ten and keep out till half-past twelve, at earliest, while his room was done. Should he go out and have tea somewhere and then come back and tackle this troublesome "Thirdly"? Or perhaps he might put down a few notes and headings now, to fix that lovely but possibly elusive "syncytium" idea for example, before he went out for his refreshment? He switched on the electricity and sat down again. To realise a new difficulty.

The electric lamp was disgusting. It was weaker than any he had ever seen before; the bulb was a fading, old one and a minimum one at that; it was inadjustable and it was so hung that the shadow of his hand and arm fell on his writing. It paled the pencil marks. He tried the other bulb and that was no better. Together the two lamps with their cross-shadows gave hardly a light to read by, much less to write down a difficult argument by. It might seem brighter later as the twilight deepened, but for the time it enforced, beyond contradiction, that his spell of work was over.

2

Time to Burn

"And now," he said, "what do I do with the rest of the day? Tea perhaps. If one can get tea anywhere after six. And then?"

He surveyed his apartment with ever deepening distaste. Should he come back here and read? In this greasy light? Reading was all he could do, for plainly he was written out for the day. He might sit and think – about Stella? (And then he would be wanting her.) He could not imagine a room less adapted to inactivity. He could go round to the club but in the evening the members crowded in and debated, for the most part, local political issues that bored him. It was not good debating; it was all borough council allusion and repartee. He regretted he was not a member of a larger and better club.

He had never felt the need for a reasonably comfortable room to sit about in before. There must be public libraries available, but so far, in the pampered career, he had had no particular use for public libraries and reading rooms. He had applied for a British Museum reading-room ticket but that had not yet arrived. There were one or two people he might ring up, but probably they would be holiday-making now and out of town, and anyhow it would be a little awkward to say, "My father has turned me out of doors. I feel rather like a lost cat this evening. May I inflict myself on you?"

Of course if Mary Clarkson was in town, she'd be only too glad to see him, but there were one or two reasons, shadowy reasons perhaps, why he should hesitate about that.

Why not go for a long, wholesome walk? He had been told to go for walks and not make his lameness an excuse for physical indolence. He could clump along now as well as anyone and hardly notice that his gait was different from the common run. With a stick he could do his three and a half miles an hour for any number of hours. That walk idea was a good one. He had never explored London as a good Londoner ought to do. It might be a corrective to his too speculative, revolutionary planning, to go observantly through the streets, watching, listening, seeing the various pulsing, human crowd which is the living substance of the alabaster block. It might allay his nervous unrest. He could observe to his heart's content or walk through it indifferent to it all, thinking his own thoughts. Just now with the stir of the IRA outrages and the intensification of the Air Raid Preparations that were going on, there ought to be a definite feel in the air. Little involuntary lapses from mechanical routine, perhaps...

Presently he was sitting in an ABC consuming dry toast and butter and doing his best to be observant and stimulated. But his mind was too jaded for new impressions. If there had been anything remarkable there he would have missed it. He felt he had never seen such ordinary people, such ordinary waitresses, such ordinary passers-by. "God must make them by the thousand," he thought. "He must rattle them off." Whatever they had to say about the current crisis had already sunk below the level of excitement. "Arrest of the UB girl," said a newspaper placard but no one seemed to care a rap about the UB girl, whatever she was. He paid his bill and made his limping way to Camden Town and up Haverstock Hill and Hampstead Heath.

There was a certain stir of war preparation going on, blimps floating in the air far above the house roofs and a string of lorries of men in training, bent upon some instructive task, threaded their way through the general traffic. It did not seem to amount to very much. He disliked the way in which the world was drifting steadily from a darkling peace atmosphere towards a permanent state of siege so intensely, that he ignored it as much as he could. It was his business to discover the way to end this universal state of siege and evoke a new way of living, but it was not his business to understand these probably not very intelligent war devices. He believed that the dividing line between peace and war had already vanished and would never be restored. He had been writing and thinking about that so much lately that now he could think about it no further. He tried to. His mind, he found, was as pale and dry as a recently cropped field. All he could summon was a sort of snarl at all these people working so earnestly and cheerfully upon the details of war-making, while they would not give ten minutes' consecutive thought to the work of making the New Peace. Even if he worked things out to the last snag and wrote it all down with the vividness of a sky sign, would they care a rap or stir a finger? Damn them!

He began to think of Stella again and then still more of Stella. Or rather Stella became a motionless symbol of desire and longing in his mind. He was not really thinking with any consecutiveness about her. He was merely continuously aware of her absence. He walked along the ridge towards Highgate. A lot of flickering searchlights were waving about in the twilight and exasperatingly incomprehensible red spots were appearing far up in the remote sky. This irritated him. The dome of heaven seemed to be further off than usual, as though it had withdrawn itself from these earnest war inanities. A thin haze, though scarcely visible itself, had veiled the stars. The people who flitted by irritated him also. Mostly they were young couples, more or less interwined and talking in undertones. They made him acutely aware of his own loneliness. And not simply loneliness but isolation.

Everybody about him seemed busy upon things that they took quite seriously, things with substance in them, while he had been doing nothing all day but work out the conception of a revolution that would certainly seem fantastically unreal if it were put beside any one of these lives. His thoughts would seem the flimsiest fantasy to any of these busy anti-aircraft workers, to all these murmuring lovers, to nearly every living soul, indeed, that expressed itself in the haze of lights of London down below there. What was he? Nothing more than the almost disembodied ghost of a highly improbable future...

He was seized with a doubt whether he should go on as he was doing towards Highgate or turn back towards Hampstead. It became a painful irresolution. He wrenched himself round.

It occurred to him that this vacuous state of mind, this loss of reality, might perhaps be due to hunger. He would go down into London and get something to eat. He hesitated outside one or two pubs near Swiss Cottage and again failed to make up his mind; then as he got down into London itself, a highly appealing inn, the Volunteer, made up his mind for him and he found himself in a warm murmur of company, before a tankard of ale and a steak and kidney pie. A sense of substance returned to him. He sat in his corner and he no longer felt the outcast phantom he had been upon the Hampstead ridge. He was flesh and blood again, not just a distressed whisp of revolutionary theory out of touch with an earnest, stolid world. He would have liked to talk to some of these people about this jolly tavern, about the food, about the parrot in the corner, about the closeness of the weather, but he was shy of starting a conversation. They sat in couples and groups eating, drinking, talking, or rather just making remarks.

"Seems like Hitler's thinking twice," said a gentleman behind him.

"Seems like it," said his friend.

"You can't tell," said the first gentleman.

"You're right there," said his friend.

End of the remark sequence.

It was really not so difficult. The tension of Gemini's mind relaxed. He began to construct remarks in the model supplied. "Parrot's a bit quiet tonight," was a good one. Then for a reply, "Saving it up." Then like the doxology, "You've said it."

It was like saying "You?" to someone in the dark and getting an answer "Beside you." Nothing more. What he wanted was just some common, human contact before he went back to that cheerless room.

He looked at his wrist-watch.

It was only half-past nine. He felt he could not go back yet to that room, that damnable room. Two hours, at least, before that. He might go into some cinema. There was one, he knew, at Madame Tussaud's close by and he seemed to remember one or two in Baker Street. Or he might get in for the second house at the Holborn or Pavilion? That would be better, because that would be solid flesh and blood stuff. He tried to start a conversation with the waitress by asking her advice about these shows, but she was a girl up from the country and busy with many things.

He wanted Stella. He wanted Stella intolerably. He was not quite sure where she was, whether she was at that hydropath at Weston-super-Mare or with her mother at Barnes or with her Uncle Robert. Most probably she was with her mother at Barnes and so within half an hour of him, fenced off from him by a flimsy prohibition. He struggled with the idea of going right off to Barnes now, weeping mother or not. Marching into the house, bearing everything down before him. "I want my Stella," he would say, "and I want her here and now. She's mine! Come!"

and out he would go with her and carry her off with him to that dismal room of his, suddenly made glorious. That would put the Odalisque in her place and surprise Etty's *Bather*. A preposterous dream, pure reverie, and yet one he dwelt on disturbingly.

Quite suddenly it came into his mind that he ought at least to ring up Mary Clarkson, though the odds were all against getting her. If for no other reason than because he could talk about Stella to her. He could not understand now what it was had hindered his ringing her up before.

But anyhow he ought to ring her up. It was his duty. He had never thanked her for the loan of her cottage. He had told her nothing of the explosion of Uncle Hubert and his breach with his father. For all he knew she was under the impression that he was still down there with Stella. She ought to understand about that.

He doubted extremely whether Mary would be in town. It was highly improbable she should be in town. At any rate, there was no harm in trying. "Telephone?" he asked.

"In the corner."

He stood waiting for a reply and he was surprised to discover that his hand trembled.

"Hul-*LO!*" came Mary's familiar voice to his enquiry. "That's my Gemini! I'm all alone in London on my way to Paris. Come right along and see me and tell me all about this war talk. I thought you were down at the cottage..."

"Explain all that," said Gemini and put down the receiver quickly. He didn't want to answer her questions until he was face to face with her.

3

Mary Clarkson was at Home

Mary admitted him herself. She opened the door discreetly. "Come right in," she said – "I'm all alone. I've only got a loose wrap on. This stuffy weather…"

Mary was smooth-skinned, dark-haired young woman round about the early thirties. She had a slender, shapely body and bright brown eyes and whimsical eyebrows. Her mouth, which was slightly askew, smiled readily and when she smiled it became more askew and one cheek dimpled. Her wrap was of some soft, figured, silken stuff and it was held together chiefly by a clasp and her own slender-fingered hand. It left her long and interesting neck exposed and gave a glimpse of her pretty shoulders.

"And how was it with that blue-eyed angel, Gemini?" she asked over her shoulder as she led the way along the passage. "Was she all your fancy painted her? Tell me what has happened."

"A sort of explosion. Someone gave us away. Her mother's family have old-fashioned ideas…"

"Yes?" said Mary. She sat down on her sofa, or rather she arranged herself frankly and attractively upon her sofa, and awaited Gemini. He walked past her, without looking at her, and stood staring at her unlit electric radiator.

"Somebody gave us away."

"People will talk. That was bad luck. And then there was a fuss?"

"There was a considerable fuss. I did not know people really had those ideas still. Her mother seemed to think that her daughter's fate was worse than death, and an uncle with a vast moustache and immense riding-breeches went and told my Spartan father – "

"Oh-wo!" said Mary.

"You may well say 'Oh-wo!' They descended upon us together. I was disowned and cast out in a brace of shakes. The old man was pure Tincture of Quinine. Stella has gone back to save her distressed mother's life. And it's a pretty lurid mess altogether."

There was a pause.

"May be that isn't so bad."

"*How* isn't so bad?"

"You were there – a week?"

"Six days."

"Pure passion? You love her, Gemini?"

"I just can't live without her any more. I can't tell you – . She's – . One can't *say* these things, Mary."

"You can't. And with the passion still glowing and mounting, came the end. Before you could be tired, before you had a hint of repetition. At the very crest. No fatigue. No satiety. No chance of any sort of jealousy. *Lucky* Gemini. You've had perfection. Naturally the real world seems a black place to come back to."

"Don't mock, Mary. I'm most damnably miserable. I'm in love with Stella – all over. I want her and I want her. And so far as I can see I may not set eyes on her again for weeks or months."

"It's hard lines on you, my dear. But all the same – . Perhaps we don't begin to feel the real edge of love – . Perhaps we have to be wrung to get the quintessence of love out of us."

"I could dispense with the wringing. I want Stella."

He stood looked obstinate and slightly puerile, with his hands in his pockets, and an air about him of reproaching Mary for his deprivation. She sat with a pretty, bare arm along the back of the sofa and studied his averted profile.

"You want Stella," she said and reflected. "Gemini! How long do you think Stella might have lasted if the uncle with the big moustache hadn't intervened?"

He turned to her and stood sideways. "What do you mean? Lasted?"

"If it had gone on. At the pace I guess things *were* going on."

"Have *you* never been in love, Mary?"

"One case at a time, Gemini."

"I'm in love. I'm utterly, absolutely and completely in love with Stella. I want her. I want to live with her. I ache for her. And you talk of the pace – . We *had* only four more days left..."

"But then you meant to go on – at intervals. Quietly. When you got a chance."

"Until we could marry."

She nodded her head gravely. She looked at him steadfastly and the wry mouth broke into an amiable smile. "And now. It is only going to be rather more difficult. That's all. She will go on with her studies."

"If they let her."

"And you will go on with your work?"

"If I can. But while I want her – . I can't work. It's so hard to explain things to you, Mary. You are different somehow. It isn't – . It isn't all just a case of physical passion."

"I quite understand that, Gemini."

"It's far more her personal quality. It's real love, Mary. If she came into this room and stood there – ."

"You'd want to cry."

"How did you know that, Mary?"

"I happen to know."

"It's *her*. It's not desire. It's not in the least desire. It's an intolerable longing. You don't understand."

"Perhaps I know more about love than you imagine, Gemini."

"You've always seemed – . But you *have*, Mary! – to take these things lightly."

"How do you know, Gemini? What do you know of me? Anyhow I know your heart aches. Would you like to talk to me about her? Sit down here on the sofa by me and just talk about her. It will do you good."

"Perhaps it will," said Gemini, and sat down.

"Well?" she said. She moved a trifle nearer to him and watched his face with a faint, affectionate smile. "Tell me about her."

"She has," he said, "a peculiar straightness and clearness of mind."

"Like that voice of hers."

"You've noted it. Clear-cut and decisive like a clean, bright sword. I suppose, Mary, I have really a more vigorous brain than hers, more copious and original, as people say, but she has a quality of discrimination and judgement... I have a feeling I shan't be able to go on thinking and working now without her... The need of her mind close to mine..."

He stopped short.

"The need of her mind close to yours."

"Yes."

"Dear Gemini," she said, "how well I understand this," and she ran her hand softly through his ruffled hair. He seemed to be unaware of her caress. "Poor heartache!" she said. "It's dreadful to see you of all people miserable."

Very gently she stroked her cheek against his forehead and kissed him in the corner of his eye.

He sat very still and she made no further move for a moment or so. He seemed to be lost in thought. He was reeking with self-pity.

Then she kissed him on the mouth and then with increasing significance kissed him again. He turned towards her, put his arms about her shoulders, from which her wrap had slipped, and gave her kiss for kiss.

While she detached his collar and stud, he was moved to speech.

"Oh, Mary," he said, "if only you knew."

It was his last attempt at conversation.

4

Reality

Gemini sat on the floor with his back to the sofa. Mary brought him a whiskey and soda and put it conveniently for him. She had also got one for herself. She stretched herself full length upon the sofa with her flushed, subtly triumphant face close to his. "*Well,*" she said, ruffling his hair. "For the last half-hour or so there has been a singular dearth of conversation in this flat, Gemini. I think the time has come now for human speech again."

Gemini was still visibly despondent. "What is there to be said?"

His note was a note of tragic self-condemnation.

BABES IN THE DARKLING WOOD

"A lot of things, my dear, and some very important things. And first and foremost, you know a lot more about yourself than you did an hour ago."

"I do," said Gemini, ruefully.

"Do you realise that when I answered you on the telephone, you knew as well as I did that was bound to happen?"

Silence.

"Answer me."

"Perhaps I had a vague sense of it as a possibility."

"You had. That was as plain as daylight."

"No, I don't think I had."

"The first answer was right."

"And here I am."

"Looking needlessly perplexed. You have been perfectly natural and rather silly and charming. And *so young!*"

"I'm older now. I'm much older, Mary. I thought I knew how I stood to these things. Now I don't. I would like to throttle myself. Mary, does *this* seem all right to you?"

"Perfectly lovely," she said, and kicked her pink heels in the air.

"But haven't you – a real lover?"

"Am I in love with anyone, you mean. No. Is anyone in love with me? Not that I know of, though the imagination of man's heart is only stupid continually. I love you – and most bright and lively people. I make love less than you think, but on this close, heavy evening, everything was for it. But love! Not for many years have I had that hungry craving for everything, give and receive, from another human being. I can't imagine the man. What a marvel, what a lovely he'd have to be! The silliest of Plato's *Dialogues* was the one where he said, or somebody said,

Socrates or somebody, that human beings were all made in pairs and split and separated and sent to look after each other. I've never met my pair. Or anything like my pair. Can you imagine him? I think that even with the people who are really in love with one another, heartaches and all, there's a lot of — accommodating illusion. Not that your Stella isn't a lovely piece of life. She's a darling. But now, Gemini, here are two remarkable bits out of my mature wisdom. First you are far more honestly and deeply in love with Stella than you were, in your state of jangling nerves, two hours ago."

"That's certainly true," said Gemini.

"And secondly, if Stella knew of this – incident – "

"Don't you tell her!"

"I think it's up to you to tell her, and sooner or later you will. It will ooze out from you. But I can hold my tongue on occasion. Nothing has happened tonight – nothing. It's obliterated. If she knew of this, I say, she would be far less upset about it than you imagine. If she's been living with you for six continuous days and nights and hasn't got your measure in these matters, she's not the girl I take her for. See? What would bother her most would be the question of whether you liked making love with me to any comparable extent... Can your intelligence grasp that?"

"I think it would hurt her – anyhow. It would hurt her most abominably."

"You're still very young, Gemini. I don't know... Most men keep that sort of pompous puerility, I suppose, all their lives. *Why*, I can't imagine. They don't want to hurt the poor dear innocent little, leetle, *leetle* woman. The female of the species, let me tell you, by the age of fifteen has a clearer sense of reality in these things than most men have to the doddering end of their days. The stuff women in love have to put up with! Oh!... Well, well."

"Wise woman you are, Mary."

"You stifled a yawn just then. Oh yes you did. Let your wise woman friend tell you to dress now and be off home."

"You seem to get a lot out of life, you know, Mary."

"One way and another, Gemini. I am a student of human behaviour. I am – how shall I call it? – an experimentalist in *moeurs*."

"I've heard it called all sorts of things," said Gemini, "but never that."

"There your intention was rude."

"Didn't *mean* to be rude."

"High time you were home. It's nearly twelve and I have a train to catch early tomorrow." She stood up.

"Get up," she said, "look me as honestly in the face as you can and kiss me friendly-like like one friend kissing another..."

In the taxi-cab Gemini found a great desire for sleep struggling with remorse.

Back in his gaunt apartment, he did his best to keep awake and think this business out. He felt the situation required it. He sat on his bed, urging his mind to the task. "How can I tell her?" he asked himself again and again.

"Of course the whole thing was inconsecutive – irrelevant. As – what's his name? Cottenham C Bower put it..." (Yawn.) "If a thing is irrelevant that means it doesn't really matter. So why trouble her with it?... But suppose somehow she found out. Of course Mary would never actually tell her or anybody, not for the sake of telling, but she might easily let it out by way of illustration when she was talking... I wonder how Stella would look and what she would say if she found out in some roundabout fashion..."

Not for the first time, there came a flash of resentment at Stella's power to enforce her standards upon him. If she found out before he told her, he would feel like a sneak...

He would feel like a sneak. She would make him feel like a sneak. And yet had he really behaved like a sneak? He tried, with his drowsing mind, to recall the exact sequence of events – quite unsuccessfully...

Or a cad? By certain standards... All sorts of people would agree that he had behaved like a cad. He found that offensive word beating upon his mind. In some way his father and Uncle Hubert blended now with an accusing Stella. He felt their convergent disapproval. "You have behaved like an intolerable cad, Sir. Cad. Cad. Cad... Within three days you have betrayed her. Betrayed her..."

He was nodding. He sat up with a start. "Think this out," he said.

The thing to do, he told himself, was to dismiss that amazing and unexpected interlude altogether; forget about it. Treat it as if it hadn't happened. And never do anything of the sort again. Never. Never. Wipe it up and say no more about it – according to the excellent precept of Uncle Shandy...

Manifestly this – all this – could not go on. This London was too easy and not exacting enough. He must do something strenuous – go away. He couldn't stay here in this too convenient London, to be prey to these spasms of bored desire, these dangerous pieces of stagnant time.

Before the rest of his friends came back from the holidays. Before all the old associations came back... He must make a break. He must do something strenuous and grimly serious. The war in Spain was no longer a possible refuge from perplexity, but there was, for example, Russia. One could always go to Russia. And there were things to be done in America. Or shipping before the mast... And – all sorts of things.

He was too tired to think. No, not tired but drowsy, softly and overwhelmingly sleepy. Never had he felt such a Midsummer Night "exposition of sleep". No good trying to think any more now. He must face this harsh situation tomorrow.

He dropped his clothes about him on the floor, as though he was still living in a world of ministering parlour-maids, and he got into that firmly simple bed. It did not bother him in the least that the lights moving about in the street outside were reflected in an ever-changing pattern on the ceiling. The street noises signified nothing. Hardly had his head touched that severe bolster-pillow when dreamless sleep submerged him.

Chapter Two

Stella has Time to Think Things Over

The Married Life of Mrs Philip Kentlake

Mrs Lucy Kentlake, Stella's mother, had her daughter's blue eyes and an expression of generalised anxiety that was all her own. She moved quietly about in a world that she felt might pounce upon her at any moment. She had a mouse-like unobtrusiveness and a mouse-like tenacity for crumbs. She took after her mother, who died of the shock of producing her. She was quite unlike her elder stepbrother Hubert Polydore or her father, who were both sudden, startling characters who seemed to like making people jump. They admired her, they idolised her, they thought her angelic, and they saw as little as they possibly could of her. Her father married for a third time and unhappily. His third wife was vociferous and alcoholic. She drove Hubert to those seaside livery-stables, from which he never completely emerged, and Lucy was sent away from home and brought up by two maternal aunts who kept a boarding-school for young ladies.

Her behaviour was impeccable; she learnt all she was given to learn and nothing that it was undesirable to know; she was most useful in the school; she took the LLA at St Andrews and the licentiateship of the College of Preceptors in her teens, and she was alert, but not brilliant, at games, always excepting croquet where she shone. She was a good pianist and a careful wearing-down chess player. Her mathematics were so good that it was a matter of great regret to her aunts that the family resources did not allow her to go to Cambridge, where she would certainly have been a Wrangler, perhaps even "above the Senior Wrangler". Also she read a good deal, often wondering at the things she read in what was recognised as literature, but never saying anything about it to anybody. She peeped a little at art when nobody was looking, and she thought that the classical world must have been a terrible time to live in, before Christianity came along and adjusted its costume. Her aunts felt she was destined to a distinguished educational career. They deplored a certain limitation of her opportunities and they wished at times she had more self-assertion, but that they thought would come in time.

All these quietly bright hopes were shattered by a botanist.

Philip Kentlake ought never to have been allowed to be a botanist. But the aunts did not understand this before it was too late. He came down to give the Windstromer Lectures at Bristol, and there seemed no reason at all why Lucy should not attend the course. She went off in her figured sateen, shy as a violet and looking as pretty as any bright-blue flower you like to name.

Now this Philip Kentlake was the younger brother of that Dr Kentlake people were beginning to hear about, even in those days. The aunts knew that Dr Kentlake was a brilliant writer, but nobody had ever warned them that he was a sceptic. Nor did they know that Philip, when he was quite a boy, had wandered off to the East collecting specimens, had lived for a time in Cochin-China in a quasi-native state, before he came back to do some startling experimental research upon mutations at Kew, researches and discoveries that had involved him in controversies in which his mixture of rudeness and exasperating brilliance had given grave offence to all the leading figures of the botanical world. It was beyond the imaginations of the aunts that botanists could lead stirring lives. They thought botany was knowing the Linnæan name of everything and drying it between blotting paper for a *hortus siccus*, and what could be nicer than that? They had heard of the loves of the plants but they believed that these were singularly free from the slightest suspicion of coarseness, an example to the whole animal kingdom; and they saw Lucy go off with a box of coloured pencils and a brand new note-book, without the slightest apprehension of evil.

Philip Kentlake was not quite the sort of man Lucy had expected but unfortunately he proved a very interesting sort of man. He had large, irregular features that gave a false impression of power, a shock of fair hair, very heavy eyebrows, and an upper lip that fell over the lower one in a queer, oblique way that made you want to look at it again. It was determined and it was irresolute; the mouth of a man at once obstinate and impulsive. He had an extremely ingratiating, soft voice. She had expected something much more in the vein of Charlotte Brontë's Mr Heger, a botanical Mr Heger with whom a delicately green and quite inconclusive affair of mutual attraction might be possible.

She followed the lecture with close attention and when question time came she was the only student to ask intelligent questions or, indeed, to betray the slightest indication of understanding the lecturer's not very luminous exposition of Mendelism and de Vries. The rest of the class sat mum, entirely on the defensive. It dispersed in due course and left the two together. He offered to show her some microscope slides and a series of photographs of plant experiments. He promised to bring and lend her a book at the next lecture.

The aunts, suspecting nothing, rejoiced at the prospect of adding botany to the school curriculum, and imagined a soundly Linnæan lecturer in restrained whiskers and a frock coat, knowing all the plants of the world by name and repute. They thought that plants were all green things with gaily coloured flowers; they knew only the bee and the common orchid, not the rarer orchids; they did not suspect the indecorums of which fungi can be capable.

Philip Kentlake had long felt the need for a steadying influence in his life. He was getting bored by this genetic stuff, which was becoming more complicated and less exciting every day. He had been trying to paint and showing signs of being a colourist, and he had had several bright but ultimately disconcerting love adventures. He could not refrain from using his attractive voice and his solicitous manner on women, and afterwards it was difficult to get away from them. His income, derived chiefly from research grants, scientific writing, a small parcel of investments and gifts from his brother, was precarious. He felt that to have love at home always at hand and a real need for an income would pull him together and make a man of him. This little piece of earnest delicacy, he felt, was all too good for him. Something he would really have to live up to. He walked with her in the Dean's garden after his last lecture and suddenly surpassed her wildest dreams about him, by asking her very humbly and sweetly to marry him.

She burst into tears, tears of horror and hysterical resolution. Aunts or no aunts she meant to accept. Never in her life had she refused a crumb that was offered her. She made a considerable resistance before she accepted him, would not let him kiss her on the mouth more than once, and went off in a mood of dismayed but implacable resolution to her aunts. They felt it was dreadful; they thought every marriage was a betrayal of all that was best in woman; even before they saw him. When they saw him, they felt their little niece had a depraved heart. He was not at all what they felt a botanist should be. He was almost sinuously attractive. Not very much was said, but much was implied, and there was quite a lot of sudden clutchings and weepings. "Such an end to our dreams!" But when they called in her father and her brother, they seemed to think it was a perfectly natural thing for Lucy to marry. All they insisted upon, with a faint flavour of menace in their voices, was that Philip should be "good to our little girl".

"You don't know what our Lucy means to us," they said to him, and except for the sentiment of the thing Philip felt that they did not know themselves.

Philip would allow the aunts only the shortest time to replace Lucy in their school. Nothing would put him off. His brother Robert appeared, a dreadful man, a sort of superlative to Philip who never looked at you and seemed to see everything, and he made two alarming remarks. One was that he had often seen Philip in love before but never like this, and the other that if anything in the world could sober down Philip it was Lucy. She went off in a dove-grey costume for a brief honeymoon in Brittany, and Philip proved a gentle, skilful but insistent lover. It was all very dreadful and secret and beyond her aunts' imaginations. "I suppose," he remarked, "I have never known what a pure woman was before", and further that he rather liked it. For a time he did like it very much. He found a freshness in a young wife who was shocked and protesting but never sincerely inappreciative whenever he made love to her. She insisted upon darkness and the decorum of a nightgown; it was a sort of inversion of the fable of Cupid and Psyche; and you never made any allusion to the indelicate side of marriage during the day.

So it was that Stella was conceived before her parents had ever seen each other in the costume of Adam and Eve.

Then the magic began to wear off this new aspect of life for Philip. He was guilty of occasional facetious remarks and one day he came suddenly into the bathroom before she could snatch a towel. "I didn't half know how pretty you are," he said, but that did not altogether reconcile her to this exposure. Her horror of nudity was rooted too deeply to be dispelled by a few words of flattery. Regretfully she had to realise that he was a rude man, a very rude man. A certain impatience presently replaced the worship and deliberation of his earlier approaches. The ruder and more enterprising he became the more she shrank back into herself. He actually proposed to paint her without her clothes, making a picture of her for everyone to see!

"Very well," said he, "then I must get a model."

"In my home!" cried Lucy in horror...

By the time Stella was four years old she was already living consciously in an atmosphere of tension. She could not remember a time when her mother was not a martyred woman and her father an inexplicable series of incongruous acts. Sometimes he was wonderful and delightful beyond measure, dabbing fantastic pictures for her or singing confidential songs to her in that soft, rich voice of his. Sometimes he was incredibly powerful, lifting her to the ceiling, holding her up above all the world. ("Put her down," said Lucy. "You'll drop her.") In the garden at times he would whistle and dance and the whole world danced with him. He took your hands and you danced too. You went on dancing while he clapped his hands to the rhythm. Nobody in all the world could play the tin-whistle as he played it. Or he would take you for a walk and tell you the names of flowers and make nonsense rhymes about them. The older Stella grew the more she appreciated him. But sometimes he was still and moody, telling his daughter, telling his own pet little Stella, not to bother him, even to "shut up". When he went to the attic with the skylight to paint, you had to keep out of the way. He would come down later for a meal and say, "I've done something. I've really *got* something," or he would come down moody. "I'm no good. Painting is *hell*."

"Oh, Philip!" Lucy would say. "Not in front of the child."

There were breakfasts of silent tension; mother still and reproachful; Daddy muttering "Oh *Lord! What* a life!" and getting behind the newspaper.

At first Stella felt the restraining influence of her mother chiefly in relation to herself. Mother was frustration. If you let yourself go in front of her, she would say, "Stella! Stella! Is that the little lady?" If you wanted to do anything very much, you had to conceal it from her or else she would say, "Do you think you'd *better*, Stella?" Then it became plain that Father suffered from the same restraints. "Don't tell your mother," Philip would say, and by the time she was seven Stella was a blind partisan. "My father right or wrong," was her unformulated principle. They were fellow conspirators in a hundred small breaches of their uneventful life.

Yet it tried and perplexed Stella sorely that her father could have the heart to go away from her as he did when she was eight. It was the manner of his going that hurt. He might at least have let her know he was going. Had she ever told on him? Had she ever let anything out? But he never said a word about it to her, never left a note for her, never said anything by way of "Goodbye". He just vanished out of her life.

After two days she asked: "Mummy, where is Daddy?"

"Don't ask about him," said Mother. "Don't mention him."

"Why?"

"Never mind Why…"

Two days later she asked: "But, Mummy, where *is* Daddy?"

"I don't know," said Mother. "I know no more than you do. *Oh! Oh!*" And she wept and would not be consoled.

Then he must have written, and the stagnant sense of absence was replaced by the appearance of Uncle Hubert, very audibly indignant, about the house, except in the actual presence of Stella, when he became leakily discreet and talked artificially about irrelevant topics. Mother wept in gusts and was seized by tear-storms and went out of the room at unexpected moments. "Gaw!", Uncle Hubert would say in heart-torn sympathy. "*Poor little woman.*" Her eyes were swollen, her face was tear-stained and she never produced a handkerchief that was not wringing wet. "You must take care of your mother now, Stella," said Uncle Hubert. "You're all she's got."

"But where has Father gone?"

"You'll know that when you're older, little lassie. There's no need for you to know of such things before your time."

"Has he gone to Paris, Uncle Hubert?"

"Bless my heart!" said Uncle Hubert. "Now where did your little ears pick up *that?*"

"He used to say he'd never be able to paint unless he went to Paris. Not really paint."

"Gaw!" said Uncle Hubert. "He told you that! As though one couldn't paint anywhere! That's his excuse. I never heard such *rot*. The truth is – but never mind what the truth is."

Stella remained attentive, but Uncle Hubert said no more. He just encouraged his moustache and muttered.

That night Lucy decided to break things to her daughter. "I have something very, very sad and very, very serious to tell you, darling."

"About Father?"

"About your father. He has gone away from us. He says – he says. Oh! he says he does not want us any more."

Grief in a torrent.

The child sat up in her chair attentive, enquiring and profoundly unsympathetic. She decided to ask a question.

"Has Daddy gone to paint in Paris? He always wanted to paint in Paris."

Mute assent.

"Why haven't we *all* gone to Paris?"

"He says he doesn't want us there. He says it wouldn't be Paris with us there."

Stella looked at her mother and said nothing. She said nothing because she did not know how to formulate the shadowy question in her mind. But if that question could have taken form, it was, "Did he say *us* or *you?*"

Lucy perhaps read something of the unshaped thought beneath her daughter's stillness. She felt Stella ought to get things right from the outset.

"He's (wow) deserted us," she cried with a new access of grief. "You have no father now. All we have now is each other. My poor darling, you do not realise yet – . Oh, my *poor* darling!"

She embraced Stella with effusion.

Stella had nothing to say. She submitted passively. She was thinking very hard about mothers and fathers and all sorts of things and, in particular, what life with Mother as her only parent was going to be like. She was markedly thoughtful at afternoon school. The girl with whom she was trying to be confidential friends noticed it and asked direct questions.

"I think," said Stella, weighing her words carefully, "I *think* my father has eloped."

"How *romantic!*" said the friend. "Is she very beautiful?"

Stella considered this. She found it a most disagreeable idea that her father should have eloped with anybody but herself. "I don't think he has eloped with anybody," she said with conscientious precision. "I think he has just eloped."

2

The Insatiable Mother

Uncle Robert had larger features than his brother Philip, and a habit of delivering careful but inexplicable judgments at the slightest provocation. His nose in particular was larger and rode high. He did not look at you as he talked; he seemed to be looking at the Real Truth of the Matter above you. He had a considerable private income and so he claimed a certain financial authority in the readjustment of the situation. His words to Lucy were formally sympathetic, but his expression was one of happy serenity at the turn things had taken. It all went on over Stella's head, but she kept her eyes and ears open as the most deeply interested party.

She caught Uncle Robert alone in the garden. "Uncle," she said abruptly. "I think I ought to go to a *good* boarding-school now. Mother – "

Uncle Robert held up his hand. "Never explain," he quoted from Oscar Wilde. "Never explain." He was always accustomed to speak to Stella as one adult to another. "There *are* no good boarding-schools, my dear. Especially for girls. Human nature is such that there are not. But you can go to a great day school in London. We can manage that. You can both live in London. Picture galleries, museums, libraries, theatres, films, choice of friends. You will have to be careful not to get a cockney accent. It is very easy and insidious. That is the worst danger. I will give you a life ticket to the London Library as soon as it is possible. How about that?"

He'd got it all ready. A great and inextinguishable love for him sprang up in Stella's heart. She nodded, too full for words. She nodded three swift little nods.

"*You'll* be all right," said Uncle Robert hastily as Uncle Hubert appeared from the house. Uncle Robert, she realised, could give one the ghost of a wink, just like Father used to do. And though she did not know it, he was marvelling at the feats of heredity, so that Stella could have her mother's blue eyes and fair hair (but coarser instead of its being silky) and yet have Kentlake peeping out of her every expression…

Discussions went on and, though they had a way of stopping short when Stella came into a room, she heard quite enough of them. Mother, it seemed, wanted a divorce. "Let him be free," she said, "I will not be selfish. He never really loved me. If anyone else can make him happier – ," and Uncle Hubert, in duologue with Uncle Robert, held that "Lucy ought to have another chance while she's still fairly attractive." But Uncle Robert seemed to oppose the divorce idea. "You can't divorce a man for going off to Paris to paint," he said. "It's desertion perhaps. If you have any reason to suppose – . If there *is* anyone else..."

"If you knew him as well as I know him," said Lucy...

"That's not actually evidence," said Uncle Robert. "What I mean is, is there anyone in particular?..."

Oddly enough Stella never learnt if her mother divorced her father. She never saw him again and she heard very little more about him. His name was taboo. Perhaps he wasn't divorced ever. He died suddenly when she was thirteen and her mother wept copiously and put her into the most emphatic mourning. It set all the girls at school asking inconvenient questions. If he painted any worthwhile pictures he did it under some different name and she never heard anything about them. No stepfather, no potential stepfather even, ever appeared. Uncle Robert had his way about the London schooling and kept his eye upon her by occasionally taking her out to lunch at bright and amusing restaurants and three or four times to matinées and once to Covent Garden in the evening to see an opera by Rossini. That was a great occasion.

He always took her out alone and he was always charming to her, informing, watchful and heartening. He never did anything

BABES IN THE DARKLING WOOD

to disguise the fact he had not the slightest use for his sister-in-law. He treated her always with disentangling politeness.

Disentangling dutifulness was Stella's form of conduct. She called her mother "darling" and "dearest" by request, unconsciously she reduced these endearing words to the coldest of formalities, and she acquired a habit of solicitude for Lucy's little ailments while really she was thinking of quite other things. Lucy was very wary of chills and draughts and it was necessary to fetch shawls and smelling salts for her with conspicuous assiduity. "I don't know what I should do without my Stella," she used to say. As Stella grew up, Lucy developed a tendency to dress in practically the same clothes. "We are so alike, we might be taken for sisters."

A remote expression was Stella's only comment.

As time went on Stella could have given points, in the art of unobtrusive detachment, to a cat. She would turn up at home with the cook's latch-key about midnight and an air of having spent a studious evening in her room. If her mother asked questions she was always truthful but restrained. "It was Phyllis Buxton's birthday party, darling. I asked you about it weeks ago. You do forget things, sweetheart, Phyllis Buxton? She's a cousin of Lord Rampole. It was *dull*, but you see I *had* to go, hadn't I, Mummy?"

Even before she went to Newnham Stella had extended her freedoms to an occasional weekend with imperfectly specified friends. Newnham had been dangled before her nose by Uncle Robert for a year before it was actually achieved. He had realised a growing restlessness in her and he appeased it with anticipations.

"Adolescence, inexperience and freedom," he reflected "make a highly explosive mixture." And he looked up some of his earlier writings. He had always been a great Liberator of Minds, and now he understood better why so many parents protested at the wide circulation of his books. Did he go too far? Was he too outspoken? He reconsidered his reasoning and found it clear and sound. He wouldn't abate a word of it. Growing up is what youth is for. "She's got to live dangerously like all the rest of creation," he said, and went off to climb dangerously in Switzerland, away out of call when the crisis arrived.

And now it seemed to Stella as if the whole edifice of her freedom was shattered. She felt defeated and fierce. She played the insulted young lady to Uncle Hubert and got him well in hand, civil and taciturn and prompt to open doors, before she reached home, but she knew the real battle would begin when she met her mother. During most of the journey home she rehearsed possible gambits. They were all rather in the form of argumentative statements in reply to a possible indictment. In the end she was completely unprepared for her mother's greeting. The little maid opened the door to them and ushered them in to Lucy, sitting motionless in the twilight with a tear-stained face before an unlit fire. She remained motionless, tragically motionless, while the servant was present.

"Well, here we *are!*" said Uncle Hubert, trying his best to cheer things up a bit, and the situation hung in silence while the door closed behind the little maid.

Then Lucy turned slowly, weeping now more distinctly. She wiped her eyes. She gulped and spoke. "Why have you *done* this to me, Stella? Why have you *done* this to me? Didn't I love you enough, my poor child? Wasn't I enough for you? We were so happy together, you and I. Just we two together. Oh, my dear! My dear, dear child. I have no harsh words for you. None. I forgive you. I forgive you. But the grief, the sorrow you have caused me!"

Then Stella should have howled aloud with love and penitence and flung herself into her mother's arms and Uncle Hubert, choking with emotion, should have left them together, stealing away. But instead Stella stood unresponsive in the middle of the room and considered the problem before her. She had the irritating habit of waiting for a moment as if to make sure her mother had finished.

"I'm sorry, Mother, you have taken things like this," she said. "I really do not see why there should be all this fuss. As though something horrible had happened."

Lucy stopped weeping in sheer astonishment. She clenched her sodden handkerchief in her hand. She stared at her daughter. "You mean," she said, incredulous, "that nothing has happened?"

"All sorts of things. We were having a lovely holiday, Gemini and I – I told you I was going to – until Uncle came down uttering the most extraordinary threats and abuse."

"You mean to say," said Mrs Kentlake very solemnly and slowly, "that nothing whatever happened. That you stayed with a man in a cottage for six days and nights and nothing dreadful happened."

"Not until Uncle came down, dear," said Stella. "*He* was dreadful. I never heard such language, Mother."

"Well I'm *damned!*" said Uncle Hubert with emphasis and got out of the room hastily, before Stella could say anything ladylike and unanswerable to him.

"He didn't even *attempt*," began Lucy still more portentously, in a low deep voice.

"Mother, you are *disgusting*," said Stella. "I didn't think it of you."

"You mean – ?"

"I mean just that," said Stella.

"But – ," said Lucy baffled.

She wanted to ask definitely whether her daughter was still a virgin and so forth and so on, but so great was her agoraphobia of plain language that she was no more capable of putting such a question directly than of playing matador in a bull-fight, naked before ten thousand people.

"If I could only believe that it was all right," she said with a wistful incredulity. And then: "But it isn't all right! It isn't all right. I feel it."

"I think, Mummy, your imagination runs away with you," said Stella, facing it out sturdily. "*Everything* was *quite* all right."

"You really *mean* – "

"Oh, Mother, how *can* you? It's indecent."

That was as far as they got in the way of éclaircissement.

There was very little doubt in Mrs Kentlake's mind what the true answer to her unspeakable question was, nor any doubt in Stella's of her mother's opinion. But Lucy had come to her limit of plain speaking. She shifted to another aspect of the situation. "But suppose it *is* all right," she said. "What are people going to think about it? What are people going to say? What am I to tell them? Have you thought of that? No one will believe – ... Going away with a man! Staying in a house with a man. Night and day. No chaperone. What is the world coming to? No decent people will receive you."

"No decent people are going to bother about it, Mother. And they will thank you not to be bothered about it. You haven't moved with the times, darling. You poor dear, how worn and wretched you look! Let me get your smelling salts and make a cup of tea for you. Or a cocktail... I know you don't touch them usually, but we shan't have supper for half an hour yet. Just a little *weak*, heartening cocktail."

"It's letting you go to Newnham. It's trusting to your Uncle Robert..."

Stella went to mix two dry Martinis and see what there was for supper. She was very hungry. It seemed a hundred years ago and in another world that she had waved good-bye to Gemini, standing in a deflated state on Mary Clarkson's porch. Here she was back from love in fairyland, with Mother rather worse than ever. "Drink that, Mother," she said. "Oh, it's not nice. No. I know you can't *bear* alcohol. But swallow it down. As medicine. It will do you good. It's your duty, darling. I don't think very much of cold mutton and trifle, by way of a fatted calf. Never mind. Let's both have a wash and get comfortable. No good crying over spilt milk, Mummy."

"Spilt milk!" said Lucy in a harrowing whisper. "I *knew* – "

Stella passed on hastily to another subject. "I suppose Uncle Hubert will be back in time for supper. He'll get his own cocktails, I expect, in own of the pubs in the Broadway. I think he might just as well have caught the late train down. His horses must be missing him. And now, dear, since nothing has really happened, let's try and pretend that nothing whatever *has* happened, that everything is just as it always has been. Let's put a brave face on all these *dreadful* suspicions and misunderstandings – and talk about something else. Come," she said, and put her arms about her mother, lifted her up out of her chair and kissed her for the first time since her return.

"If I hadn't believed your Uncle Robert," said Mrs Kentlake, yielding to Stella's familiar ministrations...

So it was the Prodigal Daughter came back to her mother. And from that conversation onward Mrs Kentlake never made the slightest pretence of supposing that her daughter was still an innocent who had to be sheltered from the terrible realities of life. It released things long pent up in her being. The great interdict upon Philip's name was lifted, and in the next few days she began telling Stella, with a gentle, persistent reiteration, particulars about her married life, about her own goodness and physical modesty and the coarseness of the human male, that she had been burning to tell someone, in gross and detail, for years. She had, Stella realised with deepening dismay, a powerful, negative preoccupation with sex. "I want you to understand what men are before it is too late."

Stella's father became a satyr.

"I did my duty by him," said Lucy. "Painful and degrading though I felt it all was, I never refused him. I was resolved that at any cost he should have no excuse for leaving me. And when I was expecting you..."

"Darling," said Stella, "don't you think these memories distress you? They do me."

"If I can warn you in time. If only I can give you an idea of what can happen to you. I suppose there *are* men who are simple and pure... There was a Mr Pramble, a clergyman at Weston-super-Mare..."

But the simplicity and purity of Mr Pramble of Weston-super-Mare are no part of the present story...

"I can't stand very much more of this," said Stella to the looking-glass in her bedroom. "Why doesn't Gemini write to me?"

The looking-glass was too small to show her all her pretty body at once. She desisted. She sat naked on her bed, hands clasping her shoulders, clinging to herself.

"Feeble and fearful and foul," she said, "and it's infectious. The dirt is entering into my soul." And then: "Five days and he hasn't written. Or have they, perhaps, intercepted a letter? If only one could telepath! Gemini my dear! Gemini my lover! Gemini! Are you there?"

3

Uncle Robert Intervenes

Stella composed a letter to Uncle Robert with unusual care. She studied it and recopied it. Yet she made it seem fairly spontaneous.

"Dear Uncle Robert," she wrote. "I hope you have had a grand holiday in the Alps. I hope you will return in splendid form and that I shall see you soon. I want very much to see you. Something has happened that I must tell you about. I have a lover and Mother is making a terrible fuss about it. It came out by accident. We, Gemini and I, did our very best not to bother anyone about it. It was, we felt, our affair and we are honestly and simply in love. We had a chance to live together for some days and we took it. Somebody seems to have told her, and all the Hopkinshire clan, Uncle Hubert and all, are up in arms. The serious side is that unless something is done Mother may prevent my returning to Cambridge and so cut off my education in the middle. She has always been against this Newnham idea, a sort of jealousy. For her it was something which came from Father's side and which released me from her. She hated it, but she accepted it because she can never refuse a gift.

"I do not know if she has written to you or whether she will. She is not good at writing letters, especially if anything has to be explained, and I guess she will wait until the beginning of term and then write and tell you that something vaguely *awful* has been discovered, and that in consequence I can't go back to Cambridge. If so, dear Uncle Robert, I shall go mad. I do not know anything in all the world so clinging as my mother. She does not mean to let me go, she has never meant to let me go if she could help it, and that is what her mother's love amounts to. She is less like a mother than a small,ced, resolute octopus, and this fuss about my having a lover just restores the grip she was losing. Uncle Robert, Help! SOS Uncle Robert, and my love. You will stand by me?

"Your Stella."

Uncle Robert was as good as ever. He sent a telegram to Lucy: *"Coming tomorrow see Stella before term important can you put me up night if necessary?"* and he appeared, nose in the air, with that invariable confidence of his that he was quite all right and knew it, when all the rest of the world was wrong.

At the earliest opportunity Stella left her mother and uncle together in the garden in order that he should be informed officially of the crisis in her physical and psychological development. There was an interval of ten minutes or more. Evidently Uncle Robert had considerable difficulty in delivering his sister-in-law of her terrible disclosure. There may have been reluctance, sobs perhaps and tears, a whispering circumlocution. When they reappeared in the little parlour, however, it had all been done. Mother had a shrivelled, dismayed expression and Uncle was saying, in that smooth, clear, gentle, self-satisfied voice of his, the most appalling things.

"You talk of purity," he said. "My dear Lucy, have you ever attempted to think what you mean by that word? You seem to attach the utmost importance to the assertion that Stella was formerly pure and that now she is impure. Let us consider these words, simply for what they are. Pure means unmixed. Well, she was always mixed. Every living creature is mixed. She is no more mixed now. What are you making all this fuss about? She hasn't been chaste. There again you have a fancy word. *Chaste!*"

"How can you say such things? In front of Stella and everything!"

"My dear Lucy, let us keep the question right way about. I'm asking you how *you* can say such things."

He took possession of the hearthrug and prepared to discourse at large. "I must reason with you, my dear. I must try and get you to see things in their proper light, because so much depends upon it, so far as Stella is concerned. You must not overpower her by sheer bad language. People of your intellectual quality run about calling people impure and unchaste and doing the most cruel and stupid things about it, and the words, if you will only give them a little patient scrutiny, mean either something totally different or else nothing whatever. I insist, you *must* scrutinise them. We shall never get anywhere if you won't do that. They are just terms of vulgar abuse that have cowed you. Why do you let them cow you? Yes, Lucy, impure, unchaste and so on are all mere vulgar abuse – ladylike vulgar abuse, priestly vulgar abuse. I can't help it if you have never learnt to speak English properly... Lucy, you must listen to me. You have to listen to me. It's no good staring into the grate and pretending not to listen. It was you started this. Purity, you said. Lost her purity. Purity is a chemist's ideal and practically unattainable even in the laboratory. Think of it, Lucy, there's not an atom in the world that doesn't lead an irregular life. It's been proved... Chastity, if it means anything, means leading one's sexual life in obedience to priestly law – and nobody in his senses believes in the priestly control of sexual life nowadays. The bare idea of chastity is nasty. The *droit du prêtre* has to follow the *droit du seigneur*. You don't know what that means! I guess you do, Lucy. Purity! When some German half-wit begins to blether about *pure* Nordics, meaning some de-pigmented Alpine square-head or some sadistic lout of a de-pigmented Wend, we begin to realise the absurdity of the word. But most people use it all the same. Pure English! What's pure English? That Latin-Teutonic bastard... Pure art! Pure water! Pure balderdash! All that has really happened in Stella's life is that she is growing up, and it's a pity, Lucy, that you never grew up in as wholesome and gracious a fashion. Not too early and not too late and quite charmingly..."

Lucy choked. "Oooo," she said.

"But come back to these words of yours. The older I grow the more I am amazed at the stupidity of the words by which we guide our lives. Purity! Chastity! Perfection! *There's* another word, perfection! A key word, Lucy. The most humourless of words. All these absolutes disregard the universal play and looseness and freshness and fun of reality. They impose the pigeon-hole limitations of the human mind upon the incessant uniqueness of every event. Yes, I know you don't understand me, because you have gone through life shirking every possible sort of mental stimulus. It astounds me, Lucy – it keeps on astounding me more the older I grow – how women of your class and quality go on, year in and year out, disregarding the most obvious deficiencies of their own minds. I cannot understand why you don't question something now and then, if only for the fun of the thing. What do you do with yourselves all the time? I confess I can't imagine; I can't imagine. Have you never read the parable of the buried talent? But Stella here understands. More and more young people are shaking themselves free from these primitive obsessions of language. Classes and counting. Number and logic. Everything dealt with as though things were made in identical sets. Og, King of Bashan, was the first logician. In the beginnings of human thought and for a few thousand years or so, it was natural and excusable that men should make a magic of counting – Eena, meena, mina, mo; one, two, three and so forth – but surely we are past that now. What are millions, what are billions · and billions of billions? What are infinities and infinitesimals? Mere conveniences of the mind, Lucy. Mere conveniences."

"How can you say such things!" protested Lucy, but almost inaudibly. "Billions of conveniences! The bare idea!"

"To play about with such things now at our present stage of intellectual development is sheer perversity. You get it at its extremest depravity in that super-superlativeness that makes Indian thought, for example, the pretentious accumulation of bubbles it is. Orgies of multiplication. Everything threefold or sevenfold – with a cartwheel of arms and legs thrown in. Sterile arithmetical indulgence. Leave that sort of thing for half-witted quantity mathematicians to live in forever if they choose. Let them worry away at their formulae and conventions and symbols as though they were the only realities, let them announce their solemn discoveries of expanding and contracting universes and atomic whirligigs and so forth and so on to their hearts' content. It's a pretty game that only becomes crazy, Lucy, when you forget it's symbols you are dealing with and begin to dream, as a patient of mine did the other day – quite an eminent physicist, Lucy – that he'd upset a hive of the square root of minus ones and was being horribly chased by the swarm. Serve him right for having such things in his head! Keep in mind that these symbols are nothing but mental conveniences for ever and ever – "

"Oh, Robert!" said Lucy. "Don't use that dreadful word again."

Uncle Robert stopped short. He lowered his nose so that he could actually look directly at his sister-in-law. "I believe, Lucy," he said, "that I have been talking to you a little over your head. I am sorry. You started it. I forget exactly how you started it, but you did. It's the lecture-room habit of presuming upon helpless hearers that leads to this sort of discursion. Let me see – . M'mm."

He resumed his contemplation of the Real Truth of the Matter. "All this arose, Lucy, out of your gross attack upon our Stella here, clean and straight and natural as she is, on purely abstract and illusory grounds. Why! You might be a Roman Catholic! My customary indignation with your confusion of abstractions with reality ran away with me. Let us come back now to the matter in hand. I don't think there is anything wrong in what Stella has done and in what has happened to Stella. Nothing at all. And so I do not think that anything has to be done through it or because of it. And there we are!"

Lucy gulped. "I can't argue with you, Robert. She cannot return to that horrible college."

"For rather more than an hour, Lucy, I have been talking the most luminous common sense to you and you haven't listened to a sentence. You have simply waited for some word upon which you could put some indelicate construction. Stella is younger than you and I, she has to face a darkening and dangerous world, and she wants the most releasing and strengthening education that she can get. On the whole the best she can do in that way is Cambridge. It's not, as you would say, *ideal*, but it is the best she can do. Therefore she has to go back and finish at Cambridge."

Lucy shook her head mutely.

"How can you prevent her going?"

"I shall write to the Principal. I shall write to everyone. I shall tell them what has happened. Oooh!" The unhappy woman gave way to a fresh storm of tears. "I forbid it," she said thickly through her handkerchief. "I forbid it. I want my daughter. I want my daughter."

"And now let me make a proposal," said Uncle Robert.

"Wan' my daughter."

"What you really want," said Uncle Robert, "is a congenial companion of your own age, with whom you can discuss the depravity of the times in length and in detail, and indulge in a little mild religiosity. You don't want Stella. You *detest* Stella. But you do, Lucy. You know you do. Perfectly natural too. You think she's a hard little devil. Why deny it? A hard little devil, and so she is, thank God for it!"

"How can I afford – " began Lucy.

"I am quite willing to make all that possible if you can find any congenial friend or relation to share your home. I agree you should not be left alone. You want a gossip. That's what you want. Gossip backwards out of life – which you have never really been *in*. But the young must escape, Lucy. The young *must* escape."

"My daughter is everything to me. How can you – you a man! – how can you understand a mother's love?"

"It is my profession, Lucy. I understand it, and if I may say so, I understand it unpleasantly well. You have to let her go."

"I want her here."

"Don't you realise that she will never live here again? She has grown up."

"But what home has she except here?"

Uncle Robert surveyed the Real Truth of the Matter above Stella's attentive head.

"What Stella will do," he said, "if she takes my advice, will be to run away from home. To me. She will find my home bookish and unfeminine and very much to her taste. I shall welcome her unscrupulously. I find the project extremely attractive. I have never even attempted marriage, because I knew my intolerable habit of talking intolerantly and intolerably would have ruined any normal union, but this relationship will be different. Stella and I will get on together. She'll have to listen to me a lot – but always somebody has to listen to me – and her alternative, Lucy, seems to be that she'll have to listen to you. I've no doubt of her preference. What sense is there in your preventing this, if I secure you what will really prove much more congenial companionship. Much more congenial. You *must* know someone of your own style and generation of mind. Even now you have probably someone in view...?

"In all these arrangements," proceeded Uncle Robert, still with his eye on the Real Truth of the Matter, "there will be no stipulation to prevent your talking with your intimate friends of the terrible ingratitude of your unworthy daughter, of how her mind was corrupted and turned against all that you consider the niceties and restraints of life, first by her own natural, inherited, original sin, then of all people by her own father and lastly by myself. I do not expect you will make these or any other accusations outright..."

"Woo woo," in protesting confirmation from Lucy.

"Nevertheless you will say them in your own way. You will say them and frame your life in accordance with them. I think we may consider ourselves in practical agreement on that. You see how clearly and plainly everything works out if you deal with it lucidly and literally. And all this time Stella has been standing there and not saying a single word..."

"And was there any word," said Stella, "which it was necessary for me to say?"

"None whatever that I can see," said Uncle Robert. "But the practice of superfluous expression is almost universal. The normal patient insists upon it. And even if there *had* been a possible word or so, I admit I do not see how you could have got it in. Edgeways. No."

He considered the outlook for Lucy.

"So much for you, Stella, You can go on now, free to face the grim and terrible problems of your time and generation. But you have to keep it in mind that you have hurt your mother profoundly, you have outraged her mental habits and shattered her hopes and expectations for you. You must stay here with her for a few days and give her all the help and comfort you can until she can establish a more equal companionship. For my own part, Lucy, I think you might very well go back to that Weston-super-Mare hydropath for good and all, where there will be a continual coming and going of people with very much your point of view. You have in such places already the beginnings of a great system of Parks and Homes for outgrown mothers and outgrown wives, women endowed with a rich and sentimental disposition not to keep up with things, whatever happens. I have a study in hand now of Retiring in the Human Species and the retiring disposition generally. This house Stella can help you to settle up. I am told it is a type of house easily disposed of. That done, Stella will resume her studies and come to me in her holidays and try to get ahead with shaping her ideas before this war, this universal collapse into ferocious idiocy, that is hanging over us, really breaks. I give it six weeks or a couple of months. Certainly not six... That I think completes a statement of what has to be done. Oh! except for one thing. I hate hurting you, Lucy, and so does Stella. In the classical phrase, it hurts me more than it hurts you."

"Boo hoo."

"Stella has to tell you she is sorry. Oh, you're sorry, Stella. You'll know later if you don't know now. You've got to tell her by word and deed how sorry you are... And that, I think, clears up the whole business. Yes."

"You know I *am* sorry, Mummy," said Stella, bending over her weeping parent.

"My lill' Stella," choked Lucy, and grabbed at her daughter's arm, as though she still hoped to snatch her back from Uncle Robert...

Uncle Robert did not worry. He knew better. Moving with his customary high elasticity, he went to the door that opened upon the garden, with an air of leaving the question ransacked and settled for ever, and turning his mind to other things. There he stood astraddle.

He seemed to be looking right through the sky to the Real Truth of the Matter, and considering those blue expanses and their unstable and incalculable clouds as a tolerable but by no means perfect display of refraction and condensation. There they were and you had to make the best of them. The sky. It was all you had. It had its dawns and its sunsets and its moonlight and so forth, and some of these effects were as lovely as Stella, but that was no reason for pretending there was something essentially ineffable about them. None whatever. Given another spectrum the whole display might easily be a lot better. Oh! Ever so much better...

4

Gemini's Thirdly

Gemini's letter reached Stella while she was still at Barnes. It came in a large envelope depressingly like a literary manuscript. Of course that was exactly what it had to come like, one Prig to another. Yet somehow she would have liked something, a precursor or something, rather more in the quality of a caress. She took it away to her own corner of the garden, seated herself on a wooden bench, satisfied herself that her mother was not hovering, and then began to read.

She was glad he recalled the glories of *Stellaria holostea*. Just enough and not too much of it. It had, she agreed, to be a serious letter.

And for no clear reason she was glad he had not used a typewriter...

She read his Firstly and Secondly with grave attention. She thought it pretty good. It read like the notes for a literary essay. It was compressed and in their own accent of thought. And then she came to:

"Thirdly, last and culminating article in this memorandum, we agree between ourselves that we love each other exclusively."

Then the pencil scribble came abruptly to an end. There had evidently been a break; the letter resumed in ink upon four sheets of the unattractive notepaper of the Maston Street Labour Club, and then returned to pencil upon a pseudo-parchment manuscript paper. Indecision, erasures and afterthoughts squeezed into the margin, became more frequent, and two pages of straightforward writing, she guessed, had been recopied from passages too blurred and patched with corrections to send.

Her expression of intelligent approval changed to a livelier interest. It seemed as though Gemini had discovered for the first time that he did not know in the least what he meant by "love", and had in his own peculiar fashion set out to thrash out this terminological unpreparedness forthwith. Stella knew very thoroughly what she meant by love; she had no doubt about it and she was sure that she was in it from top to toe. She found his perplexities dismaying. You just loved and did all you could to please and delight your lover and your lover did the same by you;

you got together whenever you could and all the rest of life was transfigured against this golden background, and what else could there be in it but that?

But Gemini didn't see it like that.

She had had gleams and intimations of their difference even during that honeymoon in Mary's cottage. It wasn't so much that he loved less than she did, as that he loved quite differently, with reservations and moods and not ungrudgingly with the whole of his being as she felt she did. While she had waited for his letter she had had spells of that same uncertainty about him, and now his letter had come she found no assuagement but an immense intensification of her sense of difference and separation. It wasn't that she felt he was insincere or deceiving her in any way; she realised that he was trying most resolutely to define a profound difference between them.

"About this love," he began.

Just think of it! "*About this love!...*"

"The unexpected things that happen to a mind – ! A bullet is a little thing you can toss up and catch, a germ is so slight that it is invisible. But hit the germ or the bullet at a certain pace, under certain circumstances, and your universe is changed and your world, if it is not wiped out altogether, is swung round into quite a new direction. The germ in our case is that same Cottenham C Bower who set us talking and differing on our last night before the things of this world fell in on us."

"I never liked that man," was Stella's comment. At the time she had felt she had not left very much of Cottenham C Bower. Yet here was again!

"You seemed to find him from the very first mention of his name a thoroughly dislikable man. I found very little to dislike in him. Less as I read him. You invented a shameful shamefaced sexual life for him, right on the spot. It wasn't fair on him. I think an adoring wife and five rather spoilt children, carefully spaced, is much more probable. He probably calls his eldest son 'Junior', and his eldest son calls him 'Pop', Quite regular and decent. But him mind is a slow-masticating mind of very high quality indeed. He writes in the rather over-technicalised style Americans affect, largely I believe as a protection from the ravening journalist, but he does assemble his material with a kind of hard thoroughness and a sense of relative value. He's not the pompous imposter you think he is; he's not an anti-feminist. He's just damned enquiring and intelligent, a Prig of a high order, and the Queen and King of Prigs have to treat him with proper respect, and not go just taking an aversion to him. He says in effect to us: 'You two are in love. You want to make it the supreme thing in life. In the name of criticism, of scientific balance,' he says, 'I ask you to reconsider that. I want to suggest that life is too complicated to admit of that much passionate simplification. I want you to see it from a novel, profoundly revolutionary and extremely illuminating psychological standpoint.' That at any rate is practically what he says. It is what he would say, Stella, if he knew what it was he was saying.

("I'll make myself clearer in a bit, Stella. I am trying to get myself clear first.)

"Love, he argues, can be temporarily overwhelming. That is no reason why it should dominate the whole pattern of life. If you fall out of a window it is a temporarily overwhelming necessity that you should fall. But that is no reason why you should not try to fall with bent legs on your feet. If you survive your fall you have to take up the general assembling and control of your life again. The fall is everything only while it lasts. If you are chased by a bear, you can't for the time study the differential calculus. You have to think exclusively of the bear. But the study of the differential calculus may be an integral part of the ruling conception of your life and the bear an adventure of minor importance as soon as you have escaped."

"Escaped," said Stella, and stopped her reading for a second or so. "And where does this take us, Gemini?

"A fall from a window," she mused. "A bear?"

She read on.

"Now when we say that we love each other exclusively we state a phase of life and feeling as though it was an integral and central part of our two existences. But we are much more to each other than all that. We want to make a pattern of life for ourselves in which we two and our intertwining mental strands are dominant. We have been in Paradise together, dearest heart" ("H'm," said Stella with dubious approval), "but that is neither the beginning nor the end of us. We liked each other no end before we thought of kissing. If we go out of Paradise, we go out hand in hand. Your clear cool straight mind is lovelier to me than your body and more yourself..."

That was all he had written in the Labour Club. He had broken off at that point. Or what was more probable, he had stuck.

"I realise I am *not* the bear," reflected Stella, and looked at the pencilled sheets. "No. He isn't even thinking of me as the bear. My clear cool straight mind? He hardly let me see the wood for the trees, but I feel already that she-bear in pursuit. That other she-bear... Already!"

The "Thirdly" resumed, closely written in pencil and in quite a different style.

"The more I read over the excellent Cottenham C Bower, the more I translate him into normal English from his awful combination of technicalities and adapted slang – imagine it! for this one book he has a glossary of 'fifty-one terms used in this book'! Suppose every book had that! It takes us half-way to Jimmy-Joyce-land! Only in his case the words do mean something and you can't afford to miss one of them, – but he gets more and more convincing and interesting the more you English him. 'Soul, spirit, mind,' he has no use for these words. Think of it! They 'beg the question', he says. Beg the question! It is a stock phrase of his. We are always using words that 'beg the question'. That's why he makes his own terms. He treats the psychoanalysts as if they were half-way back to the Middle Ages. He scraps such expressions as the Unconscious, the Subconscious and so on – how does he put it? – 'a convenient mythology of exploration that has served its purpose and must now be abandoned.' 'Fictitious regions of the mind; no more real than Asgard.' There's a poser for you, Stella. What and where was Asgard?"

"As if I didn't know," said Stella, and went on with Gemini's exposition.

"In all this he is using and developing the language of this new Behaviourist conception of life, which, when you come to work it out logically and completely, is in fact an absolute reversal of ideas which men have considered fundamental ideas from the very beginnings of speech. It is no less than that. It is coming into human thought like a still small voice, and it means a revolution far profounder – than Darwinism for example. Pavlov and Watson unfold their ideas with a certain obscure elaboration and hardly seem to realise the astounding quality of their implications. That is where Cottenham C Bower is so important. He blurts it out. It's only as I read him and so get Pavlov, Watson and Co. at second-hand, that I realise where their stuff has taken us. Let me try and make this plain.

"The right-out Behaviourist does not see a man as a simple unified mind or psyche at all. He sees him as – something – how shall I translate that something? – as a neuro-sensitive apparatus. This neuro-sensitive apparatus extends all over our bodies; it includes not only ganglia but the circulation, glandular secretions, anything with excitability and a kick in it. (Hold on, Stella. Don't let it repel you. I'm saying it as plainly as I can.) That cerebral cortex, that grey matter of yours, about which animal-ecologists make such a song, that last triumph of evolution, with its vast storage and linking up of reactions, is only the crowning and co-ordinating region of the complete lay-out. Headquarters. And all the time, day and night from the moment that a 'neuro-sensitive apparatus' – you or me, Stella, for example – first wriggles, to the moment when death overtakes it, it is going on, things are happening to it.

"You know the story as it is usually told. Your heart beats, your little tummy (your dear little tummy) peristalts; you blink the superfluous tear from your eye, you scratch the tip of your nose because it itches, and all that is *below the level of consciousness*. 'Threshold of consciousness,' you find it in the textbooks. But the Behaviourist won't have that phrase; he never uses the word 'consciousness'; he won't have it that *you* scratch your nose. Your knuckle just scratches your nose. It is a little affair between them.

"And things are going on when in the vulgar language of everyday life you are sound asleep, a multitude of natural, irrational things. They go on, a series of living sequences like people going about their business in a great city. Each of these reaction and event systems is as aware of itself while it lasts as you or I are aware of ourselves, but few of them get put on record even for a time. Just as Mr Smith and Mr Brown go about their suburban affairs, sufficiently and completely, without getting into the papers or going on record in any way. Some of the sequences and businesses may be very silly businesses. Some may get mixed up with secretions, pressures, muscular movements or external sounds. Then they may create such a disturbance, make such a fuss, that they startle the body generally and the recording apparatus in particular, into increased activity. In normal speech you wake up. Forthwith a rush of exterior stimulations, arousing memories and established reactions, pours in upon – not you altogether, but into that arena of the neuro-sensitive apparatus which for the time being you imagine you are. There is a rapid expansion of activities. Before that occurs, the activity of the awakening moment dominates everything else. It was a dream, yes, but the dream was for the moment *you*. It was the ruling sequence. Then, as the expanding system of outside reactions becomes dominant, it begins to recede into insignificance, overpowered by the new ascendant system. Usually in a few moments the neuro-sensitive apparatus (you) can recall hardly anything but a few vivid aspects of the dream that ruled it so recently, and event that much it is busy rationalising.

"Now the normal man, when he has rubbed his eyes and yawned and so forth, imagines he is 'all there'. But the outright, lucid Behaviourist would implore you to reconsider and dispel that assumption. It is only that another more vivid reaction-memory-and-event-system has established a by no means perfect control over what are called the voluntary muscles of your body. It is the body that holds the mind together, says the complete Behaviourist, and not the mind the body. The body has to go where the dominant system in the neuro-sensitive apparatus takes it, but all the time an immense variety of other reaction systems are going on and either deflecting or replacing the dominant system.

"You see the idea? The tremendous idea? It is not a consolidated John Smith who wakes up. It is John Smith No. 214, let us say, John Smith who had a row with his employer yesterday and who wakes up as the indignant employee. He goes on at once, as he gets up and dresses, to rehearse a spirited, but not too spirited, conversation with the Governor. Or it is John Smith No. 618, who sees his wife's portrait on the mantel and remembers a system of resentment and jealousy. Her offence becomes the centre of his being. The recalcitrant employee is simply not there. The body of John Smith, under control of 618, goes down to breakfast in a dark, unloving mood.

"All these John Smiths from John Smith 1 to John Smith 5,000 or John Smith 5,000,000, have a common core in his belief that he is really one person, because they are not only all aboard the same body, but also built round a similar conception of himself, his *persona*, as Jung has it. But really, says the Behaviourist, they are a *collection of mutually replaceable individual systems held together in a common habitation*. One ascends; another fades before it. If the systems vary, you call John Smith moody or inconstant, and if they vary widely you may have such contradiction that at last you have a double personality. But whatever system dominates at the time, owns John Smith, and unless it has something comparable to the scientific training of a Behaviourist or his disciples, it believes itself to be wholly and solely John Smith.

"All this I think is rather lovely stuff. It grows upon me as I think it over. Need I point out to you that this description of a man as a sort of armoury of selves like a bag of golf clubs, first this one and then that going into play with its body owner, is supported by a thousand phenomena of forgetting and remembering, of double personality, of the changes of what we call character that appear under different stimuli and at different phases of life?

"In the non-social animals, in a cat for example, the dominant reaction-memory-and-event-system is all that the animal for the time being is. It is fear or it is lust or indolence or hunger or a craving for caresses. There's no self-consciousness about a cat. But in highly social, co-operative animals like dogs, monkeys and men, there is a complication due to the necessity to behave one's *self*, the necessity to sustain a *persona* in relation to other individuals. Systems involving self-conscious restraint appear, which seem to be almost entirely unknown to such non-co-operating animal innocents as cats. The *persona* may have its own unconscious variations of course, but it is at least pervaded by a desire for consistency.

"These conduct systems of reaction require a story or stories of what we are, in order to hold our *selves* together and to put our *selves* over to other people. The neuro-sensitive apparatus of these socially self-conscious animals can no longer do a thing and forget about it almost completely until the next occasion, cat-fashion. Their conduct systems, whenever they invade other and simpler systems of reaction and become dominant, set about attacking the independence of our moods and impulses and trying to draw them together. They go about like ushers, like governesses, like policemen, like drill sergeants, pretending to impose an impossible uniformity of discipline upon the mute unconscious mutual elbowing of all the other drives and reactions in us in their struggle to dominate our bodies.

"I am being long-winded, Stella, but I can assure you trying to understand Cottenham C and succeeding, and so coming to realise the whole tremendous new system of thought that opens out behind his jargon, may well make a man proud and garrulous. But you see how he and the school in which and with which he is developing his ideas, face the problem of self-conscious living, the problem that is to say of bringing a vast disorder of conflicting sub-personalities into a real effective consistency – almost like trying to govern and consolidate a world empire – and how his *Expansion of Sex* is merely an application of the general conception of Behaviourism to one particular bunch of drives. He might have done it just as well the self-assertion, the inferiority-superiority drives of Adler. But he chose sex.

"Here, he says, taking up the sex systems, is first the drive of desire. It becomes urgent with adolescence, and it remains as an active recurrent physical need (a necessity almost) until the onset of middle age. It lingers on after that with diminishing force simply because there is nothing else to blot it out and get rid of it. 'Nature still remembers.' In other words that old sloven Nature never cleans up anything after middle age, just leaves it lying about. The desire drive is primitive and that makes it powerful and persistent. In itself it can be excited, gratified and allayed by any tolerably attractive member of the opposite sex. The social consequences of such gratification are nowadays easily controlled. In restraining circumstances, when there is no complacent mate about, it can make young John Smith shut his eyes and imagine a companion and get his relief by self-abuse or substitutional perversion. Cottenham C, by the way, thinks all perversion is really substitutional or accessory, but that, and particularly the 'accessory', opens one of his heaviest chapters. I won't go into it. It doesn't concern you and me. We are normal.

"When the primary sex drive accumulates power and becomes dominant in John Smith or Jane Smith, we say the poor dear is amorous, lascivious, 'on heat', and these isomers – I beg your pardon, these alternative personalities – of John or Jane Smith drive on to relief, setting aside at last every antagonistic system. If that happens to such individuals only now and then, they may do their bit of promiscuity, not get found out, and stifle the memory, or, if they are religious, they may get rid of the sense of inconsistency by repenting and confessing, or else they may dispose of it by distorting their memory or inventing some special excuse for it. Lots of people go over their memories and fake them almost deliberately. If they are more frequently under the sway of urgent desire than that, they may become defiantly promiscuous, even propagandists of promiscuity. Our Mary Clarkson is a case in point."

"Plainly," said Stella, her intuitions flashing like sparks from an incendiary bomb. "Yes. But why bring her in just here, I wonder?... Yes, I wonder... Well?"

"But complicating the primitive lust-drive of John Smith, which we might call John Smith No. 2, is a whole system of alternative John Smiths which may prevent John Smith No. 2 from ever getting complete control. First Nature has introduced a strong element of whim and selectivity into this sexual business, so that a simple rational act with the most available person, get your relief as an animal does and think no more about it as an animal does, fails to work. For example, elaborating John Smith 2 and taking all the simplicity out of him, we may get the complications of falling in love and being in love. We two know a lot about that, Stella. In the place of John Smith No 2 appears John Smith 256, loving and very desirous, but the faithful swain."

"?!"

"I won't go on developing this. You can see Cottenham C's line of country, and how he presents the tacit struggle for predominance among systems of neuro-mental reaction, as being the underlying reality of conscious existence! It is, I repeat, a new psychology altogether. I must confess I find this new psychology tremendously plausible; and you can imagine for yourself how he brings in religion, laws, customs, honour, as systems complicating and competing to control the general behaviour of the human being. That general behaviour is merely the rough total of its constituent medley, a fact of which human science is now for the first time, he says, modestly but firmly, becoming clearly aware. Unhappily so far only in the unreadable jargon of Cottenham C.

"We rationalise that resultant behaviour, more or less, as our *persona*. Cottenham C spreads out his survey of sex from its first struggles in the growing family group against taboos and how it developed the sense of sin – he agrees with the psychoanalysts that the sense of sin is fear of the disregarded taboo – and he goes on to trace how the sex-complex systems grew, never losing their primal urgency, as human laws and institutions grew about them. Every extension of the range of the neuro-sensitive apparatus brought with it its reference to sex. You have St Augustine bewailing it and Origen getting rid of it in the most drastic fashion. 'Who can deliver me from the body of this death?' And so forth and so on...

"One minor thing I find very good in Cottenham C, and that is his treatment of reverie. In order to get the *persona* straight and as consistent as possible, these conduct systems, these governess systems which concern themselves with the behaviour and promises and reputation of a human body, ignore a number of aberrant drives and impulses, and push them away into what a psychoanalyst calls the Unconscious, but which, according to your Behaviourist, is merely a multitude of reaction systems 'out of contact with your main directive system.' You see the difference? The psychoanalyst says they are down below in a dungeon, the Behaviourist says they are at large outside. All the difference in the world there. Jung, if I remember rightly, calls this accumulation of inoperative mental stir the *anima*. It often contrasts very markedly with the material accepted and rationalised in the *persona*. It stirs and thrusts, says the psychoanalyst, beneath the conscious life. It skulks and agitates, says the Behaviourist, on the edge of the waking life. J B Watson uses the words 'introspective' and 'observational' to express practically the same contrast in the point of view. A lot of this repressed or excluded stuff may get active in these comparatively inactive phases we call day-dreaming or reverie. The ordinary ruling behaviour-system lapses, and all the things that have been suppressed and forbidden become day-dreams; something much more actual and nearer the control levers than dreaming proper; much more realistic; the honest little clerk becomes a terrific gangster or a recklessly successful financier, the young curate becomes a romantic rake.

"The reverie may never take control at all, but at times it may grow so vivid that it captures the behaviour-control from the *persona* and sets things in motion Then *pro tem.* the reverie becomes the *persona* and the *persona* fades to the complexion of a reverie. The clerk embezzles; the curate gets a nice lay touring costume and slips up to town. They are not the knaves and hypocrites we think they are. They are turn-overs. The embezzler's reverie, which is his abandoned *persona*, becomes a dream of self-justification; the curate comes home with a discourse on the 'higher purity' of nudism and natural love and a scorn for the meretricious bonds of matrimony. In that way the old *persona* elbows its way back to recover control and moralise the life again. Rationalisation among the ruins after the act. Cottenham C gives a long list of cases varying between mere perplexing inconsistency in behaviour to a plainly split personality."

This part of the letter came to an abrupt end. The next portion seemed to have been written in a bad light with a softer pencil. But Stella did not go on to it at once.

She was wondering why Gemini was beating about the bush like this and writing sheet after sheet of summarised Behaviourist psychology. She disregarded altogether the very lively interest and self-satisfaction he betrayed in every line he had written. For the time that meant nothing to her. She was too preoccupied with her personal problem to realise the complete sincerity of his scientific detachment. "It's as if he had something to tell me and didn't quite want to come to it," she thought. "Or as if he had something to tell himself, and felt same reluctance."

Stella crossed her legs and sat forward, elbows on knees and letter in hand, staring at her problem. "I wish I wasn't so clairvoyant about Gemini. It's the Kentlake side of me... Not an endearing trait for a lover..."

It was Uncle Robert who had said once, "My perspicacity made marriage impossible. I should have been an intolerable husband." She remembered that.

She became a clairvoyant with the letter in her hand.

"Mary Clarkson, the she-bear. She sets Gemini System No. 2 going, system No. 2, very primitive and uncontrollable. Am I crazy with jealousy and suspicion, or is it all as clear as daylight?..."

Just how far it had gone, she was reluctant to know. She reproached him. Couldn't he manage somehow not to fall out of windows and not to come across actively aggressive she-bears?

"Something I have to stand. I love him, confound him!, and none the less for it. But why did he let it happen?"

"It's happened. It's going to happen again. I'm not a fool, Gemini. You rascal! You lucid rascal! I suppose there's a thrill in scampering through the wood. Not my sort of thrill... Suppose some day some she-bear catches you for good and all: what becomes of the pattern of our associated lives and all the rest of it then?"

She turned to the last part of Gemini's letter. "Enough of the general theory of Behaviourism," he resumed.

"Agreed," said Stella.

"Let me write now of James Twain. I find I am all that Cottenham C says I am."

"Yes," said Stella, "I thought so."

"I am a jumble of motive systems and London is no place for me. It's full of beaten tracks and old associations. The old responses light up and take control. I try to get on with our problems. I do my honest best, Stella. I work until I am fagged and when I am fagged I am least able to produce new reactions. The old tracks are so easy. The cocktail party calls; the late studio party. And sweetheart, you disturb me. You. I'm in love with you and full of desire for you and it troubles and distracts me and makes nerve storms in me. I'm full of desire. More than I have ever been. You are so near and so inaccessible. I'm doing no sort of good here. Everyone talks of war in the autumn if Hitler, that atrocious fool, launches an attack on Poland. (Why didn't we fight him over Czechoslovakia?) If so, I shall be stuck here in England and more broken up than ever. With this game leg. I have a desperate idea of going straight off to Russia *via* Sweden now. Before all the doors shut. I want to see what there is in Russia. Is Russia a great promise or a stupendous lie? Is human hope still alive or is it dead or stinking? I want to get the *feel* of the Russian crowd. With the stir of travel, new things and my eyes full and London far away, this laxity will drop away from me..."

Pause for contemplation.

"I called him a rascal," said Stella, "but this is plainly honest!... I suppose it isn't dangerous out there. Yet. Who cares about a casual she-bear, if this is the real Gemini?"

She read on. He was giving the ship he meant to sail by, the particulars about visas and money; his mother had been a trump about that...

"I wish I could go too," said Stella. "If only I could go too."

She folded and refolded the letter, and stuck it into its envelope and put it on the seat beside her. Then her hands went into the side pockets of her jacket.

She felt rather ashamed of herself. She had guessed the facts and guessed them all askew. "I did you wrong, Gemini. I got you all wrong. I underestimated you. I mistrusted you. I've been a jealous little fool. Now you explain, I see perfectly... Perfectly. Yes"

She stuck her legs straight out in front of her, and looked at her toes. She consulted them gravely. "Perfectly," she assured them. Then she dropped them.

"Yes," she said. "But what a business it is, this living! All these *drives*, these – what is it? – sequences of reaction and memory!... Hunger of the heart for love. Hunger of the spirit for a right life and a world done better. Hunger for clear knowledge. All these hungers and a score of others, going on at their own pace, almost independently of each other, inside one bothered skull. What an awful image that is of – what does he call us? – neuro-mental apparatuses. A vast cavern of unrest, with lights being lit up here and put out there. And things that come up behind you out of yourself and get hold of you and push you where you don't in the least want to go. Easy to get afraid of life. I begin to understand better, why poor little Mother sits down and squeals and squeals whenever anything looks at her."

And just at that moment came poor little Mother's voice from the verandah. "Stella darling. Te-e-ee."

Stella thrust that bale of a letter deeply into her jacket pocket. "Coming, darling," she said, emerging slowly from her shelter. There was Mother...

Mother?

"The way I've been thinking," thought Stella... "I don't *think* like her. I *see*, because I'm a Kentlake. But the way I *feel?* That injured sense of proprietorship? Am I, after all, more of your daughter than I supposed?"

"Where have you been hiding?" said Mrs Kentlake as her daughter drew nearer. "I got hot scones for you and they'll be half cold. And almost our last tea together! The last ten days anyhow."

"Then I mix you a cocktail, one of my best, as a peace offering," said Stella.

"You had a letter, dearest?"

"Yards and yards. All about nothing," said Stella. "Airy nothings, Mummy."

Mrs Kentlake combined sympathy, sentimentality and sadness in a timid controlled smile.

CHAPTER THREE

Search for Reality

Jealousy in the Night

That same night Stella had a most unpleasant dream about Gemini. She saw him coming with that halting step of his through a wood towards her, smiling with those dear brown eyes of his, looking radiant, holding out his hands. That was very pleasant. That was in the key of her going-to-bed thoughts.

Then. instantly the dream took an evil turn. She realised he was not looking at her, he was looking at something close to her, jostling her. And she became aware of a naked woman wrapped in a bearskin, a taller, lovelier and more supple Mary Clarkson, who was instantly interlocked with him in a passionate embrace, and he was holding her head back by the hair and kissing her, exactly as he used to kiss Stella. Stella had a queer intimation that she was dreaming, and yet for a moment she could not awake and escape. She thrust out her hands to separate those two bodies. But they were phantom bodies. It was no more than a dream. It wasn't real. She screamed denial. "No! No! No!" she cried. "*No!*"...

She woke in the darkness with the faint ghost of that dreamland cry in her throat and anger and misery in her heart.

If she went to bed a Kentlake she awoke her mother's daughter. She lay very still for a time. Then she whispered to herself: "I *can't* stand it, I *can't* endure it. What am I to do?

"It's all very well to say this is how you ought to behave and this is what you can do. What limits all this, is what you can bring yourself to do."

She sat up in bed. She adopted a tone of reasoned protest. "Look here, Gemini," she said. "I *must* keep you. I will stand anything I can stand, but this is something beyond me...

"And you, Mary. If wishing could do it, you'd be dead now. Dead – and if it hurt a little... Anyhow you'd have to be dead... *You* played all this on me... He loves me, you'd say. I know you'll say that. He just made use of you. Does that alter it? Damn you, Mary, why couldn't you leave my man alone? Leave him alone, I say! Love or no love! Leave my man alone... Because I can't stand – that sort of thing. Oh damn Mary! Curse Mary! What does she matter anyhow? It's Gemini that matters. You *fool*, Gemini! You weak Cad! When I love you... Don't you understand? – I love you... Oh! What am I to *do?*"

Her voice in the darkness stopped abruptly. Presently it said, "Ugh!"

She made an effort to lie down and go to sleep and then she sat up again. "*If I go to sleep,*" she whispered, "*and that dream comes back – !*"

Another immense pause.

When she spoke again her voice had changed. It said passionlessly: "Now what would a Kentlake do?"

The answer came in quite a colourable imitation of Uncle Robert's voice and manner. "If you are afraid to sleep because of a nasty dream, keep awake. Obviously. Keep awake. And if you are troubled by a fact look it in the face and talk to it. As I do. Disagreeable facts are like disagreeable dogs. Do nothing suddenly and just talk to them and talk to them. No dog will bite you while you do that. No fact will bite you while you do that. It's all perfectly plain and simple. There is no such thing as an overwhelming fact and the only facts that injure you are facts you run away from... The mere fact that you *can* talk, shows that you are *not* overwhelmed."

"Obviously," said Stella, concluding the speech. "Yes, obviously. Thank you much, Uncle Robert."

She sat quite still for a little while longer. Then she turned on her light, slipped on her dressing-gown, re-made her bed, washed her face and hands, combed her shock of hair severely, brushed it hard and combed it again, said "Yes, I remember," to the comb, and got into her cool chintz arm-chair and sat like a judge enthroned. She spoke *ex cathedra*, so to speak. "Now Stella, my girl, stop all this pillow banging and saying you *can't* bear it. What have you to bear? What does it all amount to?

"You have an idea, a very strong idea, of what love has to be. You have every right to that idea. But you have no sort of right to impose it upon someone else. None whatever.

"You love Gemini. Very well. Do you propose to love him as he is, or do you propose, what is quite unreasonable, to love him as you want him to be?

"Obviously you have to love him as he is, and if so you have to suppress this undertow of nagging criticism in your mind. That is *you* speaking, Uncle Robert. You have made me see things like that.

"Only you see I *just* can't," said the spirit of Lucy rising suddenly out of the depths, choking and then diving down again.

"I can," said Stella Kentlake. "But it is going to hurt. Like hell..."

"There is a curious thing to note about your behaviour in this affair," said the Kentlake strain, "and that is your strong antagonism to Gemini. Yes, Stella, your antagonism. You have been trying not to see that, but damn it! you *must*. Of course you see it. Out with it! Directly you had become his lover and given yourself to him – and you did it, my girl, with both hands and very thoroughly – you began your rebellion. Maybe all lovers are like that. They recoil like guns. You felt you had outraged your own freedom – your precious individuality."

"But then," said Lucy, sending up a bubble from the depths, "*he* criticises your treatment of *him!*"

"I *said*, maybe all lovers are like that," said Stella Kentlake. "That ungrudging, perfect love of yours is nothing more than an ecstasy dream. So now come down to the cool clear facts. Let me remind you of a certain conversation, of certain conversations – in Paradise. Then he was all for dalliance and love and you were all for the high line. In that pretty lane. It was *you* who said first, 'Let us talk of high and serious matters'. It was *you* complained – . I can remember exactly what you said: 'We won't always talk nonsense'. Did he do more than take you at your word? He was very glad to take you at your word. He found it a nice change. He began to talk to you of politics, of ideas, of ambitions. He talks very well, better than you can. (Do you really like that?) And what did you do? You didn't do it deliberately; it was just your reaction, but still – you did it? – you immediately started a new resistance. He wasn't absolutely in earnest, you discovered. He wasn't straight."

"And he isn't straight," said the shadow of Lucy.

"You of course were. And how can a man be straight or go straight, when he is finding his way into life? He has to try things over."

"If you call Mary naked in a bearskin, trying things over!"

"That seems to have taken him, quite as much as yourself, by surprise. That bearskin is your invention. Yes – pure dream. After all you're not even positive it was Mary. Much less Mary in the skin of a she-bear and nothing else. And isn't he trying to get away from the ambushes in which he was caught?... And she too perhaps was taken a little unawares."

"Is it *me* who has always got to be reasonable and forgive?"

"Yes. Why not? What's this love of yours when it comes to a try-down? The fact of it is you've got a lover, a good live lover, who's as good or better than you deserve, and the more you control that antagonism – it is, I admit, the normal shadow of love so that no love can be solid without it, but still it has to be kept in its place – and the more you adjust your conduct to him and your circumstances, the better job you are going to make of the life of Stella Kentlake. And that reminds me, young woman. You pledged yourself to the World Revolution. Do you remember that parting?"

"We said, 'Mizpah'."

"That was the least important thing you said. The really important thing was 'We two devote ourselves now – now and forever – to releasing that happy world of abundant living which is buried now in this clumsy, blood-streaked lump of alabaster'...

Or words to that effect. Or have you forgotten that lump of living alabaster altogether?... How much time have you given to the great revolution since you came back here to Barnes? Have you read a book? Have you considered an aspect? Have you moved a step forward?"

"How can I, until I go to Cambridge?"

"He has. And consider how you read that letter of his! Which he has spent some hours upon. Have you read it at all – except between the lines?"

"In this atmosphere? With Mother?"

"That's an excuse, but a poor one. And now come down to this sex obsession of yours and talk to the trouble. You and Gemini have devoted yourselves to the continuing World Revolution. Isn't that going to hold you close to each other all your lives? When you are sixty, let us say, and very old, you may come to the very end of love-making, but you won't have come to the end of world liberation. Even now you two ought to be hard-working student revolutionaries – all the time. When you can get together you can be love-playfellows and the sunshine can go mad, but that's incidental... Yes, Stella, incidental."

"But how can we be bound together if we don't have that?"

"Well, I guess you will have it. If only you don't criticise; if only you take what you get."

"Suppose a time comes when he doesn't even want to be my lover-playfellow any more..."

"You'll still have the Revolution to hold you together. Unless of course you were only playing with that idea."

"Perhaps love doesn't go on, love without end, for anyone. Very probably it doesn't. It's like every other living thing that happens; it has a beginning and a climax and an end..."

"Even for yourself that may be true, Stella."
"But that is unthinkable..."
"How do you know?"
"I know. Oh, I know. I shall keep on. I shall hold on to love, and Gemini – . I shan't leave go. I *won't* leave go. And Gemini? What will Gemini do? I know, I know it my bones... It will be queer to see him excited by somebody else. What shall I do then?

"I'll certainly have a bad time and I'll have to stand it. I'll certainly have to stand it and make as little fuss about it as possible... He needs someone he believes in, to believe in him...

"How far will these others get between us? How much will they take away from me?... Children anyhow must come before them. I *won't* bear children that aren't love children. They would feel like parasites, a foreign growth in me, a disease...

"Perhaps when a child comes one feels differently. Maybe. After all, according to him – how does he put it? – in the incessant stream of sexual impulse, one changes all the time. Sufficient unto the day is the evil thereof. Hold fast to the Revolution, for that is a lifetime interest, and take each challenge stoically, stoutly, as it comes... And that," said all the Kentlakes, "is everything we can say tonight. You don't begin to know yet, Stella, what a human being can stand. 'I *can't* stand it' is the road to nothingness. Think of where it has brought your mother. Stoicism and the Revolution. That is Life. Whimpering and saying 'I *can't*' is Death. Go to bed on that, Stella, now, and sleep like a top. Go to bed, Stella, I tell you..."

She was yawning. She threw off her dressing-gown and stood thoughtful with her hand on the light switch.

"Good night, Gemini dear," she said. "Forgive me. I'll read your letter properly tomorrow. Bless you and keep you, Gemini."

And she got into bed, rolled over, and slept like a log, even as the Kentlakes in her had told her.

When she came down to breakfast in the morning, Kentlake still, her mother watched her preoccupied expression for a time and when remarked: "You haven't slept well, darling. You aren't worrying – ?"

"I'm worried about the lease, dearest. There's something in it... I ought to run up to town tomorrow and see about it."

"But what is it, dear? Perhaps I – ?"

"It's technical," said Stella. "But it ought to be seen to."

"Of course if it's *technical*," said Lucy. "Oughtn't some man – ?"

"I'll see to all that, Mummy," said Stella. "Up there."

She went to the post-office, sent a telegram to Gemini to be sure of getting him on the telephone, and telephoned to him at the office after midday.

She went off the next morning by bus. "I hope it isn't anything serious," said Lucy, watching her depart, strung up and resolute. Her daughter returned, late in the afternoon, no longer jaded and anxious, but bright-eyed, happy and assured. "You were away such a time," said Lucy, regarding her. "Did everything go well?"

"Everything," said Stella.

"There won't be any more trouble?"

"No. It's just something I ought to have seen to before. But now it's all right and we'll be moving in a week and you'll be settling down in Weston-super-Mare and I shall be under Uncle Robert's benevolent wing. Darling, it's so nice to have things settled. It's so good to know exactly where we are."

She put her arm round her mother's shoulders, squeezed her and kissed her anxious forehead with an unusual warmth of affection. "And you waited for cocktails until I came back!" she said. "I feel I could mix you a cocktail today like no cocktail that ever was."

Lucy's suspicious deepened. "Was it so *very* technical?" she asked.

"Like *that*," said Stella, her hand describing an upward spiral in the air as she danced out of the room to get the cocktail outfit. Lucy shook her head and drunk her specially good cocktail, when it came, with an expression of infinite resignation. But she asked no more questions.

2

Stella Returns to a Focus of Human Wisdom

Stella sat in the train that was taking her to Cambridge, to stay with Uncle Robert until the term began. She had finished the packing at Barnes and got through the dispatch of her mother to Weston-super-Mare with as few scenes of abortive tenderness as possible. She packed the cocktail shaker very carefully. "Anyhow I taught her to drink," she said. "I suppose she'll try to make them now for herself. In her room, in secret. She'll give up the ice, I expect, and settle down to straight Martini and gin."

In the train she had forgotten her mother. She was thinking of the resumption of her graduation work and Uncle Robert and Gemini and the Revolution. She was not so much thinking as musing, strolling though a ramifying jungle garden of more or less correlated systems of mental activity. They took her hither and thither, so that she could not determine whether the garden had even had a plan in the past or whether she would presently discover it was growing into a plan. So far as she had a guiding idea it was the problem of just exactly what completing her education meant and what Cambridge had still to do to her and for her. Was it really doing something, or was it pretending to do something, or was it just forgetting her and her needs and dreaming of itself as something pleasantly important until catastrophe happened to awaken or kill it?

She wanted "activating". She had recently acquired that word. She did not, she realised, go on reading or thinking as Gemini did. She had none of this peculiar facility for finding the books he needed to carry him on, much less his odd trick of going on and on with a line of thought, oblivious to things about him. She wanted somebody... What exactly did she want?

"I wish I had someone to talk to about these things – who wasn't so mixed up with passion and feeling as Gemini is. Somebody who would talk things out with me impersonally..."

Love, she thought, separates people's minds. They care too much then for the effect they are producing to talk freely. But if thought matters as it seems to matter, one ought to be able to go on hammering out ideas with people you don't care a rap for, if they are intelligent and interested in the same questions. I at any rate can't do that. But Gemini does. He can guy the domestic life of Cottenham C Bower and yet respect him as a master...

"Strange, I'm going back to the very centre of the intellectual life of this most civilised country, I'm told it is, in the world. In some ways perhaps it is. I've been here two years and there is not a soul I can talk to about fundamental things, not a soul."

She had tried already to get to grips with one or two of the other girls and a don or so. They all seemed to slip away from her approaches. There was the question of God. Some of them had no word or phrase about the framework of life. They "believed" breathlessly and silently. At the core of their worlds, it would seem, was the unspeakable, a large nothing which had once been a person, surrounded by a defensive halo. Ssh! They thought themselves deeply religious, but indeed they were the completest atheists, living and thinking their entire lives outside that central Holy of Holies, going near to it only on tiptoe, reverentially, in manifest dread lest He should pop out upon them. He never did. This God of theirs couldn't say Bo! to a goose. Others seemed still stranger to her; they were consciously pious, they not only prayed but proselytised – until she asked questions. These others would come after her, sit in her study for a time exhorting her to believe.

"*What?*" said Stella. "What exactly?"

She must pray to believe, she must ask for guidance.

"But if I do not believe whatever it is how can I pray?"

"But try it. You don't understand the happiness."

"Honestly, Susan, I don't believe in that happiness of yours. I've watched you. I don't see any difference between you – and the unsaved."

"You don't know."

"I *don't* know. I'm not in any particular need of happiness, but I want to get things clear."

"If only you'd *pray*."

Usually if Stella pressed her sceptical questioning there was a headlong retreat; pursuit gave place to avoidance. What was this Triune God of theirs? Why had he such an inordinate appetite for fulsome praise? He might make Susan happy in some sort of mystical love affair, but why didn't he drop that sort of flirtation, and up and make his whole world happy? She gave a crude imitation of Uncle Robert in these blasphemies. She was given to understand she was just too *awful*.

And all these young women, by nature and necessity, were thinking about sex. But what did they think? And what did the wisdom of all the world focussed here in Cambridge, indicate about these matters? Last year as her love affair with Gemini had developed, she had watched her fellow students and the younger dons with a keener eye. They were all alive, all feeling things, probably up to all sorts of things and they were all, all of them, masking this inner turmoil and getting hardly any help from the experience round them. It was plain to her that in many practical realities they were more ignorant than slum girls. Yet she felt she could see a little into them through such chinks as for example the poetry they read – which was not always the poetry they talked about – as the self-betrayal of their make-ups and their evening costumes, as their attitude to pictures, their behaviour in the presence or absence of men, the expression of their unguarded faces when they listened to music or sat lost in reverie. They had, she perceived, their drives, their urgencies and their retreats. But a veil of fear and self-protection was wrapped about everything they said and did. They would not talk plainly and simply. They did not think plainly. They were embarrassed even by their private thoughts. They resorted to circumlocutions at the very approach of truth, they blushed and flushed and recoiled.

There was indeed a bawdy set of girls, who professed a tremendous knowingness, were proud to get drunk, pretended to viciousness, told broad stories and swapped dirty witticisms. She played up a little to these broad-minded ones; she could jest with

BABES IN THE DARKLING WOOD

the best of them, and whenever she did so she was reminded of a wonderfully intimate, flushed and red-eared talk she had had with another little girls at the age of eight. "Let's tell each other," the other little girl had said, "the very *rudest* word we know. The very *orflest.*"

Some of these girls boasted by implication of lovers, always very vaguely. Stella was inclined to think to think that the doers were not among the talkers, and that upon a hundred aspects of this problem at the warm heart of life, they were even more perplexed and rudderless than herself. What was holding them back from clear ideas? Were they all going to fall into sexual situations and then rationalise them afterwards? As she was doing.

It was the same with politics and social conduct. They were separated by great gaps of imperfect realisation from the textbooks they had to read. On these matters they talked very freely and quite uncritically and irresponsibly. A lot of them professed an ignorant and implacable communism. Even when they were not actually active communists they were agreed that Karl Marx was a tremendous authority upon political and social science. *Why*, they did not know. They thought strikes and hunger marches the quintessence of politics and Soviet Russia heaven on earth. Others were obviously impressed by the virile personal charm of Sir Oswald Mosley. Another group read the poems and prose pieces of Mr T S Eliot with an almost mystical edification, and others again seemed to derive a secret and altogether incommunicable satisfaction from the teaching of Gerald Heard, Aldous Huxley, J B Priestley in his profounder phrases, Yeats-Brown the Bengal Lancer, Gurus and the cult of Uspensky. They all betrayed a strong disposition to discipleship.

All of them shirked saying things for themselves; instead it was "I wish you would read" or "If only you would come and hear".

But what is the good of ideas you cannot state for yourself? That you haven't picked off the tree and made your own? How can you have them, if you cannot state them? Some of them had fixed on this or that writer or teacher; others had a Gemini in the background. "What does Cambridge think of this or that?" she would ask herself, and answer, "Just any old thing. It's a jumble sale."

So what on earth was Cambridge to Stella or Stella to Cambridge?

Newnham was congested now by a brawl of hefty young women who had been evacuated form Bedford College, London, during the air raid panic. They brought nothing specific with them in the way of ideas. They added nothing but numbers to the general effect of mental confusion. Stella found no intimates among them nor heard anything to show that London University was educating with any greater comprehensiveness than Cambridge. The London idea too was "just any old thing".

She fell back at last on Uncle Robert, the omniscient, the assured. It was only after term had begun that she did this, but what he said will best fit in here. "Uncle Robert," she said. "One doesn't get *down* to things here. I don't seem able to talk about realities with anyone. It is *my* fault? It slides away. Aren't they actually interested, or are they interested differently?"

Uncle Robert answered her questions on various occasions as this or that occurred to him. What he said at one time was supplemented or illuminated by later or by previous *obiter dicta*. But for the purposes of our story it is convenient to gather all he said and conveyed to her as if it were one sustained discourse, framed in the particular talk that centralised these things in her memory.

For fiction, like memory, if it is to be explicit, must practise the economics of selection and concentration.

3

Uncle Robert Tells the Real Truth about a University Education

Uncle Robert stood at his large window looking down on St John Street and King's Parade. He looked down that vista of college façades and gatehouses as a well-prepared speaker might look at his superfluous notes. He lifted his nose somewhat and directed his mind to the Real Truth of the Matter. He spoke in his usual self-satisfied, unhurrying, gentle voice.

"I quite understand the quality of our expectation, Stella, and the astonishment and dismay with which you realise how excessive that expectation was. I have been expecting you to come along. I admit I told your mother Cambridge was the best place for you. Relatively to your home and Barnes, it was...

"But now that all that is settled, we can look more deliberately into the real truth about these Universities. They make – they have always made – a profession – at any rate they have had a plausible air – of taking young people, out of schools where they have been prepared under university direction for the great experience of graduation, and of imparting some sort of ultimate wisdom and mental habits unknown to the commonalty, *initiating* them into a mastery of life...

"Initiation. That is what you thought they were going to do for you. That is what Hardy's *Jude the Obscure* imagined. That is what our poor befuddled humbugged lower classes believe goes on up here to this day. They really believe that people who have been up here are mentally better than people who haven't. You cannot believe what they imagine! Education – at a University! Excelsior and their is nothing higher. They look up to it with their mouths open. Crumbs fall to them. University Extension! Oh generous beautiful words! You, Stella, were to be one of those precious educated. The concentrated sort, not the extended sort. And now after two years you find you have got nothing whatever, nothing makes you different, or stronger or better. Eh?"

"That's what I'm telling you," said Stella.

Uncle Robert looked over his nose at her.

"It is what you have been *trying* to tell me," he corrected gently, and resumed his contemplation of Trinity. He had had his hands in his jacket pockets. He now stuck his thumbs into his waistcoat pockets and lifted his nose a little higher.

"No doubt," he said, "no doubt, all these queer processes round and about the earth which people call education, did begin as something of that sort. *Initiation*. Only you see they've forgotten about it. They've clean forgotten about initiating you, Stella. The medicine man took off the youth and put him in a hut and starved him and did things to purify and clean up his mind. Have they ever done anything to purify and clean up the mess in your mind, here or at school?"

"I – ," began Stella.

He held out a restraining hand.

"I don't want you to answer, my dear Stella. I don't want unnecessary answers. I ask these questions for rhetorical effect. Obviously. I am perfectly well able to answer them myself. In fact I insist upon answering them myself. And as I was saying – or going to say when you interrupted me – a century ago, a trifle over a century ago, in the eighteenth century, this University *was* initiating men into a world, *was* telling them the how and what and why of things in general with a certain effect of assurance and authority. It was, perhaps, not a real world, it was the highly artificial world of the Hanoverian Settlement. But anyhow it was a world. Nothing threatened it fundamentally. Everyone believed or pretended to believe so completely that for most of them at last it became a genuine belief, in the Thirty-Nine Articles, the Three Creeds, the verbal inspiration of the Bible, the Chronology of Bishop Usher, in their own knowledge of Greek, and indeed in the whole Anglican bag of tricks – you have been to Church, Stella? You know about it?"

"Naturally, at school and at home. Oh, hundreds of times. I've even attended a Confirmation Class. I wasn't confirmed, but the Head thought it might do me good to attend."

"Did it?"

"Not a bit. But I learnt to imitate the Reverend Mr Blarningham's cough better than anyone. I would make all the girls scuttle back to their places. I used to go into that corridor..."

"I suppose," resumed Uncle Robert, in that sweet detached voice of his, "all the dons of the days of the Protestant ascendency really believed in their stuff. Actually believed. Yes. I think we have to assume that. It was their philosophy, their wisdom. This, they said, is Truth. This is the beginning and the end. They were not what one could call liars. Everything had steered them to conformity. They had bouts of doubt perhaps, rather like measles – which leave you immune for ever. They helped one another through those. They read their Greek philosophers, but they must have read them very badly, and under direction; very few of them really mastered Greek and even their Latin was rotten; and besides that, Aristotle and Plato had been broken in, so to speak, to the Anglican system, by means of notes and glosses. They read *bits* of them, you know, just bits. Mostly from cribs. They didn't read them as *whole* authors. And how can you understand a man unless you have ransacked him and know him up and down and inside out? And they read a sort of classical history, all togas and dignity, and as little as possible about the filth peltings and the free fights and murders of the Capitol, they learnt nothing about the brutal realities of the Roman Empire, they just learnt the golden legend of the Empire, that glorious mirage of the past and they had also their history of England from 1066, which told them exactly how to set about politics. And that was really all they knew. All.

"Greek! That was the crown of their imposture. Few of them learnt it better than a failed BA. Babu learns English. A few industrious ones acquired that minute knowledge of its stereotyped phrases and idioms which is scholarship. To use a stereotyped phrase was 'Good Greek'; to make a new one was a sin against all the canons of scholarship. Their Greek was as dead and finished a language as that. A pompous, useless supererogation."

[And then it was, or on some other parallel occasion, that Uncle Robert disposed of what he called the great classical imposture. Greek and Classical Latin, he said, excitedly read and hideously mispronounced, had captured the Universities in the great boom of the Renascence. At that tremendous onset Clerical dog-Latin retreated with its tail between its legs, There had been a great and releasing clash of ideas for a generation or so, when eager men read the newly disinterred Greek literature for its contents, for the stimulus of its unfamiliar ideas, and then the scholars, grammarians and examiners seized control of the new media. For a brief period it seemed that Latin and Greek might live again as the double-barrelled *lingua franca* of the escaping spirit of enquiry, might intermingle and coalesce and absorb new elements, as every living language is bound to do. The new natural philosophers were quit ready for that, they used Latin for a couple of centuries, and made a serviceable nomenclature, mainly out of Greek roots. But the pedants would have none of that. They were horrified to hear Greek words that would have puzzled Plato and half-breed phrases that outraged all grammatical decorum. They had the new learning, but they still had monkish minds and monkish ways of teaching. They flogged the life out of that possible European language.

Meanwhile the European vernaculars, with no exclusive prejudices, were picking up anything that seemed useful from any speech in the world and growing continually in flexibility and power. Impatient minds were refusing to pass through the narrow disciplines of the unamalgamated, inadaptable classical tongues before they launched themselves upon natural philosophy, when they had a living language of their own now, as good or better. English in particular, though it never learnt to spell, became the most assimilatory, various and expressive language in the world. German, Russian, asserted their possibilities. French checked the natural abundance of its growth by the Dictionary of the Academy, yet still it served better than its parental Latin. So Greek and Latin died a second time, and the Universities, which had invested their little alls, so to speak, in the classical tradition, had to fight against the spreading realisation of their death. Some day, some intelligent student, probably an American, blending psychology and intellectual history, will write of the desperate fight of Scholarship to retain its ascendency over a world that had no use for it. He will trace how the papers in Classics were given disproportionate marks, how in every school the brighter boys were stolen by the classical side; how for a century and more the European intelligence struggled like Gulliver against the bonds of a perverted and dwarfed education.]

"Think of it!" said Uncle Robert, "a language reduced to quotation! Even the best scholars did no more than quote. It was the fashion in Parliament to produce long spouting bits of those awful booing and baaing sounds in which Greek abounds, and the greatest triumph possible was to cap the quotation. Those who did not understand assumed an expression of intelligent appreciation. That went on until less than a hundred years ago. But never is it recorded that anyone during that age of triumphant Greek broke into free Greek speech; never. Never a lapse into discussion. Never even a contradiction or a new witticism, fired across the floor of the House. They never forgot themselves in Greek to that extent, because they were never at home in it. Could there be more convincing evidence of the utter imposture of that scholarship of theirs? They had never taken in and digested Greek; they just regurgitated it. Quotation," said Uncle Robert, "is the triumph of memory over thought. A scholar is a man who wears second-hand clothes and lives in a junk shop. Yes, But these anglicised Grecians, these scholar-gangsters, cornered education in the English-speaking world, obstructed its modernisation, crippled the minds of the cleverer boys, distorted and enfeebled the understanding of the entire community. And here we are!"

[Stella remembered how one day her uncle had seized upon a little pamphlet that had come to him from India. "Perfect," he had said, "perfect", and for a time would not hand it over to her. "This you see is what happens when a highly intelligent man tries to master a language which is not his natural idiom of thought. Just as this sounds to you, so would the good Greek of a modern classical don have sounded in the Academy. Only his mispronunciation would probably have been hideous, and this gentleman would have been only a little chi-chi. Don't make any mistake about the matter; this man is a good clear thinker. But read his scholarly English!"

It was entitled *Beef*, and it started off bravely:

"Guess assertions from lapsing intellectuals, the spirit of deliberate maligning, the fossilised mind that will neither learn nor unlearn things, the bankrupt structure that feeds on the reminiscence of dreamy past, never trying to live up to facts or admit facts, rather suppressing facts, to keep up superciliary snobbishness, these are the factors that breed and keep up canards in every field that do not die out easily though disproved. Then there is the wishful thinking that can only spot others and not oneself.

"To turn to the precise subject being dealt here in, let us tackle the popular conceptions, rather misconceptions – one by one.

"There is the talk about beef causing leprosy current even with the intelligentsia of the country at least in Bengal which the beefeaters stand almost apologetically and the non-beefeaters assert aggressively. In the interest of truth and the better understanding of ideological groupings, the myth has got to be liquidated once for all. The findings of scientific facts and data and social study with a pair of balance, a pot of fire and a bottle of acid warrant it..."

Uncle Robert stood over Stella as she read. "And so it goes on." He said. "I do not believe there is a classical don in existence whose Greek is better than the English of that. I doubt if there's a score who would even attempt as much. And yet in the interest of this imposture, English education has been bedevilled for two hundred years.]

"No doubt in those grammarian ridden days the University *did* in a sense initiate. It gave the young Anglican gentleman all the advantages he needed over the illiterate, a sense of superiority, a class freemasonry, a code of behaviour and an acceptable way of taking the problems of life as they came to him. It trained him to the importance of scholarship. He realised the practical superiority of conformity to lucidity. He belonged to an élite, he felt; he was a Monarchist, a sound Churchman, a Patriot. He put over a bluff of learning and refinement. It produced such men, little T S Eliots by the hundred, as a rotten carcase produces blowflies. Without an effort. Mental blowflies. T S Eliot is a rare and precious thing today, he blows importantly, outstandingly, but in those days T S Eliots were ten a penny, unpoetical, unaffected T S Eliots. They buzzed about this place and they rose in fresh annual swarms to spread themselves and their maggots over England. They saw to it that our Blakes and Shelleys, our Gibbons and Godwins and Wilkeses, our Benjamin Franklins and our Tom Paynes – for those early Americans were *our* men, Stella – led properly fly-blown lives. Nice people were trained to make grimaces of genteel distaste at their names. These flies spotted on all that might have saved the English. They crawled over art and criticism... They buzzed America away from us...

"And then even that initiation began to deteriorate. But not enough and not fast enough to be cleared away. Nothing arose to replace it. It is an obscure and complex history, Stella, and no one with the necessary patience and humour has written it. Bit by bit that Church of England initiation ceased to be the one and only way to an educated life in England. An increasing number of dons became dimly but sufficiently aware of the benefits of knowing Rothschilds and cultivating Manchester and the Midlands. They dropped their cultural exclusiveness; they called it 'abolishing tests'. Jews began to come here, Dissenters of all sorts, and at last the younger and lustier dons threw their celibacy over the windmills and there was an outbreak of wives, often quite uneducated wives, a reinforcement of ignorance.

"And Newnham and all that, of course.

"That's roughly how it went. But they didn't, you see, try to adapt their initiation process to the new realisations that came flooding into the place, with these relaxations. They were too busy with other things. It was the business of nobody in particular to adjust that initiation course. And nobody did. It remained the main course. Bits of it that were compulsory were made optional to avoid offending the newcomers. Paley's *Evidences* used to be in it as an essential, a smattering of Greek, something called 'Scripture'. They're no longer considered indispensable for enlightenment, but they still hang about. Disconnected alternative subjects have been stuck in. My poor

Stella, you're not the only person to come up here and feel baffled. What is it all about? What can it all be about? I quite understand – quite. All the intelligent ones feel baffled at the menu of these degree courses. All of them.

"The old Anglican initiation hung on here, scotched but not killed, during the whole period of English liberalism, and it wriggled back to political power in this last monarchist and clerical counter-revolution of the Frightened Thirties, which has recaptured our poor fly-blown Empire, to steer it now rapidly, so rapidly now it terrifies one, towards military and economic disaster. Think of Lord Halifax with Lord Lloyd behind him in the Foreign Office, think of our triumphant Archbishops and our stupid broadcasts, read *The Times*, watch the confident smiling and bowing and posturing of the Court, listen to the wartime buzz of the pulpits, the press, the streets. One might think all of our once great and mighty England dead and decayed beneath these crawling swarming Anglicans. Where is God's Englishman now? Where is the England of Milton and Newton, Gilbert and Bacon, Darwin and Huxley, Cromwell, Nelson, Blake? It is not only you youngsters who are baffled. The whole country is baffled to hear the voices that claim to speak for it now. The world is baffled by the awful legacy of those teachers who would not learn.

"Sometimes I think I might write a history of it all. But again I might not. History rushes on. Much of it may never be written now – with understanding. I am a man, Stella, as you know, of immense and terrible perspicacity, but let me admit to you that I am an impatient, unscholarly man. It would require a stupendous effort to put one's mind in the place of the average don of a hundred years ago and then trace all that has happened since in the average donnish mind. I should have to read books, not as I do read books, like a cock scratching for worms, but patiently, sympathetically, frowstily. I should certainly have fits of rage with the stuff. There would have to be a boy down below with a basket, ready to catch the books I shied out of this window and bring them upstairs again.

"No. Not in my line. But viewing it generally – . Tick if off, phase by phase, the phases in – what shall I call it? – the senile decay of our University education. First of all there was the realisation of evolution and geological time – the Huxley-Darwin challenge. Obviously and complete and through readjustment of the general initiation was called for. Obviously. These dons, not only as educated men but as educators, were *challenged*, to occupy themselves urgently and fully with this – this stupendous modification of the time-scale, and with the plain need to replace the orthodox Creation Story by a new conception of life, a conception of life as something unfolding, creatively indeed, but without any special acts. Manifestly the realisation of evolution pushed the old story of the Fall of Man into mere mythology. It had to be reconceived or abandoned. An entirely new interpretation of sin and salvation became necessary. If the world were still to brood on sin and salvation. What did Sin mean in the new light, and what were we being saved from now?

"Curious chapter that was in the history of human thought! And of the honour of the human mind – if we can talk of such a thing.

"Did they stand up to that challenge? Not a bit of it! Were they going to have their dear old assumptions turned down, merely because they had become absurd? Not they. They lied – they lied to themselves, because *au fond*, when put to the test, they were uneducated, lazy-minded conservative men, men who *could* find refuge in an internal lie. They wouldn't learn. So they went on here for decades pretending that old exploded initiation of theirs was still the Truth, the whole Truth and nothing but the Truth. The young came up to them, agog to know whether something important had happened to the world of thought. They held out stoutly – they hold out to this day – that it really didn't matter in the least. To this day you can go right through. To a BA degree here in the blackest, most self-satisfied ignorance of the modern vision of the process of life in time. In that matter alone this venerable man-making organisation is, as a man-making organisation, a hundred years out of date.

"But that, you know, Stella, was only the opening failure on the part of University education to keep up. Quite a lot of people, some of them embedded in various colleges and cells here, although they didn't care a rap for the unfortunate undergraduates, were indulging the most fascinating curiosities, were going on with biological research in various forms. Embryologists like Francis Balfour for example, Among other things that interested them greatly were the questions: 'What is a species?' 'What is an individual?' 'Are there individualities of different orders?' 'Unicellular, multi-cellular, metameric?' 'How is a colonial organism related to a shoal or a herd?' And so on. More particularly: 'Do individuality and species really extend to the inanimate world?'

"Has anyone here ever put that particular question to you? Yet it lies at the very root of philosophy, These biologists found the age-long riddle of the One and the Many changing its character under their eyes. It was all so obvious, that already, fifty years ago, excited students were running out of biological laboratories saying: 'But then Beings are unique! Atoms are unique! Plainly. So physical science is making false assumptions. You daren't go a yard with this box of bricks logic of yours unless you check up by experimental verification'. Biological science knocked the bottom out of physical science (which is something fundamentally different from biological science) seventy years ago. Physics has been floundering and mathematicians have been trying to straighten out their bent philosophy ever since. Pragmatism broke loose asking of every pompous theory: 'Does it work? Try it first!' This ruthless logic your dons here used to talk about is really – how can one put it? – an over-confident unconscious deviation. Like the strutting forward march of a man with one leg slightly shorter than the other.

"That was evident, but did they call attention to it? Logic is as true as the flat earth theory. It keeps on getting more and more out of the straight with every step. Obviously everybody up here ought to know that. From the beginning. But do they know it? And have they ever hinted that this language stuff they expect you to do your thinking with, is a muddle of terms so worn and misused as to be almost completely defaced, phrases out of obsolete metaphysics, rash assumptions from the childhood of science? No, and no one has ever warned you that such an opposition as that of substance and essence, or of matter and spirit, on which they build so much, is the left-over rubbish of barbaric natural philosophers centuries and centuries dead? Yet all these criticisms concern the very groundwork of thinking! They cleanse and clear your mind. How can you be a modern rational being if you do not know about them?

"These long wrangles between the Realists and the Nominalists and the Neo-Nominalists again which these orthodox dons still minimise, were a tremendous struggle of the human mind to escape first from dogmatic theology and then from the sterility of the classical tradition with which theology presently allied itself. Nominalism was stifled and maligned, but it was a rebellion of clear-headedness. It was a struggle that needs plain telling now, because we are still under the shadow of the classical imposture. What do you know, Stella, of Occam or Roger Bacon, of Copernicus and Galileo and William Gilbert? You've heard their names as starry names. But disconnected names. But do you know anything of the slow, persistent, intellectual revolt in which these men played their parts? Ultimately observation was liberated. Ultimately. At long last. Escaped rather than was liberated. And those names were outstanding in that desultory war of liberation. Observation got out of prison. The human mind in a state of apologetic humility went back at last to observed and verifiable fact, and these natural philosophies that people call the natural sciences were released. Outside the schools and the Universities. There the classical-clerical held on, the monkish bawling and shouting and beating.

"European education has been a conservative and reactionary process – always. Has anyone ever attempted to put the points at issue between Realists, Nominalists and Neo-Nominalists before you? On the contrary. The classical scholars came as a reinforcement to clerical orthodoxy and fought Neo-Nominalists tooth and nail. Tooth and nail? Yes, and then, being elephantine rather than toothed and clawed, and finding they were getting the worst of it in spite of every advantage they held, they sat down upon it and pretended it wasn't, and never had been, there...

"Then take this movement to clear up the meaning of words and rescue all you young people from stereotyped phrases and thinking with bogus terms. There's Ogden, Richards and that lot. I've given Stuart Chase to you and his *Tyranny of Words*. Maybe he's not the wisest and most original of those who have worked in this matter, but his book is clear cleansing undergraduate stuff. I've made *you* read that, Stella, but how many of these young victims below will encounter it? See that your words *mean*. Half the time they don't mean. Or they mean too much, any old thing you like. Do these dons who are supposed to initiate you, care? Not a bit of it, they just go on teaching you young people to parrot. Parrots themselves. Semantics has been a challenge for twenty years. You would have thought it would have set a teaching University alight from end to end. You would have expected terrific and illuminating logomachies… Did a leaf stir?

"So it has gone on. The old initiation has rotted to pieces; and no other initiation has been developed to take its place. No vision of the history of life have they given you, no wisdom about the nature of things, no discriminatory use of language. What *have* they given you, Stella?

"They have taught you a little Latin, less Greek, some French, German and any Italian word that you might meet in a musical score. Have they ever pointed out to you that there is hardly a single word in English, hardly an idiom, that has a precise equivalent in any of these other languages? Languages correspond – yes; but roughly and loosely. Because all language is still loose and inaccurate. Not a hint did they give you of that. Not a nudge at question-begging phrases – "

"Question-begging?" flashed across Stella's mind. Where had she heard or read that quite lately?…

H G Wells

"And for that matter, philosophy – ! Have they let you know that apart from a lot of balderdash about *this* school of philosophy and *that* school of philosophy, there must be such a thing as philosophy itself? A common groundwork for modern thinking, a common basis for the uptake of life. One doesn't read Lucretius for chemistry nowadays or Pliny for natural history...

"You know better than that, Stella. You know that you began mentally as everyone begins, with what we call a common-sense view of life. You just saw what you called facts. They all seemed to belong together. Seeing was believing. And people told you facts. Hearing was believing. Then one day you had the shock of seeing one thing you saw plainly and believed in, plainly contradicting another. I remember the shock *I* had when I saw a penny under water within easy reach of my hand as I thought, and when I picked it up I found it wetted my sleeve. So it was I began upon that branch of natural philosophy called optics.

"You found too that things people told you in perfect good faith, evidently in good faith and not making them up for fun, didn't make perfect and complete sense with other facts. Uncertainty dawned upon you. You said *This is Queer*. You asked *Which is right?* What were these inconsistencies? That was the beginning of philosophy for *you*. You started trying to restore the consistency of your outlook on the world. That *is* philosophy. What else can it be? Obviously.

"Everyone has a philosophy, even if it is a mere tangle of unsuccessful attempts at reconciliation. Even if it is tacit and hardly knows of itself. As the contradictions and attempted reconciliations increase, the philosophy grows. All the so-called sciences are applications of philosophy to particular regions of factual difficulty. They ought still to be called natural philosophy.

BABES IN THE DARKLING WOOD

But some of these teachers of philosophy here will talk of 'scientists' – preposterous word! – and oppose them to 'philosophers' as though they were cats and dogs who are bound to fight when they meet. What they mean by a 'scientist' or 'science' *per se*, I cannot imagine. There aren't such things. They seem to think a 'scientist' is a man who goes about measuring and weighing things and being stupid about the results. Biologists and physicists are all the same to them...

"Everyone is some sort of a philosopher. Obviously. There must be riddles in the life of a ploughboy. 'It don't stand to reason,' says he, and worries. The one and only difference that *can* exist between a relatively educated and a relatively uneducated man, is just how far he has a living philosophical process going on in his mind and keeping his mind together in some sort of order, or not. Our world is full now of the most urgent contradictions, and obviously philosophy must be getting more and more down to things and into things. More and more. It is – for a few perspicacious people. Modern philosophy grows daily; far clearer than the ancient stuff and with a vastly bigger grip. It keeps pace with the march of knowledge, as knowledge gets out of mists of the past and looks about. It is eternally contemporary. The philosophy of my lectures and practice is an absolute repudiation and reversal of the standard philosophy and phraseology they cling to here – an absolute and complete reversal. I build on Pavlov and Watson and the Behaviourists, of whom they still pretend never to have heard. What they teach is no more than a bit of mental history on its way to the discard. That is all the philosophy you will get here – unless you *specialise*, as they say. *How* one can specialise in the science of sciences, is beyond saying! For all general teaching purposes, philosophy has gone out of the University and left no message when she is coming back. That's why they haven't even *begun* putting your mind in order. After two years of it! Have they begun to put any minds in order up here? Ask your fellow undergraduates... Need I go on? Have I answered your reasonable and intelligent question, Stella?" He moved his head sideways for a moment, almost interrogatively.

Stella knew better than to answer.

"And instead of warning you about these things, consider what they put you through for graduation. So earnestly, so solemnly they do it. They put you through it without the faintest notion of why and wherefore. It's *done*. So they do it. Ask them why and they produce a sort of parrot answer. The stuff 'trains the mind'. It does, in bad habits. It 'strengthens the intelligence. It enlarges you.' Like a bladder. My God! Hear them discuss anything real! Like balloons at a gala dinner, waving about when a draught blows in. Some of them popping in the flaring gas-jets.

"They've forgotten long since, how it all came about, generations ago here they forgot. Most of these teachers here have never been out of the scholastic world since they were prize-boys from a preparatory school. Climbing the scholarship ladder, hand over fist, up and out of any reality. The less they thought and questioned the faster they learnt – and here they are! Outstripping all the minds that said 'Yes – but'. How can these dons know anything about life? I ask you. The stuff's pumped into them and they transmit it, a little flatter, a little less real with every transfusion. If you are going to call two-thirds of these dons educated men, then trained dogs are educated men, and taxi-drivers and postal sorters, who know which street joins on to which all over London, are the most highly educated men in the country."

At this point a note of compunction became evident in Uncle Robert's voice. He was obviously trying his utmost to be just. His voice sank so that he was almost confidential. "There's a certain amount of scientific research done here, I admit, but that's a side-show. It has to be sterilised for examination purposes before it reaches your lot. There's mental activity here no doubt – in the recesses of the place. But it's secret. They don't talk about it. There's even, I observe, a certain scared, apprehensive modernity in some of the syllabuses. But they never join up the new stuff to anything else. And as for imparting it to the eager young! They don't know how. They don't care. I'm talking of that, mind you, of the education of the young for life. I'm talking of the generation that has to make over the world. I'm not talking about research. We've been adding faculty to faculty to faculty here, since 1918. Very, very considerable amounts of good detailed work there may be. Not the slightest question. No doubt of it...

"That has nothing to do with initiation, the educational function. Nothing whatever. I am talking of this place as an educational place, of what you are getting from it now. I am talking of the dons as teachers.

"These teaching dons, I say, have burked revolutionary thoughts for a hundred years – as teachers. They sit now in their little Gothic rooms while the drowning minds of the undergraduates who came to be educated and initiated, swirl in the planless sluices of the curriculum and wash out again as ignorant and unformed as when they washed in. Look at them down there, those three poor credulous boys coming out of

Trinity now, with their mortar-boards and their bits of gowns, clutching those books that nowadays take them nowhere... What can those men be? A year ago there would have been dozens of them. They would have *inhabited* the place... Probably tripos men finishing up, or medicals. But has anyone come up this term? I don't know. A few boys of eighteen may come up for a year and a bit before the army gets them. Next year, will there be a mortar-board left in Cambridge? I never thought of that before, Stella, but will there be? Look at these youngsters in the street; in all sorts of uniforms! Imagine it! Cambridge with the last rag of a gown and the ultimate disaster of a cap, *gone!* Ah! Dr Furbelow. Look, Stella, at that old humbug on a bicycle. He will be here to the last."

Stella had come to the window and stood beside her uncle.

"Ripening for a legendary University character, pedalling with an almost mystical precision. Fearfully aware of himself. Fearfully unaware of our immense world.

"I doubt if he has noticed for a moment what is happening to Cambridge. What *is* happening here? That never struck *me* so much as it strikes me now as I talk to you. Yes, Stella. The signs are out here now that the last pretences of initiation are packing up – to go to London or Wales or the trenches or hell. Leaving Cambridge to the owl and the bittern and Dr Furbelow on his bicycle, still quite unaware. He will bicycle across the empty weedy courts and through the vacant cloisters. He will go faster and faster because there will be fewer and fewer people to impede him. Three-quarters of these young men are called up already. Mostly they seem to be Air Force youngsters. Some in khaki... I've no idea what those are... Just doing mathematical and technical training for the war, I suppose; the very last pretence of initiation abandoned. Off *they* will go presently... Will anyone come up next year? A few women perhaps. A handful of boys in a hurry..."

Uncle Robert started blankly at his own idea. "Are we in the twilight of graduation already? Are we looking now at the last of the undergraduates? Will they come back as they did in 1919? Is it going to be that, twice over? Not if my reading of the war is correct. No. So far as education a people is concerned, this place is a failure now – a dying failure.

"That would not be so bad, if there was anything better to succeed it... But what will succeed it? A world where one never graduates. Where one goes on and learns and learns to the end. And how? World University? With every man and woman alive, a learner?...

"Can that be anything more than a dream?

"To me it seems cold common sense. Common sense – in a half-witted world."

He was silent for a moment. Then he resumed his upward tilt. He looked over the Cambridge skyline into the eternal and incessant sky.

"One thing at a time," he said. "I was talking about the way in which life and faith seeped out of the initiation here. And still it falls below and falls behind. They are shirking a new challenge now. The world of mind is turning round under them and they still hold on to the idea that it is fixed. There is something more now for them to keep back from you, the enormous revolution in our ideas about the human mind that has been in progress since we began to understand what was meant by conditioned reflexes. As I turn my mind to your problem, I am astonished to think how completely my ideas and practice contradict the ideas still current in these schools, how clouds and myths have dissolved out of my mind. I must give you a book I came across the other day – it's a little stiff to read at first but it is worth the trouble – Cottenham C Bower's *Expansion of Sex*. He's an American and rather pompous, but his matter and method are illuminating, if only because they show how far we have travelled in the last few years. Contrast him with MacDougall for example, whom probably you *have* read. I think I must set you that for an essay. MacDougall clings to the old conception of a soul, a psyche, an undivided *self*, as a starting-point, and deals with all the problems of psychotherapy as the breaking up of that original unity. Cottenham C Bower starts off in absolute contradiction. He assumes without discussion that so far from the mind being broken up, it has never yet been got together. How's that for immortality, spirituality and all the rest of it? We are only just beginning to get it together now. Psychology, you see, has ceased to be an analytical process and becomes a synthesis. You know this man doesn't even argue about it. He ignores the other way round as though there was no need for an argument."

"Cottenham C," said Stella, cutting in. "Cottenham C Bower. Of course I know about him. Gemini has written me sheets about it."

"Your young man seems intelligent and up to date," said Uncle Robert. "But the University? Has *that* said anything?"

"Nothing in the syllabus."

"There are people, I know, who will tell you that this sort of thing is still too novel and abstruse for young minds. They will say you must first give them the old stuff out of which the new arose. Assuming it was simpler, which it never was. That is just making up father's old pants for Tommy. Won't do, Stella. It is the right of the young to assist at the development of new interpretations. The only way of beginning any subject for them is to tell them as plainly as possible what we know and think today. On the very day of the teaching. Then bring in the old stuff so far as it explains and leave it out when it doesn't. But what they give you here now for this silly graduation of theirs is just a meal of canned food, stale and decaying canned food. Is it any wonder that you find the bright youngsters turning from that to eat cheap, fly-blown stuff from the barrow at the corner, which at any rate has hormones... You see, the real truth about these universities nowadays is that nobody really wants to initiate you and nobody wants you initiated. You are trying to see the world. When you ask them to help you to see, you offered nothing but the blackened spectacles of outworn ideas. There are books here, Stella, and myself. Apart from that there is no light for you here. And if there is light anywhere, I agree with you, this is where light should be."

4

Tilbury

Late in August Gemini had started for what even in those last days was still the ambiguous wonderland of Soviet Russia, the land of a vague millennium obscured by enigmatic shadows. He would not let the darkening Polish situation deter him; the gathering threat of war; rather it quickened his eagerness to go before disaster prevented him. He sailed by the Swedish liner to Gothenburg on a Monday, and Stella, with the tacit acquiescence of Uncle Robert, spent a Sunday and two nights with him in a little hotel in Chelmsford before his departure.

The things they did have been done a billion times, but such is the magic of sex that it seemed to them that nothing so full of pride and loveliness, so brave and exquisite, had ever happened upon earth before. Once Stella wept with tenderness at the thought of their parting, and Gemini embraced and kissed her through her salt tears...

They made the cross-country journey to the Swedish Lloyd liner and found themselves upon the pier at Tilbury mingling with the crowd from the London train. It was a mixed swarm, many Swedish people, schoolgirls and the like, recalled from holidays or schools in England by the threat of war; all sorts of rather inexplicable people, Germans, Poles, American journalists and so forth getting out of the country in time. And there were as many more people to see them off, with an unusually acute sense of parting in the sunny air.

A few English businessmen were there, one very concerned about a vast consignment of grape fruit, endless cases spinning down from the crane into the hold, which might be the last grape fruit in Sweden for a long time. Stella and Gemini had said all the things they had to say several times over; she wanted to weep because Gemini was going so far away from her and she wanted to laugh because he was glad to be leaving all the she-bears and cocktails of London behind; and they stared about them at the bustle of the embarkation, saying very little.

"And so this is Stella Kentlake," said a cool bright voice. "I *knew* somehow you'd be here."

And Gemini said, "It's *you*, Dione! M'am!"

She was a very neat, pretty, slender, tall lady who might have been about thirty-five and was indeed forty-four. She was not a bit like Gemini, except for something about the eyes; she was very fine-featured, clear-complexioned and dark-haired. Her neatly closed lips, the frame of her face, the fine eyebrows and a faint remoteness and unreality, sent Stella's thoughts flying away from England, seeking eastward until they pounced on ancient Egypt. That was it! The genetic Fates, the dance of the genes, had reconstructed a dynastic Egyptian lady to be wife of the Cadi of Clarges Street and Gemini's mother.

She smiled at Stella primly. It was a smile without effusion or any emotional quality. "I don't want to invade your parting," she said, "but I have got something here for Jimmy – "

"But of course I want you to know her, Dione dear, Dione M'am. I know you will like each other," said Gemini. "It was lovely of you to come."

"I slipped away," said Mrs Twain. "They told me at the bank that the Swedish exchange was likely to begin jumping. So I've got you fifty pounds of kronor in this envelope, against anything that may happen. It may be all nonsense, but it may save you trouble." She produced an envelope from an unobtrusive little bag she was carrying. "Put it in your *inside* pocket, Jimmy. And button your pocket. And your coat. And is your passport in order? I haven't told the Cadi you are going yet. I don't see why I should. But I suppose he will see the stamps on your letters."

"You are a darling, Mother," said Gemini. "Fancy your thinking of that!"

She looked at Stella. "One thinks of a lot of things when one's only son goes off to see the world – suddenly. At first I thought something must have happened to this – this love affair of yours, some lover's quarrel, and then I realised. I realised the sanity of it. Before this, I was a little afraid of meeting you, my dear." She added "my dear" as though she pinned it on to sentences. "Then

I told myself I must get over that. When I found, Jimmy, you were not on the train at Liverpool Street I knew at once I should find you both here."

"You're glad you came down, Dione M'am?"

"If it doesn't vex you. If I don't seem to come between you."

"It's the loveliest thing that could have happened," said Stella, and met a glance of detached friendliness. It was free of any quality of real liking or dislike. There was approval and acceptance.

"James, you ought to be going up that gangway. We'll come too and say good-bye to you up there. They'll tell us when it's time to come ashore and we shall be hustled off. That will make parting easier. Perhaps all partings ought to be hustled."

She seemed to reflect on that for a moment and then found Gemini was leading her by the arm and a satisfactorily self-possessed Stella was walking at her other side.

A number of small happenings engaged their minds until the hustling began. "Among these Swedes one doesn't feel tall," said Mrs Twain.

"But slender," said Stella.

"Slenderer than ever," said Mrs Twain with that faint smile of hers. "It's a wonderful world which gets itself all tied up in war because the Germans believe they look like Swedes – which you know they don't in the least. The only Nordic-looking real German I ever knew was a Pomeranian, and *his* head – it wasn't at all right shape. I used to look at it from behind. It was awful. It was just as though he had mumps at the base of his brain. And then it went up quite flat and tilted forward. One can imagine the most extraordinary things happening in a brain like that. And of course those Pomeranians and the Prussian blonds aren't German. They're Wends."

The hustling time came. Mrs Twain kissed her son on his cheeks and was kissed on the cheek and then turned away, turned away deliberately and looked at the river ahead, as Stella gave Gemini her last hug. "Darling," whispered Stella, "darling", through their kiss. "Come back to me. Write to me. Don't get lost anywhere. Don't go astray." Then louder to Mrs Twain averted back: "That's the second warning, Gemini."

Mrs Twain turned about again. She spoke to her son. "Good luck, my dear," she said. "Don't forget me if you are in any trouble."

"Am I likely to?" he asked.

"Dear boy," she said, and then to Stella: "I want you to come with me, in the train to London, if you will." And then directly to Gemini, after a moment of shy hesitation, "She's quite a dear, Jimmy." She was doing her utmost. She added as if by a sudden inspiration, "*I'll* look after her."

"Darling Dione," said Gemini.

They went down the gangway without a word and stood side by side looking up at Gemini, very far off already. "Jimmy has meant so much to me," said Mrs Twain, in a detached conversational voice as thought she was talking about scenery. "He has been my life almost, since I was nineteen. It doesn't seem to be real that he's going away, going so completely away... It isn't six weeks since he was living at home. Then one thing after another. This, this ship and all. And the war over there like darkness gathering. It can't possibly touch him... But it feels strange."

Stella said nothing and stared up at Gemini.

They were dropping the gangways and casting loose. A gap appeared between the landing-stage and the side of the ship and widened slowly. There was a throbbing of engines and a churning-up of the unclean Thames water. There was much waving between ship and shore, shout, last messages. There was a violent altercation about a forgotten packing-case. But Gemini stood motionless.

"If there is really a war," said Mrs Twain, "he will have to come back. Of course he will have to come back. He can't get into it over there. He may come back quite soon. I hope he will not be disappointed."

Gemini began to recede. "Mizpah", murmured Stella softly and lifted her hand. Gemini lifted his hand slowly.

He became smaller and smaller, a mere grey dab at last surmounted by a pink dot, and then just part of a vague dwindling crowd of people on the upper deck so that Stella could not distinguish him. Something aboard reflected the light of the setting sun and blazed quiveringly and blindingly, dimming everything around it.

"We may get a compartment to ourselves," said Mrs Twain, and turned about slowly. "There will not be nearly so many people to go back."

Stella wanted to take a ticket. "I'll pay for you on the train," said Mrs Twain. "They come along for tickets."

Half the compartments were empty.

In the carriage Stella began the conversation. "It is the loveliest evening," she said. "He should have a smooth crossing."

Mrs Twain, lost in her own thoughts, said nothing. She did not lean back in her seat, she sat up, as she was evidently accustomed to sit up, with her nicely gloved hands oh her lap, and looked in front of her as a neat-headed cat might look at a fire. Presently she said, as if she was talking to herself, "I was married before I was nineteen."

"Yes."

Mrs Twain reflected for a time and when she spoke again the things she spoke of had an unexpectedness that took Stella's breath away. She said things of incredible intimacy about herself, and she said them as though she talked of strange happenings in a distant planet. She spoke as though a small china image of herself had fallen into mud.

"I did not know what marriage was," she said. "I knew nothing. It was – a shock to me. Jimmy's father was impetuous – inconsiderate perhaps. I have read – have you ever read? – the books of Mrs Marie Stopes. She tells one all sorts of curious things. About men and sex. Anyhow it wasn't at all like that. I had two miscarriages. Such a mess, my dear!" ("Such a mess, my dear!" She said it in an even, detached voice – as though she was speaking of the misfortunes of same cat.) "Then Jimmy was born and after him I have had no more children. No. I learnt, well – things. I felt I was justified. I *was* justified…"

She looked out of the window and then turned to Stella. "But that, you see, is why Jimmy… Losing him is like an operation. One of those major operations when they take quite a lot of you away. I hope he will write soon. He has meant so much to me. He has been almost all my life, he and Women's Rights and Mrs Eddy… I don't know why I tell you these things. I suppose I feel you ought to know."

She turned to Stella and smiled her pale smile.

"Mrs Eddy?" asked Stella.

"Christian Science. I do not think I could have gone on living without it. You realise there is no such thing as bodily pain or physical evil. It is all imagination; it is within your control. And when disagreeable things have to be endured, you can realise they are not happening. You can treat them. You can fix your mind upon something else. It all passes off."

"But Gemini – ?" asked Stella.

"I could never persuade him. Nor his father. They have hard minds. His father hates doctors, but I think he hates Christian Science more. More even than he hates the Vote. James hates nothing, but he laughs at things. I wonder, will he always go on laughing? I wonder where he is now. I wonder if he is unpacking his things. I am afraid that at home I did rather spoil him. I always unpacked his things. It looks a beautiful evening. Sometimes it can be very rough on the North Sea."

"Have you ever been seasick?" asked Stella.

"Once," said Mrs Twain. "When my faith failed."

"And you never take any sort of medicine?"

"Never."

"But if you feel really ill?"

"I treat it. I get additional treatment if I feel I cannot manage it myself. There are Gurus in London – wonderful Gurus. They give you distant treatment. And then the illness goes. All evil is imaginary. There is nothing in the world between us and complete happiness but want of faith in Christ Scientist. Just hardness and want of faith. All this war talk, all this sickness of the world needs only proper treatment. Then there would be none of these dreadful preparations for killing, none at all. A little while ago people were saying 'No More War', and if they had kept on there would be no war. But, you see, they faltered."

She said it without sorrow or dismay. She remarked upon it as she might have remarked upon some picture on the screen. She was more and more like that remote Egyptian princess, restored to the world but still marvellously aloof from it, denying it was there.

"But don't you do a lot of work for the Rights of Women?" asked Stella, probing still for some core of reality.

"I go about and lecture," said Mrs Twain. She went about and lectured on equal standards for men and women, on the right of a wife to a living wage and of the mother to state endowment and so on. She had her arguments clear and neat. She went about the country and stayed away from home for days. "But does Mr Twain object to your going away?" There had been arguments in the past but he was very reasonable. "You see," said Mrs Twain, "I have my economic independence. There was some money in my family. Fortunately. We discussed it all years ago. All men want to dominate. I see that very plainly. He dominated at first absolutely. Until I got my own money he hardly let me have pocket money. He hates freedom – for anyone. Now it is different. I respect his rights. What can he do? Since Jimmy went away to school and college I have been able to do a lot for the Movement. I suppose now – "

She stared in front of her as though she looked at something she had not seen before: "I shall be able to do a lot more."

She sat still looking at that unexciting prospect. Presently she spoke again. "I want to see what I can of you, Stella. We might meet quite often. I suppose you will get the first news of him now. We must tell each other." She smiled wanly. "I shall have to treat myself for heartache. I suppose losing one who has occupied one's attention so much, *must* leave a heartache. I don't know what to do about his room and all his things yet. I've wanted to keep them exactly as he left them so that he could return to them. That is childish. He will never return. Whatever happens *he* will never come back to his home. Something different will come back to us... It may be better, I suppose, just to pack them all up and store them. I must try to forget about him as he was and think – there can be no harm in thinking – of what he is going to be. And not brood upon it."

They parted at Liverpool Street. She kissed Stella on both cheeks, dry, close-lipped kisses, and went off, erect and trim and self-controlled, the heroine of two miscarriages, the lady who submitted to the "rights" of her malignant husband when occasion required, and who contrived to escape from it all, even from any excessive love for her son.

Dione, Dione M'am; he had never once called her mother.

Stella watched her go. "And the Cadi," she thought, "caught that fastidious, silken, unreal thing young and ignorant, and married her and mauled her and shocked her beyond endurance with reality. And all the rest of the story has been her desperate attempt to escape from the ugliness of life. Her lecturing is escape, her Christian Science is escape. She is afraid of her love for Gemini. If she can, she will escape from that. And that is a life. Going away there and not looking back. That is a whole life, the beginning and the end of it. Even before we've begun to think about it, something happens to us; we're twisted for ever; we're knocked on the head...

"I suppose this is what Aldous Huxley means by detachment... Save me from detachment...

"And the poor old Cadi! The clumsy male brute who snapped at a butterfly and could never get it out of his mouth again!... Somehow I feel he had a case...

"I wonder when I shall get my first letter from Gemini. Better not begin thinking of that yet. I suppose he will scribble something from Gothenburg – or write on the boat. But that won't tell me much. Will he get to Russia? Even if there *is* war with Germany I suppose he will be all right in Russia. Russia wants no wars. No good thinking about it yet, Stella. I wonder if he's still up on deck, looking back at England. (Time you found the Cambridge train, Stella.)... I wonder where all those soldiers are going. What sacks they have to carry! Gas masks and all sorts of nonsense. Like the White Knight!... If it wasn't for his leg I suppose he would be in khaki...

"The Cambridge train?"

Book Three
Nightmare of Reality

Chapter One

The Guide and Friend in the Deep of the Forest

Gemini Vanishes

There came only a postcard from Gothenburg, with the date stamp of August 21st. Gemini had had a good crossing with an "interesting collection of human samples" and "gaggles of Swedes going home in a panic". Further he added, "May have to go to Stockholm to reach destination *via* Finland," and then squeezed into the corner, "American journalist (half Pole) suggests Warsaw."

This Stella sent to Mrs Twain with a note: "For your information. Please return." Mrs Twain had received an even briefer dispatch. "Sea perfect. Did you treat it? I believe you did. All's well. Love."

After that Stella had to wait six days and then came a real letter on hotel paper from Stockholm. This Stella did not send to Mrs Twain; she typed out all that was good for her.

It was dated August the 25th and it had come by air post. "I don't understand this war business," said Gemini. "This Ribbentrop treaty between Germany and Russia has given these Swedes the jitters and our sudden treaty to defend Poland has made them worse. The Russian change of front is – queer. It is extraordinary to come from the stoical indifference of London here and see the crowds outside the newspaper offices and the placards at the street corners. These people have the neutral habit of mind, not the peace-keeping habit but the neutral habit, which is something quite different. They have been accustomed to look on at wars, sell munitions and supplies at tremendous prices, and disapprove highly. Almost as bad as the Americans. But this Russo-German treaty has knocked them out of that. They have always balanced between Russia and Germany. Some still think that perhaps French and British imperialism may save the situation for them, but the German propaganda here has been very good indeed and they have an idiotically exaggerated idea of German competence and British decadence. I'm no great patriot, but that irritates me. We English criticise ourselves hard and good, but to have these bloody outsiders echoing what we say about ourselves with a superior air! No! The middle and upper classes have been inclined to suck up to Germany all along, and trust their blond complexions to see them through if some quasi-annexation does occur, but Russia is a different story. Now they are mobilising in a blue funk. Has Hitler sold them? They are setting to work upon munitions, and they hardly dare even talk to an enquiring Englishman (me) for fear of being accused of a breach of neutrality. Never have I seen a land so fair and so frightened. I wonder what sort of show they will put up if they do get dragged in. Sturdy people, but with the habit, for more than a century, of trusting to other nations to hold the balance of peace.

"I want to get into Russia more than ever. Before anything happens to prevent it. I want to find out what this Ribbentrop deal means. Is there going to be a second partition of Poland? It's Czarism back again. Has Hitler devoured Stalin or has Stalin devoured Hitler? Where's the anti-Comintern now? Where's the anti-Bolshevism of Franco? What happens to Japan? Italy? This sounds like café-table talk. That is precisely what it is. There are two men here making for Russia from Scotland, a little ambiguous, but I think enquirers on my lines. There are two or three English correspondents and an indiscreet young man poking about from the Embassy. There is a young American, Gavin Peters, who wants me to go with him to Warsaw. He wins. His stepmother who brought him up was Polish, and he speaks Polish and some Russian. I like him and I like a sort of detachment about him that keeps one's head cool. And we start tomorrow *via* Danzig for Warsaw. Anything may happen there. If things get too hot for us, we can retire gracefully *via* Lithuania and see what is happening to the Baltic states and so get at last into that even more mysterious land of Russia. Gavin is a seasoned American correspondent and knows how to get to things and how to make a get-away at the crucial moment. And he talks pretty well. I couldn't have a better travelling companion. That's my plans, Stella. Will you tell them to Dione M'am?

"And now, darling – "

The rest was an unforced lapse into endearment and tenderness without the faintest shadow of philosophical generalisation. It was totally unfitted for Mrs Twain's eyes, and it need not concern us here. Suffice it that it was so entirely personal and intimate that you would have missed most of its allusions, and some of it was pure little language and the drawings he had made were both nonsensical and improper. It pleased Stella mightily and took her back to Chelmsford and Paradise. She laughed aloud at it. So that for a little while when the writing changed she did not read on.

Abruptly the letter had returned to the realities about Gemini, but now in quite a different vein.

"I have been talking to a Swede, who might have come out of Ibsen – William Archer's Ibsen. He likes to exercise his very good English on me. 'Don't you think,' he said, 'that there is something in our atmosphere, something that has never been here before, something brooding over us all, like an enormous menace?'

"Not bad for the beginning of a conversation.

"I said I thought the Swedes were taking the situation much too seriously. 'What can touch you here? *We're* in for it if you like.' 'Yes,' said he. 'But I am more sensitive. I see through things. The restaurant life goes on,' said he, 'the buying and the selling and the going about. Cocktail parties and dinners. If anything there's a bigger throng in the streets than ever. But this is because they want to see other people. They don't like being quiet at home any more. They don't like being left alone. You see – all this place, all this country – plainly – it is all under sentence of death. All of it'.

"That was nonsense, but somehow it got hold of my imagination. You know the sort of suggestion that sticks like a burr.

"There was nothing like it in London. You can darken London, you can evacuate London, but you cannot make that unresponsive mass afraid, but here under the clear clean air there *is* this reasonless, instinctive apprehension. I can't tell you how bright and clear and happy a city Stockholm is – *must* be normally – and how this feeling of 'this is the end' overhangs it now.

"I struggle against the fancy. I put it to Gavin. There isn't even a war, I argue. The British Ambassador is going back to Berlin. There may be more appeasement. It's part of this rotten situation that you never know when and how Chamberlain will give way. Mussolini, the Pope, Roosevelt, everybody is sending telegrams and warnings.

" 'Yes,' he says. 'But I know what that Swedish fellow had in mind. This *is* the end. It's the end for all these little European neutrals. Tomorrow, if not today. It's the end for their way of living. Take a good look at old Stockholm, sonny, for you may never see it like this again. Under sentence of death? Now that you call my attention to it, I see that it is. By the by, you've got to see the celebrated Town Hall, while it still stands.'

"We went, and it's a wonder. It's super-Gothic. It's ultra-Nordic. Those Germans don't know how to begin being Nordic. I'm posting you some views. 'Say good-bye to it,' said Gavin. 'I always say good-bye to European cities nowadays. I used to say *Au revoir!*'

"You see he's been getting this fear infection...

"And such a beautiful day, everything saturated with the clear northern sunshine.

"Well, I won't twaddle on, Stella, with this descriptive matter. We have to be aboard the steamboat in an hour. The next letter you get will come from Danzig or Warsaw or any old place. I still find this was too senseless to be credible.

"Between us anyhow it's *Au revoir*. No good-bye for us.

"I must make an end now."

And so he made an end.

It was to be a far completer end than any he had anticipated. No letter, no post-card even came to her from Danzig nor Warsaw nor anywhere else. No news came by any other hand. Five view-cards of Stockholm dropped in a few days later and then absolute silence closed over Gemini. He vanished as completely out of her world as though he had never existed.

She waited. She waited over-long perhaps. But when at last she began enquiries, she found herself confronted with blankness.

The Germans invaded Poland at dawn on September 1st and Mr Chamberlain, greatly daring, declared that England was at war on September 3rd. Following on the treacheries, indecisions and swift military collapse of Poland, the Russian armies entered that country from the east a fortnight later. Then with the restoration of Russian ascendency over her former Baltic provinces, the dislocation of communications intensified. For three weeks or a month letters might still have come to Stella and it might have been possible to get news of Gemini through the consulates and correspondents who still carried on. Then that hope receded. She did not know what paper had commissioned Gavin Peters and it was only by pestering a much overworked American Consulate that she found out. But the newspaper people had nothing to tell her. He had been in Warsaw as late as Sunday the 26th, and he had sent a short news telegram and asked for money, but it had been impossible to get it out to him. Several refugee trains on their way to Lithuania had been bombed, derailed and machine-gunned, there were no casualty lists of these slaughters, and his people were very anxious about him. No further news had come from him. "He's a very resourceful fellow, is Peters," reflected the man in the newspaper office with philosophical detachment. "But that won't stop a stray bullet. Did you know him well?"

"I knew someone who was with him," said Stella, and wished she could strike people dead.

And that was as far as she got in tracing Gemini. In the orderly world of her upbringing, which was now breaking up with such incredible rapidity, the disappearance of a single person had been a mystery, a strange event to be studied and traced down to its sources, "news", a matter of universal concern. Already now social disorganisation had reached a pitch in which people without number could be lost and swallowed up in the gathering darkness, and no one would help you, no one wanted to help you and no one seemed to care.

She reverted to her old fantasy of telepathy. She knew it was foolish and yet she got a kind of comfort by sitting up in her bed in the night and trying to "get through" to him. "Gemini darling," she would say. "Gemini, are you there? Tell me where you are, darling. Gemini dear... Oh! *speak!*"

Then she began to have dreams about him. Very unwisely she had read part of the White Paper of Nazi atrocities in the concentration camps and elsewhere. It gave a hideous frame to her apprehensions. She would see him tortured and manhandled. But one thing she would not see, one thing she should not accept, that Gemini was dead.

Sometimes, scarred and bleeding and always with a dreadful slash athwart his face, he called to her in his dreams. That slash was a whip slash; it came out of the White Paper and it was always there.

"Mizpah! my darling," she said. "I am here. The Revolution, the block of alabaster, the grains of mustard seed. All we talked about. Trust me, I shall never forget. Only come back and tell me what to do, because I can love better than I can think. And how am I to live without you?"

"You may have to," whispered the Kentlake strain, running dark and cold like an underground stream in her mind. She would not let it rise to the surface.

2

Work and a Dream

Stella fought gallantly against her intimation of disaster and utter loss. Her intellectual life was more and more dominated by the idea that her job now was to get on with the understanding and promotion of that World Revolution of theirs. That was the real business of the Queen and King of Prigs. While the King away hunted and explored for reality, she had to get the house of her mind in order and have facts and schemes ready for his return. She had to animate a few remembered phrases and metaphors in forms that would interlock with and grip things as they were. She found that none so easy. But if this war was to stop men from learning, that was all the more reason for women to keep the lamp alight.

She went to Uncle Robert's new course of lectures on Synthetic Psychology and she had another talk to him and she got him to act as her informal director of studies. She was already through the first part of the Moral Science Tripos, and in a fair way for Part Two, but she was beginning to crane her neck more and more to see what was going on in the Modern History and Economics courses. "Naturally you do," said Uncle Robert. "You begin to realise that in spite of Church, State and snobbery, there is a modern education in the raw scattered about here. Smothered in the other stuff. Things some of the younger dons are getting for themselves – in part – anyhow. Let us see what we can pick out for you."

Her director of studies in Newnham was disposed to admire this awful intruder, this volunteer *privat-docent*, who had stuck his unsolicited lecture courses into the University as though they had a right to be there, and she let Stella range according to his suggestions. There was no hurry for Part Two. So she read hard, thought hard, wrote up her notes and did gratuitous essays and summaries as though Gemini might turn up any day and read them.

That and some hard walking and hockey kept Stella going through the days. But the nights were not so easy to deal with. That cold cruel thought she was suppressing came very near to the surface then. And there were defensive dreams in which Gemini figured hale and triumphant and friendly, explaining everything away. Even that scar would vanish. Or it ceased to matter. She would tell him of her reading and about Uncle Robert's flashes of intuition and unreasonableness. Gemini would tell her what he thought of Uncle Robert. He had never said very much about Uncle Robert; he knew him only through his books. There was sort of appreciative antagonism in these dream reveries. It was as though Gemini felt that Uncle Robert might run away with her mind.

One night she had a more consecutive dream than usual and one that left an exceptionally clear and vivid memory. She dreamt that she and Gemini were wandering in a dark wood at twilight; it was a very dark wood and it was growing darker. There had been bits of sky shining through the leaves and branches overhead, but now the trees were coming together into an impenetrable roof. But she did not stumble. She did not think of that. They walked with the wraith-like certainty of dreamland. The trees made way for them. She walked into a deepening apprehension of darkness, and she knew that however she walked the forest would grow darker and darker. And it was queer that she and Gemini had said not a word to one another for quite a long time.

That was very queer, very queer indeed. Because he must have a lot to tell her; he had had extraordinary experiences; he had done all sorts of things. Perhaps he did not know how to begin. Perhaps there was something about him, so that she had to begin. She said one or two things to him, but he did not answer, and it dawned upon her that although he was walking close by her side he was also at the same time a very great distance away. Was he changed in some way? Was he limping? She could not see. And then she began to lose sight of him altogether, because the wood was growing blacker and blacker; it was as if a succession of black gauzes was being drawn between them. She was quite sure she had seen him at first, quite sure. But now he was altogether invisible.

She put out her hand to touch his and she could not feel him. Had he ever been there? Someone had been there, and it had seemed to be Gemini. Someone who was more Gemini than not was there. Someone was there. But it was someone else who was hardly Gemini at all. It was someone else. It was answering her mute enquiry. It was not speaking aloud, but it was speaking as it were in her brain to her. It was saying, "You are lonely and very much afraid."

"I am afraid for everything."

"Not now," said the silent interlocutor.

"Not now. No. I was for a moment."

The presence remained with her, close and beneficent in the black, but saying no more. "You are a sort of mind that sustains," she thought. "You give confidence. You put things right. Or I should be very lost here, very lost indeed. There seemed to be a path. And there is no path. But what are you? I thought you were Gemini. Something of Gemini. Something very like his mind. You are not for example something in minds, in the mind of Uncle Robert for example?"

"Uncle Robert," came the answering thought, "is a mere superficiality. He is like a submarine periscope with no submarine to it. He can see everything and do nothing. He made that clear to you. Perspicacity is not enough. I am more than that."

"Yes?" she said.

"I am the Guide who will never fail you. I am the Friend who will never desert you"...

"It is so dark here. If only I could take your hand."

"If you believed, you would not want to take any hand..."

"But tell me. Tell me."

She drew nearer to the Unseen.

The secret of courage, the essence of faith, something deeper than thought was coming to her. The ebony darkness about her became positive. It became an intensity of vision that transcended sight. Something immensely wonderful seemed to be pouring into her mind, and at the same moment she realised with dismay that she was dreaming and on the verge of awakening. She felt that something ineffable was slipping from her and she struggled in vain to retain it.

H G WELLS

3

The Secret Fantasy

This dream of a responsive presence in the heart of the dark forest left so strong an impression upon Stella that in her waking state she could still feel it was real, more real than many memories. It had conveyed the profoundest things to her, things deeper and truer than anything that had ever come to her mind before, but the pity was that all that was actually said was gone; she knew quite definitely that what had been said was the clue, the complete satisfaction of every distress, and it had left her again. Her mind was like Psyche when she awoke and found her arms were empty. Just at the end, between waking and sleeping, she had felt the onset of this evasion, and she had made an attempt to grasp something, a sentence, a phrase, a word. For the fraction of a second something like "Oom-be, oom-be", had assumed the quality of the fundamental secret. Even these magic syllables became uncertain.

"What *was* it?" she said, and sat up in bed and beat her forehead.

There was no sense in mystical words. "Oom-be?" What had put that into her mind? Somewhen ages ago, far away in Asia, A kindred mind, she realised, had been through exactly this same experience and had emerged at last with the same empty substitute for the unspeakable reality. So it was that "Om Mane Padme Hum" fluttered from every praying-wheel in Tibet, the symbol of a lost significance, and the Lamas in their Red or their Yellow Hats congregated to preserve, earnestly and jealously, the memory of a forgotten secret.

Something revealing, confirming and sustaining, had come very near to her, and she had lost touch with it. Nothing but that sense of an approach remained.

She determined to take her perplexity to her teacher.

"Uncle Robert, I want you to talk about something... Is there a God?"

"Billions, I should think."

"But do you believe that below and above and in everything there is a God?"

Uncle Robert lifted his nose towards the Real Truth about God. His thumbs stuck out of his jacket pockets. "There are some words, Stella, that ought to be forcibly removed from circulation, and 'God' is one of them. It is like one of those defaced and flattened coins that may be sixpence or a bit of a krone, or a gulden or anything, that a cabman may cheat you with in the dark. The word 'God' has meant so much in the past that today it carries no definite meaning at all. For most people it is merely an expression of prejudice. With a certain magic quality. If you say 'I believe in God' they think you are good and on the side of everything respectable. If you say 'I do not believe in God', you are just awful. But if there *is* anything in existence like that All Wise Maker of this present Imbroglio to whom people pray today, then he will be there and he will be the same whether you call him 'God' or 'Hi or any loud cry'. Or are we to suppose him so far short of normal intelligence that he does not know himself by any other name?

"That seems to be the position of these people who want to start religious wars against anti-God Russia on behalf of their sacred word. Or the sacred investments that it seems in some way to sustain. In the name of God! – guns! A God by any other name would rule as justly, and if that 'All Wise' and so forth definition holds, he would at least have the wit to know his own without a label. You can bring up one divinity after another to me and I can say definitely of each one, it is absolutely impossible to believe that there can be any such God as this; the universe may be insane but it is manifestly not idiotic. No one has ever yet produced anything under that title that I find credible. No one at all.

"These various Gods of the Christians would fill a museum. They have hardly a thing in common. They are not even like a family portrait album. One of these Christian Gods is an imbecile egotist who created mankind to worship and praise him for ever! Can you imagine it? All of the Christian collection seem to have made some sort of mess of their creation and have become very sentimental and complicated about saving mankind or some favoured section of it from the consequences of that dismal muddle. Some seem frankly to admit the existence of rivals. They are jealous Gods, they say, and they become very menacing and trumpet the great commandment – from Sinai was it? – 'Thou shalt have none other Gods but me'. But why go through these variations in absurdity? Frankly, Stella, theology, except as a study of human trial and error in the statement of moral forces, has no interest for me.

"God means anything in fact from a luck fetish to a mathematical formula. He's a holy terror of a parent. He's always a bit of a devil; never quite able to exorcise himself or his world. Queer that he's always male, Stella. It's remarkable your friend Lady Rhondda has never rounded off her six-point charter by insisting that the universe is a matriarchate. Tradition too strong for her, I suppose, even in her thinking.

"What I do find worth emphasising is that under no circumstances has the human mind ever got to regarding God, any God, as the final and fundamental fact of existence. There is always something deeper and greater than God at the back of men's minds. They don't for instance make him the ultimate reference. They say he is Good. They say he is angry, resentful, merciful or what not. Why? Because they individualise him and want relationship with him, and so he has to have a character. Over him and above him there is always something else, a Standard by which he is judged. No God at all but a Super-God. I wonder if you have noticed that?"

"That's just why I asked you to talk, Uncle. I've had a sort of dream. You see – "

"Are you going to talk to *me*, Stella?" said Uncle Robert suspiciously over his nose.

"I'll be as short as possible."

"Go on," he said, "go on", and listened abstractedly, twiddling his fingers behind him and occasionally punctuating with a grunt or so...

"That," he interrupted when he had heard enough, "is very interesting, Stella. That is an intelligent dream. It does you credit. And I am quite willing to be your soothsayer and interpret your dream for you. Listen:

"Firstly, Stella, in my efforts to direct and enlighten your mind, I have done my utmost to impress upon you the entirely untrustworthy nature of language. Everybody alive suffers from an impediment in his speech. Intelligent statement is still merely an ideal, and life is full of unspeakable things. We say what we can and try and fix our thoughts. Generally we fix them too much – and a little wrong. Man has got along so far with metaphors, analogies, abstractions and symbols. We are continually transferring meanings. And about some things and particularly about this that came near to you in your dream it is better to attempt no words at all. Leave that at least as something unspoken. Directly you give it a name, you will want to have relations with it. You will. Directly you name *anything*, you want to have relations with it. 'Guide and Friend' you called it. Something holding out a hand to the personal you. You see? Well... *It* isn't either Guide or Friend.

"I know perfectly well what was in your mind. There is a rightness about things, a direction like the magnetic field that turns the compass needle north. It is above and below and throughout all things. It is in your conscience and apparently it comprehends a rational order among the atoms and the stars. The stiller you are, the more definitely the direction of these lines of force appears. And there it is and there is nothing more to be said about it. You know good from bad because of that. It is no more a God than it is a Sacred Cow or a Little Liver Pill. The Quakers seem to have some sort of apprehension of it, but Quakers are all muddled up with Christianity. Now if there were Quaker-Atheists!

"How this ultimate rightness has to do with life is beyond telling. Maybe it is a necessary thing to life, so that as life becomes conscious, those valuations are found to be in operation. This, which is something far more like a magnetic field than a person, insists that truth is of greater value than any falsity, and that certain patterns of conduct become us best. Whatever it is, this isn't God or any sort of God, because, as I have pointed out to you, all the Gods men have ever invented are and must be subject to it.

BABES IN THE DARKLING WOOD

"Gradually, Stella, the psychologists, the anthropologists, are getting all these Gods *taped*. They are almost as multitudinous in origin as they are in character. It is a rash thing to try and reduce the history of the idea of God to a simple story. It is trying to say what happened in billions and billions of minds over tens of thousands of years. Fear played a large part in most of these processes. I suppose this fear and propitiation of the Old Man of the Family-Tribe may have had even a dominant share, but there was also that more ancient thing, going back to the earliest ancestor who shrieked and ran, the fear of the killer at large, the beast of prey, the enemy in the ambush and the dark, and then the Old Man became a champion. He was not only the Holy Terror who imposed his taboos upon the tribe long after he was dead. He was the great helper and defender in reserve, the avenger of his people. It was natural for masterful men, not sure that they were sufficiently masterful, to project themselves into a God for whom they spoke. They half-believed in him themselves and interpreted their wills and fancies as his. There were the priests' Gods who were bumped about in an ark of the covenant or hid behind the veil of the Temple in some Holy of Holies, and there was the radical prophets' God who queered the pitch of the priests' God with pestilence and thunder. A God may be fear, may be self-projection, may be magic and fetish. It's like the genus *Canis*, no end to its varieties and mongrelisations. There's *Deus Ferocissimus*, with thousands of sub-species. He gives no quarter. He punishes the dead in hell for ever. The type of that species is the Fundamentalist God of Tennessee. There's *Deus Jehovah*, always breaking his promises to the Jews, *Deus Brahma* – not quite so relentless. *Deus Amans*, the friend of the nuns. It's vast miscellany, Stella, from the totem divinity of some remote savage to that oily Anglican divinity, now prevalent here, *Deus Suffocans*, the self-projection of Cosmo Gordon Lang, a sort of thin spiritual grease-film right across the English sky. I wish we could put them all away in a museum now and get on with a rational life..."

"And you think my dream – ?"

"Your dream, Stella, was a very profound dream. Don't spoil it. Don't speculate about it. No one has the mental apparatus to do that yet. There is truth, there is righteousness and right conduct in us and our universe. Things are so. In the confusions and hates of life we may stumble about and be misled, but the stiller and calmer you are, the more you are aware that it is so. I doubt if anyone can get beyond that. Maybe no one will get beyond that for a very long time. Ages. Perhaps it can all be accounted for in a perfectly natural, rational way. Life couldn't exist in us without its being fundamentally like this when you get right down to it. That may be arguable and provable. It alters nothing.

"Accept it, Stella, and leave it alone. Someone, I forget who, said once: 'By faith we disbelieve'. That wasn't bad. Don't try and make a will or a person out of it. Don't add your own little private mystery to the endless doll shop of the gods. Set up your altar to the new Unknown God, and however secretly you do it, along will come a Paul presently, all bluff and epilepsy, to tell you that this God 'whom you ignorantly worship, Him' will he 'declare unto you'.

"Be still and secret about it, Stella. Say nothing about it, because there is nothing to be said. Talk, and in a little while the still darkness will be yours no more. The confidence with which it filled you will be at an end, and you will be hopelessly perplexed. The soul hunt will begin. The forest will be filled with torches and lanterns and strange noises. They will all be claiming that this Guide and Friend of yours is their God and that they will tell you all about Him. He is unhappily a little tongue-tied, they will admit, but never mind that: they will explain. If you want immediate attention they can supply it. You will find the smell of incense and candles growing stronger. There'll be a dance of Bishops all gas and gaiters, and the Buchmanites will be inviting you to participate in the profits of God-guided businesses and all sorts of shared-out lucky tubs. And voices that boom and voices that intone and sweet little choristers singing like tethered skylarks. And sidelong priests edging towards you ingratiatingly. And there you will be, Stella."

"But if I do nothing," said Stella, "I may forget."

"Once you've been there, you'll go there again," said Uncle Robert.

"Have you been there?"

"I *live* there," said Uncle Robert calmly. And added: "Practically."

She stared at his self-complacent profile.

"But – " she began vaguely.

"I ask you, Stella, as your teacher, as your Guru, so to speak, not to say a word more about it. I ask you to keep all this to yourself. I have never talked so much about it before. I have practically told you by what I live, move and have my being. *Over*-explicitly. It fills me with a sense of indelicacy. I doubt if anyone so young as you are can really do without some sort of God; the less God the better, for Gods *do* corrupt so; but still a God – until you really grow up. Which may be in ten or twelve years' time. Until then you still have the child's craving for support. You need a sense of personal care. This something in the darkness seems like protection. Well – talk to this something if you must, but never expect it to protect you, never expect a reply. Above all, don't attempt to make a ventriloquist's stooge out of it. Until you are grown up, keep it secret, and you will never want to talk about it later. And that, Stella, is the beginning and end of all my Theology. Clear and clean as a wind-swept sky."

He turned to her with an unusual gravity. "And now, Stella, my dear, run along. The lecture is over."

"I think I've got you, Uncle," she said.

"I think you have."

From the street she looked up and saw him at the window gazing over the Cambridge skyline at the Real Truth of things, but, she fancied, with rather less than his usual arrogance.

She made her way back to Newnham very thoughtfully. She wished she had Gemini with whom to talk things over, and that passing thought expanded to heartache and distress. When would she hear of him? What was happening to him? She was trying to get all the particulars she could about the bombing and flight from Warsaw, and none of them were reassuring particulars. Russia, it seemed, was having some sort of trouble with Finland, but nobody seemed to think it would lead to war. Gemini had probably got to Russia. That she thought would be the best thing to happen to him. Russia, she knew, would never make a war. All her generation knew that. But it was queer that no letter nor telegram nor message came through. She tried to read. She gossiped with two of the Bedford College girls, but she could not get interested.

She went to her own study and pretended to read, and sat with her mind stagnating about Gemini. She went down to hear the late news bulletin. The radio never told her anything, but she always went down.

She returned to her study and copied out some stuff again until boredom stayed her hand. Then very slowly she undressed and got into bed. Nowadays there was no fun in undressing before the mirror. Desire was dead in her, for Gemini had passed beyond all thought of caresses and had taken desire with him.

She lay thinking for a time and then suddenly she turned on her side and pressed her cheek into her pillow and closed her eyes. "My Guide and my Friend," she whispered very softly, and lay quite still and sank listening into a dreamless sleep.

Chapter Two

Gemini in Poland

Gavin Peters Appears

One day early in December Stella received a letter that looked so ordinary and businesslike that she left it beside her plate unopened until she had read the newspaper. The paper was ablaze with the Stalin-Molotov attack on Finland. "So ends the last illusion of sanity in the world," she said. "Why have they done it?" When at last she took up that unobtrusive letter addressed to her in typescript, she thought it was probably a receipted bill.

But her muscles tightened as she read.

"Dear Miss Stella Kentlake,
"I want to see you if possible right away. I must. I have some money I must pay someone and I have news for you, not so bad as it might be and not so good as it might be. But good rather than bad. I was with Jimmy Twain in Riga on November 17th and he was alive and well then, still scheming to get into Bolshevik Russia. It was an obsession. He wrote to you from there, I know; he was writing a long

letter and I happened to see it was to you, and I think he wrote some others; we both sent cables too and I sent a dispatch, but nothing of that seems to have got through. I don't know how letters or cables were going. They just took your stuff and your money and didn't send it. There was a Russian censorship, I believe, as well as the Lettish. You never knew where you wouldn't find the next tangle. Riga was in utter confusion; swarming with Polish refugees, Jews, expropriated Balts trying to get to Germany, spies, Germans, Russians, frightened people of all sorts. The hotels and everything stacked with people trying to get away. We had the greatest difficulty in getting a room and a change of clothes. We had to buy everything. People would not take us in. We were unspeakably filthy and verminous after what we had been through. All that is a long story I had rather tell you face to face.

"Jimmy was splendid from first to last. I left him, and I know it might look as though I took his money and deserted him, but there was no time to go back for him, there was only one seat on the plane and anyhow he was so set then on the Russian idea that he would not have come. The Stockholm planes even then were booked full up to March, three months ahead; it was just one passenger who hadn't turned up that gave me a chance. I admit it looks like a sort of desertion, until I explain. But think! after all that had happened, could I have deserted him like that? Nothing seemed to knock the pluck out of him. It was just that made me do as I did. I thought at the time I would get round by Abo to Helsingfors and then communicate with him. I didn't think whether he had much money with him until

BABES IN THE DARKLING WOOD

I was halfway across. Then it dawned upon me he might be stranded. My idea was I could send back help for him from Finland, and it was only when I realised that maybe I had marooned him in Latvia, that I began to feel anxious. It was only when I tried to get contacts I found I had lost him. It's just over twenty-three pounds, I make it, I have of his. He had a sort of decisive punch in that limp of his. Something between an imp and a prizefighter. You see he made one feel so sure, so very sure, he could take care of himself. He was getting rather mulish and irritable at the end, I admit; the more uncertain the Russian outlook, the more he wanted to go on, and I think perhaps he may have got right away to Leningrad or somewhere in Soviet Russia as soon as he learnt I had left him. But all this I can explain better when I see you, as I hope you will let me do very soon. For three months we were together, and for two of them we were lost and hunted men, always continually in danger. I must tell you. That makes you know a man if anything can. And I never knew anyone to compare with him, a sort of splendid pluck. I would go back to Finland or Russia or anywhere if I thought I had the ghost of a chance of finding him again. But all this I must tell you, and the sooner the better.

"Gavin Peters."

"Yes," said Stella. "The sooner the better."

She sat stiff and stern and her hand was trembling so much she could not hold the letter still to read it. "I don't like you, Mr Gavin Peters. I don't like your slanting, loopy handwriting. Why can't you keep the lines straight? My Gemini was splendid, until you left him. And then it dawned upon you he might be stranded. And you've suddenly decided to hand over that three and twenty pounds...

"Shall I tell Uncle Robert? Shall I tell Dione M'am?...
"I'll see him first."

2

The Story of Gavin Peters

Stella liked Gavin Peters even less when she saw him, but then she had been accumulating dislike and suspicion against him. She was afraid at first that she would be lacking in self-control, but when she came to the meeting she found herself steady and deliberate. She decided to meet him at Gilbert and Susan's Coffee House where they could sit in a corner and talk freely. He appeared as a tallish blond young man threading his serious way among the tables to her corner. She had told him she would be in the corner nearest the window. He had deposited his hat and coat in the cloakroom. He swayed right and left. He had long slender hands which he held as though they were in readiness for the keyboard of a piano. He had a temporary entanglement with a chair, but at length he got to her.

"Miss Kentlake?" he said.

"Will you sit down, Mr Peters?" she said. "Would you like coffee or chocolate? They're both good here."

"May I have some chocolate? It's been such a cold journey down."

"Cigarette?"

"I have some, thank you. Won't you try one of mine?"

"Presently perhaps," said Stella, and gave her orders.

There was a slight pause. He had bright coppery hair with a crisp wave in it that was so hard and definite that it seemed as though it might be artificial. His skin was white, a sort of dead white; he had a foxed complexion. And he did not attempt to meet her eyes. He stared straight in front of him.

"It's hard to know where to begin," he said, and seemed relieved when the waitress came back to verify her order.

"You said one black coffee and one chocolate?" said the waitress...

"Perhaps..." said Peters, when the girl had gone again. "I don't know. The first thing, I ought to hand you over this money of his. Twenty-three pounds, I make it."

The long narrow freckled hand went halfway to a breast-pocket, hesitated and thought better of it.

"That belongs to his mother," she said, and then by an afterthought; "or his father. You don't know who his father is?"

"Not an idea. He never talked very much of his people. He was full of the war and what was to come out of it. Had he quarrelled with his people? He sometimes gave me that impression."

"His father is the magistrate, Mr Twain of Clarges Street. He's rather a hard man..."

"They call him the Cadi. Yes, I've heard of him."

The hand started again for the pocket-book and was called off.

"I want to know about Gem – about James Twain. Afterwards if you will, we can have a meeting in London and you can talk to Mrs Twain about that money. It has nothing to do with me. But tell me please about Warsaw and Riga and everything. Why did you get into such trouble? And what was he going to do when you saw him last? How was he then?"

"When I last saw him, Miss Kentlake, he was fit. Perfectly fit. He was thin. I admit he was thin, but fit and resolute. Lit up. He had a tremendous reserve of nervous go."

"Where do you think he is now? Have you any idea?"

Peters, still staring at nothing, put his forearms slowly and deliberately on the little table, and spoke with an air of profundity. "He might have got right down to Moscow. He might have got by way of Estonia to Finland. He might be almost anywhere, all round the Baltic. I would say, almost certainly I would say, that he can't be dead. I couldn't believe that. He had a vitality... You see there've been ships going, planes going, here, there and everywhere, people being evacuated in crowds. There's been a lot of crazy interference, but also plenty of opportunities of slipping through. I should say, knowing him as I do, that he got into Russia, and got there pretty certainly before this Finnish business burst. There was a fortnight, after, after I saw him last in Latvia, before the door was shut. Up to the very last everyone believed that the Russians would make a deal with Finland. Now if he got to Leningrad, say; what might have happened there? I suppose they were packing off most of the Intourist people and the Society for Cultural Relations tours and all that. Sending them home. Exactly what he would have dodged. He would have avoided any British representatives, because they, too, would have sent him home. He particularly didn't want to come back. He knew some German. He had a little book, *Russian Self Taught*. He was always nibbling at that. It's a difficult language for an Englishman, but he was quick – and he had a good ear for sounds. Sometimes he would try bits on me. I guess he took his chances in Leningrad. He was very keen on that Mass Observation stuff, asking people questions, he had a technique of doing something odd suddenly so as to get them off their guard and talking and all that. That may have got him arrested as a spy. That isn't so dangerous as it sounds. They wouldn't want to shoot him; they'd want to ask him questions. Russians love an argument. They have curiosity. They haven't the feeling an Englishman has – if I may put it that way – that a fact may not be quite respectable. They don't mind being mixed up with a fact, any old fact. They love being told things, though they never seem to make anything of what they are told. They play about with it and leave it as a cat might a rabbit's foot. If I had only one bet, I would say he was under arrest in some Russian prison and most probably in Leningrad. You can't tell, but that's what I should say."

"And then?" said Stella. "Will they torture him?"

"Russians don't torture. But – they'll bother him a lot. No end."

"*Bother* him! And what can be done for him?"

Peters made a grimace to express entire intellectual bankruptcy. "Technically England is still not at war with Russia, but if I may say so, you English have been almost as incompetent in handling Russian problems – "

He left his metaphor incomplete. No metaphor could express it. "You talk about your wonderful Empire… It's up against Russia from the Baltic to the Pacific and it has been for generations, and yet I doubt if there is such a thing as a Russian teacher in any single one of your public schools. Imagine it! The cheek of trying to run a world empire on blank ignorance and bluff! Cutting facts dead unless they wear the old school tie! 'Don't know you, suh.' An English representative in Russia is deaf and dumb. And since he has been trained not to talk with his hands... Generally they get to hate the Russians because of the impossibility of any sort of understanding... Though I don't see why they should expect *every* Russian to learn English on the chance of meeting them... They get together with Germans and people and swallow what they are told. Or they get vamped by interpreter girls... When you dine at the Embassy – I did once – really – yes I did – you pretend you are not in Russia... Well, none of your people, such as they are, are likely to be of any help in fishing out Twain..."

The arrival of the coffee and the chocolate truncated these reflections. Peters became unhelpfully directive in spreading the table, moving the coffee and plates and chocolate cups with his long hands thoughtfully and slowly as though he was playing a game, and Stella watched his sedulously averted face.

"And now," she said, "will you tell me about your time with him? I know you both went aboard a steamboat for Danzig. That was before the war began. What happened then?"

He featured immense intellectual effort.

"One thing followed after another. It's hard to get it into a consecutive story. Things didn't lead up to one another. Each seemed to blot out what had gone before. War was coming – plainly. But how was one to tell that the Poles were going to be wiped out, as they were? They were sold from the beginning. By other Poles. You can always get a Pole to do in another Pole and blame you for it afterwards. Like the Irish. Don't I know them! Fight we can, most of us; it's the in-between time when we go wrong. The Germans started the war at dawn and went straight for the petrol dumps and aerodromes. It was like keeping an appointment. They went by the map, and the country, which should have been under autumnal mud, was as dry and hard as concrete for their tanks. That was too bad. That was our bad luck. Our Polish air organisation was caput from the world go. Warsaw was being bombed in a week. The British and French might have bombed Berlin, otherwise, and refuelled and got fresh bombs in Poland and dropped them on the way home. But there was nowhere left for them to go in Poland..."

Stella interrupted. "I want to know about – James Twain."

"I know," he said.

She sat quite still.

"It was all just the usual thing in Danzig and Warsaw. Walking about streets, sitting and talking and looking and listening in cafés, and hanging about in hotel lounges. Bits of night life – always with the hope of getting a light on things. One never does. One gets drunk. *He* never did. *He* doesn't get drunk. I forget – for the life of me I forget – whether we stayed two days in Danzig or three or four. It was very Nazi and excited and unfriendly and, as he said, we had a sort of unwanted feeling. If we stopped to look at anything, someone wanted to know what we were looking at. We were always having to show our papers and turn back and all that. He thought the city a lovely old place and very clean. He had no idea what a lot of cool clean cities with cathedrals and fine public buildings the Baltic has to show. Englishmen are Baltic-blind. India turned their heads. We got that same feeling we had had in Stockholm, only worse, of something – something hanging over everything. Anyhow we were in Warsaw a day or so or more before the war broke, and there again it was the same thing. Everyone very excited and military and quite sure they were going to win the war. They had no idea. They thought it was going to be a war with cavalry raids and loud cheers. I spent hours and hours trying to get through to my people in London –

I know now that I did get through to them but I never had a reply. Or everything might have been different."

"What was he doing?"

"Taking it in. I told you, didn't I? – He wrote a long letter to you. Maybe that's all charred and burnt in some railway siding…"

It was clear Gavin Peters had to move on in his own style. He flowed on with digressions, evasions, repetitions. She listened with knit brows, intervened when he wandered, brought him back to the point, cross-examined him. "And where was Twain then?" She had to ask it a dozen times.

Gradually the story took shape.

It became eventful with the bombing of Warsaw. "He didn't like being bombed. He took it as a personal insult. He wasn't a bit afraid; he didn't seem to think he could be hit, but he was as indignant as if someone had just missed him with a lump of dirt in the street. He went out as if he was looking for somebody with a head to punch. The Polish anti-aircraft defence was obsolete and feeble; the Germans just did what they liked. I was for taking shelter but he simply dragged me out. Three or four streets away there were houses burning, and the streets were littered with broken glass and bits of masonry. Then we came to the salvage people and mangled bodies. I didn't realise. He'd never seen anything of the sort before. Never. There was a poor little kid all torn to pieces. Its poor little bowels spread out. Quite dead, you know. He swore. He danced – danced you know – and shook his fist. '*You* bloody Germans,' he said. "You filthy swine!' And then he was as sick as a dog."

Stella pushed her coffee away.

BABES IN THE DARKLING WOOD

"You don't mind, my telling things like that?" said Peters, looking up at her for the first time.

"It's just a qualm," she said. "Tell me everything. I can stand – what he stood. You go on."

She looked at him reassuringly and, by way of evidence, drank some coffee with a steady hand. "Go on."

"It was just a healthy reaction." He pulled himself together. "You mustn't think he was afraid. Not for a moment, M'am! He was never the least wee bit afraid. I never saw him afraid. But he used to get angry. A sort of white dangerousness. I couldn't get him to come back in, under cover. 'You go to hell,' he said. He mixed in with some sort of ambulance people. He couldn't carry a stretcher because of his lameness, but I think he was getting people out of the wreckage. I didn't see him again for a day; or more, and then he came in dog-tired in the late afternoon – stains of blood on his coat like a butcher – and threw himself down on the bed and went off – it wasn't so much sleep as exhaustion – complete exhaustion. Meanwhile I'd been getting information..."

"You see," said Peters; "it wasn't that we were driven out by the bombs. But the Germans were coming round us like this and like this." The long hands surrounded an imaginary Warsaw. "Things looked bad for us both. He was so furious, I was afraid if it came to a storm and street fighting he'd get caught with a rifle in his hand. I did anyhow get him away from that. I did do that. Even if that didn't happen, he might have got shot as a British spy, and the best that could happen once they got hold of him would have been to be a prisoner for the duration. Not good enough. And *I* wasn't so safe if they found out I could talk Polish and smatter a bit of Russian. I'd have to play the Star Spangled Banner, loud and clear, one hundred per cent. The thing to do was to get on to one of the trains that were still running into Lithuania. By way of Vilna they went. The sooner the better. We had a fight for it. Even to get on with tickets. Up to the last I was afraid he'd want to stand down for some woman. That didn't arise, anyhow."

"When exactly was this?" asked Stella.

"September the eleventh," said Peters. "He gave me the money and I took the tickets. I remember the date stamp. He went and got a big piece of ham and a lot of chocolate and we had our flasks. I told him to get that. I don't think he'd have thought of food if I hadn't. He'd got all the old *civilised* habit of expecting everything to be on tap. He quite thought there'd be a wagon restaurant... Things are changing... Do you mind if I have some more of this lovely chocolate and those sweet biscuits? There wasn't a thing on the train. The train down here, I mean. And thinking of that train makes me hungry again."

"And you got on the train?" said Stella, picking him up again. "You got on that train."

"Do you know I forget almost everything about the first evening and night of that train journey? There was a sort of feeling that the Germans were all round us. We were huddled up together in the darkness and the train rumbled along slowly, stopping sometimes for a minute or so or an hour. Those waits were the worst of it. You'd see flickers from lanterns outside and hear people asking silly questions from the windows and getting short answers. They were afraid of air attacks, afraid that bridges might be mined, afraid of rails torn up. Now and then someone would come up at a station and flash a light on us for a moment and then I would see Twain sitting up and scowling at the universe in general and the Germans in particular. He sat up stiffly with his hands on his knees most of the night, and I kept wanting to tell him to lean back and fold his arms. But he was so irritable. I don't think he slept at all. The corner seats were all taken, but I just remember lumps of darkness that sniffed and sweated and snored and stirred... Stuffiness and a sort of hot dirtiness. Children crying... Somebody drunk and singing down the corridor... Then slowly everything became visible. Such a warm red dawn! Such a lovely September morning! All that flattened-out country with its silver birches and its oak and willow scrub and its fields and thatched houses, as if it was asleep, nobody about very much, the most peaceful-looking land you can imagine..."

Gavin Peters became more intent upon his outstretched hands.

"They bombed that train about the middle of the next day. We didn't know they were on us until we heard the zoom of the planes. Then a lot of conflicting shouting. Lie down! Take to the woods! People didn't do very much at first. It was so incredible. Then the train stopped with a concussion and threw everything about. They'd hit the engine. People began tumbling out in a disorderly manner and running for the woods and any sort of cover before the planes came back. A lot were throwing themselves flat on the ground. Others were lying down in the carriages and corridors. Some got out and crawled under the carriages. There were two planes. We got down and Twain was swearing. 'Come on,' I said, for he seemed to want to stay there by the train and fight somebody.

"They machine-gunned that train five times, three down and two up. They came down so close we saw their goggle faces looking at us. They enjoyed it. They not only plastered the train;

one of them went after some poor devils who were running in a scatter up a field to a wood. I heard the hard rattle of the machine-gun and a woman screamed like a knife. And – ...they went off waving their hands like schoolboys..."

He looked up at her in frank realisation of the monstrosity of the fact he was stating. "Like schoolboys, you know," he said. "It was *fun* for them.

"They'd made an utter mess of the train. It was alight in two places, belches of sooty red flames coming up in the sunshine. The engine was off the rails on its side in a cloud of steam. People standing about rather helplessly. A few business-like. A doctor at work already near us. Some on the ground groaning and writhing... Some crumpled-up dead."

"And where were you?" asked Stella patiently.

"Wet through."

Stella stiffened with self-control.

"You see it was *then* that he saved my life."

She did not see, but she waited with her fists clenched.

"It happened so quickly. At the first machine-gunning it was just Heaven's mercy we weren't hit. Then I saw close by the track a sort of ditch canal. I don't know what it was. Irrigation perhaps. I made a plunge for that and he came with me. It was too deep for me and I couldn't keep my feet. I should have drowned. I should surely have drowned. I slipped against the bank and got mud in my mouth and eyes. I was – I was just simply out of control. He held me up. He got behind me and stuck that game leg of his into the bank, sort of hoisting me astride on it, and he got out his flask to give me a nip of brandy. 'Hold up, Gavin,' he said. 'It isn't the end of the world. Duck. They're coming back.'"

"Yes," said Stella.

"*He* didn't duck. He said what he thought of them and put my head down under water when they came near. And then when it was all over, he helped me crawl out and we started doing what we could for the other people. We were soaked to the skin but we got dry somehow. Just dried with the mud on us. One couldn't do very much."

"What became of the train?"

"There we were, and then I remember he said one of those civilised things of his. Grim as things looked I couldn't help laughing out loud. 'There ought,' he said, 'to be some sort of relief train presently.' I suppose it was natural for anyone brought up in England, to expect three or four policemen to turn up and take charge of things, and then ambulances and nurses and doctors to appear, first aid and all that. Only here there wasn't anything of the sort. Presently we saw some dark figures coming out of the woods, first one or two and then others, sort of slinking out of the woods, and some bending down over the one or two people who had been peppered in the fields. These newcomers were not – how shall I say it? – not a bit friendly, not a bit helpful. They came in little hesitating bunches towards the train. It was like cattle in a field coming up to something strange. They were mostly peasants who'd been hiding, I suppose, from the German light tanks, and I suppose we seemed just part of the war to them. Presently some Polish soldiers turned up from nowhere, stragglers, I suppose, from the army, which had been caught between the drive from the west and the invasion from East Prussia. No officers that I could see. They were ill-grown blue-chinned young louts, worn out and sullen, glad to get food and drink from us but quite unwilling to take orders from anyone.

They stood about and looked on and made remarks in undertones to each other. The doctor and two of the conductors of the train and one or two railway men made a sort of council, and presently a priest turned up. Officious, well-meaning little man he was. Catholic. He scolded those soldiers for being unhelpful, but it wasn't any good. One or two helped for a bit and then knocked off again. The others sat about in groups beside the line.

"There was nowhere to take the injured and no stretchers for the wounded. There was nothing to do but to camp in the train until some sort of help came from somewhere and hope the Nazi airmen had had all the fun they could get out of us. I believe a messenger was sent on to the next station, fifteen kilometres away, the priest said, but if so he started late, and nothing came of it. The doctor and the priest didn't like the look of the soldiers and didn't want to send possible helpers away. We got the fire under in the burning carriages so that it wouldn't spread, and we mad a sort of hospital out of the end two cars and put the uninjured people in the others, five or six cars – it was quite a long train. I remember remarking on the queerness of it to Twain. There we were in the sunset, a sweating, blackened little group of people trying to get back from bloody massacre to some sort of social order... And we'd almost fought to get on to that train!"

He meditated for a moment. "It was one of the loveliest sunsets in the world. Like pink fish-scales... It was only as the twilight deepened that we realised that we were practically without lights. Just a flash-light or so and a few matches..."

He paused exasperatingly.

"I don't know when the plundering began or how it started. Somebody may have offered those soldiers or some of the peasants money, or shown them jewels or something. Naturally most of the people in the train had their valuables upon them, I doubt if the soldiers would have thought of that if it hadn't been put into their heads. I was fast asleep and then I heard Twain shouting 'Peters! They're robbing people. Come and tell them not to.' Then there was a bit of a struggle and a woman began screaming and weeping and imploring. 'It's all we have,' she said. 'Give them back to me.'

" 'Where are you?' I said. His voice answered, 'Come and tell this fool here to ease off me.' I scrambled out of the train. Not too soon. It was starlight – not a trace of a moon anywhere, but a sort of clear darkness. There was a fellow holding a bayonet to his chest and saying, 'Hands up!' In Polish naturally. 'Hold up your hands,' I shouted just in time, 'or he'll stick you. What's the matter?' 'They're looting,' he said. 'We've got to stop it. Something is going on down the train there.' '*Your* hands too,' said another soldier behind me. 'We don't want to hurt you,' they said. 'But don't try to teach us how to behave. It's only reason that you – bourgeois he meant but the Polish words he used were, well, coarser – should pay up a bit. You'll have the Russians here before very long, and *they* won't stand any of your nonsense.'

"I think," reflected Peters, "those fellows came from Lublin. They had an accent – a sort of Russian smear. I could hardly understand them. One I heard speaking German. They sounded like factory workers.

" 'We want to go down the train to our friends,' I said.

" 'Go right up the line, comrades, and clear out before trouble begins,' said my man. 'We're not taking any risks. That little priest down there is asking for trouble. He'll have only himself to blame if he gets knocked on the head.' And then I remember this fellow asked me if I knew the stars. He wanted to know which was south, and I showed him the North Star and explained. That was a townsman anyhow. 'We aren't going to hurt anybody,' he said, 'but we can't have all this loot carried off, out of the country. We've got to expropriate it. *Expropriate*, comrades. Understand?'

"What was happening down the train we never found out. They took our watches and our flasks, confound them, and told us to clear out. They never touched our pocket-books. They didn't search us. They were jumpy, in a kind of guilty hurry. I heard the voice of the little priest and a jumble of other voices, I suppose there was some sort of resistance, but we could do nothing. Maybe there was a capitulation. Maybe they just took what they could and cleared out. Maybe the peasants joined in. We heard a shot or so and then everything was quiet. We had to do what we were told. What else was there to do? They made a sort of parade of orderliness. That's the Bolshevik style. Lucky they weren't Nazis. They marched us by the black masses of the burnt carriages and the engine, and we had to guide our steps beyond that by the gleam of starlight on the rails. 'Keep your hands up,' said our soldier. 'We'll give you five minutes by this English watch of yours, and then we'll shoot along the line, and shoot again if we hear any more of you.'

"We staggered along for a time and got down the embankment for a bit when the shots came. Then we crept back to the track and kept along it, because it was too dark to leave it."

Peters became sententious again. "If it wasn't for Twain I don't think I should have seen any symbolism in it. But he had a generalising mind. He would have made... I mean, he *has* the makings of a great journalist. It was what attracted me to him first. He was always shedding the freshest, most original crossheads. He made you feel that an experience isn't worth having unless it means everything, so to speak. 'Civilisation!' he said. There was the train, a kind of black lumpiness in the general night; in a word or so he made it look like the dead body of his nice cut-and-dried civilisation. It didn't signify anything more. It wasn't going anywhere further. It was done. And there were the looters like rats gnawing at the body, and after that, what was going to happen to the poor scared robbed passengers, and what sort of help could there be for the wounded and dying? We two had no aims. Except to get away... It was no good going back. Even *he* saw that. What could we have done?"

"But I thought you said there was a town fifteen kilometres off. That's only ten miles for help."

"That was the next station."

"But didn't you get to the next station?"

"That was our idea. I remember now. Get help from the next station. We nearly fell into a river. The bridge had been bombed. We saw the tangled ironwork against the sky and pulled up in time. It made me laugh. Even *he* laughed. 'There's no sense in it at all,' he said. You could hear the river far down below among the rocks laughing and chuckling like and idiot. It wasn't light enough to walk about freely. We squatted on some dry grass and slept in a sort of way until daylight, with our hands round our knees – it got pretty cold before dawn – and then, you know, our wanderings really began."

The wandering reminiscences of the wanderings proceeded...

3

Note of Interrogation

The Coffee House clock proclaimed the hour of five. "I suppose I ought to be getting back to London," said Gavin

Peters suddenly. He was still in Lithuania. "To make a long story short – "

"I feel you've hardly told me anything yet," she said; "I want to know everything. Don't make it short. It was very good of you to come here. What I would like to do next is to meet you again in London with Mrs Twain. And then you can settle about that money."

"Of course, that money," he said, and the hand fluttered towards the pocket-book again. "I certainly ought to see his mother, especially if it's her money..."

So the rest of Gavin Peters' story was gradually unfolded and straightened out, but never completely straightened out, over a lunch table and in the coffee room of the Hypatia Club. His thoughts were obsessed by the fact of his desertion of Gemini in Riga, he was always drawn towards that and never coming to it, and the intermediate events had to be patched together from his sudden swerves into fragmentary accounts of individual adventures. He told her how they decided to follow the river south and then to work round to the eastward, and so get on to Lithuania by way of Vilna. He knew there was a second east and west railway line, somewhere to the south of them, but that they never seemed to be clear about. Some east-going railway they followed for a time, and they sheltered for some days in a small town called Wiczlicze. There they got a room and food and cigarettes and pulled themselves together. They could get no contacts by telegram or telephone to Lithuania. They sat in a café listening all day to an old gramophone, and they were loth to take to the road again. "Until we got a little red blood into us, going on was more that we could face."

Babes in the Darkling Wood

The Russian march into Poland had not begun at the time of their train disaster, and Peters and Gemini did not hear of the invasion of Poland from the east until, in the last week in September, they actually saw Russian cavalry.

As the story unfolded, and looped back and went on again, the two women did their best to get a consecutive picture of Gemini. They had glimpses of him is a state of astonishment. "I never realised," he had said over and over again, "how artificial and accidental a thing our old civilisation has been. So flimsy against destructive forces, so hard to set up again. You hit at it here with this war, and – there isn't anything left of it. We're down on dry earth and naked animal humanity. Who's going to put all this back? Who can?" He kept on saying that sort of thing, it seemed, and he kept on saying, "In Russia. In Russia we shall find a new order. There, something better is beginning."

But these reflections were interspersed with uglier experiences. These were things that were already half suppressed in Peters' mind. He told them in the manner of a reluctant witness. They had starved and got ill. It dawned upon Stella that she was hearing about a land in which metalled roads of the Western type had never existed. There was no countryside in the English sense at all. Some phrase of Peters' made her see a straggle of low thatched cottages fenced off in half-acre yards from one another, with a very broad mud-track running amidst them by way of a village street. There would be dust pits in the middle of the trail round which the cart-tracks skirted, dust pits that would become foul morasses as soon as the rains returned. Dead animals occasionally. Once a dead old woman. A sprawl of rags and grey hair. At places they found recent tracks of light tanks, probably German tanks. The houses would be deserted and empty, or dark figures lurked defensively in them. Then, after two false starts, he forced himself to tell a frightful thing. In one isolated house there had been a massacre; "God knows why. Perhaps they were Jews"; and peering in on the chance of food, they found a stinking mass of rags. They were turning to go. "My God!" Gemini had cried, "there's something moving!"

"It might have been a rat," said Peters, "but we looked again and saw it was a hand. We both tried to get it out and do something, but it died. It never moved again... It might have been a boy or a girl with dark hair... You see – Things had happened to the face. It left us empty with horror."

" 'We must just go on,' said Twain. He limped along. He never said a word to me, for miles. He kept talking to himself."

When they were starving they stole a chicken. A pale gleam of amusement appeared in Peters' face. "What would you do with a chicken, if you didn't know how to get its feathers off or how to clean it, and you hadn't a pot to cook it in, or a fire? When we caught it, we thought of roast chicken, beautiful roast chicken... We dragged that bird along with us for five or six kilometres and then – well, we tore it up and gnawed it raw. And it made us ill. But we were almost always ill, disgustingly ill. Filthily ill, we'd eat half-ripe berries and gnaw bits of bark. One place we found a lot of swedes. Everything we ate seemed to disagree with us. We'd lie up in the woods. No one to look after us. Getting iller and filthier and filthier. He'd never been ill in his life before without somebody tucking him up in bed. He thought that happened to everyone. I suppose it does in England. If it hadn't been for the drive in him, I should be lying in those woods now. Just a sprawl of rags and bones. Dragged about by birds and things. It was he made me go on."

At last Peters got by way of Vilna and Kaunas to Riga, and came to an ambiguous evasive explanation of how he left Gemini behind him there. He added little to what he had already told Stella in his letter...

"And now, Mrs Twain," he said, with an air of conclusion, "I have to pay you that twenty-three pounds. They've been burning my pocket, I can assure you."

Mrs Twain looked at the money he counted out upon the table without offering to take it.

"And so," she said, "the story ends on a note of interrogation."

"If ever, in any way, I can do anything more – " said Gavin Peters.

"I am quite sure we can rely upon you," she said, and stood up slowly and held out her hand. He stood up as she did and produced a card from his depleted packet-book. "If you want to contact me."

Stella, with two chairs and a table between them, did not hold out her hand.

She watched Gavin Peters going off as bravely as he knew how. "I wonder what he has left out," she said. "I wonder what he has put in."

Mrs Twain was tucking away her money in her bag. She looked at the door through which Peters had just vanished. "I think you are unfair to him. If it had been Jimmy who had left *him*..."

"And don't you feel like that?"

Mrs Twain considered. "I control it," she said.

(She controls it? Thought Stella. Or doesn't she feel? Is this detachment of hers innate or is it habit become a second nature?)

Mrs Twain meditated for a further moment and then began almost cheerfully to consider that next step to take. "I suppose we must go on trying find out from consuls and people like that, what happened to Jimmy. I wonder if what are called Private Enquiry Agents would be of any use to us? Or someone in the Foreign Office? I wonder if one offered a reward? How helpless women are really! Always thinking of getting 'the man' to do it – from the plumbing upward... Ages of subjection..."

CHAPTER THREE

Gemini in the Shadows

The Finding of Gemini

One chilly morning before the great cold and snowstorms of January 1940 locked up the country altogether, Mrs Twain came down to breakfast a little before her husband. His *Times;* he read no other paper; and his letters, awaited him. Her own correspondence was piled beside her place, *The Daily Telegraph*, *The Christian Science Monitor*, and various circulars and letters. As she passed his armchair to go to her own she halted for the fraction of a second. The topmost envelope bore what she recognised as Swedish stamps. Not her business, she reminded herself. She helped herself at the sideboard and examined her mail with her usual air of serene detachment. Her husband appeared and clattered over the bacon and eggs. Then he sat down. "Hul-*lo*," he said. "What's this?"

"Shall I pour your coffee, William?" she asked.

"Please." He opened the letter. He became very intent upon it. "My God!" he muttered. "Oh my God!"

It was evidently profoundly disturbing to him, and she realised at once that he was torn between a desire to talk to her about it and a still stronger desire to let her know that it concerned Gemini and torment her by not revealing its contents.

Long years of self-training enabled her to lapse into a pensive contemplation of a second-hand book catalogue as though she had no other interest in the world. Then with a faint sigh roused herself, drank some coffee and turned to *The Daily Telegraph*, regardless of the grim face that watched her from the other end of the table.

He did not touch his *Times*, she observed. He made only a pretence of reading his other letters. He pushed his kipper away from him half consumed. He returned to that crucial letter. "There are things I must attend to at once," he said.

"No more coffee?" she said.

"No."

He hesitated. Then very deliberately he placed that significantly empty envelope upon the table-cloth where she could hardly fail to see it, gathered up his letters and marched with an air of gloomy preoccupation to that austere sanctum, his study. He slammed the door – at her. She was not to be told; she was not to know. But she was to feel that she was to blame... Very well.

She trifled for a time with the residue of her correspondence. Then she walked slowly by his place to the door. She leant over to see the envelope for a moment; she would not touch it. The address was not in Jimmy's handwriting. It came from Sweden. She saw the date stamp *Flens*. She must find out where this Flens was. Jimmy must have got back to Sweden. And what had that letter told and what had she to do? She knew that whatever it was she would hear in a day or so. William would not be able to keep it back from her. It was something dreadful, but it was something living. If Jimmy was dead, William would have behaved quite differently. That would have crumpled him up completely. Had the young man been arrested? Was he just in some monetary difficulties on his way home? At any rate he was out of Russia and out of Finland. That was to the good.

To a casual observer the goings and comings of Mrs Twain that morning would have betrayed nothing remarkable. She dressed warmly and carefully; her fur cloak which had been a birthday present to herself was a particularly well-chosen one of mink; and she went about her business with an effect of quiet, unhurrying orderliness. Yet a closer scrutiny of her proceedings would have revealed a very active and at first rather confused mind. She began with the London Library. There she asked for books about Sweden and was shown where to find them. She read discursively. She found particulars of the size and position of Flens. Then suddenly she was off to Cook's in Berkeley Street to find out how one got to Sweden under war conditions. Cook's enlarged upon the difficulties until she risked an assertion that her only son was in hospital there, and then Cook's became imaginative and helpful. Then she taxied to Lincoln's Inn Fields to see her lawyer. She had long ago achieved a separate passport and he was very helpful about visas. Then she appeared at the Swedish Consulate. She wanted to know all about Flens. When a lady wanted to know all about Flens then it was plainly the duty of all honourable Swedish men to see that she did so. That was the atmosphere she created. Was there a prison there? Was there a hospital there? They were most helpful but there were limits to their knowledge. "But you have a telephone directory of the region? Couldn't we perhaps find out from that?"

The Consulate admitted that this was a bright idea, and with some difficulty produced an old directory. It dated from 1935.

There was, she learnt, an excess of possibilities. There was indeed no prison, but there were no less than five hospitals in the district, one public and one psychotherapeutic, the clinic of Dr Olaf Bjorkminder, and after a moment of quiet reflection she copied down all their addresses. The Consulate was left congratulating itself on its own resourcefulness in producing that telephone directory. Her next visit was to the Hypatia Club, that celebrated cock and hen club in Albemarle Street. She sat down to pensive tea. She realised she had forgotten her lunch, and she supplemented her tea with two boiled eggs. She ate slowly, composing a letter in clear and simple terms adapted to a Swedish reader who did not know very much English.

Then she sat reflectively at a writing-desk for a few moments before writing in identical terms to each of those five addresses. She asked if there was a young man named James Twain in the establishment. He was the son of her husband Mr William Twain, the well-known London magistrate, and she was his mother. If so, would they please send her a <u>full and complete report</u> (underlined) of his present condition and outlook? There would be no need to limit expenditure if he was in need of special attention. Mr Twain was much engaged in his magisterial duties in London, but she hoped to be free to come over to them very shortly. No doubt she would find accommodation for herself in the neighbourhood. If a diagnosis of the case had already been sent to Mr Twain, it would be convenient for her to have a duplicate copy if they would be so kind as to have one made. She read over with great care what she had written, she addressed her letters by air post, stamped them and saw that they were posted. And so home with the sense of a day well spent.

She had a bath and appeared at the dinner-table with a general effect of never having been out-of-doors. It was their custom to dress for dinner, and she found the Cadi in his usual dinner-jacket. He had, she observed, tied his tie very badly, an unfavorable omen. "I think it's colder," she said. He made no reply.

She affected indifference. The parlourmaid, whose trimness aped her mistress', served the Coquille St Jacques and the white wine and went noiselessly out of the room. The door closed behind her.

Then the Cadi spoke. His intonation was dry and hard.

"So you gave my son money to go to Sweden just when war was breaking out?... Did that girl go with him?"

"He went to Sweden, William, because he felt he had no place now in London. He wanted to see the countries round the Baltic – and get away from everything. That girl, as you call her, did not go with him. No they haven't parted, but he went alone. You have heard from him, I see. Why do you try to torment me? Tell me what has happened to him. Where is he?"

He stared at her with hostile eyes and then barked a string of short sentences at her with a pause between each.

"Out of his mind."

He repeated; "Out of his mind. In a hospital there. My son. A lunatic, to give it the proper word. The son on whom I built all my hopes. In a Swedish madhouse. The son whose heart you stole from me. In a madhouse. And how? Blown up at a railway station. So everything comes out. Why did he never write to us? What was he doing out there in Sweden? All that time?

Concussion! But they say there his mind must have been affected before... Mad... I knew he was wrong-headed but I never thought he was weak-headed. And so it ends. That career! That career that might have been so brilliant... *God*, how I counted on him!"

He forgot his hatred of her in his own accumulated self-pity. He pushed his plate away from him and covered his eyes with his hand.

Behind her masks of self-assurance Mrs Twain was smitten with an unwonted sense of inadequacy. She found herself sorry for his wretchedness and she had not expected to feel that. She had expected anger and denunciation but not unhappiness.

She had known this quarrel impended ever since she had seen her son off at Tilbury; she had rehearsed it, always as a quarrel, and how as she looked at her husband, she realised as she had never done before the power that lay in his possible self-abandonment. Suppose suddenly he wept. It would be unendurable. What defence had she if he wept? If suddenly he became a martyr?

"You said he was no longer your son," she began. She said that by sheer inertia. It was part of that preconceived dispute, and she felt as she said it that this was now mere useless recrimination.

She decided that to save the situation she must abandon all antagonism. At once, she must do this, before he retorted and began to boom at her, or did whatever else he was disposed to do. Her tone became matter-of-fact. "He has not been in Sweden all the time," she said. "I had a letter from him some months ago, but that – . He was in Warsaw. And I have heard since through an American journalist that he went to Riga. I ought to have told you these things, William, but I did not know how you would take them. I did not know whether you wanted to know about him or not."

"But how did you hear from him? When did you hear from him."

"You see, dear" – she was becoming more and more the dutiful wife – "I did not know whether you would like to see I was having letters from him. I thought it might annoy you. So I asked him to write to my club. But there is nothing to hide. I was distressed, but I did not know how you would take things. I was waiting for a suitable occasion for telling you. This American – "

She paused to arrange her facts. The Cadi must not know about the money or the real facts of the Riga desertion. She knew his immense capacity for self-righteous vindictiveness, and she did not intend to expose Peters to his pursuit.

"Go on," said the father, with the flatness of a broken-hearted man. "Tell me."

She skirted the truth neatly. The young American had promised Gemini to tell her all about him.

"Why didn't he bring a letter?"

(Yes, why didn't he? Quick, Dione!)

"They parted unexpectedly," she explained. "There was no time to write. There was a letter – yes, he *said* there was a letter, but it never got to me. They had left it at the hotel. The plane was just going off. So Gemini gave him my address at the Club. Asked him to explain things."

"And he told you – ?"

"They had had a hard time, William. They were in Warsaw when it was bombed. They tried to get to Lithuania and their train was bombed and wrecked. They wandered about the devastated country. They starved. They were ill. They seem to have had dysentery. They almost died in the woods. But – *our son*, William, kept that American alive by his courage. Saved his life twice. And at Riga he still wanted to go and see things for himself. He was obstinate, as you are, William, when you get an idea into your head, and he hated giving in. As you do."

"But what happened then?"

"You know that better than I do. And now, William, may I see the letter they wrote you and what they told you?"

He too had been prepared with a sheaf of recriminations for a quarrelsome dispute. But in his own possessive way he cared for his son and at the back of his mind there was a respect for his wife's capacity. "You have always thwarted me about this boy," he said. "But now – . You share my loss. You share the responsibility. Much of this is your doing. I see no reason why you should not know what I know."

He produced his letter, grudgingly, and handed it to her.

She took it, and rang for the maid to clear away the untouched course while she read it. She read in silence and her husband watched her. Gemini had been standing on the platform of a station at Flens when a box of ammunition and then a whole carload had exploded, twenty yards or more away from him. He had been knocked senseless and had been picked up and carried to a hospital, suffering from cerebral concussion. In the language of the latter he had "an injury to the conus medullaris, manifestly a haematomyelia". (Now what might that mean? Did William know? He must have found out, or he would not have handed over the letter. She must ask him, and it would please him to explain.) This had "released a long-suppressed anxiety hysteria, which had converted into motor paralysis and blindness". (What was "converted"?) There was "a complete withdrawal of the libido into the ego". That sounded stiff and a trifle improper; Freud and all that. "An abandonment of will". "A resistance to any relief". "No wish to get better". "Intense irritability and a clinging to an almost comatose apathy". (Comatose apathy? That was just understandable.) He had been removed already, as soon as his parentage was ascertained, from the general mental hospital to the clinic of the well-known psycho-therapeutist Dr Olaf Bjorkminder, who declared the case required long and the most persistent treatment. The unfortunate young man needed extreme quiet. He should not be moved, at any rate for some time and until Dr Bjorkminder was able to acquire an ascendancy over him. His mind had turned against everyone in his family, against his father, his mother and particularly against a young lady with whom he had evidently been in love. He called her by a peculiar name, *Stellaria Holostea*, the botanical name of chickweed. He had said repeatedly, "Keep that little weed away from me. She is all over me. She will stifle me." Evidently she symbolised something he wanted to forget. He disliked everyone who recalled his former life to him. This was very common in these cases. His parents must take it to heart. If they would trust Dr Bjorkminder, a time would come, and he would be the first to advise them, when their presence would be helpful. But not now. Now they would simply disturb the treatment.

The maid had gone again. Twain was not eating, but he drank a glass of Pommard.

She read over the phrases in the letter he could best elucidate. He explained them as well as he was able. He had evidently consulted some specialist. He was equal to haematomyelia, a sort of temporary stroke just at the back of the head here, he indicated the place, and he said libido was the desire to live. "I thought," he said, "it meant something much more unpleasant. Something – well, Freudian. Apparently that is not the case. These technicalities are, like most medical technicalities, glib and obscure – I always make my medical witness talk plain English in court– but the general drift is quite clear."

"And what have you told this Dr Bjorkminder?" she asked.

"I have wired that no expense is to be spared."

She meditated on that and Dr Bjorkminder, with the cultivated mistrust of a Christian Scientist.

"One of us ought to go there," she said.

"But he says so emphatically No."

"That is why I think someone ought to be on the spot."

Twain drank another glass of wine. "But I have already wired no expense is to be spared."

"We cannot have it said that you left your only son in strange hands in Sweden. That you just threw money at him and left him…"

He stared at her and then with no further pretence of eating got up and stood before the fire. She remained seated at the table. She spoke evenly.

"You cannot go," she said. "You have all your work here… There's all these cases with foreigners now. Who would look after them as you do? You have your duty to the country. You see through them so clearly. But one of us has to go. So plainly – I must go."

"You?"

"One of us evidently."

"But you!"

"Would you have people say you let your son – ? You see, William, he may die. Don't you care for him?"

BABES IN THE DARKLING WOOD

"Care for him! Ten thousand times more than you do. How can you understand what he has been, what he is, to me? At the back of my mind there is still a desperate hope that somehow this dreadful thing may make some change in him. Don't you see that? There you sit, as though all this frightful tragedy mattered nothing. As though it was a story told! Have you a heart? He is my son, I tell you, you green-blooded woman. He is my son."

"Is it *necessary* to tell me that, William? You forget that to a certain extent he is mine also. Plainly it is my duty to go. And I am going."

"Going. Do you know what going means? In this weather? In this war?"

"I suppose it will not be quite so comfortable or as safe as usual. Perhaps one might charter a plane. I do not see that it alters the fact that I have to go."

He looked at her with a gleam of that reluctant admiration which so often put a resentful edge upon his hatred of her. He knew not only that she would go, but that the chances were she would get through it all unruffled and ladylike, reducing the ocean, the enemy, and if need be the entire mental home, to the completest normality, and that she would do every sane and sensible thing that had to be done with an air of enquiring aloofness and the completest success.

But he had to assert his position.

"No," he said. "I can't let you go. I forbid it. If anyone goes, I go. You have no imagination, Dione. You do not *begin* to imagine the danger of such an expedition."

"I don't *want* to disobey you," she said.

"But you mean to go?"

"Yes, I feel called upon to go."

"You do it at your own risk," he said, but she realised she had won her point.

He became clumsily facetious.

"They'll torpedo you. They'll blow you up. You'll have to take to the boats. They'll machine-gun you in the water. You'll strike a mine. Up you'll go. Head over heels. I hope you'll have time to treat the situation – *treat's* the word, isn't it? – before you come down. If you start to go I'll put the Defence of the Realm Act in operation against you. I'll say you're in possession of secrets likely to be useful to the enemy."

She perceived the matter was settled. "William," she said, "you haven't eaten a mouthful. It distresses me. The dinner is spoilt, but there is still a cheese soufflé and some more wine. You must keep your strength up." She touched the bell.

Mr Twain returned to the table and poured himself a third glass of wine, "Well, since we've hammered things out," he said, "perhaps I might – "

He ate now with appreciation. "If only you would be franker with me. If only you would tell me things. You have so strange a distrust of me. That lies at the root of all our troubles. After all – we love him. Well, don't we? We love each other through him. Maybe what has happened may draw all three of us together. I am glad, even now I am glad, that at last we can co-operate again. Maybe the outcome of this may be what I have always longed for – a family consolidation. He can be cured, evidently, and then we may find him a different man. It is significant that he does not want to see that girl again. That shows an awakening of conscience... Sometimes I know I make fun of you, but I assure you, Dione, that I have an immense respect for a sort of courage and clearness in you. Tonight, I admit it, you have helped me.

This cheese savoury, by the by, is *excellent*." He finished the decanter and raised his glass to her. "Courage," he said. "After all – . I have a conviction that things may still come right between us, Dione. After all, if we had him over here to care for him together... You mustn't stay for ever in Sweden, you know. You have your duties here."

He looked at her with an ingratiating smile.

So that was how the crisis was to end.

For some weeks she had not, as she put it to herself, been "mauled". But it was evident that so their reconciliation would have to be crowned.

But soon she would be in Sweden and in full possession of herself for quite a long time.

2

Stella Has to Restrain Herself

For ten days, breaking the treaty of mutual information they had made, Dione M'am said nothing to Stella of this Swedish news. But she sat and thought about it a great deal. Then when she had had a long letter from Dr Bjorkminder in easier English adapted to the feminine intelligence, and when she was quite clear about everything she meant to do, she telephoned Stella at the College to meet her at Uncle Robert's house, and she went down to Cambridge through a snowstorm that delayed the train. The great man was out skating; she had just caught Stella in time to prevent her joining him.

Stella appeared in a state of vivid interrogation. "Well?" she said, after they had kissed. "Is there something?"

"Something to tell you. Yes, Something not too dreadful, Stella. If you come to think of it. No. But not – not happy. Our Jimmy is alive."

"How do you know that?"

"I knew it ten days ago."

"You knew it ten days ago! And you never told me! You promised – "

"He is very ill."

"All the more reason I should know. I want to go to him. Ten days! Ten precious days! Where is he? But why, why didn't you tell me at once? Ten days ago!"

"Let me tell you first, dear, how things are. Then I think you will understand. He is in Sweden. He is in hospital there. He is – Listen. He has been hurt and it has affected his mind. He doesn't know anyone. No one at all. He has turned against life and everything. The clinic people ask us to send no one. They say they do not want him disturbed. I am going over alone, and even I may not see him. But I have to see about him. I have written to them and got a long report from – from the institution. But I think I ought to go over and see the institution. Everything perhaps is not quite right. One never knows. Mr Twain thinks everything must be all right because the fees are so high and the man who runs it is quite well known. I am not so sure. I want to see."

She stopped at that and sat still.

"But I want to see, too."

"I understand that, I have thought that all over. That is why I have made this delay. From what they tell me, you had better not go – yet... You see he doesn't know anybody. And his poor ideas are all upside down."

"But can't I nurse him?"

"It's so natural to say that. I knew you would say that. And I don't think you can. I have thought it all over...

"I believe I've never done so much hard puzzling-out of things in my life. For years now I seem to have been lazy... Now somehow I feel I must look at reality much straighter than I did...

"I thought even of going without telling you, but I knew you would never forgive me that. But I *must* go without you. I don't know what will happen exactly, but I think I shall bring him back to England. And then perhaps – "

"But Dione M'am!" cried Stella, using that familiar name for the first time, "don't you see I cannot endure this? Don't you see? He's my man."

Mrs Twain sat prim and still weighing every word she used. "I suppose," she said, "I *am* distressing you. It's because it is so difficult to say things. Especially if one is not quite clear about them oneself. I wish I was clever. I think I ought to tell you... His poor ideas are all upside down, I said. Among other things, dear, he has taken a violent dislike to you. They often do. I have asked several people and read books about it. It is really nothing, but it is just the phase he is in. It means nothing."

"But if I went to him!"

"I've been asking about that and other things, for all these days. I wanted to be quite sure. You must not go near him on any account. You've got to stand back, Stella. A time may come... It will certainly come..."

She went into one of those calm silences of hers in which she collected her thoughts. When she had them arranged, she spoke again.

"All these scientific people and psychologists, they know so little about men and women. Just bits – and prejudices. There've been too many men at it and not enough women. It is naturally a woman's subject. It's such a pity. Women observe so well and write it down so badly. They come at once to practical conclusions and throw away and forget all the stages, rapid stages they are, by which they got to those conclusions. So that they don't seem to think at all, and men talk of their intuitions, half envy, yes, but half contempt.

"Well; I don't think, Stella, it *is* your business to nurse him. I don't think a man should ever know that a woman he loves has seen him at a disadvantage. Of course we all see them at a disadvantage, but they ought not to know that. I think it turns him against her. Men, Stella dear, are irrational creatures. They are entirely dependent upon us for a certain reassurance. You know I am what is called a passionless woman. I really cannot imagine what it can be to be a passionate woman. I know one ought to take everything God has made calmly and intelligently, but I must confess the phrase 'passionate woman' *disgusts* me. Happily my reputation as a respectable – as a Puritanical woman makes them behave decently when I am about…

"Well, you have to realise, Stella, that almost every man in the world finds it necessary to believe that he is beyond all comparison warm and wonderful, in fact incomparable as a lover, that there never has been and cannot be anyone to equal him – if not in the eyes of all womankind then at least to the lady on whom he confers the – the privilege. She is understood to be dazzled. She is enslaved. More than one if possible. Some of them, like Casanova and Frank Harris, have written long books about their gifts in this respect. They make the monkeys in the

Zoo seem quite delicate little creatures. They call it virility nowadays. But probably you read more books than I do. These modern young men! You never know what you *won't* find on the next page. They really ought to be book-trained just as cats are house-trained... What I want to say – I do so wish I could arrange my thoughts better – is that with men this is not just an obsession which a man may or may not have. It is part of their peculiar make-up. They want to be convinced that they are gifted and uncommon – in this respect. In the Middle Ages it – it affected their costume. When they get that reassurance, then they can go about their business and look the world in the face. Otherwise they suffer a sort of gnawing humiliation. It demoralises them, they get restless, spiteful, unbalanced. All the rest of their make-up seems to be saner and better-brained than ours... I'm afraid I'm rather running on, Stella?"

Stella answered a little doubtfully. "You know very little about Gemini and me. Really you don't. But go on, Dione M'am."

"Yes, let me finish what I set out to say. I have always been an unapproachable woman. No one has ever made the faintest suggestion that I should – what is the word? – *betray* William – except one or two men who had had too much to drink. Then it amounted to nothing more than foot and knee pressure under the table, or following one about the room with a desirous stare, or breathing one's Christian name, flavoured with alcohol, very close to one's face."

"Slugs and snails and puppy dogs' tails.

"And that's what little boys are made of," quoted Stella.

"No. What I have tried to say isn't that. A woman is the custodian of this peculiar and special pride – which is necessary to a man's full existence. And that is why he doesn't want her to pet him or nurse him. Particularly a young man, who is at his best when he is full of pride and illusions about himself, doesn't want that. Stella, if you go now and nurse him and mother him and see him ugly, feeble, unshaved perhaps – if you witness all those endless things that humiliate a man who is seriously ill... He'll be grateful to you, Stella dear. Very, *very* grateful. When he knows about it afterwards. And as soon as he gets well and strong again he will look round instinctively – he won't be able to help himself – for someone who doesn't know so much about him, who will be able to say 'You're *wonderful*' to him..."

"Gemini," said Stella, in a tone of denial that got no further.

"And particularly as he is," said the wise woman, and was silent, having said her say.

Stella stared in front of her.

"My Gemini," she said. "My poor Gemini."

"Will you do as I ask you?"

"I'll do anything or nothing, whatever is best for us. You see I love him, Dione M'am. *Real* love."

"*I* love him," said Dione M'am. "I suppose there is nothing in the world I love a tenth as much as I do him. But I want him to be happy, I don't want to monopolise him – "

"Nor do I – " began Stella, and stopped.

"True love," speculated Dione M'am, "gives and gives and it never even looks to see what it gets in return except to be sure of the giving. And that is all I know about it. But then you see, as I have said before, I am a passionless woman. It seems to me at any rate, that for men and women love means something absolutely different... How can I know? I've never wanted anyone in the world to say 'You're wonderful' to me. I am quite sure I shouldn't like it. At the best it would be an impertinence. It would affect me almost like being pawed about. Maybe this 'You're wonderful' business is the quintessence of" – she always hesitated with a faint distaste at the word – "*passion*, for men and women alike. But outside passion, we women can and often do love, really love, and we do it in a way no man can ever do.

"But these are things, Stella, very hard to talk about – even to you..."

3

What was Left of Gemini

In the clinic of Dr Olaf Bjorkminder Gemini lay inert, recognising no one, answering no one, a Gemini so withdrawn from life that he seemed to want neither to live nor die. He was curved up, she thought, like an embryo, and the most she saw was a scrub of hair and a very red ear. He had paid not the slightest attention to her entrance nor to her voice when she said his name. "Jimmy, I've come to see you."

Dione M'am stood by his bedside, unweeping and pensive. It had never occurred to her before how widely the cult of Christ Scientist swerves away from the problems of mental disorder. She had brought a book with her to read in the place, a book that had once come to her as a revelation. She had never re-read it since. But she had read thousands of other books in between and changed her knowledge and standards so that now this *Science and Health, with a Key to the Scriptures*, which had stayed and grown in her mind as a symbol of emancipation, revealed itself as a volume of pretentious gabble. It had nothing to say about a troubled mind that was in the least helpful in the case of Jimmy. It seemed to be written entirely for the edification of prosperous middle-class people suffering from greed, sedentary habits and those intimations of mortality that come in the fifties. It related a series of triumphs over dyspepsia, flatulence, the drink crave, the tobacco crave and so forth. Why had she ever accepted it as a great release? High over the North Sea she had asked herself that question.

She remembered dimly that her husband had picked it up in the hall in those remote days when one still got books from Mudie's, and how he had jeered at it. With malice as though he scented antagonism. That had counted in its favour. And involved with that was something more, the precious suggestion that the reality of one's feelings could be denied and driven away from one. That had mattered a lot more.

Anyhow it was no sort of use to her here and now. All the Christian Science in the world could not touch the hard reality of Jimmy's inert body and inaccessible mind.

Dr Olaf Bjorkminder hovered about behind her and she wished he wouldn't. He would not go out of the room. She wanted to tackle this problem for herself, and he seemed to her chiefly occupied in pronouncing incantations to distract her mind. She walked round the bed, turned back the bed-clothes to expose her son's face. "Jimmy!" she demanded, "don't you know me?"

"Ssh Ssh!" said the doctor, making disregarded gestures of disapproval.

Jimmy seemed to shrink from her and attempt to retract himself into the bed-clothes. He never opened his eyes. All the light and life had gone out of his countenance, it had become a shrunken replica of his father's at its worst, mulish and grimly bitter. "What's the *good* of her?" he muttered.

The doctor tugged at Dione's arm.

She bent down to listen. "What's the good of anything?" said Gemini, and lapsed into an obstinate silence.

"Jimmy dear," she whispered.

"Is this my patient?" asked Dr Olaf Bjorkminder. "Or is it yours?"

Mrs Twain raised her eyebrows slightly. But the great psychotherapeutist was no reader of eyebrows.

"I do not think you grasp the elementary idea of our method," he said, holding the door open for her.

"I'll do what I can, Dr Bjorkminder," she said, very meekly.

4

The Psychoanalysis of Dr Olaf Bjorkminder

Uncle Robert turned over a letter he had received from Mrs Twain. He was trying to construct a picture of the writer of this delicate unfaltering calligraphy which went on without acceleration, enlargement or any sign of fatigue, to its clear and self-conscious signature. It was acutely self-conscious. Inaggressive but self-conscious, with a needle-like stiletto pointing defensively towards you. And at times she underlined. He wished she didn't underline. It's a way of poking words into your face. He didn't like having words poked into his face.

He knew this lady had been in his house talking to Stella, and he knew of her journey to Sweden, but he had never seen her. "A sort of primness" was as far as he got.

She was remarkably clear-headed in discussing a very difficult matter, and she never betrayed the slightest emotional undercurrent. She was writing about her shattered only son and what was being done and could be done to him, and yet her shrewd comments had at times a levity, a gleam of amusement. "I approve of you highly," he said to the letter, "but I am not at all sure that I like you, Mrs Twain. But I give you full marks on the question of Dr Olaf and generally. You've sized up the old humbug. I couldn't have done it better myself."

She had introduced herself briefly. She said she had read most of his books and lately she had been re-reading them. She liked reading them, and she had a feeling of agreement and friendly confidence in him. She liked his humour and the flavour of his wit. She used to read them for pleasure, but lately all these things that were happening, the war, Stella and her son's disappearance, had seemed to wake her up from "that kind of looking-on" at life.

She told compactly her disillusionment at re-reading the gospel of Mrs Eddy and how she woke up to the fact that Christian Science was a mere device for detachment "<u>from the stresses of reality</u>. For years I have been nothing more than an intelligent looker-on, even at myself." Nothing had seemed to concern her, and now everything seemed to concern her, and she wanted to understand – particularly she wanted to understand the trouble in Jimmy's mind. Books had become absolutely different. She wasn't a reader any more; she was a learner. "It has never occurred to me before, but literature is about life. It is addressed to you personally. So all good books ought to leave you different about life. Queer not to have observed that. Queer that the sort of people I have lived among never realise that."

For nearly a fortnight she had been trying to understand the realities of Jimmy's case, and she found herself lost yet still interested in a huge, tedious literature of psychoanalysis. "I've read everything in English and French I can find in the clinic's library. From the masters downward. Government reports on shell-shock cases and so forth. Such a lot of it is so true and illuminating and such a lot of this psychoanalysis seems to be pure assumption – presumption – imposture. I don't know what to do, and the only possible person I can think of to tell me, advise me anyhow, about what they are doing to my Jimmy, what has to be done to him and how I can set about it, is you.

"You can tell me books to read. You can tell me so much more than that."

And then abruptly she launched into a description of Dr Bjorkminder.

"I think the best way to put it all before you is to describe this gentleman. He is large and blond, his hair is untidy and the collar of his blue shirt gets into trouble every morning when he ties his tie; he weighs, I should think, about two or three stone more than he ought to do, and it affects his breathing. It affects his poise. Most of the additional matter is in front, so that he has to lean back from it to balance it. He is a fine large 'blond beast' of a man who might easily become overwhelming. I should be terrified if he really shouted, because allowing for everything else there must still be enormous resonating spaces in that big head of his. Nevertheless he <u>does</u> lean back. His English is rather clumsy and, after he has made an explanation and I ask questions about it, he shows signs of losing his temper. But no more than involuntary signs. He is evidently far too anxious to keep Jimmy in his clutches – clutches – you begin to see how I feel towards him – and annex me, to risk a storm.

"It is not easy to estimate his intelligence because of the language difficulty, but the impression he gives me is that he is what one calls a <u>highly</u> intelligent man of the type that learns, remembers, passes examinations and gets trained. Without a bubble of resistance."

There was a gap in the writing as though Mrs Twain had sat back to think a long time.

"He is always saying," she resumed, " 'Tell me all your thoughts. All you have to do is to let your thoughts flow unrestrainedly. Then we could begin something'. Coming from him such a suggestion seems indecent to the last degree. But that is precisely what I want to do to you. It is like bringing an exercise to you for correction. I want to run on and let you know exactly what I make of this business. I may be all wrong.

"I see it like this.

"In the first place am I right in believing that all this psychoanalysis grew out of the treatment of mental cases by hypnotism and that sort of thing? They seem to be always referring back to the Salpêtrière in Paris – "

"OK," said Uncle Robert. "You sit up and take notice when you read, Madam."

"Then along came Dr Freud in Vienna, and he was one of those people who have genius and see things quite plainly that other people cannot see at all, and he jumped at the idea of a great underworld in our brains, the subconscious, and invented a new <u>technique</u> of getting down into it and experimenting in it. He was taking patients and helping and curing many of them of their mental twists and tangles, but the much more important thing to him was <u>what he learnt</u>. He was essentially a man of science. His practice was his laboratory. Am I right in that? He produced a crop of disciples who all call him Master and fall away from him. Is it blasphemy to think that his technique of exploration was something as great as the idea of gravitation or evolution, the beginning of a new age for his science, a new birth, and also to think his methods of application in practice were not nearly so good? Is it right to suggest they were <u>premature</u>? Is all this reasonable?"

"You know that as a well as I do," said Uncle Robert.

"There was evidently much competitiveness among these psychoanalysts. Those disciples were irritatingly disposed to go one better, or to claim to go one better, than the Master, and to advertise the fact. After all, for a lot of young men this new mental therapy seemed to promise a lucrative profession and I should think for many of them a gratifying one.

"You see how I come round to Dr Bjorkminder and stab him in the back. In the course of his attempts to violate my personality and induce me to tell him <u>everything</u> about myself, he has let me know most of the essential facts about himself. He began to be psychoanalysed as a medical student, and he tells me he has been done over twice since. He is an addict even if he is not an adept. What difference it has made to him I cannot discover. If he had a twin brother in manganese or oil or something unpsychic of that sort, it might be possible to judge. But he appears to have been an only child.

"To come now to his treatment and what he is doing and what he says he is doing to my Jimmy. Apparently he has to gain his confidence and acquire an ascendancy over him. He has to become a sort of Father-God to him. So far Jimmy has given no sign of accepting him as a Father-God. Rather on the contrary. Even as a little boy Jimmy was reluctant about the Deity – any Deity. However, Dr Bjorkminder is a man of great perseverance, especially when no expense is to be spared. When that ascendancy is attained, then apparently there is to be a lot of questioning and answering which will lead to the discovery of an Oedipus complex.

"You must know more than I do about that, and about its little under-nourished sister, the Electra complex. I am afraid that my reading in the past has been rather discursive, and all I knew about Oedipus before I began to look things up, was Shelley's *Swellfoot the Tyrant*, which was an unkindness to George the Fourth's gout. I ought to have read the translations of Gilbert Murray but I never did. Those popular Greek dramatists wrote what everybody nowadays says are masterpieces, the wrote in Greek, which is cleverer than any living poet can do, and who am I to judge? — plays all about gloomy misunderstandings, accidental innocent breakings of taboo, particularly some <u>incest</u> taboo, parricide, matricide and at last really <u>terrific</u> killings, Sin, Fate and Blood. That sort of thing seems to have appealed strongly to a kind of boyish streak in the Athenian mind. 'Sadistic' is the word. They liked their drama, if I may use such words, <u>bloody awful</u>. There was a time when he was about thirteen or fourteen — I used to call it the Red Indian stage — when my Jimmy would have loved that sort of thing. And the Fat Boy in Pickwick was a case. Why not a Fat Boy complex?

"Freud seems to have found a key to the puerile imagination in all this stuff. So far as I can put things together, he began by quoting it for purposes of illustration, and then he built upon it and built it, until he built it right into his theories. But what does it amount to? Boys feel they own their mothers, and when they become aware of sex, they are naturally apt to think of women first as rather large and over-developed physically, manifestly women, round women, motherly women, and not girls. That is all the mother complex amounts to. 'Not mamma, mammae' is what the young male has in mind. Girls think of adult men as persuasive and masterful and a pleasant relief from the pinching, hostile little boy they meet. That is all I can find in the father complex. Forty loves eighteen and vice versa. What do you think? Anyhow here we have, in the person of Dr Bjorkminder, the Oedipus complex (with little sister Electra singing seconds) as the key to all human behaviour. <u>All</u>, he says. I have asked him twice, because I could not believe at first that anyone could be so silly. Hitler, for instance, is a man who has 'failed to deal satisfactorily with his Oedipus complex.' But you know all about that sort of thing.

"And the object of his treatment, he says, is to get down to the Oedipus complex in Jimmy – in other words to discover an incorrectly repressed incestuous passion between him and me. He is to be questioned and badgered about whether there is any antagonism between myself and my husband, whether he has ever taken sides between us in any domestic difference, and if possible I am to questioned and badgered about whether I preferred my father to my husband and so on. All these are things that <u>verge upon reality</u>, and none of them have the least touch of the obscenity and profundity that Dr Bjorkminder wants to thrust upon them.

"And then at last when our guilty secret is laid bare, what then? That I cannot discover. Something is going to be dealt with and dispelled. But what and how?

"It makes Dr Bjorkminder uncomfortable if I ask. It spoils the game. But you see what lies before Jimmy if he stays in this place. He is being bored profoundly. He is being badgered to agree to something outside sense and decency. He is being tired and worried and he is <u>getting cross</u>. He is putting up a grand resistance. And he is taking just a little notice of me now in a grumpy way. Particularly on the rare occasions when the doctor is out of the room. He feels we are allies so far as he goes. 'I don't listen to that Nazi,' he said one day quite distinctly. 'I don't listen to a single word he says.' If things go on, I am afraid that something will click over in him and he will get out of bed and assault the doctor.

"I wouldn't mind that so much if I thought that he was in proper condition to carry it off. But I doubt if the poor boy weighs as much as eight stone now, and he used to be ten, over ten. What Dr Bjorkminder weights I cannot imagine. But if he should <u>throw</u> himself on Jimmy. Jimmy would have no chance.

"I am writing you all this, Dr Kentlake as <u>brightly</u> as possible. I am not trying to do so. I have never learnt any other way of writing. In reality I am profoundly distressed. Jimmy is being worried and wearied and I do not know what is to be done about it. He wants something quite different. He wants rest. Before anything else he wants rests. Nowadays I know it is getting less and less easy to find rest. The breakdown pursues us everywhere. But in England somewhere, somehow. In some <u>pretty</u> place as spring comes on. Just for a time. But I want your approval that he should be brought over, and I want your moral support – I have to ask this – with his father. That is everything I have to say. I ask your help, but I feel quite sure I shall get it, or else I should not have written."

"You'll get what you want," said Dr Kentlake, and reflected.

"And incidentally," he added, "anyone but a trained psychologist wouldn't have much trouble in realising what is the matter with you, my dear lady. *Dear lady!* You see how one slips almost unconsciously into the manner of an elderly actor in the green-room when one talks to you."

He reflected for a time upon the Real Truth about Dione M'am, and then he went to his writing-desk to compile the necessary letter of release.

Book Four

Trumpet Before the Dawn

Chapter One

Psychosynthesis of Gemini

Window on Tranquillity

One sunlit day in early March, Gemini became aware of himself in an extremely comfortable bed in an extremely comfortable room. The broad window was closed, but it was so brightly clean that it might have been open for any diminution it made in the clear tranquil lucidity of the grey gable and the budding grape-vine spread out upon it, outside. Some rascal sparrows were rustling among the stringy branches, and a very delicate sprig of ivy reached out beyond the window frame. He lay for a time observing these things in complete contentment.

He moved his left arm. Then he remembered dimly that that arm could not be moved. It was paralysed. It resumed its old position and he could no longer move it.

Slowly his mind became clouded. Something had happened. Something was going to happen. There was an argument; there was a struggle going on. He had to be prepared. He turned over and drew up his legs and clenched his fists. The sunshine, the ample comfort of the room vanished from his consciousness.

Someone had come in. One of them. One of those people who were trying to put over a lie upon him, who were trying to stand him up again for no good at all, for another overthrow from this malignant, pitiless, hideous universe that had already proved itself too much for him altogether. All his retractions and resistances intensified. One of those people had come in. Presently something would be said. Or they would begin carrying him about somewhere. Lately there had been a lot of carrying about. Airships and sailors and that railway train. Higgledy-piggledy events. All these disturbances were, he knew, attempts to get him to react. Whatever they said or whatever they did, he wouldn't lift a finger...

He couldn't move his arm anyhow. That was paralysed beyond hope...

He had never moved it...

Then nothing began to happen. Nothing began to happen with a quite positive emphasis. Someone had come into the room, and now there was such a stillness... Yet it was a fact that there was someone in the room...

It couldn't be that damned old Nazi come back. That would be too bad. But *he* had evaporated ages ago... Probably he had never been anything more than a delusion...

Gradually, without letting himself know what was happening, and quite noiselessly, Gemini's eye opened and his range of vision got itself over the edge of the bed-clothes.

He had been quite right. There *was* somebody there.

But this individual was not taking the slightest notice of Germini. And he was a complete stranger. He was standing with his back to the bed and staring out of the window. With his nose, as far as could be seen and inferred, a *large* nose, in the air. And presently he spoke aloud.

"*Alauda?*" he said. "*Alauda* won't do. What the devil do they call a sparrow? I shall forget my own name next."

He spun round on his heel before Gemini had time to do more than harden the expression in his eye to a defensive blankness. But this intruder – he was really an intruder – seemed to be entirely indifferent to Gemini. What on earth then was he doing here?

"Go and look it up, I suppose," he said, and went out of the room. Gemini heard the door close behind him.

For a little while Gemini's mind was chiefly occupied by a queer little question. Had this stranger, as he passed, winked ever so faintly at him?

Gemini discovered himself as a slightly indignant neglected mental case. Here he was all crumpled up for defiance with nothing to resist. *Alauda* indeed! *Alauda* was ridiculous. It was the lark. *Alauda* something or other. Of course, *Alauda avensis!* The name for a sparrow was *Passer, Passer domesticus*. Everyone knew that. Everyone. And he had gone to look it up! Let him.

For a time finches, buntings, tits and canaries, growing rapidly more faded and confused, flitted about the world. And with them as they passed into cloudy indistinctness, the clear and precise young naturalist who had dabbled a year or so ago with the idea of a contribution to pre-history based on their distribution, faded out of existence also. When Mrs Twain came with a meal for the patient, there was not a trace of this temporary return of that lucid young man of science to the body over which he had once ruled. That body was an inert lump again, with one arm completely rigid, tenanted by an irrational resentment.

Nevertheless it was not quite the same inert lump it had been in Sweden. She had restrained herself not to note it in any way, but since Gemini had been installed in this back room of Dr Kentlake's looking out so placidly upon Mortimer's high-walled garden with its vine and mulberry tree, he had on two or three occasions betrayed a certain interest in his food.

She had been instructed by the doctor never to show the slightest concern about her son's thoughts or feelings. "Braised onion," she remarked to all whom it might concern; "cheese savoury and apricots. I wonder if the savoury would be better for a little grated parmesan."

The indifferent body seemed indisposed to respond.

He took the braised onion. And then very indistinctly came a word, and that word was "parmesan".

For all her ingrained calm Dione M'am felt like shouting and weeping, for in that word she recognised a long-overlaid streak of individuality. It was the voice of someone she loved very much. Who was still there. It carried her mind back to the days when Gemini was a little boy convalescent in the day nursery and being rather a greedy little pig about his food.

He had always shown a wholesome interest in his food. Somewhere he had been hidden away ever since in this now contracted body, and it was as if he had peeped out and spoken to her, through it, using its lips. But she did not make the slightest attempt to hail that momentary appearance. She knew better now. That would have roused all the new resistances that had captured him and were keeping him under. She slipped away to get the parmesan, which he took without a sign of appreciation, and afterwards she reported this moment of relaxation to the doctor.

Babes in the Darkling Wood

He displayed no excitement. "He's there," he said. "Obviously, he's there. Why tell *me?* Didn't I tell you? And in a little while I will have him back and talking to me. *You* will come later. You're more mixed up with his emotional selves than I am. I'm going to have just a little trouble on one point, and then I shall be talking about all sorts of things with a perfectly sane James Twain, your brilliant son – who will still for a long time shut up like a fist whenever you come near him. As you will see."

"As I shall see," said Mrs Twain.

She knew she would. She had fallen under the spell of Uncle Robert's confident omniscience and she was quite unable to challenge his statements. But something in her own make-up, perhaps it was the Christian Science habit of mind, rebelled against this subjection. She wished she could challenge, she wished she could detract. She wished she could get him expounding and defending his treatment while she pricked him with needles. Towards the end of Dr Bjorkminder's reign she had done a lot of that sort of thing, and found infinite satisfaction in it. But Dr Kentlake didn't argue. He just said things, and he did not so much answer questions as slap them out of existence like a fly-flapper. In secret she invented derogatory names for him; "Old Uncle Nose-up and Knows Everything" for example; names she was acutely ashamed of as soon as she made them. But still she hoped on, hoped she would hit upon something to satisfy the hidden rebellion of her heart.

She made a difficulty one day. "I have been trying to understand," she said, "just how your treatment really differs in the end from psychoanalysis."

He turned his face towards her and looked at her with extreme suspicion over his nose. "Well?" he said.

"In both cases you give the patient a clear picture of what is the matter with him, and then he is supposed to realise that his obsessions *were* obsessions, so that they — they no longer dominate him."

"They only difference between the two treatments," said Uncle Robert, "is that the things told the patient are diametrically opposed. Just that. We wind up in each method by telling the patient exactly what we believe to be the matter with him, and making him conscious of his problem. Then he ought to be able to take control of himself. Only the psychoanalyst tells him wrong, and I tell him right."

"But diametrically opposed?"

"When I say *diametrically* I *mean* diametrically." He paused as if he had said all that needed to be said, and the lecturing habit prevailed over him. He lifted his nose and the discourse flowed. "These psychoanalysts are in the last phase of one of the most fundamental of human errors. It is almost a congenital error — it is one of the vices of the language we speak — like the absurd opposition of matter and spirit. These psychoanalysts believe — as everyone has believed since thinking began — that there is a concrete continuous thing in a human being called the mind or the soul or the psyche or the self. But now all that has been undermined. These psychoanalysts believe, as all the world before them has believed, that in mental disease this simple, originally unified something goes to pieces, as people say. They treat every morbid mental phenomenon as a splitting, a falling away, a deflection. So that this subconscious of theirs is a sort of cellar into which things are dumped by the consciousness, the one way in. All the manias and phobias, all the secondary selves and complexes are thought of — without any further enquiry — as

Babes in the Darkling Wood

stuff of the original self in rebellion. That is how the problems of human conduct and human mental disorder have been treated by priests, teachers and rulers since the beginning of history, up to and including – your friend Olaf. Only now – as anyone who has read my books or followed my lectures must know, cannot help but know, the idea that the mind is not something that can be taken to pieces but something that is being put together, is breaking like a dawn upon the human intelligence. Pavlov, Watson, and so on and so forth, each tugging back the curtains and letting the new light shine a little plainer. It's not anyone in particular who has discovered it, it is growing apparent to us – that that unified soul, that psyche, that individual self, is a basic delusion. A human being is not like a ship with a properly appointed captain more or less in control and a vast tumult of mutineers battened down under hatches. No, he is a ship that has never had a properly commissioned captain nor definite sailing orders at all, and which is constantly open to the attempts of fresh experiences and suggestions, to take control and put the old officers in irons. You can turn every history of a mental case that exists, right round, and it will instantly become simpler, clearer and more controllable. But I am constantly saying this, I am repeatedly making this contrast between the old dying idea of personality as an analysable unity and this new and entirely revolutionary idea..."

He had been running on and suddenly he stopped short.

He stopped short and brought an accusing eye down to his hearer and remained for a terrible second silent.

"By now you know all this as well as I do," he said.

For the first time in her life she found herself afraid of a man she did not dislike and despise. She lied. "I wanted to get everything clear. I thought if I put it as an objection…"

He ceased to scrutinise her. He returned to his normal impersonal manner.

"If you are not very careful you will become an argumentative woman," he said. "It is quite plain to me that you knew perfectly well what the answer to your question would be. Deliberately you made that objection. Why? Everything you said, was said for the sake of self-assertion. At times your character falls short of your intelligence, Mrs Twain."

He paused. "I tell you these things for your own good."

He turned away from her and appeared to forget her. He looked out of the window and then sat down at his writing-desk. After a moment of desperate self-control, she decided to leave the room.

She made her way to her own apartment in a state of outward serenity and inwardly boiling indignation. The housemaid on the landing stepped aside to admire her ladylike calm and return her faint yet friendly smile.

Dione M'am's indignation was entirely with herself. She had given herself away not only to Dr Kentlake but to herself. For a time her self-reproach was so lively that she could think of nothing but her desire to do something to reinstate herself. But the idea of giving her motives and acceptable turn in his mind was like crawling unobserved up the beam of a searchlight. The only thing for a sensible woman, if she might still consider herself a sensible woman, would be to let the incident drop and hope to forget about it. He had said what he had to say and it was unlikely he would recall it. Yet all the same – !

At this point any lady less self-possessed than Mrs Twain would have said "Damn!"

The real business in hand had nothing to do with these trivial and entirely insignificant personal reactions. Which were so annoying simply because they meant nothing at all. She must concentrate upon the outlook for Jimmy and the campaign that lay ahead.

She sat saying over her lesson to herself.

She had no doubt of the validity of Dr Kentlake's ideas. She had learnt his phrases. All the "reaction systems that had constituted" the son she knew were still latent and ready to be reawakened in his brain. But together with them now were these new strands of association, and mostly they were experiences of fear, horror, helplessness and the desolating failure of his hopes and world-outlook, that right up to the moment when the explosion at Flens had knocked away his last resistance, his brain had been struggling most desperately to square with his *persona*, his conception of himself. Then they had defeated that previous self altogether. They were established in control in his brain, and though that control might be wrested from them, never more would they leave it altogether. The old Jimmy might be recalled and put in effective possession of himself again, but they would be waiting to emerge as vivid nightmares, as momentary evil hallucinations, as sudden moods. The reinstated Jimmy had to be informed and trained to deal with that affliction. These rebel streaks in his personality were as much a part of him now, as a buried splinter of shrapnel or his broken foot.

Since the return to England there had been a marked tranquillisation of these invaders. At first she had had to listen to disordered cries; he had sometimes cried out very dreadfully in the night; and also time after time she had crept near and heard the muttering tale of his troubles.

She never succeeded in piecing together a consecutive story of his experiences, but gradually she assembled a sort of framework for them, a frame of bitter disillusionment in his baffled search for a new world. Once he produced a phrase that took her back to Gavin Peters' story of their Polish wanderings. "Stank," he said. "Stinking rags. It stank; it stank and it was alive and someone had stamped on its face."

But most of the other things that obsessed his mind seemed to have come to him after the parting at Riga. He would mutter aloud: "Children in bits, like rabbits torn to pieces and thrown about by a giant lunatic! Good old Providence sitting up aloft!...

"Little...bloody...oozy...bits of human bodies...

"Joints. Choice cuts. Bones I knew the names of. The acromial process; the femur, symphysis pubis. Funny to meet 'em lying about in the street. The blasts seemed to have peeled the flesh off. Omo-sternum, exactly like the joint out of a butcher's shop, and that – that squashed woman. Ugh! that woman, wrong way up. Bah! Who would want to have anything to do with a woman again after that? Love! Just playing about with entrails? Bloody entrails.

"Filthy fraud of a world...

"Planes over! Russian planes. Planes from the Land of Promise setting the proletariat of Finland free and bombing them to hell. Run! Run! Run!...

"Don't go in there. Don't go through that door, I tell you. They got it there yesterday. There they are, all among their silly little furniture. I went in because the little china clock was striking, and there they were, scattered about among the things.

Sewing machine – bought on the instalment system I suppose – and an old lady with bloody grey hair and her mouth open, clawing at it. Father had got his newspaper and slippers nice and comfortable, only his armchair had gone over backwards and his head had splashed off on to the wall and the cigar was sort of gummed on. Funny in a sort of way – like Harry Tate. The children had been tossed about more, and the bits of the table were all mixed up with them. Still something domestic about it all. Not a particularly big bomb. One of Molotov's whiffs of liberation...

"The fighting wasn't so bad. I don't complain of the fighting. Like football on a foul day. You bowled them over. Rat-tat-tat-tat. Over they went. The thing jumped about against your chest...

"It was what the fighting left behind...

"Those still woods... Oh those woods! Silent, silent. That uncertain, drifting flake of snow. The light going. Night. Creeping down with a knife in its teeth. Benighted! Not here! Mustn't get lost among all this. Not lost, for God's sake! Mustn't get lost here. Why did we come this way? They've left me behind. Push on. Never mind your heavy feet. It's a road anyhow. Broken trees, broken machinery, broken weapons, heaps of broken men, hedges and rows of bent and broken men, all muffled up and motionless. Don't let that fellow with his arm out get hold of you. He's only shamming dead. Keep clear of him... What was that? Snow off a branch? Not it... Ya-aa-ah! It wasn't me. I didn't scream... I've heard sounds before, but this, this is hearing stillness. No rats. Hardly a bird. Too cold for them. Heaps of stiffs – the peace of Stalin. Peace that passeth understanding. Keep on, Gemini, keep on... Ugh! what's that?...

"Don't speak too loud! Go by. Get by. *Creep* by.

"Run now! Don't look back. Men ahead. Slow up. Get your wind. No! I didn't hear anyone shouting. I tell you I wasn't shouting. Nothing. I was just running to keep warm...

"Wait until the summer. Finland will be flyland. Happy flies! A flies' world it is. Thousands of flies for every human being. They breed and breed. I'll tell you something. We're just there to feed them and kill each other for them. God's a fly, the Master Fly, the Lord High Bluebottle. Makes his pathway *in* the sky and rides upon the storm. The flies are his Chosen People. Why not? Just as reasonable. Don't be so – so anthropomorphic. The great God Buzz. Beelzebub. Closer to fact. Much closer to fact... Stick to fact... Great is truth – and it stinks... For the Lord High Bluebottle loveth a stink, and the savour of burnt offerings is very agreeable to him...

"What do I care for life? how it goes on or how it goes off? I won't play at it. It bores me. I won't even go to the trouble of ending it. No. Starve myself, you say? You think I'll starve myself? Why? And why not, Dione? If I like food now and then, why should I starve? And if I dislike food, why should I take it?...

"What is the good of Dione trying to argue about it? Why can't she live her own thin dismal life such as it is and leave me alone? She had a baby put upon her, she didn't want it, and now, why can't she leave it alone? She's just as bad as the old man. He and she shoved me into this bloody world and then they both go wanting to live by me and in me and through me and all over me. Parents... Parasites... Crawling flies like the God that made you... Get off my face... Leave me alone, I tell you. Leave me alone..."

2

The Man at the Table

That man had come into the room again.

As usual he had gone to the window and stared out in silence for a time, and then he had begun muttering to himself, He didn't seem to realise there was a patient in the bed. "Better bring the stuff in here," he was saying. Then he went to the door and said to someone outside, "Bring it in. No, not there; sideways to the window." They were carrying something in, a table or something. They were putting it down under that fellow's direction. "Yes," said he, "that's right." Then the others went out of the room and there came a pause...

That man was fiddling about with something...

Apparatus? They weren't going to use apparatus? Electricity? Galvanise him? That would be too much.

The wary eye looked over the sheet again.

"I'll want the book," said the intruder to himself. "Where the devil did I leave that book?"

"What's that thing you've got there?" said Gemini.

"Damn!" said Dr Kentlake. "Don't *you* wake up now for goodness' sake!"

"Who are you!"

"Now I have to talk to *you*," said the doctor in a tone of forced patience. "What is it?"

"I ask who you are? What am I here for? What are you doing to me?"

"Nothing whatever," said the doctor, absent-mindedly drumming on the writing-table with his fingers.

"Then why am *I* here?"

"You had to be stuck somewhere, I suppose. I wish you'd be quiet – just now."

"But this place is some institution – ?"

"It's the visitors' bedroom in a private house in Cambridge. I'm sorry, but I'm very busy this afternoon. Can't you leave me alone for a bit?"

"But who *are* you?"

"This is my house. This is the only quiet room available. They are making a noise out in the front and I want to read over something I have written – "

"I'm a guest?"

"Unfortunately yes. My paying guest. Is that enough?"

"No. Who are you? Just another patient, I suppose. How are they treating you? They leave me alone for *hours*."

The invader chuckled. "If I tell you who I am, will you lie still and let me get on with my work?"

Gemini's eye was suspicious and expectant.

The doctor sat down at the writing-table before him and ceased to regard his interlocutor. "My name is perfectly familiar to you. We've just missed meeting dozen of times. Last summer particularly. I am Dr Robert Kentlake."

Silence from the bed.

"So that's that," said the doctor.

"I won't have anything to do with the little beast. I've done with her. I dislike her – *violently*," said Gemini.

"I suppose you're referring to my niece Stella. Charming terms you use! May I say that I don't care a dam how you feel about her. Possibly she reciprocates your sentiments. I don't care. My business is philosophy. And now will you let me get on with what I have to do?"

BABES IN THE DARKLING WOOD

"Don't you let her come near me."

"I said I was a philosopher, didn't I? Not a pimp. I'm entirely indifferent to whether you two young people get together or keep apart. I don't want to hear about it. What I have to do this afternoon is to prepare a brief discourse upon the views of a certain Cottenham C Bower, a psychologist of whom you have never heard. It is one of a series of ten or twelve on fundamental ideas which have to be embalmed or canned or potted or whatever you like to call it, upon steel gramophone records. As I have never done anything of this sort before, I want to write the stuff down and try it over, before I face the fatal instrument."

"I know all about Cottenham C Bower."

The doctor's eye remained fixed on the cornice. He answered like a man who humours a fool. "And pray when did *you* hear of Cottenham C Bower? You went down from Oxford – it *was* Oxford, wasn't it? – some years before anybody heard of him. And so far as I know Oxford has never heard of him to this day. Suppose now you go to sleep."

"Everybody has heard about Cottenham C Bower and his *Expansion of Sex*. He's not a psychologist; you're wrong about that; he's a biologist – a zoologist or something of that sort – at some Western University. Radnor Smith? That's the name of it. Not Western – Georgia. A biologist. That's how he got his freshness of approach."

Uncle Robert disregarded the correction and continued to talk to the cornice. "So far from everyone knowing about Cotteham C Bower, there are probably not a couple of dozen copies of his highly glazed, thinly printed – masterpiece, in the British Isles. And he writes in a strange home-made jargon that makes him almost as unreadable as Anrep's *Pavlov*."

"And he's worth the trouble."

"I agree. And since you won't go to sleep and will talk, I shall read you over slowly and deliberately the gist at least of this lecture I am proposing to clarify and can for the use of students throughout the world. For some teachers anyhow are beginning to sit up and take notice to that extent. Any criticism you can manage to express with civility I shall be very ready to consider. If you object to this and will go on interrupting, all I can do is to go upstairs to one of the attics, leaving you to that sulky meditation which seem nowadays to be your constitutional habit of mind."

"Sulky meditation," said Gemini, reflecting.

"Sulky meditation," repeated Uncle Robert firmly.

He left that to soak in for three seconds and then began to recite a compact summary of the essential difference between the new psychology and the old. The Gemini who had written long expositions of these matters to Stella, Gemini the young essayist and reviewer, Gemini the King Prig, emerged from the darkness and despair in which he had been hidden so long and listened with intelligent appreciation. Unconsciously his bodily attitude relaxed.

The memoranda went on. Gemini made the remarks of an intelligent equal. He suggested amendments. Dr Kentlake considered them with respect.

For the better part of an hour Uncle Robert kept this resuscitated personality upon the surface, playing it as an angler plays a fish, which is hooked but which is still a long way from being landed. The gaff and net must come later. He broke off abruptly. "I have some notes of various cases of mental trouble upstairs. Very important for purposes of illustration. They're not arranged yet. Maybe you'll like to hear them when I get them into order, this evening or tomorrow."

He sighed, got up and went out of the room, not even looking at his guest, and he left that humped-up body in possession of a very perplexed tenant.

"Where exactly have I been?" Gemini was asking himself. "Evidently I have been ill. I read up all that stuff in a dismal little room near St Pancras. I remember writing about it in a room with a groggy table. I kept putting bits of paper first under one leg and then the other... Some accident? Run over or something? I don't in the least remember."

He could not remember. Presently he dozed off, and as he dozed unpleasant dreams assailed him. He was confronted by Stella Kentlake and she was deriding him because he was impotent. It was in the manner of their old familiar bantering, but now it was shot with contempt and cruelty. She taunted and pressed herself upon him, and he thrust her away from him and struck at her, and her body altered and became a thing of horror. Diabolical monstrosities of slaughter crowded upon him. Yet all this was laced by a faint perception of unreality. He awoke with a sense of effort, he awoke because he wanted to awake, and as he did so every item of that nightmare diminished and vanished, leaving nothing but a pervading aftermath of distress, and his long-matured resolve never to confront Stella with his intolerable shame.

He lay for a time crouched in his familiar pose with his paralysed arm in its old position; yet still aware of himself as that same Gemini Twain who had in the past read and learnt and criticised and reviewed philosophical, psychological and theological books, with such gusto and acuteness. He was aware of himself as that same self, but with a puzzling sense of some of undefined intervening catastrophe. There had been some terrible revelation, some huge humiliation and defeat. He had discovered himself to be delusion. He tried to understand this and the thought weakened and faded in his brain. He sank back again out of sight of himself into a weak delirium...

When Gemini floated up to the surface of consciousness to discover himself once more in that tranquil room, he did not know whether he had been away for ten minutes or a day or a week. A phase of confusion, all illness, had intervened, but none of that was himself. Kentlake was at the window softly whistling something very familiar. It was something of Brahms', one of the symphonies, the one haunted by a memory of the finale of the Chorale. But he hadn't got it quite right. How did it go?...

The doctor ceased to whistle and turned to the writing-table.

"Now to struggle with these case histories," said the doctor. "I had better read it over to you and you must tell me what you think of it."

The young man listened attentively.

The doctor made a correction or so, cleared his throat and began to read.

"At any time," he read, "a brain and body may be invaded by an experience or a group of experience and their associated reactions, so strong, so vivid and alien to what has hitherto prevailed, that they do not mesh with their predecessors, they spin free of them, and for a time they may put these others quite – out of the limelight. What do you think of that phrase? Limelight?"

"Nothing the matter with that," approved Gemini.

BABES IN THE DARKLING WOOD

"Suppose you take the body, the brain, the individual, or whatever you like to call him, and put him into strange and unaccustomed circumstances so that he is only rarely and weakly reminded of those previous groups of reaction-systems in which he has hitherto lived, he may develop a complex network of new associations and responses to rule him, while personality number one recedes into the background more or less completely. You hear people say India or Scotland or University life or the sea *made a new man* of so-and-so. But the old school of priests, moral teachers, criminologists and so on, refused to see it like that, because they were obsessed by the idea that individuals began life as integral minds or souls, complete and whole, and that anything of this sort must be a breaking-up of that original unity. Most religions are based on that soul idea. To weaken it, the priests and lawyers think, would undermine moral responsibility. They would call that new man case, a case of schizophrenia, or perhaps, in a milder case, of mere absent-mindedness and wool-gathering, schizothymia – and they would say that there had been a more or less complete splitting of that primary unity. But the real truth of the matter is that there never was anything to split. Something has been added. Schizophrenia is one of those countless question-begging words that confuse human minds. Palestine in AD 33 was really very much nearer the truth when it talked of diabolical possession, though so far as I can see there is no reason whatever to suppose the new complex in control is necessarily any more or less diabolical than the assemblage it supersedes. That, I think, is a fair statement of the modern point of view?"

"Yes," said Gemini, "you put things clearly. Much more clearly than Bower does. But his gibberish may be deliberate.

Some of these American fellows, I think, don't want to bump hard and good against religious persecution, – that can take ugly forms in a land of lynching journalism. So they put it thin and high and technical where only tall people can see it. What you are saying is that instead of starting life with souls, we are putting souls – which never have existed hitherto – we are putting them together…"

"It is very fortunate we are so like-minded," said Uncle Robert. "It is saving us a lot of time. And now I am going to read over to you a case history, which I think brings out these – "

"It will be my own case," said Gemini with a smile.

"Obviously," said Uncle Robert, lowering the Kentlake nose and bringing the phantom Kentlake wink to bear upon him.

"I don't mind," said Gemini, and reflected for a while. "We've got over the ground in marvellous time, because both of us have a preoccupation with the same techniques of thought. We're of the same mental world and in the same subjects. Yes. You're the master and I'm the junior, but that's how we stand. But what I'd like to know, Sir, is this: How would you have set about me if I had been someone entirely different? I mean, suppose I had been a chess player or a footballer or an experiment chemist or a young priest or a stockbroker or a drysalter – whatever a drysalter may be or do?"

"That would have been more roundabout. But fundamentally we psychotherapeutists are always after the same thing, we are always trying to get a clear idea into the mind of the patient of what has happened to him and then leave matters to him. You clear up and disentangle his misconceptions about himself and then hand him back to himself for treatment. As a rule you revive the central interest of his habitual work, and then get him to ask what is the intrusive trouble that is shoving it aside; why he forgets, why he doubts, why he is better sometimes and sometimes worse, why his energy comes and goes. Obviously different people are required to arouse that main interest again. Obviously, the people who have had only a weak main interest in life, give way most easily to this so-called schizophrenia. They don't much matter anyhow.

"But about this getting back to the main interest. Only a consummate ass would have the conceit to think he could mug up a technique so that he would really put himself into intimacy with another man's speciality. More especially any sort of artist; most of them invent a private, self-explanatory jargon of their own. Makes them very hard to get at. For a painter I think I should bring in some irritating art critic, or some nice little handbook of art through the ages, just to startle and infuriate him. Or, I'd get him a congenial pupil.

"A chess-player, now would be easier...

"The young priest, I'd have to attack myself – a frontal attack, and make him defend his religion. Him, I'd have to make a new man of, because evidently psychosynthesis cuts all the ground from beneath the feet of any sort of dogmatic faith. Obviously. But I'd have to begin upon his original beliefs. The treatment of a case depends very largely upon the nature of the intrusive matter. In the case of a mad priest one might possibly have a fundamentally sexual disarrangement. But the Church has its own empirical way with such cases, and there is a lot to be learnt from the Church. Knowing old bird, the Church. It has an entirely different idiom of thought from us moderns in speaking of the same factual realities, and that brings out all sorts of things that an apparently similar way of stating things hides. I've never had a mad priest come my way...

"Come to think of it, here is a whole world of thought about which I know nothing. What is the orthodox theology of madness? Here is an immortal soul and it goes mad. It commits some crime of violence and gets violently killed. What is it comes into court at Judgment Day? And what becomes of it? And again, what of a mental defective incurably addicted to abominable things? I have no idea how the Church handles such problems...

"The stockbroker? It is difficult to put oneself in the place of a man who is given over to arithmetical triumphs and emotions. Possibly he would have an amateurism on the side and one could try to make a real man of him by developing that. But suppose he is just simply a devoted stockbroker... Perhaps a lethal dose of sedative," reflected Uncle Robert.

"You never knew my father?" asked Gemini abruptly.

"I've never had the pleasure."

"It isn't much of a pleasure," said Gemini.

"Is he a stockbroker?"

"No. But he invests with great wariness and cunning, with an occasional lapse into gambling, which almost always goes wrong, I guess, and he never admits his losses. A very secretive man. He lives in a whole world of false values. And he is viciously unpleasant. I have spent a good many hours thinking him over. As himself, and also as an element in me. Somewhere, quite early in his life, he suppressed something, quite possibly a precocious sexual drive. Whatever it was, he forced it under into his secret private life. His marriage must have been an explosion. Like taking a neglected, deformed but powerful dwarf out of a cellar. He decided he had to subdue himself to established values, contemporary established values. He is the deliberate conformist. He does not believe there is a God, but he fears him... Yet I bear him a natural affection. I have a feeling at times. If only I could lift that enormous lid he has pulled down upon himself and just say 'Hello' to something... Perhaps it's gone long ago. Perhaps it shrank to nothing..."

"We're just gossiping," said Uncle Robert, considering the transient animation of the young man's face. "Let us get back to our patient."

3

The Real Truth about Frightfulness and Gemini

"If he can be considered a patient," said Uncle Robert. "But are you? I'm much more disposed to deal with you now as a reasonable man with a kink, something that has got into your make-up and lies in wait to trip you up. A kink – and something else..."

A shade of obstinacy qualified the candour of Gemini's face. "Call it a kink if you will," he said. "But I know I am a permanently damaged man. The more you recall the intelligent interests of my past, the more you intensify my realisation of disillusionment. I have lost something for good and all; my faith in myself... Human beings become too wise, so that at last they can perceive nothing but complete failure. That may be the end of all human wisdom. You mayn't have got there yet. I have. I know too much of the ugly side of life ever to face it again."

"I know enough of what you call the ugly side of life to put it in its place with the rest of things," said Uncle Robert. "These disappointments of yours, which you call disillusionment –

ultimate disillusionment, eh? – are just the discovery by a young animal that the whole world isn't made for it. It finds that each and every toy may break and that there's even a bag of guts in Venus. Most faith and religion is an attempt to run away from that realisation and forget about it. Obviously. It tries to impose an ever-blessed-Virgin upon you who is just solid goodness all through, like marzipan. You don't believe that anyhow. So suppose you go on and through with your disillusionment. Maybe there's more disillusionment ahead for you still, and even this terribly terrible discovery of the cruel and obstinate independence of things isn't ultimate. Maybe you will find, as I have done long ago, that the grim face of reality is no more final than its opening grin."

"You can say that," said Gemini.

"I *am* saying it," said Uncle Robert.

"You can theorise. After all, you've led a very civilised life. You sit in a comfortable study. You seem to have sat in comfortable studies all your life. What do you know at first hand of the things I have been through? – the things that have flattened me out – to this?"

"So you think me a mere amateur of suffering, eh? Nothing bloody about me? How do you know what things have happened to me? I won't plunge into autobiography, because in your mood of inflamed egotism I should bore you extremely. I'm not going to start swapping experiences with you in a sort of game of 'beggar my neighbour'. A man may get deeper into life in a quiet room in Wimpole Street than by running about during the worst of air raids. I will just tell you I know infinitely more about disillusionment that you do, infinitely more. And leave it at that."

"But," began Gemini, stopping short.

"Infinitely more. So don't argue. These horrors you make so much of, this sort of horror, does not as a matter of fact involve any exceptional pain and suffering for anyone but the spectator like yourself. None of those dead you saw ever knew that they were dead. None. They had no time. They were shot in the head or frozen or blown to bits. So they suffered nothing. Those who were injured were stunned to begin with and then generally they found themselves surrounded by attentive helpers, carried in ambulances to hospital wards, bandaged, drugged. Have you ever seen photographs of any of them who didn't look fairly well satisfied with themselves? I put it to you.

"Even the minority who really had agonising damages probably didn't suffer anything like the torments endless people have undergone in bed in peace time. There you are all laid out for pain without distractions. Even in the extremest cases, however, pain comes and goes in waves. Or the mind gives way and stops registering. It's been a problem that has always left inquisitors and high-minded conscientious men of that sort baffled. They're not quite sure when a thing really hurts and goes on hurting. They have the satisfaction of shocking and disfiguring and twisting and degrading their fellow-creatures, it gives them a stupendous sense of power, but they are never sure whether their victims really appreciate it; even writhing and groaning may be a relief. Nature's a careless old harridan, but careless is not merciless... An immoderate dread of pain is part of the equipment of every young animal. Naturally. As you grow older you can grow wiser, and some of us do."

"You will tell me presently that I was the one spoil-sport at a rather jolly party."

"No, but I do tell you that the amount of pain in the world is vastly exaggerated and there is a great difference between things looking horrible and being horrible. Except for the cerebral mammals this is probably an almost painless world. Where there is instant reaction there is no pain. And the time factor only comes in with the deliberating animals. Face up to the real truth of the matter. You saw human beings and bits of human beings quivering, dying, dead, torn to pieces. The point is that that distressed you. It was *you* who got the pain. It was *your* memory which carried off this slow-healing scar. Which is still tormenting you. Those people, even the ones who seemed most vividly alive and hurt were stunned, benumbed, automatic or half-conscious. They were not feeling anything like what you felt, or what by transference you imagined they felt. It was natural and right and proper that you, as an unsophisticated, social animal, should feel pity, indignation and fury at the time. Even the mothers of solitary animals feel like that about their cubs when anyone hurts them. But, get it clear in your mind that those were the emotions that worked you, and that when the crisis was over and you'd done your indignant bit in the mêlée, they had served their purpose. Get that clear."

"I admit a certain plausibility in your argument," said Gemini, doing his best. "It reduces an air-raid almost to a pleasantry."

"It does nothing of the sort. These air-raids you saw were outrages and crimes, *but* they are not revelations of any unsuspected cruelty in the nature of things and that is what you are making them out to be. Everybody must die somewhen and somehow. Dying of cancer when there is no friend handy with the lethal dose, can be infinitely more dreadful... Never mind that... But the real truth of the matter is that a beautiful picture defaced or a lovely building wrecked, something a picture or a building cannot possibly feel at all, can be just as horrifying as any of these living casualties. Just as horrifying. More so. Ask any cultivated person who tells the truth whether he'd rather see Leonardo's Monna Lisa destroyed or half a dozen babies... Well, we won't argue that point. It's a question of degree. The fact remains that what has bowled you over, Twain, is not any foul discovery about the world. No sort of black revelation. You knew it could stink, you knew it could pinch, you knew it could make ugly faces and alarming noises before you were two years old. Like every other sane human being you had established a normal system of disregards for all such unpleasant facts. You had got into that 'it's all right really' state of confidence, without which it would be impossible to go on living. And then you fell into a string of nasty events that was too urgent for those defences. The blows followed too close upon one another. You were tired to death, infected, starved. You were done up and fagged out. Your physical resistances evaporated. And something which had always been lying in wait for you in your make-up – I'm coming to that in a moment – began to say, 'Chuck it, Twain. Throw in your hand'. Already in Finland. And that little concussion is Sweden was just what you wanted to let you out...

"Don't interrupt me! I'm treating you. I'm telling you the real truth about yourself and you have to listen. What you have to realise – you must have read it somewhere and forgotten it – it's a commonplace – is that every impulse to act in a human being and maybe in every animal with a cerebrum, carries with it a countervailing disinclination, just as every visible body casts a shadow. Some people, in many matters, have that countervailing disinclination so strongly developed, that it makes them hesitate and funk and slack, almost habitually. Yes. And you, in matters of action are one of these natural born shirkers and deserters. That's the real truth of your make-up. Generally you've kept up an appearance of being of pretty lively, active young man; after all a young male in the middle twenties is in his heyday; but always, always in your life you have had that disposition tugging at you to leave off and to go and do something else."

"I don't think you do me justice…"

"You do. You know I am telling you the real truth of the matter. You know how as a student you had to force yourself to complete things… Of course you remember. And all this mental trouble of yours, now that that bump at the back of your neck has gone down, is your wilful acceptance of the idea, wilful acceptance, I say, that life is too much for you – and you won't even attempt to face up to it again."

"Life *is* too much for me," said Gemini.

"You have given way. And now you are holding on with both hands to this idea that you need never square up to life again. You are getting better; you have the recuperative power of your youth, but your character…"

"Yes," said Gemini, "my character."

"This impotence of yours you're making such a fuss about is all part of the same thing. It's the symbol and quintessence of the whole thing. You want to make love. Every natural human being wants to make love. But you are afraid to make love because at one and the same time you think you will not be able to do so and also you think that if you are able to do so, your excuse of utter defeat will be taken from you.

"It's all perfectly plain. You would and you won't. That's the essence of neurasthenia. Sex is a primary drive; it's probably heaving about even in that depleted body of yours; but in a cerebral animal sex is never a simple drive. 'I will not' always waits upon 'I would'. As I have just been saying, every cerebral animal sets about love-making with a touch of fear. Every human being demands the stimulus of some sort of beauty, seeks it and won't be happy till it gets it. Even when sex works while you are asleep, it has to conjure up an excitement in a dream... Well, in your case, it happens that, without any immediate reference to the sexual drive, you lost your touch with most of the beauty of life during that hard time you had in Poland and Finland. You feasted on ugly things and uglier interpretations until your sense of beauty was paralysed. You've had ugliness smeared all over your universe. And now, enfeebled and frustrated, you've come down on the defeatist side...

"I know all about your last wobble before you fell over. I see it all. You'd heard a lot about the impotence of soldiers back on leave from the front. It is a sort of hard joke. Of course, they are out of adjustment. They hear about it from others. Very easily it becomes a disabling anxiety..."

Uncle Robert swung round and pointed an accusing finger.

"Of *course!* that's what you did in Stockholm. It's the key to all the things you are ashamed of. You two poor devils! Think of that poor jaded unwilling woman, trying to sell what cannot be sold. Some hungry draggled blonde. Picked up shamefacedly. Hoping to make as little submission as might be and get the nasty business over. And you who had never bought a woman in your life! Ashamed of what you were doing. Grudging her even the caresses you exchanged. Doubtful of her cleanliness. Bah!

Precautions? Eh? What a clumsy lover you must have been anyhow! Not even decent sensuality in it. Not a jest... 'This,' you said to yourself, 'is what I have always suspected of life'. And the courage ran out at the heels of your boots... and that it was beat you, and your little concussion at Flens just hammered it in..."

Gemini listened with detachment.

"Anyhow, I am beaten," he said, with invincible conviction.

4

Russia, Revolution and Reality

Gemini would not budge from his entire and baffling acquiescence in Uncle Robert's indictment.

"All you say," he repeated, "is perfectly true. I am a shirker and I am done for. So why ask me to go on with things?"

He refused flatly to see Stella. "She wouldn't want to see me," and then angrily, "I don't want to see her. Don't you understand? That's all spoilt. Keep her away from me."

Yet, a day or so later, he began talking quite consecutively and with an almost complete scientific detachment about his mental disaster.

"Things keep going on in my head round and round," he said. "I think we are dealing with something a little more complicated and extensive than you, in your desire to bully me back to life, are admitting. What has happened to me, must have happened with variations, to a lot of my generation. We were sceptics and rebels and all that sort of thing because we believed in something. We believed there was something on our side which would ultimately win. We could take liberties, we could strike attitudes, we could do this and that, but in the end things would justify us."

"Mentality of every young animal in the world," said Uncle Robert.

"And a delusion."

"Not completely a delusion. You found out that the odds are not *for* you, but that does not mean they are against you. Don't be *over*-disillusioned. That is what you are now. What one might call the Scheme of Things is absolutely indifferent to you. That may be more humiliating, but it is less tragic."

"But if you've staked everything on one idea?"

"And what has your generation been banking on?"

"It is absurd but it is true. At the back of the thought of all my generation was Soviet Russia. We did think that there something saner, more generous and juster than the outworn, self-deceiving selfishness of capitalism, had established itself. It was something more primitive and fundamental and yet wiser and scientific. We hung on to that. Men had achieved that in Russia and so they could achieve it everywhere. We were ready for any claim or statement that confirmed our faith. It helped us enormously that so much anti-Bolshevik argument, spat with malice and had an ugly face. We endured even the doctrinaire gabble of our simpler comrades. Soviet Russia gave us the background for all our defiances and braveries. Faith in Russia contained our minds and when the container broke – "

"It broke?" said Dr Kentlake.

"Obviously it broke."

"Finland?"

"Finland settled it. For me."

"But even before that, weren't there one or two little things, the trials for example? And the purges?"

"We were rather shaken by the trials. But they didn't break us."

"The Trotsky-Stalin feud? The glorification of Stalin in such a film – did you see it? – as *Lenin in October*. You saw it! So did I. Most illuminating. And various other little things?..."

"We held on. We held on all the more because of the way people rubbed all that in. Until I got to Finland..."

"And then you saw some private homes that had been bombed – just as if it were Warsaw – and you knew the whole world was evil from pole to pole."

"My whole world came to pieces."

"And you were left – you and a lot of your generation – in a state of neurasthenia – not between an old world dying and a new world unable to be born – but worse, between an old world dead and in decay and an abortion also decaying?"

"Yes, that states it."

Dr Kentlake considered his patient for a moment and then placed a chair for himself by the bedside. He stuck his hands deep into his pockets and stared out of the window. "I'd like to talk about that," he said.

"Isn't it true?"

"No."

"Well?"

"For my own part I have never thought of Russia in quite such violent terms as you do. It was never my land of hope and glory and now – I think rather well of it."

"Still?"

"Still. I think the Russian Revolution was almost the only good thing that came out of the '14–'18 war. The League of Nations rotted from the beginning; it claimed credit for a lot of international arrangements that would have done as well or better without it, and it fell down upon every vital issue; but the Soviet régime kept on and did a lot of quite considerable things. After all, it abolished what it called the Capitalist System; it got rid of most of the financial incubus on industry, it abolished most profiteering, it wiped out the great parasitic classes of landowners and rentiers altogether. We still have to do that here. I do not believe that any of that social top-hamper can ever return now to Russia. That is an immense clean-up. No wonder those classes which still dominate us here regard 'Bolshevik' as synonymous with devil. It is all very well to say the Bolsheviks did it clumsily, with a vast unnecessary loss of efficiency and freedom. Perfectly true. They only half-did the job, they cleaned up the site and then they jerry-built some unattractive sheds; but anyhow they half-did it, and we have everything still to do. A sort of mushroom growth of nasty little portfolio officials may have sprung up on the clearing. I don't take that very seriously... Or don't you agree with this? Your shock didn't precipitate you into the Tory Party, did it?"

"You think," began Gemini, interested enough to raise his head. "Still... Perhaps it was a useful clean-up. But that was just the first spurt after Lenin. All that is over. The country is a Czarism again and going back – "

"Not so fast as you think nor so far as you think. It may be necessary for a generation to grow up completely and think a bit before Russia can go on again. It doesn't *like* its official figures."

"Russia doesn't? How do you know?"

"I know. They can criticise in Russia still. They can laugh and mock at the administration. There's far more free speech in Russia than in Germany. They can make funny stories and plays about the régime. You think Stalin is a sort of monster who has killed and devoured the Revolution. I doubt whether you can even say he has betrayed it. Certainly not deliberately."

Gemini smiled, the smile of the controversialist, and Dr Kentlake noted that smile with satisfaction, because it was the first he had got out of his patient.

"You are going to whitewash the ineffable Joseph now, I suppose. Just as the other day you were making out bombing to be a sort of hot snowballing. It's a part of your treatment, I suppose."

"I'm hardly thinking of your treatment. I like arguing with you. I'm quite prepared with a case for the ineffable Joseph. From one source or another I know a good lot about him. Morally I should rank him above Hitler or Chamberlain, who are both viciously self-centred men... Narrow and simply vain..."

"But Joseph," said Gemini, "this *Saint* Joseph."

"Saint Joseph's another story. One Joseph at a time, Twain. The Josephs are a mixed lot. Putting together what we all know with things I happen to know specially, because I'm a curious enquiring sort of man and sometimes I get people to tell me things – particularly when they have something to tell – one can make a quite understandable account of this alleged monster...

"Consider first what his education was and the shape and quality of his framework of ideas. He was some sort of peasant-born Georgian, he still speaks Russian with an accent, and he went through the narrow and special training of a seminarist, until he heard talk of Marxism, and read what came his way about it. What was it came his way? It must have been the hard, doctrinaire stuff of little pamphlets and furtive meetings in one of the very provincial towns. I can find no evidence of any other reading. I ask you – think of all he cannot possibly know! Then, because he had a sort of adventurous boldness, he became an active comrade, he raided and robbed in the cause, outlawed himself, fled, hid. From that time on to the October Revolution he was an incessant worker for the Party. Incessantly, he was doing laborious, detailed things, and never taking out his working ideas to think them over. Again I put it to you – think of all the things that even ordinary well-read people like you and I know almost as a matter of course, about which he must be either completely ignorant or have only the vaguest smattering. Trotsky in his attacks upon him is always sneering at his want of culture. He likes treading out music with a pianola, for example, to the great disdain of the culchad Trotsky. But anyhow you must, before you judge him, try to assess the furniture of his brain. You must try and work it out in hours, and find the maximum he can have given to reading and thought – allowing also for forgetting and misunderstanding."

"This is process you might apply to almost any public leader," said Gemini.

"You might, and you ought to do so," agreed Uncle Robert. "You may ask, 'What can the Pope know of Darwinism and Socialism and social life before he pontificates about them?' It is a perfectly legitimate question. You will find it cannot be very much more than a very few hours of reading. A few score hours at best, and that, mostly in ill-chosen books. You can apply this same analysis by hours to anybody of whom you predicate omniscience, and after you have applied it to a few type cases, if you can still believe in the possibility of an individual, all-wise dictatorship, then I submit you are a mental defective. All human beings today still think in blinkers – narrow because our education is narrow – and until you consider what blinkers this or that individual or this or that group is wearing, you cannot begin to deal with him or it...

"But to return to our Stalin, Twain. My point is that he sees a world entirely different from the world we see. He really sees it in perfect good faith as a struggle between the bourgeoisie and the proletariat and as hardly anything beyond. Both his bourgeoisie and his proletariat are fantasies, but in *his* brain they are solid realities. And he sees the bourgeoisie as incurably base, and the proletariat, the disinherited, embodied very largely in himself and his associates, as good. He sees the governments of all the world outside Russia as wicked and incessantly scheming to attack and destroy the Revolution, *his* Revolution. He sees this with hardly any complications, and I am convinced to this day that he is still as devoted to the Revolution as a good mastiff is devoted to its home. But he has all the traditional self-righteous Marxist intolerance. From its very beginning, Marxism has cultivated narrowness of mind as though it were a supreme virtue, and has made the imputation of evil motives a normal controversial method. Our Joseph never had a chance of escaping that.

"The inner group of Bolsheviks, even in the days when Lenin kept a sort of rule over them, never really discussed or considered, they resisted and indicted. And as soon as Lenin was gone, they flew at each other's throats. Stalin felt himself underbred and so he was almost affectedly simple and rough and proletarian. Trotsky is evidently intolerably conceited, and it is plain from his own evidence that he never missed airing his genteel superiority over his boorish associate. They began to save the Revolution from each other with intensifying hatred. Each saw treason in the other's face. In perfect good faith. They were the chief actors in a brawl of petty irritations, magnified by their own egotisms to the dimensions of the Soviet Union."

"To a certain extent," began Gemini...

"Can you account for the great Trotsky-Stalin feud in any other way?"

"Go on."

"And now let me tell you that while Trotsky is invincibly convinced of his own rightness, Stalin is a modest man, defensively shy, and haunted by a profound self-distrust."

"You romance."

"I know. I happen to know. He had to keep it to himself in that atmosphere of aggressive assertion, and I suppose also that the secretiveness which all dark highlanders, from Scotland to the North-West frontier, seem to possess, sustains that. But all the time he feels the need for confirmation and correction. That is why he was so fantastically disturbed by the death of Gorki, because you see he was in the habit of going off to Gorki, who stood to him in a relation something between what the Americans call a stooge and a father confessor, and talking his views and intentions over with him. At all hours. He *knows* himself to be moody; he *knows* he has phases of irrational violence, and when he had Gorki he could go and talk and see himself reflected. He could be restrained from doing something foolish or cruel..."

"Those wretched doctors were also fantastically upset by the death of Gorki."

"That doesn't touch my explanation. He thought they had murdered Gorki to cripple himself. Pure treason! He gave them a public trail and there was no Gorki to reason with him. They were shot. That's not diabolical, Twain. That's infantile. It's quite common. Thousands of widows here in England would have prosecuted doctors and shot 'em if they had had the power. And since then there has been no restraining influence upon his storms of impulse and his blinkered judgments. He is all-powerful because he distrusts everyone to whom he could delegate authority, and because everyone is afraid of his distrust and his spasmodic forcefulness. So nobody gets near him now who does not flatter him subtly and richly. They have persuaded him that the Russian people need a national hero; they have made the satisfaction of his smouldering vanity into a public duty; the Russians have to be reassured about him, they intimate, even as he has to be reassured about himself. When you have taken all these things into account, then I think you will agree with me that on the whole, according to his lights, this friendless, rather clumsy man in the Kremlin may still be trying to do right. Have I made him human?"

"He bombed civilians and trains of refugees in Finland."

"He probably knew nothing about that. What he saw in his mind was the Imperialism of Germany and Western Europe and the elements of reaction in Scandinavia and Finland, all plotting against his sacred proletariat, ready at any time to drop their present conflict and combine against him. And Finland with its guns commanding the Neva was the appointed spear-head of the attack. So he saw it. And something that Ribbentrop took to Moscow, some anti-Bolshevik idiocy of this foolish government of ours, which we still don't know about, which is still being hushed up, clenched his conviction."

"And after all, what does all this prove?"

"It exposes the fact that while Russia is human, all too human, your crowd of young people began by over-believing in it and refusing to hear any criticism of it, and now most of that bright red youthfulness in you is slumping over on the other side. You have been betrayed, you little dears, and that absolves you from everything. Or else, the last desperate squeal of the residue of the faithful, everything is still beyond cavil in Russia.

"Which brings us back to what we were talking about the other day, the underlying timid evasiveness of the human mind, and particularly of the youthful human mind. All intelligent young people, deep down in their hearts, are scared by life. Naturally. Deep down in your hearts is the profoundest funk of any real World Revolution, which calls for just what you find so difficult; steadfast effort, self-subjugation, balance, co-operation with people different from yourself – people perhaps wounding to your self-love by the difference of their gifts and of their unusual phrasing. Far easier and more congenial to break up what those others do than to do something yourself. Your young communists are the bitterest enemies of Revolution. They have a crazy, subconscious fear of it and will do anything to cripple or prevent it. What is the easiest way out for them? Not to work with anyone who isn't exactly on the Party line. The little fastidious darlings! Far easier to wave a red flag and yell stale party slogans. Far easier for your silly young students, who have found study rather perplexing and heavy-going, to stop studying altogether and shout…"

"Anyhow," said Gemini, "for me and most of us that moral background has collapsed. What is left for us?"

"Life begins every morning," said Uncle Robert. "Grow up a bit and start a new and sounder moral background."

"With our damaged and disillusioned minds."

"With your chastened minds."

"From the ground upward."

"From reality upward."

"You ask too much," said Gemini serenely from his comfortable pillow. "It was effort enough for most of us to get out of this system of ideas here, the ideas of Christian England and the comfortable classes. We thought we had made our getaway. Communism anyhow had an air of something ready, and we didn't realise that most of the comrades would far rather, as you suggest, make an infernal machine (to plant under just anybody) than a clock. Now we know better – after wasting five or seven or ten years out of our lives. Minds do not go on growing incessantly. They settle down." ("Rubbish," interjected Uncle Robert.) "And now you ask us in effect to make a clean sweep in our minds, go back on ourselves, re-examine the words and phrases we use, ransack the facts for what you call the true operating causes, and begin all over again, correcting the mistakes and false starts of the past ten thousand years and reconditioning the world. When it is already dropping to pieces out of its accumulated rottenness. 'Re-make the world.' You really mean it. We – a rally of beaten, half-educated youngsters! How can one face up to so vast an undertaking?"

Dr Kentlake still smiled his exasperating smile at the sunshine outside.

"What else is there to do?" he said.

"Nothing," said Gemini. "One can do nothing."

"Life won't let you. While you are alive."

"I have offered my resignation," said Gemini.

The animation of their argument faded from his face. He ebbed visibly.

"Oh! I'm tired," he said abruptly. "I'm broken. *Damn* life!"

"He rolled over on the bed and turned his face to the wall and lay perfectly still, to convey the completeness of his apathy.

"Tonic," said Dr Kentlake in a sort of memorandum to himself, and reflected for a moment on the chemical nature of the human soul. What had Catholic theology to say to a mortal sin committed by a man who gets inadvertently drunk or drugged? Or to the goodness and kindness of a saint who is indefatigably good and kind merely because his hormones are in order? How ill-read he was in this attractive field! His mind returned to the problem before him. Iron? Strychnine?

"Broken or not," he said, standing up, "you are still alive, Mr Gemini Twain. Like it or not, you'll find out you have to do something about it. Every morning life begins. Tomorrow will come along and say 'Well?' to you, just as though nothing had happened."

Chapter Two

The Killing of Uncle Robert

Death-bed Scene

Just at this turn of affairs, the blind ruthlessness that flows beneath events in this world decreed that Uncle Robert should die. His death came as a devastating surprise to everyone, including himself.

He missed the kerb, stumbled and was immediately knocked down, run over and crushed by a lorry. Just how it happened was completely blotted out of his mind, and he became aware of himself vaguely as a diffused pain and a wooden rigidity, looking at his own bedroom and the face of his particular friend, Dr Hallerton. He stared at him for a moment. "What's up?" he asked.

"This damned black-out," said the doctor.

"Foolery," said Uncle Robert. "Am I badly hurt?"

Hallerton sat down by the bedside. He knew his man. "Yes," he said, "pretty bad."

"We just ask for it, Hallerton. These armlets, this idea of a white hatband, luminous buttons. All this black and white stuff. Flies in the face of the common sense of camouflage. Consider nocturnal animals. Consider the skunk. Consider the badger. Consider the giant panda. Stripes, and blotches of white upon black. Breaks the outline. Obviously. Essence of camouflage – break the outline. Black pedestrians are dim, white pedestrians are plain, but black and white pedestrians vanish. Neither here not there...

"Ought to have thought of that before."

He looked at his friend gravely. "Pretty bad, eh?"

"Pretty bad."

"Like that, you mean?"

"I have never told you a lie yet. It looks like that, Kentlake. We felt you over a bit and did a small relieving operation."

"I suppose – what is it? It's tomorrow?"

"It's the fourth of April. You were knocked down on the night of the second."

"Affairs in order. I think. All in order... Stella?'

"She's downstairs."

"Leave her. Nice kid. If you knew her mother – ! I suppose I'm what you might call crushed. Right across. Queer how little I feet. What sort of car was it?"

"Lorry – loaded with gas cylinders."

"Didn't do things by halves."

"Who?"

"God. I suppose it didn't break my bones or I'd ache more. Spinal column intact. No ribs? Just below that – squash. No definite pain. It's lying as still now as a tiger after a gorge. I feel it breathing. You won't try any more operating, Hallerton?"

"We can't without your permission."

"Shall I give it?"

"Clitterham wants to try his hand. He was here yesterday afternoon."

"Patching things up? I suppose if I lived four and twenty hours, the operation would be successful. That's how these surgeons put it? After that, the patient's strength gives way. Of course he may survive. Miracles occur. I might carry on with all sorts of tubes joined up and an artificial aperture or two. Some months – for the greater glory of Clitterham. Any scientific value in it? Tell me, Hallerton. None. Probably I should stink. I hate stinks. I don't ask you to say anything, Hallerton. We won't have that brilliant operation. You'll see I'm comfortable, won't you? I don't want to have narcotics. Something else. The discomfort is vague and a long way off. Can you hold it there? I'd like to keep a clear brain."

"Nothing particular you want to say?"

"Thank you, to you. And my blessing on Stella. They might come back now."

He dropped off to sleep quite abruptly. The doctor went halfway to the door, returned and sat looking at him. He has thirty years of experience behind him, and still the now imminent change-over of a thinking, responsive human being to a waxen image, perplexed and baffled him. It made no sense for him. A universe of thought and it vanished! Presently Uncle Robert opened his eyes again, reflected for awhile and then spoke.

"I suppose I ought to say some sort of last words. I don't seem able to fix my mind. I think, of course, but then the stuff flows away into something else. I suppose it's these drugs and things you have been putting into me. I think of something in fine Roman letters, very well cut, a sort of self-epitaph – *can* you say self-epitaph? – and then before I can read it, it becomes a vast Roman arch, and then a lot of arches, rows and rows of arches, the Pont de Nîmes, and then it goes off into a perspective of broken aqueducts. There's no sense in that... Phew!... Even if I don't say last words, I suppose I shall be allowed to go when the time comes?"

"I wouldn't worry," said the doctor. "Any time you may get even clearer-headed than you are now. Do you feel pretty comfortable? On the whole?"

"I feel humorous. Though I'm damned if I can see the point of the joke. Euphorbia? Euphoria? – Not myself really – chemicals."

He smiled amiably at the doctor. "My niece," he said suddenly; "Stella. Nothing too good for her."

"She's here whenever you want her."

"Trust Stella. If I think of anything I'll tell her. Bless her."

"I'll come back in the afternoon," said the doctor, and called in Stella and the nurse.

He left Uncle Robert regarding the Real Truth of Things above the bed with a look of disdainful penetration. So he remained for the best part of an hour. Stella sat by the bedside watching him, and the nurse watched them both. Early in the afternoon he sighed profoundly, and turned his face over sideways. The Real Truth of Things, it seemed, interested him no more. It bored him. He looked worn and tired. Presently he began talking to himself. He was evidently thinking of Gemini and Gemini's cure.

"You'll go on all right now," he said. "You've – . Recuperation. Young. But don't do it again, Jimmy. Don't do it again. No. Everyone has a limit..."

He lay still for a long time after that, as though thought had ebbed away from him, and when at length he soliloquised again it was plain he was back at his own problem. The idea of some last word, some summarising epitaph, had returned. Some austerer element in his make-up was putting his *persona* on trial.

"Ought to have done so much more. *Could* have done so much more. So much more. I've insulted people. Estranged them. Ought to have been gentler with their feelings. Never been considerate enough about those *feelings* people have. Never...yet after all; after all, if one's going to complicate things – . Complicate things. I mean complicate things about the real truth... Consider... Consideration... Considering people...

"Not clever enough for that... Couldn't have done it...

"Tha's mere excuse. Won't do. I *liked* letting them know they were fools. Tha's the real truth... I *could* have won people over... Got them to do things...

"I made cockshies of their silly little Gods... Cockshies! Whack! Bad's a bloody missionary..."

Then came something that might have been the ghost of a cough or the shadow of a chuckle, and after that he was silent through another ebbing interval. When he spoke again, he was till engaged upon that private Last Judgment.

"Ind'lence... Arrogance..."

She pretended not to hear this mumbled soliloquy. It had nothing to do with her. It was entirely unaware of her. It died down to a mere murmur, the formless shadow of speech. She thought she saw a tear run to the corner of his mouth, but she felt that was something she ought not to see. Then very clearly he protested: "How was *I* to know?" After which he lay still, very still. So still that presently she went over to him. He was intent upon his own thoughts, quite alive, but profoundly weary and very pinched-looking.

He became faintly articulate once more. She strained her ears. He was speaking drowsily, like a drunken man half asleep. She heard: "'s all ri'... Qui' all ri'. Ob—. Ob_{viously.}"

That was all. Presently he began a peculiar rasping breathing.

"Uncle dear," said Stella, pressing his cooling hand. But he made no answer. The nurse spoke close to her.

"That's just the death rattle. Don't let it distress you. It doesn't hurt him, dear. He's dead. He doesn't know. It's the air dying out of him. He's dead. Don't stay now. It will only distress you."

"Yes, but all the same I want to hold his hand," said Stella.

And she did, with a vague idea of helpfulness and protection, until that harsh breathing ceased altogether.

2

Withered Wreath

When Dione M'am heard the news of Uncle Robert's death, her lips tightened but she betrayed no excess of sorrow. Afterwards she talked about him to Stella. "He despised women," she said. "His intuitions were more like a woman's than a man's, and yet he despised women...

"I don't think he really understood women. Women are only beginning to understand themselves. They have still to find their proper forms of expression. I don't think he realised that..."

It has to be recorded that this clear-headed woman indulged, not once or twice but many times, in reveries of a conclusive éclaircissement with Uncle Robert, that was now for ever impossible. In these reveries she was unusually brilliant. Sometimes he was difficult but never impossible. She won him over; she drew admissions from him. He admitted that she had given him an altogether broader and deeper realisation of the feminine mind.

Schizothymia, the psychoanalysts would have called this sort of dreaming. It faded out as time went on to a gentle regret for him. She bought all the books by him that she did not already possess. She tried to find a satisfactory portrait of him, and she never succeeded. He had always been camera-shy. She was always beginning talks with Stella about him and never getting very far with them.

Chapter Three

Reveille

1940 is Leap Year

Gemini was sitting in a comfortable armchair at the open window that looked out upon King's Parade, the very window from which Uncle Robert had pronounced his indictment of universities to Stella and prophesied their dispersal. And now Gemini was clothed in a dressing-gown and slippers; he was clothed and for most practical purposes in his right mind. He was looking over his morning paper again. He had been reading a book, a very congenial book he found it, Chakhotin's *Rape of the Masses*, and he was questioning whether the appearance of any saving élite in the world was even remotely possible.

He could not believe it. He put down Chakhotin on the little table beside him, and turned over the day's news of the world for any sign of that will and understanding for which Chakhotin was asking. He found nothing but evidences of limited imaginations, universal suspicion and disingenuous impulses. That did not distress him. It seemed indeed to release him from responsibility. A great lassitude had taken possession of him. There was nothing to do done about it. It was deplorable in a way, but interesting.

And soon he would turn his face to the wall for the last time and be out of it altogether. Like putting down a book at bedtime. Kentlake had got out of it – not so badly.

The door opened and Stella came into the room, and stood looking at him.

He turned and discovered her.

This encounter had been hanging over both of them for some time, and yet when they came face to face each of them was tongue-tied. Each of them had changed profoundly since that afternoon in August when they had parted on Tilbury Pier. "Mizpah!" they had said so bravely. Such a long time ago it seemed now. He looked smaller and round-shouldered; his face was thinner and less confident; the hands on his chair were the white hands of an invalid. A wave of pity and tenderness shook her, so that she had to clench her hands to control herself and set her teeth to keep her face steady. And he had not thought of her as a figure in black. He had always thought of her as a challenging little desperado in trousers and a negligible shirt, the embodiment of that élan vital he could no longer face.

He broke the silence. "I've never seen you in black before."

"I feel black," she said. "Your mother is against all mourning. But I loved my uncle. Like that. If I was a straightforward barbarian I should shave my head or cut myself with knives. Anyhow wearing this black – relieves something."

He tried to recall all that he had prepared for this encounter. He forgot the question of mourning. What was it he had to say to her?

"I am sorry you have come down to me," he began.

"Yes?" she waited.

"I had hoped not to see you again."

She nodded. Not trusting herself to speak just then.

"Things are all different."

There eyes met, searched each other for a moment, and then his faltered and turned away.

"That love – "

"Well, that love?"

"Evaporated. You or anyone. I can never love again. All that is over…"

He talked lamely. He had meant to dismiss her much more ignominiously and conclusively. "That's that," he said.

She walked across to the other side of the window and posed herself half-sitting on the corner of Uncle Robert's writing-table. She took a deep breath. "Well," she said: "There's no reason you should talk like a melancholy ass, Gemini! You don't love me. You don't want to see me any more. Very well. You don't. Very well. Very natural. All the same, Gemini." (Don't cry, Stella, don't cry! Don't be a silly fool of a female. Keep your voice steady.) "We've got to talk business, you know. You don't seen to understand you are in *my* house now. And something has to be done about it. I'm afraid I must ask you to go."

"*Go!*" said Gemini. "Where?"

"Is that *my* affair?"

He stared helplessly out of the window.

"There's your father's house in London," she suggested.

He said nothing.

He was visibly dismayed. She felt a twinge of contempt. This wasn't her Gemini, she felt. This was some sort of sub-Gemini. Even in the past she had had glimpses of that sub-Gemini. Her touch of hysteria was over. She had thought this all out beforehand and it was going according to plan.

"You see, Gemini, it's like this. I – well – I love you. I've never failed you in that. But since you don't want it – put it aside. But here I am, suddenly become a very well-off young woman, and you have to consider my good name. I can't very well *keep* an ex-lover in my house simply because he was my uncle's patient, can I? People will talk. What will... Uncle Hubert, for example, think – and say? I'm sure your father too will disapprove..."

"But how can I pack? I can't *stand* the old man."

"You're fastidious, Gemini. Surely your mother can find some nice hospital – some rest establishment – with treatment perhaps."

"I'm not half cured yet." said Gemini.

"No," said Stella. "Evidently."

Pause.

"If things were different," said Stella, "I shouldn't make a bad nurse. I don't see much sense in taking a degree now. This war... I've been training in the hospital here..."

He shook his head firmly.

"I want to suggest something. I said I loved you. I don't want to harp upon it, but I want to say that again. Because you see, to be blunt, Gemini, I know perfectly well how things are with you. No, don't interrupt. It's this. Why shouldn't we go through the form of marriage? I know your dismal little secret and I won't betray you. I won't even nurse you if you'd rather not. I'll vanish upstairs again."

"No. That's too much. I can't do that. It's impossible."

"But you *owe* it to me. You've got to make an honest woman of me. Ask your father. Ask anyone. It's the thing to do. You've compromised me."

"No."

"You can get on with your thinking. You can get on with your writing. You can live in an ivory tower and all that. You will turn a brave face to the world again. No one will suspect. Trust me."

"You don't know what you are proposing, Stella."

"I know what I am doing, Gemini."

"You pity me. You have – a sort of habit of thinking about me. How long will that last? Did you ever read a book by D H Lawrence, *Lady Chatterley's Lover?* A stinking book if you like, but true. That would be our story. Think of the life there is in you."

"Lawrence, as Dione would say, was just a man."

"Yes. But Nature has a drive in her."

"There's no arguing about things that *may* be, Gemini. I understand your fear. Suppose you accept me – this is Leap Year Gemini. Suppose Nature does as you say. Suppose one day you have to divorce me…"

She paused. She looked as keenly at him as a doctor who has just given an injection might look at a patient, and she saw he winced at that.

"In the whole course of our living together have I ever broken a promise to you or told you a lie?"

He agreed with a murmur.

"Now here it is. If you have to divorce me, no one shall ever know, and of all people the other man shall never know or suspect – your real trouble. It shan't come out in court. Have I to promise you that? Am I to swear? Gemini, Gemini! Oh, Gemini! Can you believe I would ever let you down like that?"

She leant against her desk, as self-possessed as ever after one grimace of wretchedness, but now tears were running down her face. She sniffed and smeared them away with the brown back of her hand, and he suddenly remembered that her inability to produce a handkerchief of her own had been a standing joke between them at Mary Clarkson's cottage. It wasn't a joke now. He gave way to pity and mostly it was self-pity. "It's all so damned hard," he admitted dully.

"It's hell for you, my dear," she said, and knew that she had won.

"I am thinking of you," he said belatedly.

She nodded rapidly.

"I care for you – a lot."

She smiled faintly.

"But how did you come to know?"

She was inexpressive.

"But – ?"

"You talked a lot in your delirium – and refusing to see me was – odd…"

"It was Dione M'am who put you up to all this?"

"The things young women know about nowadays would have shocked their grandmothers," said Stella. "We actually begin to understand our business in life before it is too late." She became interested in the state of her fingernails. "I suppose we call it a deal?"

"I don't think I can possibly let you do it."

"Right O," she said, and, restraining an impulse to smack the face of this poor sub-Gemini or shake him until his teeth rattled or embrace him and kiss him and weep all over him, she walked meditatively out of the room. "I shall tell Dione M'am," she said. "She's the only one who will ever share our guiltless secret."

"But I haven't agreed," said Gemini.

The door closed behind her.

"No," said Gemini very firmly to the universe at large, "I cannot sacrifice her whole life... She was made to be loved."

Lady Chatterley's Lover, now how had recalled it, stuck in his mind like a thorn. His mind festered round it. What devil had brought that book to his mind?... That was a thing he could never endure. He'd get a pistol and kill that lout... And her...

"No..."

"I've done it, said Stella to Dione M'am. "It's all right."

2

Spring 1940

Stella married Gemini as she had determined and she married him masterfully in her own fashion. "You are too broken to arrange anything," she said. "You sit at that window and watch the world go by. May be you'll get the energy to write about it presently. Something very simple and beautiful... I'll be proud of my artist husband. High and above the common things of life."

She never touched him. She never came within three yards of him. She seemed to be always dressed in the same black, and he never suspected that she was spending far more upon her dressmaker than was seemly in war time. But he noted that her admirably fitting dress revealed a body a stage nearer womanhood than the girl he had loved the best part of a year since. She was less sun-tanned and her hair was a shade more golden, it looked softer and more under control, though she still restrained it by a fillet of black ribbon. The eyes he avoided were the same dark blue as ever under the broad forehead, but the mouth and chin were firmer. And in the end, he was now convinced, she was bound to deceive him after the fashion of *Lady Chatterley's Lover*, and whenever he thought of that he thought also of the painful and extravagant way in which that prospective interloper – the "lout" was the word he always used in his thoughts – would have to be killed.

"I have found a cottage," she announced, "for our honeymoon. We shall have to have a honeymoon. For appearances' sake. Then we can talk about your plans for work and everything that is happening to the world. We must understand each other about things like that. It's a poor little cottage, but cottages are hard to come by nowadays. I forget the name of the place, but don't you bother. I've got that book by Karl Mannheim you wanted to read and Hamilton Fyfe's *Illusion of National Character*. Mannheim looks rather heavy going."

They were married unobtrusively by the Registrar. To her mother she sent a letter that struck her as sanctimonious even when she wrote it. She explained that Gemini was still too ill for any ceremony. She could not dream of dragging her mother across country from Weston-super-Mare in these uncomfortable times. "When I have nursed him back to health, then I hope we may both come to see you. That will be far better, darling..."

She had Gemini helped into a car to take him to a still unknown destination. He wriggled away from the chauffeur's assisting arm. "I'm not so damned helpless as all this," he said, and plumped down in the car. He was beginning to hate chauffeurs and people of that sort.

She seated herself stiffly beside him, pulling down the arm of the sear between them with a bang.

"Now where are we going?" he asked.

"You will see. I won't have you worried," said Stella.

"This is getting a bit too much for me," said Gemini.

Stella did her best to look as serenely uncommunicative as Dione M'am.

Presently she spoke.

"I think a bride has a certain right to be whimsical on her wedding day. This cottage I have is a surprise for you. Let that be my indulgence. I've bought it."

"Very well," he said. "You carry off things with a high hand, Stella, nowadays."

"I don't mean to. It's my rotten manners. Just nervousness, Gemini. I want this thing to be an absolute success..."

"We are travelling almost due east," he remarked presently, and scrutinised her suspiciously.

"South by east," said Stella.

"Something familiar about this road."

"There's something familiar about all English by-roads, bless them..."

"The station. That church...

"But this is Mary Clarkson's cottage!" he exclaimed.

"No," said Stella. "It's mine. I bought it from Mary. Your Mary. She's in France now, being a little sister to – all sorts of people. I thought you would be quieter and more comfortable in a cottage with which you were familiar. The name of the lady standing on the doorstep and bobbing up and down is – I don't know if you remember – Greedle. She is installed as what is called cook-housekeeper. She was the best I could do in the time."

"Damn it!" said Gemini. "Don't get out first. It's my place to get out first. I won't be helped. What will that old sinner think?"

"Well, Mrs Greedle," said Stella, following Gemini's limping but resolute steps up the path. "What have you got for us?"

"Everything you like, Mrs Twain. Everything you fancy most! You can smell it from here. Irish stchoo. *And* the wine you sent."

Mrs Greedle kissed the points of her fingers ecstatically as she had once seen a French chef do in a film.

"I expected to see you looking ill, Sir," she said to Gemini. "And you're flushed with health. Quite in the pink, as one might say. It's good to see you again after you being lost and all in them foreign parts. And oh! Just a moment, sir. *Not* like that."

"Not like what?"

"Pick your good lady up like a man and lift her over the threshold and kiss her and 'ere's honour, riches, marriage-blessing to you both." A certain rich graciousness in Mrs Greedle's gesture and a transitory hiccup made it plain that for her wedding celebrations had already begun.

"You've got to," prompted Stella, between her teeth. "Sorry."

The ceremony was performed. The young couple found themselves inside their own house, a little startled and short of breath. "Where's his gift of the gab gone?" thought Mrs Greedle. "E *as* been ill after all." Stella went to the window-boxes and created a diversion. "You remembered the geraniums, Mrs Greedle," she said. "You forget nothing. They're better than ever."

"It's a great day for me, my dear. It's a great day. I'd be sorry to forget anything. You'll find I've even made up that bed for you in the dressing-room, as you ordered, though why you should want a bed in the dressing-room – "

Uncle Robert's former chauffeur appeared in the doorway with the bags. "Just show Trimble the rooms, please," said Stella. "And don't let him hit his head on the stairs."

She and Gemini faced each other in profound embarrassment. "I'm sorry," she said. "I ought to have had more sense than to employ that old sinner. She's – *tight*."

"She's tight," agreed Gemini. "I don't remember her ever actually getting tight before."

Pause.

"We might perhaps have a look at the garden or go up the lane a bit. Don't feel ruffled, Gemini. We're bound to feel a little awkward with each other, but things will settle down all right. I thought a cottage you knew so well…"

"And a Stella I know so little…"

They walked out into the garden in silence. An extreme shyness of one another had descended upon them. If anything, that shyness increased as the evening wore on. They might have been two strangers who had never met before, who were visiting the cottage for the first time, because of some story they had read about it long ago. They sat on either side of the open fireplace, in which Mrs Greedle had it a generous fire, for the evenings could still be chilly. At one moment Gemini was explaining about the weather. He talked of a thirty-three-year weather cycle and sunspots and things like that.

"Do you remember how the parson sat in that chair and talked?" he said. "He will be glad to see you wearing a ring that *is* a wedding ring."

"He ought to have married us," said Stella. "I forgot that. Do we go to church on Sunday?"

"Why not?" said Gemini. "I doubt if you'll make a good church worker. But I can pray into my hat with the best of them."

They talked of the irrepressible Balch and what might have happened to him.

("Perhaps ghosts talk like this," thought Stella.)

At length, at enormous length, came bed-time.

Stella lingered in the doorway of his room.

"You see the writing-table I have put for you?" she said.

"I think," said he, "I will read a little before I turn in."

"And so good night, my dear," she said trembling.

He too was trembling. "Our – our wedding night," he said. "I think – "

A tense interval followed.

"In another moment I scream," thought Stella.

"On our wedding night perhaps one kiss…"

"Gemini dear!" and they clasped each other…

"Kiss my throat," she whispered. "Kiss me here as you used to do. Never mind the damned dress. Tear it."

With all their lives before them, they set about their love-making with a sense of guilty haste. They never spoke above a whisper.

Next morning when Mrs Greedle came to do the rooms, she surveyed the torn black dress flung on the undisturbed bed in the little dressing-room with reproachful approval. Stella's valise had been carelessly unpacked quite in the old style. Anything she didn't want thrown just anywhere. "What my lady had that bed made up for," said Mrs Greedle, "is wrop in mystery. Some kind of lover's quarrel... All made up s'morning anyhow and him as chatty as ever. Greedle-Wheedle indeed! And chuck me under the chin if you please. 'More 'am and eggs', says she. As if there wasn't a war on!"

3

Recovery

Gemini did not seem to be in the least aware that anything remarkable had happened to him. Nor did he observe that Stella, instead of being in a black dress, was now wearing blue overalls and a careless white shirt open at the neck. It was just natural she should dress like that. "It was a grand idea of yours to come down here," he said. "It means we can pick things up just where we left off. Do you remember that Stellaria in the lane and how we peeked at old Kalikov's lump of alabaster?"

"We made a sort of symbol of it."

"We did. I wonder. What has he done to it?"

Stella felt a sudden chill.

"I'm afraid, Gemini. I'm afraid. Suppose – suppose it isn't there? Suppose he has made something out of it and taken it away! Don't let's go there yet. Let's come to it gradually."

"A walk round. Round by the fields. Why not go and see the inside of the parish church and then return the parson's call? We've never been inside that church. There may be brasses or a monument or so. And the vicarage. It will be interesting to see the interior of the vicarage. Sham stained glass gummed on the passage windows, I guess, photographs of some cricket eleven or rowing eight, a little blue, red, gold and white Virgin on a bracket and a view of Padua."

"Why Padua?"

"Why not?"

"He'll tell us what has happened down here and what everybody is doing," said Stella. "Shall I go in and put on black?"

"You come as you are," said Gemini. "I don't like your black. All the while you were in black you bullied me. I never want to see you in black again. Extraordinary the effect of that black!"

"It *was* extraordinary," agreed Stella.

"A sort of stand-offishness. I never expected to be afraid of you. And rather hostile."

"It's all different now?"

"Everything is different."

"Every Sunday we shall go to church while we are here and every Sunday I shall wear black. Just to put you back in your place."

"We shall see," said Gemini.

They found the Reverend Morton Richardson in the lush churchyard, and half a dozen sheep were feeding among the tombstones. He was wearing a soutane and a little round skullcap, that emphasised the austere precision of his face. Gemini remembered that he had once thought of him as a "wily ecclesiastic". He had rejected the phrase then, but now, in this costume, it seemed fitter. Wily – but weak. He was carrying a small violet-covered book in his hands, and his lips were moving as though he forced himself to attend to precious rather then congenial words. He looked up with a start. He regarded his approaching visitors with a certain worried dismay, as though he was trying to remember some thing. Stella held up her band with its wedding ring to him. "We're married," she said, "as you wished us to be. In Cambridge, but I wish we could have come here to you."

He took it in slowly. "That's better," he said. "I'm glad of that. Yes, I'm *very* glad of that. I – yes – congratulations. Certainly."

There was no friendliness in his response; his expression was one of fussy vexation rather than recognition. He fumbled to keep a finger to mark his place in his book before he could shake hands. And manifestly, for such forced mechanical reading as he had been doing, as intelligent as a Tibetan praying-wheel, the "place" had to be kept. It would never do to pleat his incantation. He began to talk, not so much to them as at them, a recital of the things he had to deal with and think about.

He had changed profoundly. He had lost flesh. His eyes were slightly bloodshot. He looked rattled. Under the stressed of the war situation his streak of sceptical tolerance had vanished altogether. As he talked, they realised that his never very venturesome mind had bolted back to outright High Anglicanism and to fear and defensive hostility towards anything outside it. To him they came now as a reminder of some vaguely remembered indiscretion, some reprehensible tolerance...

"I'm troubled about these sheep," he said. "Yes, I'm very troubled about these sheep. I don't quite *like* them grazing here. There's some sort of disrespectful rhyme... worms, parson, sheep, mutton – I forget. But what can one do? With this war, all touch and go, the slightest things may make all the difference. Just all the difference. Mutton we must have. More and more it becomes an economic war. More and more. Every day. More *economic*. Wastefulness, dissipation of energy, has always been our English weakness. We have been, I fear, a slack people. Against this terrible German efficiency... We have to save.

"Here we are doing all we can, Mrs Twain. I warn you we shan't spare you if you come to join us. We'll find you something to do. Everybody here is bucking up splendidly. I *will* say that. Splendidly. What can be done is being done. Mrs Smitherton-Bradley, now that her son had gone into the Censorship, is doing wonders with the Boy Scouts, and Miss Ripple of the Post Office has given the Girl Guides absolutely a new life. They collect refuse and sort it; tin cans, paper, scraps of tobacco, everything. Of such are the sinews of war. Little fellows of ten and eleven are working in the fields now – real good useful work, the farmers tell me. They vie with each other. Schools stand empty. Evacuees too join in with zeal. Little town children who a year ago had never seen a ploughed field. A wholesome rest for their poor little noddles. Then there is our little band of night watchers preventing the least leakage of light. When I have insomnia – and I *do* suffer from insomnia, wondering how all this is going to end – I get up and join them. No use wasting wakefulness in bed, I say, no use at all. In this little place alone we have fined six people. We've made this one of the blackest villages in England. We blunder about; Farmer Wildershaw fell into the old horse pond. Nobody minded. He's been in bed ever since. *He* doesn't mind. 'All in a good cause', he said. "If it helps beat them Nastys,' he says, 'I'll sit in the 'ole pond all day.' Seventy-two he is. That's the spirit of it. Everyone is on the *qui vive*; everyone alert. It's a great strain, but we have to do it if we mean to win this dreadful war. Think what those Germans may be doing!

"But there are compensations, Mrs Twain. There are compensations. Yes. A new seriousness. A higher tone. How can we tell that these days of trouble may not prove a blessing in the end? This community, when you visited it a year ago, was in a state of spiritual lassitude. We were all lax. *I* was lax. I admit it. The church three-quarters empty and maybe three or four communicants, mostly elderly people, with nothing else to do. Now I find twenty people or more seeking the comfort of the mass. Even quite young people – among the women. It all adds to my work, but all the same it is a comforting thing. Some even ask for confession – on Anglican lines, of course. Sunday tennis is a thing of the past. No one would presume. Not even ping-pong. Then at Portage House (Mrs Smitherton-Bradley's, you know) they are even restoring the good old custom of family prayers. Every day – all the household, the evacuees, everyone down on their knees, and Mrs Smitherton-Bradley reading in that proud voice of hers. After that, the day isn't quite the same for them. At first there was a little giggling among the maids, I'm told, but Mrs Smitherton-Bradley soon put a stop to that."

"Hasn't something happened to the church tower?" said Gemini. "That black side – ?"

The vicar turned his eyes with a certain reluctance to his desecrated tower.

"That's tar," he said. "Camouflage. That cuts half of it out, you see – or at least it was meant to do that. Our tower here, we discovered, could be used by enemy aircraft as a landmark. It was Mr Chrissy of Cow Point, perhaps you remember him? – he has exhibited at the Royal Academy several times – who thought of that. Insisted. At first his idea was to erect a sham spire, employing that cement stuff they use for cinemas, but that had to be dismissed on account of the expense, and then, after a certain amount of discussion, the council produced some tar. Road tar. You see that thing there in the corner where they boil it. They've left it there. The black was to cut the shape of the old tower – into something unrecognisable. Even as it is – Don't you think? But before it was half done Mr Chrissy fell from a ladder and ricked his back, and we've had to leave it as it is for the present and hope for the best. There was no one to replace him."

As they looked at the poor old tower with a wisp of ivy on its forehead, Stella was reminded extraordinarily of Bill Sykes with a patch over one eye. The vicar turned away, evidently trying to dismiss that degradation from his mind. "Everybody," he said pointedly, "has something to do. It is a totalitarian war. Absolutely totalitarian. All in. No idle hands this time. We *do*."

"By the by," said Gemini hastily, before their dismissal became complete; "wasn't there a great sculptor who lived near our cottage – Kalikov?"

"Kalikov?" meditated the vicar, pretending, out of pure wartime caution, not to know all at once. "Kalikov? Oh! He's interned. Yes, interned."

"Interned!"

"Naturally."

"But he is a Bulgarian! We're not at war with Bulgaria?"

"All the same, it was decided to intern him."

"But I heard he was going to be naturalised as an Englishman!"

"Not in war-time," said the vicar. "Yes, I remember hearing about it from Colonel Gusset. Your friend – well, this Mr Kalikov – made a very poor showing. He lost his temper with the tribunal. He tried to be sarcastic in that German accent of his, and *that* did him no good, you can be sure, with a resolute man like Colonel Gusset."

"But it's *not* a German accent," said Stella.

"It sounded German to the tribunal," said the vicar. "And he was *very* rude. Extremely rude. After all, much of his work, I am told, is far from being – well, in the best possible taste. Un-English essentially. You see – these aliens come here. They take not the slightest trouble to respect our standards of decency or beauty. Our natural amenities. None at all... What can they expect?"

"But to intern him!"

"We can't be too careful. After all, we are less than twenty miles from the coast. And I'm not certain he wasn't more or less of a Jew. All that hair of his."

"But we're not at war with the Jews! And Kalikov isn't a Jewish name."

"There are Jews and Jews, and they take all sorts of names. They are really all alike," said the vicar, and dismissed that increasingly difficult topic. "Anyhow he's interned."

"But what has happened to the things he left behind?"

"Locked up, I suppose..."

"His house, surely you've looked after his house?"

"As well as we can. Some of those East End evacuees may have broken his windows. They are terrible at breaking windows – especially in unoccupied houses. They seem to think it's what windows are for."

"But, Mr Richardson, have you done nothing?"

"My dear young lady, in these days of crisis, we have more serious things to do than to look after the personal effects of a swarm of alien invaders."

Mr and Mrs James Twain regarded each other with raised eyebrows, and it became extremely doubtful whether after all they would attend Church next Sunday. They were turning away.

"Oh! wasn't there a man called Balch?" asked Gemini abruptly.

"Balch?" The vicar was still discreetly evasive, but there was a sudden change in his manner.

"A man with a large face that slanted upward," said Gemini, "and pencils and large fountain pens sticking out of him all over him."

"Yes, he *was* like that. At first. Not so much a slanting face as a large slanting back. He always seemed to be going round corners in a hurry. Away from me. Shy, I suppose. He – he has been something of a surprise to me. No. I think – . I don't think there is any harm in telling you. Between ourselves."

He lowered his voice and looked round to make sure that there was no German agent lurking among the tombs. For a moment he scrutinised one of the sheep rather doubtfully. But it was a sheep all right. It behaved like a sheep there and then. The cleverest German agent could not have done it.

"Mr Balch," he said, still in undertones, "occupies quite an important place, so I understand, in our Ministry of Propaganda. He directs our propaganda in Brazil. Before he went away, I had one or two conversations with him. He would come in to lunch quite unexpectedly and talk things over. Essentially an *enthusiastic* type. Very quick apprehension. I believe I was of some use to him. Everyone must help who can – everyone. Ungrudgingly. Mind or body. Yes... I'm really afraid – you'll have to excuse me now."

"But did Balch know Portuguese?"

"Not a word, so far as I know. But, as he explained to me, almost everybody who *can* speak Brazilian – it is a little different from Portuguese – is apt to be a foreigner or have such foreign associations that – they don't understand what has to be put over. Hopeless!" He agitated the purple-covered book in the air to indicate hopelessness. "You can use them as translators, of course; you can even let them make records under direction; but the real matter we want to tell these neutrals – manifestly you must have a real home-grown English mind for that."

"And what does Balch give them?" asked Gemini.

"Excellent stuff. He has given them – I might almost say *we* have given them – three admirable talks upon Keble's Christian year. Admirable talks. And one on the Heroines of Jane Austen. And a talk about the origin of the Limerick and the Nonsense verse of Edward Lear. That sort of thing gets the real English idea over to these people. As nothing else *could* do. I'm told Lord Halifax thinks very highly of Balch's original drafts. You couldn't have higher praise than that. Brazil was particularly interested in the Pobble. They had articles in the newspapers."

"*Pobble?*" whispered Gemini.

"You know – 'The Pobble who has no Toes'."

"The Brazilians!" said Gemini.

"*Fascinated.* They had never known us before. In San Paulo 'Pobble' has become a byword for Englishman. So Mr Balch tells me. Ah, there *is* Mrs Smitherton-Bradley. You really must excuse me now. So much to see to. So much to correlate. She is probably wanting my advice on some new activity…"

He called after them. "*I'll* find something for you to do."

"*Will* you?" whispered Stella venomously.

"Well," said Gemini, as they walked slowly through the fields, "While I have been a special case for mental treatment, it seems that Old England, generally speaking, has gone nuts. Think of it! Tarring the church tower! The Pobble for Brazilians! Children of ten working in the fields! You can hardly call that man mad, but it's a sort of rapid chittering in the brain. Since I began to sit up and take notice again, it's become more and more manifest how widespread this sort of thing is. There must be scores of thousands now like him. Hundreds of thousands. Insanely set upon being stupid. *The Times*, for instance – completely gaga. This country, under the war strain, is becoming a gaggle of Anglicans. It's a Midsummer Night's Dream John Bull, with a Halifax instead of a head. Is there no other England? England, my England! Are you there? I begin to have a horrible feeling that this time our rulers may contrive to lose this war outright. If so, the end of Old England is going to be – you can't call it a tragedy. It isn't falling, like a tall column, with dignity; it's guttering down like a fat old tallow candle in a draught. Dithering down to doom. The youngsters fight, the sailors, the fishermen, they are all right, they get killed like men, but so far as I can see they are fighting for nothing but what that old fool there in his High Church fancy dress represents.

"Well, what else *are* we fighting for? In this mess of a war? We're just fighting because there is nothing else to do. Which reminds me that I'm not fighting at all. I've got no right to criticise unless I take risk. I'll have to tell you about that. I've an idea – from something I've read. It isn't only the youngsters without spot or blemish who are to carry all the risks. I could probably handle an anti-aircraft gun on a trawler as well as anybody... We'll talk of that later, Stella."

Stella hadn't thought of that. She had counted on Gemini's remaining a neutral. But instantly she understood that in this particular war no man who was a man again, could possibly remain a neutral. What happened to men in trawlers?...

"We'll talk of that later," she agreed.

"When I went back to Cambridge after Tilbury," she began abruptly, "Uncle Robert was very concerned about the education I was getting, and he talked a lot about it and about the Universities and the British mind and what he calls the mind of the world. I remember him lifting his nose up over King's Parade, saying – what did he say? – in effect it was this...

"Now let me see? Stand away, Gemini. I must imitate him. I can't get it unless I imitate him. I'm not mocking."

She stuck her hands into her side pockets and she tried to lift up her nose. It had always been a shapely but unobtrusive feature, nevertheless she did her best to lift it after the manner of her uncle.

"Obviously," she said, like a musician who tunes his instrument, and then she began.

She kept up her impersonation for a while and then relapsed into oratio obliqua. She reproduced in a weaker and compacter form that Jeremiad upon intellectual laziness, evasion and obstinacy with which Uncle Robert had indicted not simply Cambridge but the whole feebly pompous academic world from Upsala to Cape Town and from Tokio to Chicago. Not simply England but the whole world, he had said, was pin-headed. The species had failed mentally. What did it amount to – this World Brain of today? It was, he said, the brain of a mere foetus, incapable of steadying and controlling the great overgrown body of mankind.

"And so, as our securities dissolve away," said Stella, "and reveal themselves – how did he put it? – 'a transitory combination of happy accidents', we find mankind with its wits unorganised, no better than a horde of frightened fools, fanatics and greedy, scheming, criminal men. And then, Gemini, he lamented because he himself had done so little to change all that."

"He said that?" said Gemini.

"He said that. And – how can I put it? While he said it, it sounded true, but I didn't *feel* that it was *really* true. I felt it was just *brilliantly* true. You know! Not *real* like shots being fired at you. But now I begin to realise how daft people are getting everywhere, now that their world begins to shake. The shots are coming at us, real shot and shell hitting things about us and quite likely to hit us…"

"Maybe something worse is happening to us," said Gemini. "Maybe while all the rest of the world has gone mad, we two are going sane."

"Is being cowed, sanity?" said Stella. "I doubt it. One begins to be afraid to say anything for fear of being misunderstood, of doing anything except join in the screams and rushes of the crowd. That's not having a sane, free mind. Can anyone keep sane when the world goes mad?"

"*I* feel sane," said Gemini… "Today – I don't know how it is – down here, I feel as though for the first time for a long while I had cast off something from me and got control of my wits. Perhaps it's just the old memories of the place; the way in which we join on to the things we talked about last year, when we tried to get our ideas in order – before this world delirium overwhelmed us."

Stella looked at him with a mild astonishment. Had he no inking of the last exorcism she had had to perform so skilfully? "Thankless work being a woman," thought Stella.

He stumped along, thinking over his case, reviewing it.

"Go on, Gemini," she said. "Let's hope it's not just a temporary lapse into lucidity."

"I still don't remember all that happened before I got knocked out by that explosion at Flens. I suppose I never shall. I guess there's not a trace now of the original concussion; that bruised lower brain and so on; all that has cleared up long ago. But there is still a black-out in the memory. It left its scars. I know I developed a lot of queer irrational dislikes and phobias…"

He broke off abruptly. "There's the village green ahead. There's the old post office where that ratty little Miss Ripple presides, ratty Miss Ripple, who's put such life and fire into the muck-raking of the Girl Guides. I always used to suspect her of steaming our letters after the post office had shut. She had a huffiness. Perhaps she just saw through us. And there is ye olde English inn where Balch used to play darts before he began to expound 'England, my England,' to the Brazilian mind…

"Let's sit on this stile for a bit. Let's stop here. There's no hurry. Now that Kalikov is interned."

"Yes, let's stop here for a bit," agreed Stella promptly. "If it's there, it will be there."

"Queer," he said.

"It's queer."

He laughed. "You feel it too? That's good. I thought it might be a lit of hang-over from my concussion. I'm afraid – I don't know why I'm afraid to go on to that block of alabaster, but I *am* afraid. Some fear of disappointment?... Well, anyhow the day is young...

"I was saying – what was I saying? – I was saying I still don't know all that happened to me after Warsaw. Very likely I shall never get it clear, or maybe we'll bring it all out later by hypnotism. Uncle Robert might have arranged that if he had lived. He said I may still have dreams... One of the oddest aspects of that phase was the violent dislike I took to you. And to my mother. I suppose it was the impulse of a dog-tired man to get away from everything he had been before. At the price even of scarcely living."

"Yes," said Stella.

"I just hated you. And that was mixed up with a sort of negative obsession by sex."

Stella stuck her hands deep in her side-pockets. "Odd," she said, and assumed an interest in the scenery.

"It was as if some gigantic prohibition had been imposed upon me. I rebelled against it – in a weak sort of way. That's neither here nor there. 'Don't go back to life,' it said. 'It's bitter; it's vile'. No Early Christian Father was ever so obsessed. It was a fear. A shame. A taint of incapacity. That lasted – "

"Yes, Gemini?"

"Oh, to quite recently. But – it's simply *gone*."

Stella overcame a violent impulse to push him backward off the stile. But that sort of thing, she felt, had better come a little later. Now it might receive his concussion. Instead she said: "Got a cigarette on you, Gemini?..."

"I don't know why I was so obsessed by the question of sex," Gemini reflected, when the cigarette was well and duly lit. "After all – it amounts to very little. It's so simple. If you look at it simply."

"Yes," said Stella, wise now with all the wisdom of Dione M'am. "It amounts to very little. It *is* simple."

And to herself she said: "But think what it can amount to, when it amounts to nothing at all."

She made two or three smoke-rings and then said what she had in mind. "You remember, Gemini, how we argued and almost quarrelled about that book, *The Expansion of Sex?* Or have you forgotten? Queer how it irritated me at the time. Sex meant so much to me then.... We had a great time, Gemini."

"*Had!*" reflected Gemini. "Well – ."

"The idea was that in the case of the higher apes and man, sex has overflowed, needlessly, from its primary business of reproduction into the general imagination and will. It's rutting-time all the year round for mankind. 'When gorse is in flower', as the Sussex yokels say. I forget the exact words. Well, what I felt then, when we had that argument, I feel now. I object to the word 'needlessly'. Aren't our moralists a little ungrateful to sex? Hasn't it also been a flow of energy over the whole mental life? It's fighting-time all the year round too for mankind. Don't the two things go together? Don't you think these sexual strands impart a certain vigour? The beasts that have a breeding season go very tame and timid in between... It may be a matter of stimulation rather than sublimation... Maybe some affair of hormones. ...It's just an idea of mine."

Gemini lit a cigarette in his turn and reflected.

"There may be something in that," he said. "I must think it over..."

He was evidently not thinking it over at all. He was thinking of something else. He blew a cloud of smoke.

"And now I think we must face the secret of the lane. What is there to be afraid of? What are we flinching at? Even if the block isn't there. It won't matter – ... Not really... We have been wandering about and talking of ourselves and my concussion and the decadence of England long enough..."

4

The Block Turns Over

It has to be told and it is extremely difficult to tell. Something strange and largely inexplicable happened to these two babes in the wood. It happened. Enormously portentous it was to them, and yet it was no more than a trivial coincidence. There is no accounting for the timing of it, and still less is there any accounting for the real state of apprehension, of dread, which preceded it.

They walked with a deliberate slowness down the old familiar lane. The spring was late. The chickweed had not appeared yet, and the may buds were still flushed with purpose. The lilac was reasonably early and profuse, and the oak leaves were warm with golden promise. There were still some belated heads of elder. All the greenery was more staccato, harder and brighter than they remembered it. And this time these two young people said not a word to one another until they came to the gap in the hedge of yew.

Then, still silent, they clambered up and looked over.

It was there. The grass and weeds about it were thicker and higher, and there were many more nettles, but the block was unchanged, massive, veined and semi-translucent, the block that had begotten Gemini's great idea, their sacred symbol for the purpose in their lives.

"Oh! *Look* at the house," whispered Stella.

Every window had been conscientiously smashed, and a corner of window curtain, caught and held outside on some splinter of glass, flapped feebly against a mullion.

"Little beasts," said Stella.

"Let's climb over this," said Gemini. "Let's see a little nearer. Softly, Stella. Put your foot there."

He clambered over clumsily and helped her as a man should, though she could have popped over without an effort. She let him help her, for still she was not sure of him, and very mindful of the wisdom of Dione M'am.

They stood now, waist-deep in weeds and nettles, close to the block. Hitherto they had only looked down upon it from the oak fence, and it had seemed squat and broad. It towered now six feet above their heads.

And then it was the wonder happened. At first they hardly realised that the block was moving. Then they perceived it was coming towards them. It was approaching them with a steady acceleration. It was coming down upon them. It was pursuing them. Swiftly, relentlessly. The rank herbage was crushed and swept aside by the advancing monster. They started back with gasps of terror. They uttered weak nightmare cries...

With a soft thud, the overturned block was lying at their feet, motionless again. For an immense moment it seemed to them that it was merely pausing for a moment before resuming its advance.

The juicy scent of crushed vegetation rose about them in that tremendous interval.

"It's turned over," said Gemini feebly. "It's fallen over."

"As if it had been waiting for us to come," said Stella. "So that it had to happen exactly now."

"It's turned over," repeated Gemini. "My hand is trembling. Look. I'm not – . My nerves are still not right. Simply because a big stone rolled over. I shall dream of the way it seemed to be coming down upon us. But of course all this is perfectly natural... Something has undermined it... Growth of things under it..."

"Yet why should it have happened exactly now?" asked Stella.

"It had to happen somewhen."

"But *now!*"

"It's still a lovely mass," said Gemini, and obliged himself to lay hands upon it and feel its smooth massiveness. "Feel it, Stella," he said, and she obeyed.

"It is our block more than ever," he said. "It has given itself to us. It has taken possession of us. It has made its appeal. This is our sign. This is our recall... Recall? Let us stay here just a little longer."

"No," said Stella. "Now I want to go."

"I feel I can't leave it."

"It won't move again."

"It will never rest again."

"Somewhen," said Stella abruptly, "we must eat."

She looked at her watch and her voice sharpened. "Do you realise, Gemini, we must eat. It is a quarter to two. I remember we asked Mrs Greedle to do her best for us – at one sharp. The thought of that gives me a feeling like a whiff of distant onions..."

They went through the weeds to the gate of the little orchard upon the lane; they went slowly, and they kept on looking back.

Stella wanted to get away from the block. Gemini wanted to remain. If suddenly it had moved again towards them, they would both have been terrified excessively, but not in the least surprised...

"What's come to them punctual stummiks of yours?" thought Mrs Greedle.

They ate, they had a siesta in each other's arms, they went for a walk in the woods behind the house, but that sign and miracle now dominated their thoughts completely. Theirs were by habit and nature the most sceptical and realist of minds, and yet neither of them doubted in the least that they had been definitely told to get on with an essential duty. All the time they felt that block of alabaster pursuing them with its implacable question of what they meant to do about it. It had been a symbol before; now it was a living obligation. "Even honeymoons have to be rationed," said Stella. "A year ago we were King Prig and Queen Prig deciding just what we meant to do to the world. Now, before you go off to your minesweeping and I go back to my nursing, let us see what we can save out of those magnificent intentions of ours. We promised things to that block and it has taken us at our word."

In the woods up behind the cottage all the felled trees had been cleared away, and they sat and talked to each other, siting on two adjacent stumps and feeling as though even sitting in the woods had now to be measured and kept under control. Much of the moss had been torn and disordered when those trunks had been dragged away. Black mud had been brought to the surface and had caked in hard ridges. Gemini looked round, trying to recall some earlier scene. "The smell of resin," he said.

"I remember," said she. "Yes."

"I have been thinking over something you said – on that stile."

She became attentive.

"Gradually my mind is being restored to me. Gradually, I say. In a rush rather. You asked if sex was a small matter, and I said 'Yes'. I pushed that question aside because still I did not want to face it. But I agree. Sex *is* the quintessence of life. The *go* in life is supplied by sex – somehow. The how and still more the why is another matter. The method of its intervention is enormously – infinitely variable. It isn't logical and necessary by any *a priori* standards, but either through suppression or sublimation or elaboration or straight, clear and homely love, sex keeps us alive. I'm telling you what you know, Stella, and I understand now – everything. I did then, but there was still the ghost of the inhibition... I do now – understand everything. Stella dearest, you have brought me back to self-respect. You knew what you were doing and you did it. Thank you."

"Simply my instincts," said Stella drily. "Way I am made."

"I know exactly what you wanted me to say on that stile. Forgive that last resistance. I love you, Stella. I shall never love anyone but you."

"Say that again," said Stella. "I love you. Say it again. You needn't add the rider. Just say 'I love you'...

"And again, Gemini...

"And again, dear Gemini...

"And don't forget to say it again to me inside yourself, when you are running about the world. Gemini, I could cry and shout.

But we've had a long, hard interlude, my darling. Life and death have pulled faces at us, very ugly faces. Anyhow at last we are together again... Don't come near me. *Non bis in idem*, Gemini, which means we won't make love here again. No. But we don't forget what happened here. We're a whole year older, and we've learnt much. We were children and we're near grown up now. We should be lovers now if every scrap of this sex that brought us together was banished from our world. Which happily it isn't. You love me. Say that, Gemini. Stay where you are say that again. And don't add the rider, for that's a mere promise."

"I won't add the rider. It would be a mere promise, and I am an evasive man. I love you, and that's enough," said Gemini. "I know I shall never be as straight and simple as you. How can I be? I am the child of two complex and disingenuous people. But I doubt if I can ever really love anyone but you. Nevertheless, I won't swear that I may not stray. Even at this moment I won't lie to you. But rest assured. I shall be faithful to you after my fashion. I shall be a brute sometimes, after the manner of the old man. You've never seen me churlish yet. I shall be. I hope not, but I shall be. The dark mood comes on like a dark night, and the balance of things vanishes. All one can do is to clean up after it as soon as possible. I am a mutilated mind – though Uncle Robert has done his best to put me together again. I may talk and scream when I am asleep, and maybe at times when I am not asleep. And in phases I shall be as disingenuous as dear Dione. I may step aside when life charges at me too grimly. I may dodge even if I do not run. But however I misbehave, however I shirk, whatever ugly streaks come up, whatever I do, or fail to do, I shall come back to you, sure of you. I shall always *mean* to be faithful to you. My love for you, Stella, is a part of me now like my eyes or my right hand. In that sense I am yours, Stella, as much as you are mine. But if ever *you* fail me...!"

"Spoken like a man, my Gemini. And I, being a female woman and my mother's daughter, will always play for keeps. This is *our* way anyhow, and I am content. Let other people make their own patterns to suit their own needs. This is ours. Say you love me again, Gemini."

"I hope to go on saying it in a thousand ways for all the rest of our lives."

"Variations on a theme by nature. See if you can bore me, Old Gemini. Begin. You needn't ration *that* stuff. Don't filter it. I like it crude."

They looked at each other with grave affection.

"Stella! There is much to be said against your mother, but she did choose a good name for you. You are a star. You shine clear and you are there still, even on a cloudy night, even when the dusty daylight hides you. You have a trick of steadfastness... It isn't all Kentlake blood in you. He gave you a lot to be thankful for, but not quite that. There is blessed touch of stupidity in your steadfastness, divinely uncritical. Whether it is below reason or above it, I do not know. You're wiser than any old star and you're young and childish and feminine... Yes, you are... And at times you are going to be a very obstinate and difficult woman to deal with... And what is more exasperating, sometimes you will be right, absolutely right."

"How well you talk, Gemini. How well you talk, and how well you can play the lover still. Come over and kiss me now. Yes, my dear, *so*, and put your arm about me like this, and now go on talking, close and friendly, your face near to mine, cheek by jowl, as we go down the hill. That block of alabaster... Interpret our parable, my dear. What of the block of alabaster, Gemini? Come back to that. Expatiate."

5

Possible Path in the Wood?

"That block of alabaster. Well – .

"When we were taken by that fancy, last year, I am convinced we were taken by something altogether good for us. For our particular little minds. For us. It was a freak of imagination like a lucky pet name, but it fitted with all we were trying to get square in our minds at that time. Out of this bloodshot world there *is* a world to be carved. But we didn't realise then, as we do now, that if the right world is not carved out of this living block in a reasonable time, it will be sentence of death for everything that has made life worth living so far as we are concerned. We didn't know then that the block wouldn't wait for our convenience. We know now it is, 'Get on with the block' or extinction. We were feeling that already this morning. Even before we saw it turn over."

"We were. And if we do not do something the block is demanding of us, you think – extinction? Really extinction? It's a strong word, Gemini."

"Extinction of all we care for anyhow. Either we make the thing we desire out of it, or presently something else will happen to it. Some blind force will come upon it and smash it. It may be built into a wall or hammered to bits as road metal or broken up for a rockery or a crazy pavement by someone who has no sense of what it might become. We two want to save it for our own dream. We don't want a downfall for mankind. No. What will it matter to us that some crippled outcome of man's seed, hobgoblins and fairies, Morlocks and Eloi, emerge at the other side of this great débâcle? If *Homo sapiens* fails in his promise, then I do not care whether it is *his* degenerate descendants, post-human monsters, Olaf Stapledon's First and Last Men, or whether it is totalitarian ants or rats or mice or what not which come next in the succession. Fate may override us in the end, but that is not our affair. I am for that *Homo sapiens* who is my quintessence who is everything I desire and might be, living in this world as I would have it...

"I can see a world before me, Stella, as full of peace, order, beauty and variety as a well-kept garden, and as full of life, freedom and energy as – there's nothing with which to compare it! All that is still latent in the block. And still it will be Man's world, our world, far more than this world of today. Because you see, Stella, eye hath not seen yet, nor ear heard, not hath it entered into the heart of man to conceive, what this world might be like were every human being in it fed and lovingly educated – well educated – educated out of its inferiority complex and its spites and arrogance – and put to the job in which it could realise its powers. There is scarcely a human being alive *now* who couldn't do something well, if you could find the thing for it to do, and presently, when maybe the creatures are more deliberately born, though there will still be infinite variety, there will be no longer anything you will be able to treat as all-round inferiority. The possibilities of breeding and bettering men that are coming within reach of us... They stagger my imagination. Some things...

"I got a paper the other day from an American called Stephen Zamenhof, a paper with stores of references to other writers in the same field, and the gist of it is, the entire possibility of affecting the texture and quality of the human brain, multiplying its cells, making its fibres more delicate, by pre-natal injections. No need to wait for eugenics. We may soon be able to lift the human intelligence long before the human individual is born. Dozens of careful, intelligent men are working on that possibility... Think of a thing like that. And we haven't begun even to experiment with what can be done with the modern resources for education. We can neither see nor hear nor count nor reason as we might do. We can put knowledge anywhere, now, ready for use. We can show and store and record and discuss and clean up in a way inconceivable – even in our fathers' days. Mankind is crawling about in a state of brutish stupidity, with its head in the mud, blowing bubbles under the filthy mud, while the heavens are opening about it...

"Now that life has come back to me. Now that my pride is restored, all these things are not merely possible; they are imperative. We must realise them whatever it may mean in the way of a fight. For, after all, I know it now, as though I had never forgotten it; what is life for but a fight?

"The starveling vermin we are, Stella; we are no more what men can be, than a lump of wet clay is like fine porcelain. That means you and me, Stella darling. Do you remember how we talked in the lane last year – it is all coming back to me – and how we agreed that we were a very exceptional couple, very, *very* intelligent and privileged?"

"I remember we said we were privileged and that we had to do something about it."

"No, we said we were damned clever. I'm positive."

"Also."

"Perhaps also."

"We were very young. We were nearly a whole year younger. Eleven months anyhow. A little more. We were a very conceited young couple."

"Perhaps, Stella, we were a little wrong about our outstandingness. Conceivable, there's quite a lot of young people all over the world, not so very inferior to us, possibly some of them a lot better than either of us, but like us. All over the world there are still civilised homes turning out the class of emancipated student minds to which we belong, getting the same sort of outlook, reading the same books, staring now at the world – with the same amazement. The things we have to face, they have to face. The risks and the suffocation. Are they going to think so very differently from the way we do? Are they going to do anything so very different from the things we shall do?

"The nearer we average out with those others, the nearer we may be right. We've got things right for ourselves, perhaps, and still there may be a lot we have got wrong. Their individual accidents may be endlessly different from ours. They may find quite different ways in getting a vital drive out of sex. How are we to know? It's our luck that the vital drive falls in with our ideas of purpose. It isn't the universal rule. Sex drives you into action, but there's no reckoning on the sort of action it may drive you into. We can't get anywhere without that urgent motor, but it's our affair to see that it takes us where our intellectual conscience wants to go. That was a good book of Philip Jordan's you sent me, *Say that She were Gone*. Love as disaster. But when we've allowed for casualties of that sort – and even the man in that story did some attractive work on the right side – there is going to be a lot who will travel our way, or nearly in the same direction, and have their friends and lovers with them to sustain them...

"Quite apart from all that, there's something else I have in mind, Stella. It's impossible that there isn't *some* slant and *some* disproportion in our particular interpretation of things. But – listen! – this is very important. We two may do a lot and yet get it a little wrong, and all those others, all of them, Stella, may get their ways of spending life a bit wrong. Nevertheless, if we and they do our damnedest to get things right, that won't matter...

"No, don't interrupt. I tell you it won't matter. Matter to us perhaps, but not in the scheme of things. We may fail in whole or in part, that's what I want to say, and yet what we do – if we do it as right as we know how – may be the thing we ought to do. We may fail altogether as individuals, and every single one of us may fail, and yet the accumulation of what we do may be a success for mankind. What does it matter even to us, what becomes of us in the end, so long as we play our part?...

"What's our formula? What's the formula for the likes of us? Face our block of alabaster, so lovely and ambiguous and misshapen, and dream until we dream it plain and clear, and then set about carving it out without haste and without delay... Never live to see it! What does it matter? I see it now. It's *our* world. Full of weeds it is, like that parson, and full of nettles like my father, with that stone of promise, that block of may-be, throwing itself down upon them at our feet. We may fail in a thousand ways, my dear, but that is not saying it cannot be done and that it won't be done. Not in the least, Stella. Not in the least..."

Discoursing very bravely in this fashion, Gemini, with one arm about his Stella's shoulders, and learning upon her, and his free arm flourishing, came limping down through the trees to the garden gate behind the cottage. The sky was warming towards evening and the air was full of Mrs Greedle at her savoury best.

"It was here," he said. "It was here we said — I remember the words — 'we dedicate ourselves to the free and fearless world-state'. Not a year ago. 'Mizpah', too, we said…"

"I remember," said Stella. "Every moment…"

She was unusually silent at dinner. And after dinner, they strolled up the lane in the warm twilight.

They said very little for a time. The rustle and stir and squeaks of hedgerow life went on unheeded. At last Stella came out of her brooding…

"Gemini," she said; "You've set my brain fermenting… I've got the broad magnificent idea. But that's all. There's a gap. For a time you will have to go on making it real to me until you smooth me down to belief and confidence, which I haven't got yet. Dear windbag, full of courage now, you have to come down to my level. You have to talk real. Dedicate, *how*? Tell me what have we to get up to tomorrow. Exactly. Tell me the sort of life we are going to lead. You talked some considerable drums and trumpets coming down the hill and you set my feet marching. But are they marching in *fact* or are they marking time? I want to feel more sure than I do about the way we have to march."

Gemini said nothing and Stella went on.

"Do you *really* see a path in this darkness, Gemini? Which way do we go from here, Gemini, day by day and year by year? You, with your head in the air, and I, with my feet on the ground. Is there a path? I shan't sleep tonight until I feel sure I shall wake up in the morning with something to do and somewhere to go. Is there a path in the dimness or are there just beautiful delusions of paths? Carve our alabaster! It's fine. We have come back to that after a year in which we have surely learnt many hard things? Carve our alabaster. Gemini – what does that *mean?*"

There was a long silence, broken only by the slow swish of their feet.

"I wonder," reflected Gemini. "*Am* I a gas-bag?"

"You are," said Stella. "It mustn't discourage you. There are endless cars get about now by using gas-bags. Haven't you seen them? We can't move anything without gas of some sort..."

"As bad as Balch for example?"

"My dearest – damn your *amour propre!* There's a lot of Balch in all of us. You know perfectly well what I mean. You know perfectly well what I am asking you to do."

"I *said* I was in for a henpecked life."

Stella threw away her cigarette and stuck her hands deep into her jacket pockets.

"Will you never talk common sense to me as one man to another? Will you always keep up this damned flirtatiousness is the wrong place? Whatever I do?"

Gemini was silent for a moment.

"You're perfectly reasonable," he said. "I am still lazy-minded. I am still, as Uncle Robert said I was, evasive. All the same, I have ideas. I have ideas, and they are taking a more and more definite shape. They bubble and multiply. But I'm putting no urgency into it. And I ought to do so. About this world hidden in the alabaster now..."

She waited.

"I Balched a lot this afternoon about the things that Man could do now... All and more can be done, if only... It is just that 'if only' I have been leaving unanswered... I used to think these things would really come of themselves and that we should be carried along by the stream, cheering things on and pretending we were steering them. That has always been the weakness of the progressive liberal. And people of my temperament. Belief in inevitable progress is the end of progress, and so thank God for good old Belloc, who has always kept that under our noses. We know better now. There is now automatic progress in things. None at all. Progress is here for the taking, but it's not a free gift. I know now that this world of our desire will never come about unless men – no, *we* – make it come about. What are the chances of that great world of Man ever coming about? And how?

"Yes. And how?

"And how?" he echoed, and contemplated the sprays of the hedgerow silhouetted black against the deepening sky. The air was perfectly still. Not a leaf stirred.

"I'm not going to say tonight," he said, "whether you sleep or whether you don't. Because, as you feel – I'm not ready for it. I ought to be. Give me a day or so. I am going to think out a full and proper answer to you. I'll do it properly. I'll arrange my facts. I may even make notes. And then I will deliver a discourse to you – without the faintest flavour of Balch in it. I promise. There shall be no signs and symbols. No rhetorical evasions. I'll talk prose, dear Conscience. For conscience is what you are – ."

"Listen," said Stella suddenly...

"Anti-aircraft guns," said Gemini. "Out at sea..."

"*That* was something bigger..."

"They may have been bombing a trawler."

"Or they may not. It's no good meeting the war half-way. It is going on now like railway accidents or a pestilence. If it gets us, it gets us. We were talking of something more important. What we two ought to get to work upon – straight off from now. I'll put it all in order for you, I promise. *And* for myself, Madam Conscience."

Stella made no immediate answer. She shivered suddenly. "Let us go in," she said. "The nights are still chilly."

They turned back towards the darkened house that had glowed so warmly and confidently upon the world the year before.

6

Hope and Plan for Living

Stella left the main issue alone for three days, and meanwhile they talked of various subsidiary aspects of the world situation. Gemini was mindful of his promise. The day had turned to rain, and after dinner he lit the fire in the main room, whose familiar picturesqueness and dancing reflections from glass and brass had still to be subdued to Stella's austerer taste.

She sat down in the corner of the settle from which she had listened to the Cadi of Clarges Street nearly eleven months before, and Gemini took his stand before the crackling twigs.

There was still, she thought, a resemblance between father and son, if only in their dialectical mannerisms. Argument was in their blood. The shape of the two minds was the same, even if the ideas had been turned inside out. How obstinate is inheritance! The magisterial Twains. What case, she thought, had the Cadi's father argued, and the Cadi's grandfather? She had a momentary vision of a long gallery of Twains standing before a succession of period fireplaces and laying down the law, up-to-date. A Roundhead out of Hudibras, disposing of Hobbes' Fascism and the Fifth Monarchy Men, all in one sweeping allocution, and a bearded Twain in a long dagged embroidered robe, dealing with the hopeless outlook of those Wycliffites, Hussites and Lollards, were particularly distinct...

"And now I'm going to tell you all about it," said Gemini, "as I promised. I've thought over what you said, and I will tell you just as plainly as I can exactly what you and I have to do. It may surprise you a little – I don't know. But I must develop my case in its proper order so that you will see exactly what I mean. You mustn't object till afterwards."

Stella nodded and refrained from saying, "Silence in the court."

And this is how things looked to Gemini on the very eve of the German invasion of Holland, with the hawthorn coming into flower.

"I think," said he, "we are very much of a mind about what is happening now. We and everybody. We needn't discuss that. No man in his senses believes that Hitler and his Germans can do anything that will amount to a decisive conquest of Europe, and that is their modest ambition. They keep no promises; they love destructive enterprises. They have no stabilising ability. They have burnt their boats; there is no making peace with them. They cannot stop; they must go on with it now, and failure at a climax of smashing must be their end. They've smashed into Norway and Denmark. We may wake up tomorrow for the news, and find they are in Holland or Belgium or Hungary or Roumania. It's like a homicidal lunatic at large. This war is our immediate reality. It hardly lets us see what is beyond it. So long as the German drive, we have to go on fighting. But no one believes that this amazing pro-Nazi government of ours will do anything but break up what is left of our poor old Anglican Empire in conflict. Indeed the British Empire, except as a political hallucination, has gone already. The Statute of Westminster dissected the body. Sunk by its Chamberlains, with their incurable monopolising instincts. When Joe determined to put a tariff round it, he set a limit to its growth and started its decay. Neville is just trying to do a trade with the enemy for the ruins. That great liberal Empire that linked the world half a century ago, can never reappear. That Empire of the open hand closed up in an impossible Zollverein. There has to be something greater now than any Empire, or there can be nothing at all. On all this we two are agreed... Yes?"

" 'm," said Stella.

"We agree further that the rough shape things must take now is a steady disastrous extension of the war, world bankruptcy, world exhaustion. Somehow the stage will be cleared of this silly Chamberlain-Halifax-Goering-Hitler first act. It's none the less a pretty and silly story, because it is an enormous bloody mess. New faces will take over the fight. Possibly there will be a technical victory for the Allies — whoever the Allies may presently be. There will be a sort of victory by exhaustion over Aggression. But it may be a very close thing this time. It may be much more like a deadlock between chastened antagonists, sorry they ever began. The British Empire, we discover, has made tremendous advances in incompetence since 1918. In the hands of this government now, it is hard to believe it is any longer a Great Power; it looks far more like a loose, silly, big Power, like

China under the old Empress. It is as ungirt as America. It may wake up presently – but why doesn't it wake up now? Why didn't it wake up about Abyssinia, about Spain, about Czechoslovakia? It will come into any settlement shorn of most of its prestige.

"Even such radicals and cosmopolitans as we are, feel a patriotic ache about that, although we have to realise that so things have to be. Cosmopolitan we are by conviction, but English at heart. We were born to love this land of green lanes, and hitherto we have both cuddled the thought that the English would at least play a leading part in remaking the world. Still the truth is the truth! and Old England as a world leader seems a vanished dream. Nor will Marianne be in a position to act the vindictive hostess this time. No. The war won't go that way anyhow.

"France and Britain had their chance of making a world peace in 1918, and they muffed it. They let the Foreign Offices and old-fashioned semi-big-business and His Majesty George the Fifth, steal their peace. A lot of good our majesties and merchants and mandarins got out of that! They hardly needed to make a fool of President Wilson. He volunteered. He came over to Europe eager to take his wife to Buckingham Palace and score off the Republican Party. All that is history now, gone beyond recall. The world was full of hope in 1918. It was fobbed off with the League of Nations, which blocked everything and did nothing. This time Britain and France will have to sit down amidst quite a number of interveners. Another Armistice, but I doubt if *this* little George will block the street of London with a Thanksgiving Service at St Paul's making out that he and God and the Archbishop of Canterbury were really the blokes who settled the affair. This Armistice will be something more explicit. It will be a different sort of Armistice altogether...

Babes in the Darkling Wood

"I doubt if it will be made up by the actual combatants. It will be discussed first through neutral countries and it may even be – almost imposed by neutral action. You can't prevent discussion going from land to land nowadays. No censorship can stop that.

"About the end of the war. It seems impossible now to call off the fighting until the Germans are exhausted, and something like a general disarmament is agreed upon and provided for. It is not *our* choice that; *they* won't let us. How can you trust Germans any more so long as they have arms in their hands? And the return of the evacuated populations has to be not only stipulated for but arranged for. Before we leave off. Treaties aren't good enough. And there will have to be immense social reconstructions. Money is going bust. Both sides will have to come together upon that much, before this war, as they call it, *can* end. Anything short of that will be merely a pause for another Nazi surprise. The Armsitice will be imposed by necessity on both sides. Until there is some such fully implemented Armistice prepared, how can this fighting stop? It may ebb for a while and then break out again, but there can be no other ending for it. So that a lot of the terms of the Armistice will have to be discussed and settled – through neutrals perhaps, and in all sorts of roundabout ways – while the fighting is still going on. Maybe America may formulate these conditions. Maybe America – and Russia – have you ever thought of such a combination? – may insist upon them. Neither dare permit a Germany rampant. Then they must co-operate in holding her down. We shall get what some bright lad has recently called a war-welded federation of the combatants and the interveners, quasi-victors and quasi-vanquished, in the guise of a great tangle of special world adjustment commissions…

"That too has become plain common sense – quite recently. Suddenly it turns up here, there and everywhere. New and yet obvious. Europe is being bled down to pale reasonableness pretty rapidly. We could have the best part of the world under international commissions in quite a short time if it wasn't for the inertia of the old politicians. In two or three years at the outside. That is the most probable way out and the most possible and the most desirable. Unless this break-up of the world into a slaughter scramble is to go on indefinitely, there must be" – he ticked off his international commissions on his fingers – "an effective disarmament commission, a reparation commission, an internal commission for the restoration of the displaced populations, an air and general transport commission and a commission for the restoration of production by some readjustment of money and barter, all in operation quite soon. Their work, once it begins, may stretch over years....

"Is this asking too much of the human intelligence? At its present level? I don't think so. One world-wide federation there certainly must be after this war, and that is a federation to put an end to air-war for ever. Plainly that must stop, or civilised life must stop, and the one and only way to stop it is to set up a world commission with full powers to control the air everywhere, powers of search, power of instant suppression. No single country can be left out of that. If necessary countries must be compelled to come in. And no simple treaties or conventions will meet the case. There will be no more treaties because there is no more good faith. The air commission must be a commission with full powers, a world air-police. All over the world reasonable people and common people will be in favour of that. Patriots may object, but even patriotism may be out of fashion in a little while. And once you federate so far as the air goes, you can add other world commissions quite easily to the bundle of delegated powers. All that, we can get out of a properly conditioned Armistice. We can get it in no other way. So I take it that is the way things will have to go."

"What else can there be?" said Stella, blinking at the cheerful uprush of the fire.

"What else can there be? Utter disaster. Even countries that keep neutral right up to the end will insist on having a finger in this. It is a universal concern. They will all be under arms. They will all be entangled economically in the war. They will all have to join in with these international commissions. Inevitably they must. If not, we must all become troglodytes listening for the air-raid warning. You see the idea of a sort of Standing Armistice? Discussed beforehand. Put into operation at the cease fire. The longer those inevitable international commissions stay in being and the more extensive they are, the less disposed reasonable men will be to part with them, and the more effectively will they block the way against the old order, or the old disorder, sneaking back to its outworn localisations and appropriations. Putting the settlement in the hands of international commissions will save the faces of the combatant governments, and it will satisfy the immediate need for peace and reorganisation as nothing else can do.

"How else can they get back out of this world mess? How can they dodge such an obvious settlement? Saving face is always important in old, decaying, complicated states. All the sovereign states will be able to declare they are still independent sovereign states, except in so far as these international commissions go. They can keep all their flags and dignities. What will that matter for the time being? We are only beginning to realise how far the commissions may be able to take us to a world-wide collectivism in raw materials, industrial distribution and so on, in spite of all such face-saving residues of sovereignty. It's not so very difficult therefore to anticipate the sort of peace phase that lies two or three years ahead. The nominal Armistice will be in effect a Peace Union.

"The world will become, for all essential purposes, a federated union, so far as the function of these commissions go, long before the fact is openly recognised. But the vision is clear on the top side than underneath. What's going to happen to the under-dog in the future, and what's going to happen to free-minded, criticising people? And how long will it go on at that level?

"Who will be the people to run these settlement commissions? I think we have to get our minds clear about that. Will the present hard-faced business man grasp his opportunity and take control? He will have a great chance if he has the wit and ability to grasp it. He can say 'I know all about this practical stuff — about producing and distributing iron or cotton or food. I have this organisation here and the best thing you can do is to socialise it, socialise us — we won't mind — make our cartels and so forth world-wide — and leave me and my friends here in charge.' There you will have your settlement commissions ready to hand. 'Fuse us and use us. If not, you will have to break up all the vast network of the world's business and hand the broken fragments to politicians without any practical experience at all. As Russia did. With a vast and crippling loss of practical efficiency. Learn from Russia.'

"He will have a case there, Stella. Will he make it? Typically I think that generally speaking he is too much of a fool and too mixed up with our failing, over-inflated financial system to do anything of the sort. He lives too much in the counting-house. He has been brought up to believe that successful greed is a sort of virtue justified. He is too blinkered, as Uncle Kentlake used to say, with the social and political notions of the nineteenth century, individualism, dread of state control and all the rest of it. He does not understand the forces that produced him, and therefore he will not have the subtlety and capacity to adapt himself to the new order of things. He will come in, I think, to a certain extent. But disingenuously. He will resist and try to sabotage and discredit. He will be only one element therefore, and not the best element, in these controls.

"But he's not the only realist in the world. There must be – coming out of business staffs and technical institutions – a lot of more or less trustworthy administrative experts available, men of the type of Sir Arthur Salter or Lord Stamp, who would be willing and able to bear the main burthen of the organising. They would have had some experience in handling the shareholder, the profiteer and the politician, but they wouldn't be eaten up by that side of the business. Few of them are really devoted to their shareholders. They would soon draw plenty of recruits and assistants from the managerial class in the big trade machines, from what people call 'idealists' and from a miscellaneous riff-raff of job-seekers...

"That as much as we can say about the people who may be running the world before 1950. It's cloudy, I admit. We have our observations and suspicions, Stella, but neither of us has any profound knowledge of the social elements concerned. Young and bookish we are still. But plainly this practical Federation of the World by Armistice, this hushing-up of war by arrangement, which I believe is the major probability ahead, is going to produce a very imperfect world-organisation. It will just be a working organisation. And since we two can know about it only in very general terms, we are left still more in the air about what is going to happen to the happiness of the under-dog and the free play of the human intelligence – which are quite different things from each other, but which nevertheless have a common interest in maintaining the Rights of Man.

"There is this movement we hear about, to bring together all the Left movements of the world by a common Declaration of the Rights of Man. There was fuss about it in the *Daily Herald* some time ago, and now it has died down. It is impossible to say as yet how far it may wake up again, and what sort of democratic corrective to hard, ruthless, slightly disingenuous pseudo-efficiency it may evoke. The idea seems to be to make it the working credo of the one world-wide popular front. One talks of the revolt of the Masses. Masses? I doubt if there has ever been anything of the sort anywhere on a larger scale than a city or a fairly uniform region. 'Masses' were always a local crowd. Anyhow the idea of Mass Revolutions nowadays is a fantasy. The Masses have dispersed and disappeared. There are no Masses of illiterates with a common sense of injustice any longer in the world. For all practical purposes now, the broad base of the human community is middle-class. Everywhere people read, everywhere books go, at any social level you may meet a well-read man. By mental standards even the workers on the dole are middle-class. Nobody now can tell how far the whole world may not be following what is going on, how rapidly a certain internationalism of understanding may spread and consolidate a world democracy, and how far that may exert a qualifying influence upon these coming world-controls....

Babes in the Darkling Wood

"And here, Stella," said Gemini, putting his thumbs into his waistcoat pockets, lifting his chin, and so mingling a reminiscence of Uncle Robert with the manner of the ancestral Twains, "I have to digress into the question of human motives and what the liberation of man really means. One dominant motive plays about the human self-consciousness. It is a double-faced motive: it has its variations, but essentially it is the desire to feel right and powerful. Of all the psychoanalysts I think Adler, with his inferiority complex, gets nearest the truth about the primary nature of this motive. It springs into existence with the idea of the Ego. It is part of that idea. 'I exist and where do I stand?' The discovery and the question arose together. Babies are jealous and assertive in their cradles." ("Bassinettes nowadays," whispered Stella.) "We want to feel masterful, we want to impose a recognition of our mastery over others. We are depressed and dissatisfied if we feel unimportant. This makes us all want to get on. It's the inspiring motive of ambition, competition, ruling classes, tyrannies. We want reassurance. Acknowledge me, we say. It is the chief stimulant of personal love. We conquer one another. Of course we do, Stella. It is that which has given mankind all the leaders, the kingships, the power and the glory through the ages. Against it the vast multitudes of the unsuccessful fight – and have fought since the remote beginnings of history. The unsuccessful are driven into revolt, into not very congenial associations for collective resistance, and into the consolation of sabotage and malicious mischief. Malicious mischief (such as the Communists cultivate) is the cheapest way of getting square with arrogance. You don't get anything done, but you relieve yourself. There's your Right and your Left, Stella, through the ages.

"But wait a bit! Between Right and Left there's a Centre, which broadens out in tranquil times and narrows down in times of stress. Quite a lot of people in the world are neither crude power-seekers nor rebels. They get their sense of mastery in doing something they can do particularly well and having that mastery recognised. That ought not to offend anybody. It does, but it ought not to. You get that sort of power satisfaction in the artist, the skilled artisan, the cultivator, the technician, the man of science. Other people again get their sense of mastery in the give-and-take of home life, in little snobberies and neighbourly showing-off. The children look up to Daddy at home and brag about him at school. So long as the aggressive types leave such people alone, this Centre can and does carry on without much social and political disturbance. I suppose one might say that the stability and soundness of a government is to be judged very largely by the preponderance of these little closed systems of satisfaction, by the relative size of its Centre. Am I being clear, Stella?"

"So clear that my mind runs ahead of you."

"I'll go quicker. All through the ages a social struggle has been going on, between the energetic, clambering, interfering, grabbing, aggressive, unsated types of mankind and the mixed resistance of the unsuccessful, the contented home-life people and the people who are satisfied with acknowledged creative mastery. Something has always been done about it; and all custom, law, religion, and morality, formulates resistance to aggression. They are all of them organisations to protect the Centre. In stable conditions, a sort of general balance may be brought about, but with changing conditions dislocations are inevitable, and the energetics find new, unexpected opportunities of self-assertion. Today we are living in a storm of change.

Abolition of distance, enhancement of productive and destructive power release of human energy into unemployment or social wreckage... We both know that story by heart. I won't go into it...

"Now all the great religions of the world without exception, Stella, without exception, have begun as revolts against oppression, and because normal satisfactions were being widely frustrated. All of them were revolutionary in the beginning. Moses, as Freud has shown, was an Egyptian driven into exile who made capital out of the slavery of the Hebrews, Buddha was a bored prince shocked by the nearness of death and decay, Christ was an evacuated child, born in a manger. The whole of history, the story of religion through the ages, the story, as Uncle Robert would have it, of the assembling human soul, is a history of the intensification and then the checking of aggression, and the ebb and flow of the responding revolutionary impulse – insurrection on the one hand and persecution and tyranny on other. A half-triumph for the revolution has followed, a surrender and a compromise. That compromise, Stella, has always been a new state religion.

"Wait a moment, Stella. Let me finish this... We are living in one of the intenser phases of this thrust and counter-thrust between aggression and revolt. The new revolution, the world revolution, is only just waking up. But it is waking up, while old and new grabbers fight among themselves. The power régimes seem so excessive now, because while they fight, they feel the revolt of reason in the air about them. They feel judgement gathering. It invades their consciences if they stop to think. Thinking, they feel, is qualification, that is, from their point of view, weakness. So they try not to think of anything fresh. They hurry on with the fighting, although there is no end in sight for them except defeat. They strike out, but they strike out blindly. They stick to their flags. They turn on their own people. They stifle every dissentient voice. So they fight on until their vigour ebbs. And these commissions of settlement, I take it, this Armistice Federation, must lie in wait for them as their vigour ebbs. They will give in at last ungraciously – muttering."

He stopped and looked to Stella for approval.

"So it may be," she said. "And so may it be... And next?"

Gemini went on with his exposition.

"I want now to say something about the world of, let us say, 1960 or 1970. We must do that. The present signifies nothing at all unless we look to its future. We don't simply fight, we fight for something ahead. After this present nightmare of destruction, it is quite possible then that the atmosphere of the new dawn may feel – just a trifle bleak. We may discover in the half light the bare frame of a unified new world still wearing the rags of the old. It will be without a literature of its own, without any body of substantial thought, unless – .

"You note that '*unless*'. I'll come back to that in a minute, but you realise that outside that rather vigorous but unattractive cosmopolitan administrative class we shall have over us, who will, of course, as a class, share the natural desire of all vulgar and illiterate humanity to feel and display and impose superiority, there will be a great number of people resentful at the régime because of that disposition, and anxious to get square with it. The natural response of the uneducated human soul to successful arrogance, we have agreed, is malicious mischief...

"I'm not sure whether Hitler and even some of those others about him aren't really to be counted as part of the revolt, as part of the revenge of the inferiority complex, rather than an attempt to construct a new dominance. They are so purely destructive. I don't know. I won't go into that... No..."

Gemini hovered speculatively for a moment and then got back to his lecture.

"I think we can reckon that the rationalising forces that will produce this first World Federation by Armistice, will have very nearly spent themselves before the eighties or nineties of this century. The leading spirits will be tired out or dead. The sort of people who will be running the standing commissions for this, that and the other world controls, will be the equivalents of the rather hard, career-planning young men who go in for success in business or politics today. They will be energetic and fairly capable, but whatever touch of imagination may have leavened the original settlement will have gone. Unless – ... They will be finding new ways of achieving that nice superior feeling and letting other people feel it. They will be rather after the pattern of the leading Russian commissars now, with their Lincoln cars and their dachas and their general atmosphere of privilege and authority. Then there will come a reaction – about 1970 or '80. The very success of the new order so far may encourage the reaction against it. People will see nothing but its strains, its imperfections and its inevitable abuses, and all the good it has done in abolishing the immediate spectres of war and social collapse will be regarded as being in the nature of things.

"Remember, all the nasty little monarchies and churches and patriotisms may still be in existence, – 'mediatised' is the word – scotched but not killed, and fretting to come back. They will look harmless. They may have acquired a certain romantic charm...

H G Wells

"Unless we do something about it, there will be the same universities, much as we have them now, impoverished perhaps, the same weak, ill-equipped schools and teachers, the same thin trickle of information. Just as Uncle Robert denounced them... It is impossible to imagine the people who will handle the world's general settlement in the immediate future, troubling to do anything about that sort of thing. They will patch up that pacification by those special commissions for settlement because it is the obvious thing to do. They will do all that because they will be obliged to do it. But their idea of a new world will be a minimum new world. They will leave just as much of the old state of affairs as they can...

"Let me tell you my ideas in the order in which I have planned them out. All that was prelude. Just a recitation of our views for you to OK. It is a prelude that has rather overrun itself, and I see I'll have to put a stick or so more on the fire... What was it came next? Ah! Yes... What intelligent people have to realise, Stella, is that this world can be unified, by such a series of federated essential world-services as I suggest, without anything in the nature of a World Government or a World Parliament or a World President or anything of that sort ever coming into existence..."

"But," said Stella.

"Here, on this point, discussion lags behind the obvious realities. The state of the argument today is this; you can hear it constantly repeated; you *must* have a centre of power somewhere, which can give decisions. Somewhere there has to be a *power* government for the whole world that will say 'Yes' or 'No'. Well, that's nonsense. There is no such imperative. It is a delusion that has survived from the slavish, servile, childish past. The real truth of the matter, as Uncle Robert would have said, is that in every eventuality, there is a Right Thing to Do." Gemini's voice put in the capitals. "If only you know it. If only you know the right thing to do, you haven't to obey *anyone*. That is the basis of the liberal idea. You have to know to the best of your ability, and to do what is right.

"If you have a pestilence to deal with, for example, there are certain things that must be done. In a barbaric community, you can't get people to understand what these things are. They feel they are up against mysterious and malignant forces. They have panics. They accuse the Jews or people with red hair, or set-to upon the people who don't kow-tow to Mumbo-Jumbo and so have brought His wrath upon them. They offer up preposterously cruel sacrifices to the offended Gods. Even if the right thing to do is known by a few people, the masses need the strong hand, a dictatorship of some sort, to restrain their hysteria of uncertainty and force that right thing upon them. Or the wrong thing. They need medicine men to humbug them to save themselves. But an intelligent community is quite different; it has its information at hand. It can listen to explanations. It can do what has to be done, without asking anyone whatever to decide for it. The more it knows, the more it can dispense with power and enforcement. The more the administrators it appoints can be watched and checked. Is that sound, Stella?"

" 'greed," said Stella.

"The Right Thing to Do will be the real dictator for adult mankind..."

Stella nodded her head and remained critically attentive.

"One could say this was platitudinous if it were not that it is so universally ignored. You dictator is an imaginary omniscient being in the minds of weak-willed people. As an alternative to omniscience, they cal him an instinctive genius – as a lot of our pro-Nazis here call Hitler, which means that they believe he will always fumble through to the successful thing without knowing it. He is magic. He is their substitute, and an altogether disastrous substitute, for organised knowledge and thought. From which it follows that the organisation of knowledge and thought in the world is the central and saving business before mankind…"

It took Stella some seconds to follow him round that corner. "Go on," she said to his pause.

"I have said '*unless*' and '*unless*', Stella, and now I can explain – what you already realise (bear with me, Stella) – that that '*unless*' is leading up to the particular thesis that concerns us most. I have said we have to know the Right Thing to Do – yes – but in a thousand matters there remains no right thing to do yet, because we have not the necessary knowledge and wisdom. That it the essential thing in the situation, and it is the thing the ordinary man is not even beginning to realise. The whole human outlook is dominated by the need for an immense revision, expansion, reorganisation of our knowledge-machinery and our mental and moral instruction. We have to bring that up to the new scale of life, and at present, and particularly here in England, nobody seems disposed to do anything about it at all.

"Think of the absurdity of this. We are daring to look forward to a world at peace, where an infinite variety of local peculiarities, racial localisations, climatic response, will flourish within the network of the common world services. Necessarily it will be an order varied and subtle beyond anything that exists now. An order which is only possible therefore, on a basis of knowledge and education such as only a few of us are beginning to realise is attainable. At the present level of education, mankind may blunder in and out of war, even snatch a few more decades of peace – as we are hoping – but it will not be able to get out of its staggering progress to extinction. Presently it will resume that. The primordial antagonisms will reawaken under new appropriations and unexpected stresses, unless we anticipate them.

"It is going to be a hard saying for the Reverend Morton Richardsons of the world, but a new world, a new planetary society, *has* to have a new education on its own scale; it *has* to have a vast, ordered, encyclopaedia of fact and thought for its Bible, and a gigantic organisation not only of research and record, but of devoted teachers and interpreters, teachers by the million and priests and confessors, medical and mental counsellors by the million, and not only priests, but prophets also to innovate and reanimate its idea. And it has, as a whole community, to be responsive and participating in all that immense cerebration.

"People talk of the new order as though religious structures were going to disappear. Of course they are not going to disappear. They have to be re-born upon this vaster scale. With a sounder philosophy and a clearer creed. Every ordered society in the past has had temples and priests and teachers to hold it together, and how can an infinitely more complex world-society expect to get along with only the outworn lumber of the old creeds to hold up its thought and behaviour? I ask you. Plainly it has to be permeated by a new consciousness, and it has to have and be a World Church, that is to say it has to have a unified World Brain and World Will. Conscious of their functions. The vital job beneath the superficial political and economic commissions of the world settlement is just that, to embody this Religion of Knowledge and to put it in control of human affairs...

"Don't interrupt just yet, Stella. Don't jump down my throat with your ready understanding. Don't, above all, get ahead of me. You asked for this lecture, and you've got to have it in precisely the order in which I have planned to tell it to you. Or else I shall get lost in digressions. I've been thinking it out for three days. Maybe you've heard a lot of it before. I may have talked in my sleep. But I want to get it clear for myself as well as you. Let me go on just a little longer...

"Do you realise that the very hardest thing for anyone to admit is mental under-nourishment? Much less will a man admit his mind isn't fully capable of dealing successfully with all possible occasions. He may admit that he does not know something, but he will insist that his strong natural common sense, or the other things he imagines that he does know, make whatever he doesn't know of quite minor importance. In the whole scheme of things, this intellectual self-complacency, Stella, is the most formidable obstacle to man's escape from frustration."

"Uncle Robert," began Stella...

"Uncle Robert, I know, was always hammering away at that idea. Plainly I am basing all that I am going to say now on Uncle Robert. He understood, he really understood, that he was an ignorant man in a thickly ignorant world. It was his rôle to insist upon that. It was continually in his mind. Other people might say it, but he *knew* it. He hated colleges and caps and gowns, degrees and dignities, dogmas and authorities and all the paraphernalia of erudition and teaching, passionately, because he knew the miserable poverty beneath those pretensions. He could not see the whole system as anything but a deliberate imposture planned to exasperate himself. He underrated our common gift for self-deception. He thought all the big bugs of academic life knew themselves to be imposters. There was nothing for an intelligent human being today, he believed, but a passionate, aggressive, mental humility. Aggressive mental humility, Stella – a good phrase for his attitude? Eh?

"He realised that the very language he used was vitiated at the source, that philosophy had an impediment in its speech, that it was choked up now with scholarly affectation, and loved to hear itself lisp and stutter. He knew that such knowledge as mankind possesses lies scattered on the floor of this plundered and outraged world like a looted library, smothered in its own disorder. What he said to the world, and particularly to that part of the world which wears robes, orders, honours, crowns, mitres and suchlike – what he said, sometimes in this way and sometimes in that, was not only 'You don't know' but, with a continually increasing exasperation as his life went on, 'Damn you, you fools! You don't *want* to know. Why, in the name of all your cheap and idiotic Gods don't you *want* to know? If only for your private satisfaction?...'

"At the thought of a University Chancellor in all his majesty he quoted Swift: 'That such a creature should deal in pride!' And he was right, Stella. He was right. He knew a fundamental thing about the human mind, the hardest thing in the world to know, which is that it scarcely knows anything at all... He felt that it scarcely exists as yet. He was trying to assemble it. He was trying to put it together, strand by strand. Just as reasonable people nowadays are beginning to synthesise a federal world peace, function by function. His surely should be called the Synthetic Philosophy, and not old Herbert Spencer's stuff..."

"In the future," said Stella, "he said everyone would be a student all through his life and the whole world a University…"

But Gemini was off upon another tack.

"A queer isolated life your uncle led. *He* never found a Stella. There were things in his life we know nothing about at all. We knew him as a devastating intelligence, and that is all we know. He was eaten up by curiosity. Always he was plodding away to get at the reality of the human mind; what it was really, how it worked. And how it might work better. He seems to have divided his attention between the psychosynthesis of the demented and the psychoanalysis of the sane. Yet he too had to assume some sort of mental self-sufficiency. There was that *perspicacity* of his…"

"It was a sort of pose," said the loyal Stella. "He wasn't really self-sufficient. He pretended to be a seer in order not to call one an ignorant slacker."

"Hm," said Gemini. "I wonder. Nevertheless, he had a rightness… And that, you see, is where you and I in particular come in. He *made* us two, very largely, he made us, and we owe it to him to get something effective out of his teaching. His life was a declaration of war at this pervading, this uncritical ignorance in which mankind is blundering towards irreparable disaster, but he was still only declaring war when he died. It's we who have to go on with the war he declared. There won't be too any people at the job at first, and it's the most fundamental job at all.

"Because, you see, Stella, the one and sole *reality* in human life is mental. It always has been; it always will be. Our selves are the mental assemblage of our activities. Theology and worship, religion, philosophy, science, imagination, propaganda and teaching, are the essentials upon which all purposive action, all co-operation and material achievement depend. Violence and the forcible prevention of violence are both merely the realisation of ideas. A bomb is a whole complex of thought embodied. Of all human fools the man who shirks thought, despises 'theory' and fancies himself a practical man, is surely the biggest. He's a detached bit of dementia. His actions are epileptic. To live is to think; to act consciously is merely thinking by action; there is no other living... Agreed?"

"Obvious," said Stella. "As Uncle would have said."

Gemini paused. He flew off at a tangent. "Have ever heard a more idiotic expression than 'coming down to brass tacks'?"

"Never," said Stella with conviction.

"And you know exactly what they mean by it?"

"It has a meaning."

"Well, coming down to brass tacks, let me tell you as precisely as possible what I want to do now, and what you ought to do. I think my academic standing is good enough to get me some sort of chair or lectureship in pedagogy or social psychology or what not, so soon as the war is over, and then I shall be able to settle down and go ahead, and you, you would make the perfect head of a women's college. Have you thought of that, Stella? Because I think you will have to. You can talk to parents, organise study groups of girls, try and evolve that powerful-minded type of woman that you can't get by making them imitation men. Men's education is still overshadowed by the traditions of monks, and women's education is still overshadowed by men's and ruled by spinsters."

"We are going to have children," said Stella informatively in parenthesis...

"I think we have to hear more from the mothers, Stella. And the whores. They have their rôle, Stella. There's whores by degradation. I say nothing of hem. But there's whores by nature.

They have a case. They have always been shouted down. They have never had a fair hearing. A distinctive women's education and a distinctive women's philosophy doesn't exist. You have the generosity to be ancillary, Stella, in the old style. That's my luck. But that's not an end of *that* question…"

"It's a digression," said Stella, "named Mary Clarkson. Come back to what we two are going to do."

"Well, when the mine-sweeping and the nursing are over, and this next breathing-space releases us from our bit of actual warfare, that is the way we two have to go. We have to start getting on to that road now, with all the time and energy the war will leave us. We can begin tomorrow. We will. My stiff leg isn't going to hinder me in this sort of thing. What I have in mind, means lives of steady work and a sort of obscure eminence for both of us. It will take all the hard work, self-control and self-possession we can put into it. That class-unconscious élite, on which Chakhotin says the salvation of the race depends… We have to join up with that. We have to. Right away we can get to work. Tomorrow.

"We ought to set about this business as though we were the only people in the world to do it. Presently we shall join up with others, but we cannot wait for them to come along. When we hear of them we will get in touch. For example, we have to being accumulating names, addresses, quotations. We have to find out all that there is to be known and what is afoot in those various movements for documentation, for bibliography, for indexing, for all that microphotographic recording one hears about distantly and dimly. Or doesn't hear about. Then there is a sort of renaissance of Encyclopaedism going on, there's what you might call the de Monzie experiment, in France. There are feeble calls for that sort of thing over here too and in America. Why is there no proper response to them? The man in the street wants to *know* – acutely. Is it saturation with commercialism that stands in the way of any response? We know hardly anything of all that. People make passing remarks and go on to something else. It's nobody's business. Yet.

"What are these University Presses we hear about? They seem to print some scientific books, but they never attempt to produce a literature that would be educational for the mass of people. Have they no funds? Do the Tory dons ban them? Is the old drooling lecture and tutorial tradition too strong for them? Haven't they found the way to sell books to the general public? The *Encyclopaedia Britannica* was once quasi-academic. Why was it commercialised? Why is there no British or American de Monzie? Maybe there is, and we don't know of him. Is there such a thing as a Minister of Education in America? I don't know. You don't know. The handing-out of books is part of the world-mind machinery. But it seems to be the most fortuitous of businesses. For my own part I'd rather close ten schools than one good bookshop. Why don't the right books get to more people? Why is there a vast trade in pseudo-books; feeding the children with bran instead of bread? We have got to understand that. We have got to map its complexities.

"We ought to start a sort of private index, I suppose, to frame what we are doing. You probably did something of the sort of your reading, and also for your addresses. I did. We have to make a digest now of all that stuff and keep it up-to-date. We have to use the same methods.

"Then we have to go into the general psychology of the specialist and the don. How much is a certain conservative viciousness on the part of these types – unavoidable? I have a suspicion, derived from Uncle Robert, that whenever a man becomes what is called a scholar, he goes into a sort of rigor... Does he? Can a mind be broad as well as deep? That's the sort of job we start upon, Stella. A preliminary study of the possible intellectual enlargement of the world. Hard work, and sometimes dull and toilsome work it is, and yet it will be heading towards – the most important thing in life...

"For it becomes more and more evident that the one important thing in life is this business of thought and will which is going on in the brain. The life of a man pours up for realisation and co-ordination into his cerebrum. What is he but a cerebrum? Study, learn, teach and learn by teaching. Make understandings and more understandings. That is the reality of life for every human being. The only real mastery of life is knowledge and clear thought. All the present leaders of men argue and write, and the quality of their thought determines human destiny. They make books and pamphlets. They make speeches. Thought and expression haven't the traditional splendour of inciting revolutionary crowds from a balcony, riding at the head of one's troops into a conquered city, being crowned in some vast cathedral, but when the bands have died away in the distance, when the flags and decorations have been taken down, and all the parades and processions faded back into insignificance, thought and expression remain the reality of history..."

He stopped short. He brought himself down to the level of brass tacks for a moment and then soared again. "Well, we two anyhow have to be rankers in this endless war of the mind. Last year we were adolescent Gods, and this year; how do we stand? Professor James Twain I shall be, and you, Mrs Doctor of

Pedagogy Twain. What do you think of it, Stella? I think I've de-Balched our outlook pretty completely now. No heroics, but self-conscious, subordinated polyps doing our best on that great mental reef, which may or may not grow up to harbour – harbour? – harbour the refitting and re-conditioning of the Hope and Will in man..."

He caught her tranquil appraising eye. He pulled up abruptly on the verge of a fresh explosion of metaphor.

"Well?" he said.

"This sounds all right to me," said Stella. "But what you say has a way to sounding right to me. And yet – you queer beast, Gemini! – you haven't thought all this out in the four days we have been here, since that block turned over."

"I've been putting it together as something that *might* be done, ever since I began to read and think again. As one might do a problem or a puzzle. With no belief that it could ever be done. And no particular desire to do anything about it."

"And now suddenly you intend to *do* this?"

"Now suddenly I mean to make my peculiar contribution. I suppose I had to think that it could be done before I could think of it as something that has to be done."

"Hm," said Stella.

"And I suppose my hormones had to be put right again before I could think of it as something I want to do."

"And this is – you are sure of it – your programme?"

"For keeps, Stella. Honour bright, I mean to live for this. If we do not mean this, we mean nothing at all. This is what we mean."

She considered his assurance in her deliberate fashion. "Yes," she said; "it is."

"And even," added Gemini, "if occasionally I relax my attack on that damned block of alabaster, there is not the slightest doubt in the world that it will keep on attacking me. Better to face up to it than to run. Do you remember how it swept down on us?... Seemed to sweep down?... What else is there to do, Stella? What else *is* there for our generation to do?"

"Nothing," reflected Stella. "Nothing whatever. Thank heaven." She sighed and stood up before him. "For us. Or any generation henceforth for evermore. 'World University,' he said. A world of minds awake. And now I think we can end this day and go to bed the sober grown-ups that we are."

She was moved to call him by a title she had never used before. "Dear husband," she said, and kissed him.

He held her close to him. "Dear better half," he said...

The casements rattled.

The young couple stood listening.

"Those guns," said Stella...

"Nearer," said Gemini.

"It sounder louder," said Stella...

For a moment or so some scar among his Warsaw memories winced in Gemini's brain...

"They will pass," he said. "All that will pass. We fight by the way. To get rid of a dangerous nuisance. It is not our essential business. Incidentally our world may be blown to pieces and we with it. That cannot alter what we are while we are alive, not what we have to do."

Tail-piece

So it was, set forth as plainly and completely as possible, that two fairly receptive youngsters were living and thinking about life between June in 1939 and May in 1940. The accidents of their birth, training and character had brought them into the closest contact with the latest and most enterprising thought of their time; and through all their mental exercises they were responding to the primordial and inseparable urgencies of sex and self-assertion. Philosophy is a sign-post; it tells you the way but gives you no lift on the journey. The drive is the ferment in your blood. They desired and hesitated; they faltered and fought; we have told how Gemini went down and how he was restored to fight again. It was true that those distant guns were drawing nearer and that Stella had reason to shiver at the sound of them...

War was extending like a searching hand to grip them both.

That very night, while Gemini, after the manner of the magisterial Twains, was summarising his views for her, in front of the dancing flames in Mary Clarkson's cottage, the German armies were pouring forward through the darkness to invade Holland and Belgium. They crossed the frontiers at dawn. The news came to our Babes in the Darkling Wood on the morning radio.

They went back to Cambridge that afternoon...

After that, for a time, the intense reality of warfare in the foreground spread and blotted out their personal and philosophical interests alike. The ideas they had shaped floated above their preoccupied minds like the guiding stars of heaven in a night of cloud and storm. Gemini achieved his immediate project and got to a mine-sweeper, and Stella became a nurse, and very rapidly a trustworthy and authoritative director of nurses. Husband and wife met at rare intervals when he had leave. They scribbled letters to each other that were sometimes never sent and sometimes never reached their destination. The war, the struggle against destruction, became their one consuming reality.

The country was waking up, confused still in its mind, but roused at last to the inescapable need for fighting hard. That half-hearted "Fifth Column" government, combining strong pro-Goering leanings with an insufferable sanctimoniousness, that vague, weak government at which Gemini had raged with such apparent impotence, was replaced in effect by a new regime. The things he had thought so hotly and bitterly in the spring passed out of mind. Chamberlain became a fading ghost in the background, still gibbering self-righteously, and the quickened nation pulled itself together under Winston Churchill and set itself with a belated effort to concentrate upon the suppression of "those marching and trampling Germans."

"The real truth of the matter," quoted Gemini, without quotation marks, in one of the scrawls that did reach her, "is that our people detest militarism and at the same time take to fighting very readily. It is nonsense to pretend the mass of people are unhappy. The country is excited and you can't be really unhappy when you are stirred up. This war is going to be a near thing for us all, and we like it. With a sort of grim excitement. The one dream of old Smithers, our skipper, is to 'do a bit on his own'. He feels he has never really lived before. If we come on a German cruiser by any chance, I'm certain he'll go straight for it. He'll chase it, and he'll keep banging away at it until we are blown into the air. And we shall be cheering him on, and who knows whether we shan't get away with it?

"That's all very well for the moment, Stella. But it takes us nowhere. This can't go on for ever. We talk among ourselves here about how things are to end, but when it comes to that we are all at sixes and sevens. Theoretically all our chaps want a world at peace. But they discuss it half-heartedly, as though it was some sort of pi-jaw, and then they go and fondle the new gun we have been given. It's a lovely bit of machinery. They've never had their hands on anything so competent. Or so simple. Our dream is to bring down a raider. 'Blast that peace of yours,' they say. 'Let's win the war first.'

"Never will our people look forward. Now the bulk of them, I realise, don't want to. It's too perplexing. The peace – or anyhow the time for peace – may catch us just as unprepared as the war did.

"I have no fresh ideas about the peace. What I said that night seems to me now – just obvious. There is nothing more for me to say about it.

"I think I got the very essence of the matter for us, at any rate, in that pompous little lecture I gave you in the cottage. I think I did shape the way out and the way things should and may go. But nobody will give a thought to that sort of thing now. I believe still in our vision of life and in Uncle Robert's synthetic philosophy. I don't think either of us will ever get very much beyond that in our ideas. What we have to realise most is that the sort of full, long-range life we want has to look good and more believable, for everyone, if ever we are to get it...

"That's the practical hitch, Stella. If I have got any new idea, it's that. I mean, until life can give these chaps something as lovely and satisfying as they find this gun of ours – microscopes, observatories, stratosphere travel, apparatus for the photographic survey of the world, things that will make the rock and waters of the earth, the sky above and the unknown beneath our feet, yield a sense of power to them, these rank and file men are going to enjoy war far more than any peace they have even yet been offered. What do we promise the common man here or in France or Germany or anywhere? Nothing but to go back on the street corner. We don't even promise them something to hammer. Are they likely to think seriously of peace, when peace has no other face than the face of a tepid bore? With the nobility and gentry scrambling back to all the positions of advantage and romping about with opportunity while the heroes, etc., are back on the dole. Allowed to look on again. 'I don't fink', as we used to say. These boys just say 'Peace' because they've been taught to say it. They'll blast it when they get it... Even if the world doesn't need rebuilding from top to bottom, we ought to set about rebuilding it, carving it out and throwing it about, just for the excitement. No living thing will endure life for long, unless it is exciting...

"You remember that Armistice plan I was so full of? Was it plain common sense or utterly preposterous? It seems both to me – at one and the same time. Did I really think out that stuff, or was I just saying in my own priggish way what was dawning upon people in general? I see nothing but an occasional out-of-date newspaper here, and I'm in the dark about what people are thinking and saying. But surely it was sane, that idea; it was obvious; it would give mankind a last breathing space. Are they taking it up? Or anything like it? Shall we really get out of all this even for a time? Or is it just war now and again war to the end of the story? I sit here scribbling with a faint pencil on a scanty scrap of paper.

"Nevertheless while we live, our sort has to go on according to our nature. Our thin, strained ideas are the necessary phantoms of things to come. Priggish concentration, pi-jaw, impossible men, utopias – every discovery, every extension, every good thing in human life, has come out from such insubstantial beginnings…"

Stella had read as far as this when the bell at her elbow shrilled insistently. She read no more. She tucked away Gemini's scrawl in her pocket and took up the telephone.

"Another trainload," she said. "How many, about?… There won't be enough beds… We must get busy. I'll come down right away."

H G Wells

The History of Mr Polly

Mr Polly is one of literature's most enduring and universal creations. An ordinary man, trapped in an ordinary life, Mr Polly makes a series of ill-advised choices that bring him to the very brink of financial ruin. Determined not to become the latest victim of the economic retrenchment of the Edwardian age, he rebels in magnificent style and takes control of his life once and for all.

ISBN 0-7551-0404-8

H G Wells

In the Days of the Comet

Revenge was all Leadford could think of as he set out to find the unfaithful Nettie and her adulterous lover. But this was all to change when a new comet entered the earth's orbit and totally reversed the natural order of things. The Great Change had occurred and any previous emotions, thoughts, ambitions, hopes and fears had all been removed. Free love, pacifism and equality were now the name of the game. But how would Leadford fare in this most utopian of societies?

ISBN 0-7551-0406-4

H G Wells

The Invisible Man

On a cold wintry day in the depths of February a stranger appeared in The Coach and Horses requesting a room. So strange was this man's appearance, dressed from head to foot with layer upon layer of clothing, bandages and the most enormous glasses, that the owner, Mrs Hall, quite wondered what accident could have befallen him. She didn't know then that he was invisible – but the rumours soon began to spread...

H G Wells' masterpiece *The Invisible Man* is a classic science-fiction thriller showing the perils of scientific advancement.

ISBN 0-7551-0407-2

H G Wells

The Island of Dr Moreau

A shipwreck in the South Seas brings a doctor to an island paradise. Far from seeing this as the end of his life, Dr Moreau seizes the opportunity to play God and infiltrate a reign of terror in this new kingdom. Endless cruel and perverse experiments ensue and see a series of new creations – the 'Beast People' – all of which must bow before the deified doctor.

Originally a Swiftian satire on the dangers of authority and submission, Wells' *The Island of Dr Moreau* can now just as well be read as a prophetic tale of genetic modification and mutability.

ISBN 0-7551-0408-0

H G Wells

Men Like Gods

Mr Barnstaple was ever such a careful driver, careful to indicate before every manoeuvre and very much in favour of slowing down at the slightest hint of difficulty. So however could he have got the car into a skid on a bend on the Maidenhead road?

When he recovered himself he was more than a little relieved to see the two cars that he had been following still merrily motoring along in front of him. It seemed that all was well – except that the scenery had changed, rather a lot. It was then that the awful truth dawned: Mr Barnstaple had been hurled into another world altogether.

How would he ever survive in this supposed Utopia, and more importantly, how would he ever get back?

ISBN 0-7551-0413-7

H G WELLS

THE WAR OF THE WORLDS

'No one would have believed in the last years of the nineteenth century that this world was being watched keenly and closely by intelligences greater than man's…'

A series of strange atmospheric disturbances on the planet Mars may raise concern on Earth but it does little to prepare the inhabitants for imminent invasion. At first the odd-looking Martians seem to pose no threat for the intellectual powers of Victorian London, but it seems man's superior confidence is disastrously misplaced. For the Martians are heading towards victory with terrifying velocity.

The War of the Worlds is an expertly crafted invasion story that can be read as a frenzied satire on the dangers of imperialism and occupation.

ISBN 0-7551-0426-9

OTHER TITLES BY H G WELLS AVAILABLE DIRECT
FROM HOUSE OF STRATUS

Quantity		£	$(US)	$(CAN)	€
FICTION					
	ANN VERONICA	9.99	14.95	22.95	16.50
	APROPOS OF DOLORES	9.99	14.95	22.95	16.50
	THE AUTOCRACY OF MR PARHAM	9.99	14.95	22.95	16.50
	BEALBY	9.99	14.95	22.95	16.50
	THE BROTHERS AND THE CROQUET PLAYER	7.99	12.95	19.95	14.50
	BRYNHILD	9.99	14.95	22.95	16.50
	THE BULPINGTON OF BLUP	9.99	14.95	22.95	16.50
	THE DREAM	9.99	14.95	22.95	16.50
	THE FIRST MEN IN THE MOON	9.99	14.95	22.95	16.50
	THE FOOD OF THE GODS	9.99	14.95	22.95	16.50
	THE HISTORY OF MR POLLY	9.99	14.95	22.95	16.50
	THE HOLY TERROR	9.99	14.95	22.95	16.50
	IN THE DAYS OF THE COMET	9.99	14.95	22.95	16.50
	THE INVISIBLE MAN	7.99	12.95	19.95	14.50
	THE ISLAND OF DR MOREAU	7.99	12.95	19.95	14.50
	KIPPS: THE STORY OF A SIMPLE SOUL	9.99	14.95	22.95	16.50
	LOVE AND MR LEWISHAM	9.99	14.95	22.95	16.50
	MARRIAGE	9.99	14.95	22.95	16.50
	MEANWHILE	9.99	14.95	22.95	16.50
	MEN LIKE GODS	9.99	14.95	22.95	16.50
	A MODERN UTOPIA	9.99	14.95	22.95	16.50
	MR BRITLING SEES IT THROUGH	9.99	14.95	22.95	16.50

ALL HOUSE OF STRATUS BOOKS ARE AVAILABLE FROM GOOD BOOKSHOPS
OR DIRECT FROM THE PUBLISHER:

Internet: **www.houseofstratus.com** including synopses and features.

Email: **sales@houseofstratus.com**
info@houseofstratus.com
(please quote author, title and credit card details.)

OTHER TITLES BY H G WELLS AVAILABLE DIRECT
FROM HOUSE OF STRATUS

Quantity		£	$(US)	$(CAN)	€
FICTION					
	THE NEW MACHIAVELLI	9.99	14.95	22.95	16.50
	THE PASSIONATE FRIENDS	9.99	14.95	22.95	16.50
	THE SEA LADY	7.99	12.95	19.95	14.50
	THE SHAPE OF THINGS TO COME	9.99	14.95	22.95	16.50
	THE TIME MACHINE	7.99	12.95	19.95	14.50
	TONO-BUNGAY	9.99	14.95	22.95	16.50
	THE UNDYING FIRE	7.99	12.95	19.95	14.50
	THE WAR IN THE AIR	9.99	14.95	22.95	16.50
	THE WAR OF THE WORLDS	7.99	12.95	19.95	14.50
	THE WHEELS OF CHANCE	7.99	12.95	19.95	14.50
	WHEN THE SLEEPER WAKES	9.99	14.95	22.95	16.50
	THE WIFE OF SIR ISAAC HARMAN	9.99	14.95	22.95	16.50
	THE WONDERFUL VISIT	7.99	12.95	19.95	14.50
	THE WORLD OF WILLIAM CLISSOLD VOLUMES 1,2,3	12.99	19.95	29.95	22.00
NON-FICTION					
	THE CONQUEST OF TIME *AND* THE HAPPY TURNING	7.99	12.95	19.95	14.50
	EXPERIMENT IN AUTOBIOGRAPHY VOLUMES 1,2	12.99	19.95	29.95	22.00
	H G WELLS IN LOVE	9.99	14.95	22.95	16.50
	THE OPEN CONSPIRACY AND OTHER WRITINGS	9.99	14.95	22.95	16.50

Tel: Order Line
       0800 169 1780 (UK)
       1 800 724 1100 (USA)

International
+44 (0) 1845 527700 (UK)
+01   845 463 1100 (USA)

Fax: +44 (0) 1845 527711 (UK)
      +01   845 463 0018 (USA)
      (please quote author, title and credit card details.)

Send to: House of Stratus Sales Department
           Thirsk Industrial Park
           York Road, Thirsk
           North Yorkshire, YO7 3BX
           UK

House of Stratus Inc.
2 Neptune Road
Poughkeepsie
NY 12601
USA

PAYMENT (Please tick currency you wish to use):

☐ £ (Sterling)   ☐ $ (US)   ☐ $ (CAN)   ☐ € (Euros)

Allow for shipping costs charged per order plus an amount per book as set out in the tables below:

CURRENCY/DESTINATION

	£(Sterling)	$(US)	$(CAN)	€(Euros)
Cost per order				
UK	1.50	2.25	3.50	2.50
Europe	3.00	4.50	6.75	5.00
North America	3.00	3.50	5.25	5.00
Rest of World	3.00	4.50	6.75	5.00
Additional cost per book				
UK	0.50	0.75	1.15	0.85
Europe	1.00	1.50	2.25	1.70
North America	1.00	1.00	1.50	1.70
Rest of World	1.50	2.25	3.50	3.00

PLEASE SEND CHEQUE OR INTERNATIONAL MONEY ORDER
payable to: HOUSE OF STRATUS LTD or HOUSE OF STRATUS INC. or card payment as indicated

STERLING EXAMPLE

Cost of book(s):..................... Example: 3 x books at £6.99 each: £20.97
Cost of order: .... Example: £1.50 (Delivery to UK address)
Additional cost per book:............... Example: 3 x £0.50: £1.50
Order total including shipping:........... Example: £23.97

VISA, MASTERCARD, SWITCH, AMEX:

☐☐☐☐ ☐☐☐☐ ☐☐☐☐ ☐☐☐☐ ☐☐☐☐

Issue number
(Switch only):   Start Date: Expiry Date:

☐☐☐   ☐☐/☐☐   ☐☐/☐☐

Signature: _____

NAME: _____

ADDRESS: _____

COUNTRY: _____

ZIP/POSTCODE: _____

Please allow 28 days for delivery. Despatch normally within 48 hours.
Prices subject to change without notice.
Please tick box if you do not wish to receive any additional information. ☐

House of Stratus publishes many other titles in this genre; please check our
website (**www.houseofstratus.com**) for more details.